Robin's Way

KATE ROBINS
&
ARTEMIS TAYLOR

Disclaimer:
This is a work of fiction. All characters, locations, and businesses are purely products of the author's imagination and are entirely fictitious. Any resemblance to actual people, living or dead, or to businesses, places, or events is completely coincidental.

Paper Back 979-8-9911226-4-1
Hard Back 979-8-9911226-1-0
eBook 979-8-9911226-2-7
Audible 979-8-9911226-3-4

Artemis Publishing, LLC
2977 Hwy K Ste 340
O'Fallon Missouri 63368
USA
www.artemispublishingllc.com

Editor: Sarah Ridding - Reedsy
Interior formatting: Lorna Reid – Reedsy

Artemis

Chapter 1

MEETINGS

"Robin? What sort of name is that for a girl?"

"It's my name," I replied, somewhat irritated by the tone of the handsome young lordling towering over me, my neck cracking as I looked up to meet his gaze.

He wasn't to know I'd had that reaction repeatedly from the moment I'd gone to school. My tutor at college had been taken aback when *Robin* had turned out to be a red-headed woman with an attitude and legs that were, as a male friend had once kindly put it, rather too long for her skirt. This reaction to my name had pretty much been standard through to theological college and beyond into my first curacy.

That being so, I should not have been as curt as I was with Ryan, but he was, even at the start, irritating as well as charming. He was one of those men who knew he was handsome and clever—and he knew I knew and thought I should react with appreciation. Since I'd never liked doing what was expected, I responded according to my likes.

That was, in short, my introduction to our local lord of the manor—or at least to his heir.

This awkward meeting of two forceful personalities was occasioned by my recent church appointment, and his position, by no other than his birth.

My rector, Susan, was simply the best priest a girl could have wanted to serve her ticket under. She was a no-nonsense woman from Manchester who saw the Deanery as her challenge. Rural Suffolk was hardly home territory, and wealthy Tory landowners were not her natural constituency, but she proved as adept with them as she did with all the locals. With seven parish churches to curate, she needed a curator and had got me. Unlike Susan, I had grown up in the countryside and loved the rural life. She'd noticed, and as time had passed, she tended to let me deal with the outlying rural parishes.

Though the adoption of women vicars had happened when I'd been a girl, out here in the countryside, twenty years was but a moment, and there was some hesitation about the presence of a *lady vicar*. I'd chanced upon several comments, some overheard, others conveyed to me with kindness, and a few directed at me in person.

My favourite comment had been from Mrs Bertram, who must have been ninety if she was a day, who leaving Communion had commented: "Don't worry, love, it'd be easier for them to accept you if you looked like the back of a bus. Pretty vicars are harder on them."

She made me laugh, and I reflected that if one of the oldest inhabitants had no problem, I should lighten up with those who had. Time had shown that was the sensible thing to do. Ryan later maintained that what was really wrong with what he called *vicars in knickers* was that we made the *Tarts and Vicars* fancy dress ball problematic by being both.

Ah, yes, Ryan again. He keeps popping up. His family owned the old Rectory, which the church had flogged off in the 1980s, leaving the then vicar with a little suburban box, which made do for a busy curate. Said box was next to the Old Rectory, and it had been the habit of Lord Surtees to invite the old vicar to lunch once a month. I'd inherited the invitation.

On my very first visit to the grand home, I'd stood before the large, ancient-looking door and rung the bell. I'd stepped back and plastered a broad smile across my face, letting my dimples peek through, and had prepared to speak in a cheerful yet respectful tone.

The large door had creaked its way open, complaining as if its movement was a rare event, and it had been with some consternation that the butler had received me.

"Hi there." Noting the puzzlement on his face, I'd added, "I'm Robin… the Reverend Topham… the new curate."

I'd thought his head would explode, as his eyes had seemed bent on popping out, but I supposed the jaw-dropping let out enough air to prevent that. He'd recovered quickly, a true credit to his profession. The initial shock of my appearance was swiftly concealed behind the passive mask stereotypical of his calling, which slipped into place before he invited me in and, with practised ease, offered to take my shawl before showing me to the drawing room.

"The Reverend Topham, my Lord," he'd intoned in a low rumbling sound like distant thunder.

If Lord Surtees had been surprised, he had not shown it.

"Delighted to meet you, and so glad you could come. Though I don't often get to church, it matters in this community, and I like to keep in touch. Have you met my son, Ryan?" Lord Surtees had asked, sweeping his arm toward someone I had indeed noticed.

Lord Surtees had steered me toward a very tall sun-bronzed figure who looked as though he was channelling Michelangelo's David — and knew it. I am on the tall side for a woman, five-nine, in my heels five-eleven, but he'd towered above me — he must have been at least six foot four.

"My, what have they done with vicars? They didn't look like you at Dover Court."

Why had I not been surprised to learn he'd been to one of the country's most exclusive, and expensive public schools? One famous for producing goodness knows how many Conservative Prime Ministers?

Craning my neck upwards, politely smiling, I'd said, "Thank you, but they do say that altitude can blur the vision."

He'd laughed. "Touché, nice return of serve. Now, what can I get the prettiest vicar I know to drink?"

"A gin and tonic would go down nicely. How many vicars do you know, by the way?"

Fixing me a stiff drink, he'd smiled broadly. "If I'd known they made them in your model, I'd have ensured I knew a lot more. But you have me at a disadvantage. You know my first name, what's yours?"

"Robin," I'd said.

"Robin, what sort of name is that for a girl?" Ryan had inquired, with a broad impish grin and sparkling eyes.

And that, as they say, was how it started.

I'd have been lying if I'd denied finding him attractive—indeed, very attractive. But then I doubted that any red-blooded woman would have found herself neutral. The difficulty for me was twofold. My only previous sexual experience had been at university, and not with a man. We had, as they say, *made out*, but not gone *all the way*? I had been more attracted to women than men, a problem for an ordinand in the Church. And now, along came Ryan.

Over the next few days, I found my thoughts straying in his direction.

Monday was a welcome day off, and like most clergy, I used it to catch up with mundane things like ensuring my vestments were clean and starched. I was one of those odd women, maybe the only one, who loved the cathartic process of ironing and starching her surplice. Indeed, I enjoyed it so much that I did Susan's too. Across the period I'd served my ticket there, she said the thing she'd miss most when I moved on – apart from my cheery smile—was my laundry services. If all else failed, I could earn my living as a cleaner-cum-laundry-maid. I could not abide mess or dirty clothes. Nor, it turned out, men who thought they were God's gift.

It was my regular practice to take a long walk on Monday afternoons. The country lanes were white with blossoms, and this year, the abundance was stunning, reminding me of God's love for us—there was so much of it that one marvelled at it—and our ability not to appreciate it. The air was thick with a sweet, heady perfume, so lavish it felt like a whispered promise and a reminder of unseen grace. One could not have slapped my smile away as I paused, lost in my walk, surveying a sea of blossoms that stretched like a bride's veil across the field as far as I could see.

A single honeybee caught my eye as it flew past, unconcerned with the lumbering human as it lived its purposeful life. I knelt to watch the tiny creature, its body and legs dusted with pollen, shifting purposefully from bloom to bloom, gathering each blossom's bounty. A small but tireless contributor to the vast play that was life unfolding in this quiet corner of an immense, busy world. Watching it move, I was struck by the simple truth that each of us, in our own way, was woven into a much larger tapestry, each serving and supporting one another, or should be, with most not even realising it.

It struck me slightly humorous that here this little creature was covered in pollen, its black and gold, presented to the world, its uniform if you will. Thinking back to how much time I had expended on what I would wear today.

As we had just passed the second Sunday of Easter, I decided a gold-coloured beret would go with my pashmina and mid-calf skater skirt, and as it more or less matched my walking shoes, I thought I would present a suitably coordinated picture to any of the congregation I might encounter. Men could get away with looking like scruff bags, women clergy ought not to hold themselves to such a low standard.

The sun was still high in the sky, and the water was running slowly.

We'd had a winter notably without rain, and a hot Easter. But I still couldn't resist doing what I had always loved doing as a girl—playing Poohsticks. For those unfamiliar with Winnie-the-Pooh, well in the first place, buy and read the books, and in the second place, it consists of dropping sticks on the upstream side of the bridge and seeing which of them comes out first.

I had two willow twigs, one thicker and shorter and one longer and wispy. I leaned as far over the stone parapet as I could, briefly watching the light on the swirling water. My reflection made into a liquid Salvador Dali in the little eddies just before they disappeared under the bridge. Counting out loud, "Ready, steady, and go!" I dropped them and then raced back across the bridge to await their emergence from the mysterious regions under the bridge. The lighter, thinner one went over first; wanting another go, I rushed back and found two similar oak twigs lying near the stone wall and set to start again.

I was so engrossed in my game that it was only when he spoke that I realised I had company.

"The stick on the right will win. Want to wager me ten pence?"

Turning, there he was—Ryan, smiling broadly. "Well?"

I tried not to look as startled as I felt. "Honestly, since I agree, I'm hardly going to bet against my preference. Do you play?" I could have kicked myself the moment the words were out of my mouth.

"Depends on the game and the stakes. What did you have in mind?" His eyes looked straight into mine as his grin broadened, which I did not think possible.

"A quiet country walk, as it happens. You?" I responded, followed by the immediate urge to kick myself yet again.

"Oh, this and that, nothing that I could mention to a vicar in knickers."

I wondered if he could ever stop smirking but doubted it. My cheeks heating pink, Ryan had invested the words with a wealth of meaning, which I was determined not to get, or indeed, to investigate.

"Thank goodness for that," I said, with what I hoped was a light laugh, which I feared had probably come out as a nervous giggle.

"So, if I take the left side and you the right, let's see which stick wins—are you Pooh or Christopher Robin?" he inquired with a naughty wink.

"Why narrow it down?" I teased back, showing all the teeth I could in my grin. "I could always be Kanga or Tigger." I *really* did need to take a vow of silence, or else think faster.

"I suppose that depends on whether you're the motherly sort or bouncier?" He looked at me with his own rakish grin, leaning against the parapet, one leg crossed over the other.

"A vicar in knickers never answers such questions," I said, extricating myself from the dilemma he had posed.

"Sounds more like Wol," he said. "A wise vicar holds onto them that way."

I couldn't help laughing—he was quite outrageous, but in a flirtatious way at which it was impossible to take offence without coming across as a total killjoy.

"Quite agree, and I am a Wol vicar. I choose the left."

"I thought you said the right would win."

"That was with the willow twigs, the two oak twigs you have will work differently."

"Oh. An expert, are we? Tell you what, make it fifty pence if you are that confident."

"We poor curates are hard-pressed, you know." I smiled, looking straight back at him.

"Tell you what, if you win, I buy you dinner, if I win, I buy you a drink at the White Swan. What do you say?"

"I say that it's a way of asking me out, but I accept." I was now daring him.

"You're on. One, two, three…"

And we dropped the twigs simultaneously, before turning and looking over the bridge to the weir's edge. That childish triumph still overcame me when my twig went over first.

"Dinner it is then." Ryan smirked. "As it's your day off, what say I pick you up at seven?"

"Hey," I protested, "Mr. Fast Worker, who says I'm free tonight?"

"Well, are you?" His smile was as broad as the river.

"As it happens, yes," I admitted, my cheeks warming.

"So, seven it is? I'll pick you up from the new vicarage?"

"I think you already did." I smiled.

And so he had.

It was all very well Ryan joking about *vicars in knickers*, but it is a truth not universally acknowledged that a single woman in possession of a clerical collar must puzzle about what to wear on a date. There it was, that word.

Was this a *date* or just a casual drink and dinner? Come to that, what had Ryan been doing at the weir?

If it came to it being a date and that was the reason why Ryan had been at the bridge, then what was I doing going to dinner with him? "Dinner?" I caught myself looking in the mirror while rifling through my extensive haute-couture wardrobe. I tossed the hangers on the bed in frustration.

I looked at my reflection. *It's the pub for goodness' sake. Get real, woman!*

A tee-shirt—linen, of course—and an A-line, mid-calf length red skirt with pleats might do the trick—with red heels, of course. There, looking in the mirror, not bad if I said so myself. The question of what I was getting myself into would be resolved as time went by, so I encouraged myself to enjoy the moment—and wondered whether actually talking to myself was the first sign of madness? The checked jacket would look good, so I grabbed it just as the doorbell chimed.

"Your coach awaits you, ma'am." Ryan smiled. "You scrub up well, like the red—and love the beret. I hadn't…" And there, the silver tongue failed for once.

He stood there seemingly struck dumb, so I got in. "Hadn't what, Ryan? Expect style?" It was my turn to smirk at him, my head tilted to drive home the point. "Did you think I'd turn up in something clerical?"

For once, I had the conversational advantage, and he took it well. Being the perfect gentleman, he opened my car door. Lotus Elans are low-slung, so getting in with decorum required skill. I was relieved I'd not worn a shorter skirt; a feeling not shared by him, judging by the look on his face.

It was a glorious May evening, so we chose to dine in the conservatory, which gave us a river view. The food was, by local standards, not too bad, and our choices said much about us. In a way, it explained how the evening went. A steak, done lightly, and a pint of real ale for Ryan, the vegetarian risotto with a glass of Pinot Grigio for me said it all really. And yet it could not be denied he was fun, as long as I kept on my toes; he clearly regarded conversation as a competitive sport. But I was a good listener, and had never met a man who didn't appreciate that in a girl.

I learned a lot about him; Ryan was one of those who enjoyed talking about themselves and managed to make it entertaining. He'd done Economics at Cambridge and then had worked in Switzerland with one of the big banks. It was clear that he was no mere playboy. He had the opportunity to be, money was not short in the Surtees clan, and he had the looks and the style, but he was driven to prove something, perhaps to himself and his father. But none of that explained why he was dining me, little old me, why?

"Was that as bad as it looked?" He nodded to the gloopy risotto I'd pushed aside once I'd satisfied the need to eat a little. Ryan had been so engaged in his steak and his conversation that I'd thought he'd not noticed.

"Do you normally eat so little?" he asked, carefully setting his silverware down so as not to stain the tablecloth.

"To be terribly honest, it was not… one of the greatest meals of our time." I smiled and sipped my wine. "Let us just say that food and I have a somewhat contentious relationship."

He chuckled, and sipped his ale as well.

"But I take it that your steak was one of the better dishes they do here?" I responded, noting his comparatively spotless plate.

"Pubs do steaks well or they go under. Vegetarian dishes round here are a tokenistic attempt to satisfy young women who like to signal their virtue," he retorted while smiling back at me.

As an opening gambit, it was a good one; aggressive but elegant. It demanded a response in kind, or the game was over. I could see how easily he could get bored.

"Surely," I quipped in reply, "a lady vicar should be signalling her virtue?"

His laugh was full-throated as he threw his head back, inciting the attention of some of the other patrons, who no doubt wanted to see what might be the source of such mirth.

"You give as good as you get, don't you?" His eyes back on me, as his lips met the edge of his glass again.

"I am like John Lewis, never knowingly undersold." My cheeks were sore from smiling back.

"And there was I, thinking you might be a Tesco girl, every little helps," he retorted.

If we were going to play supermarket bingo, I would run out of road, so it was necessary to change tack.

"Oh, I am all in favour of helping, but the Lord helps those who help themselves. Speaking of which, if you don't want that last bit of bread, I shall requisition it."

"Bread on the waters and all that, eh? Speaking of which," he said with a hint of mimicry. "What on earth made you become a lady vicar?"

There it was. A direct question deserved an indirect answer, but that, I told him, could wait for the dessert course.

Predictably, Ryan ordered one of those rich puddings to which men who have been to public school seem to be prone. Equally predictably, I ordered cheese and biscuits. In response to, "What do you want to drink?" I ordered a cappuccino while he ordered an espresso. So far, so predictable.

As we settled into the armchairs in the lounge, he asked again, "So, what got you into this?"

"You mentioned 'on earth'," I replied before sipping gingerly at my coffee. "But it was more to do with what is not necessarily here but should be." I hoped that might pique his interest. Somehow, it mattered to me that Ryan should judge me by my intelligence and not, as he seemed to be, by my looks.

"Try me," he riposted, challenging me.

I explained to him that it hadn't been a case of my choosing. I'd wanted to be an academic. I'd had an excellent first from Oxford and had begun post-doctoral work on T.S. Eliot's religious poetry. Still, it had dawned on me, at first gradually, and then in a blinding flash one morning at the eight o'clock Morning Prayer, that what was calling me was the religion and not the poetry; the poetry was in response to something Eliot had sensed; I'd sensed it too. I had gone to talk with my College Chaplain, who'd put me in touch with people from the Anglican Training College, and the rest, as they say, was history. In short, I had felt a calling.

He kept silent, and he looked intently at me. "So, does that come with a pile of baggage?"

Sipping less gingerly, I gazed at him over the cup's rim, I wanted to look into his eyes. "Only with others," I said.

"How so?"

"You'd be amazed, or not," I replied, "at the number of people who think one of two things: either that I must be some sort of bra-burning feminist or that, in addition, I must be a raging pinko."

"And are you?" He was amused but kept it in, his eyes waiting for me to fall into the traps he had laid.

I was not going there, instead, I would take the battle onto his territory. "Do you suppose anyone really burnt their bra? I'd always thought it an urban myth, but I suppose if necessary, I could buy one for the burning."

He looked at me, and I looked right back, challenging him. He did not rise.

I shrugged. "As for the rest, politics does not interest me, but looking after others does."

"Well," Ryan drove forward with another thrust, "Lady Thatcher said that the Good Samaritan wouldn't have been able to do anything without money."

The challenge had been made. But if he could refuse mine, I could refuse his. "True, that, but surely what matters is that he used that money to help those less fortunate than himself? Camels, eyes of needles, and rich men are an interesting mix."

"They could mix interestingly with lady vicars," he quipped back.

"I doubt your girlfriend would appreciate that," I fired back immediately. If he was pushing onto this terrain, I'd push back. He had not mentioned anyone, but with a man like Ryan, I knew there had to be at least one girlfriend, if not a fleet of them.

"That's a fair point, but Allegra's an understanding sort of a girl, and she does so hate the country, so I wouldn't concern yourself with her."

"I wasn't," I said, my eyes locked on his, "but I thought you might want to, as she is your girlfriend."

"So," he said, shifting one of the minor pieces on the board as a distraction, "an after-dinner snifter, or does your virtue demand holding back?" There was a challenge in the way he said it.

"I wouldn't concern yourself with my virtue," I said. "It has a solid track record of success. But a small scotch and water would be good."

At that, we came together, as he ordered one too.

A silence, the first that evening, descended, broken only by the waitress bringing a second scotch—and the bill. He was obviously expecting me to go all feminist over it and hesitated.

"Oh, it's fine; after all, it's your own designated forfeit for losing at Pooh Sticks," I replied, feeling myself softly smiling to his implied question, and challenge.

He laughed at the reminder and paid up.

The silence descended again. I looked out into the conservatory where the blackness of the night was uninterrupted by any artificial light. I was comfortable with silences. I was not sure if he was.

"More water?" He looked at me, his eyes shifting from place to place, seemingly searching for something, all while his fingers tapped slightly on the table

I glanced back over my shoulder. "That might be an idea." Suddenly remembering how we arrived, I asked, "Are you okay to drive?"

"Probably a little over, but when was the last time you saw a policeman out here at this time of the night—and it's only a few minutes by car. Or are you going to come over all Miss Goody-Two-Shoes?"

"Oh"—I smiled—"didn't you know that's my *nom de plume*?"

"If it's a problem," he said, "I'll see if I can raise a cab, though out here at this time of night..." He let the sentence die. We both knew that there were no taxis out here.

"I could, of course, book us a room?" His sly grin hinted that he believed he had me at a disadvantage.

There, the gauntlet was thrown down.

I'd be lying if I said I wasn't tempted to say yes. Part of me felt that such a carefully planned game deserved its reward, but temptation wouldn't be temptation if it didn't entice you. And yes, as any red-blooded woman might be, I was tempted. But this wasn't how I wanted to end the evening. If his moral code didn't, and it clearly did not, include the same objections to a one-night stand, as mine did, then I had to make the call.

I tried to explain my stance to my mum once, but I might as well have saved my breath to cool my porridge. My reasons for not yielding to Ryan and my own growing desires were simple: as a Christian, my faith sets my moral framework. Further, I don't want to be a hypocrite, preaching one thing while doing another.

Sex is a natural human urge, just like many others, and not all of them are meant to be indulged. Take my craving for cream buns; if I gave in regularly, I'd soon find myself resembling one—soft and round. I believe God's rules are there to protect us from our worst instincts.

Perhaps I hold an old-fashioned view, my tutors often reminded me that I am entering ministry in the twenty-first century, not the nineteenth. Some might say what I do in private is my own business, but I strive to live by my faith. That's why, at twenty-eight, I am still a virgin. It seemed like Ryan might want to test these waters—hence the challenge.

"Thank you." I left it just a second before adding, "But I'll take the greater risk."

For once, I had him on the defensive.

"Yes, a night here with you carries a known risk, a drive home unknown ones, so let's be adventurous."

If he was disappointed, he hid it successfully, his smile faltering only a moment. "You can't blame a chap for trying." He seemed almost to sigh. "But your wish is my command, my lady. Your chariot awaits."

The night air had turned chilly, and I was glad of my coat and beret.

"Are you cross?" he asked, as he put the car in gear and exited the pub car park.

"At what?" I asked.

"At my attempt on your virtue?" Again, those twinkling eyes and rakish grin.

"I'd have been surprised if you hadn't. You're plainly interested, but in what, apart from the obvious, we shall see."

He laughed. "That depends on whether you want to see me again. After all, at some point my assaults on your citadel may tire you."

"If that's all you're interested in, they will, but you may get tired first." I only smiled back politely.

"Touché," he responded, turning right at the crossroads toward our gate. "Tell you what, I'm back in London tomorrow, but if you give me your mobile number, I'll ring, and we'll go somewhere more upscale next time?"

"And, was it Allegra?" I inquired, having no interested in a *ménage à trois* of any kind.

"I'll take care of that." He was smiling again, but I thought mostly to himself.

He drew up outside the box, which passed muster as the vicarage. Unbelting, he went round to my side and opened the door.

"My lady." He opened the door with his right hand and swept his left arm out, all while bowing perfectly.

I stood, straightening my back after the low seat. There was a pause, a tension. I felt a chill. It was cold. Then his arms were round me, pulling me to him, and his lips on mine. He pulled away. I had not resisted.

"Till next time then, Robin."

I watched him go from the window. My head, and heart, were giddy, and I knew I had to be careful here. As long as we'd played love chess in our heads, I'd just about held my own, but that kiss! I suddenly realised I was vulnerable in a way I had not thought of myself before. It wasn't that men had not tried to date, or indeed kiss me, it was that I'd felt in control of the process. I realised, with a dull thud, that with Ryan, I might not be.

This was something we girls had talked about at theological college, but which none of our tutors had wished to address. There were well-defined paths for men who wanted to date, but for whatever reason, including but solely, the relatively recent date at which women had been ordained, there was not the same guidance from precedent. Indeed, memory said that we'd heard more about 'same-sex attraction' than we had about dating, which was all negative.

Well, I thought, who knows? Ryan was away, and within the foreseeable, I would be off, so no point getting my hopes up. *Golly, I have hopes?* That in itself was a bad sign.

Then the phone went. *Who on earth?* I picked up the call.

"Hello?" I was unsure if at such a late hour I should announce myself.

"Is that Miss Topham, the Reverend Topham?" The woman's voice sounded serious, as if she made these sorts of calls all day and night.

"It is."

"This is Lavernham Hospital. Could you get over here? Your colleague Susan Foster has been involved in an accident."

Once I'd recovered a fraction from my shock, I said that I would do my best. I phoned Janet, the churchwarden, and explained I needed a trip to the hospital. Bless her, she came right away, and within the hour we were at the A&E department.

The doctor explained that Susan had been involved in a car crash. Her legs had been broken and there might be other damage. She was in surgery, and it was too soon to say.

Janet and I went to the prayer room and offered a prayer for Susan. So much for leaving Lavernham.

Over the next few days, I could see Susan and the Rural Dean. It was clear Susan would need a prolonged convalescence, although, given that, she should be able to return to ministry within the year. Samuel, or Sam as he preferred, our Rural Dean, was, as ever, direct. "In the meantime, Robin, I am afraid you will be taking over. You'll need to talk with the lay readers and non-stipendiaries about how you work things out, but for now, my dear, you are the vicar of Lavernham. I am pleased to say that we can add a little extra to your stipend. By the way, how are the driving lessons coming on?"

And that was that.

Whatever I had thought, it was plain that I would not be leaving anytime soon. If I had a pile of practical things to sort out. I also had the matter of that kiss to ponder.

As though on cue, my mobile went as I left the Deanery.

"Robin? Ryan here. What's this I hear about Susan?" Ryan asked.

I explained, and he was suitably sympathetic.

"I think a girl needs cheering up. I am back tomorrow night; how about a morale booster?"

Despite myself, I laughed. "As long as that leaves my morals intact, okay."

"Be with you about seven. The kiss did not put you off?"

Well, I said, groping for the nearest cliché, "A kiss is just a kiss."

"We shall have to see, shan't we?"

My treacherous heart skipped a beat.

The following day passed in a blur.

After what seemed endless phone calls, things were arranged for Sunday.

I would do the 8 o'clock in town and then Communion at 11 at Dunhelm. Stephen, one of the non-stipendiaries, would do the 9 o'clock at Clendon and evensong at Clendon Magna, Stephanie would do the family service at Arburgh at 11 and I would do evensong (traditional language) at Stopford. Little Linstead would, I feared, have to take care of itself. Lord Surtees hardly ever went, and the villagers tended to follow his lead. I checked with the estate manager, who confirmed that would be in order.

Seven Churches was just too much for our reduced contingent. I was unsure how I would manage three services, but Vera, the other churchwarden at St Hilda's was happy to act as my taxi service. It reminded me that I really needed to get on with the driving lessons, though goodness knew when I'd find the time.

When all was arranged, and I'd phoned Susan—who'd told me how guilty she felt—and had let the webmaster know the arrangements so he could put them all up on the site, I felt as though all I wanted to do was collapse onto the sofa and listen to some music. Instead, I had to get myself ready for Ryan. I could, of course, have cancelled, but as he'd come up earlier from town… gosh, the fibs one tells oneself, I reflected, as I perfected my lipstick, adjusted my silver necklace, and checked that my striped top was properly tucked into my slightly short black pleated skirt. I thought the red beret would set it all off nicely.

Bang on the dot of seven, the doorbell rang.

Chapter 2

IRINA BREAKS THE SPELL

"That red beret, just the thing. Suits you, ma'am," Ryan joked.

Of course I found him, arms folded, casually leaning on my door frame as if he owned the place, but I suppose in a way he did.

"I thought you might like the *Goose and Egg* out at Dunhelm, so I took the liberty and booked."

It was the most expensive restaurant within twenty miles, a Michelin star and rave reviews in one of the Sunday nationals.

"Sounds like the first of many liberties, Ryan," I laughed.

"That's up to you, and I make it a rule never to tangle with anyone wearing a red beret."

The Goose and Egg sat nestled in the countryside, its restored 18th-century barn exterior exuding rustic charm. Surrounded by lush greenery and rolling fields, the building's weathered wooden beams and warm, welcoming façade invited diners into a tranquil escape from the hustle and bustle.

We parked, and Ryan again leapt out to open my door. He made no secret of his careful examination of my legs as I got out.

Inside, the restaurant was a blend of cosy elegance, with exposed wooden beams and a roaring fireplace that added to its inviting atmosphere. Large windows framed stunning views of the countryside, while the soft lighting and tasteful decor created an intimate and relaxed dining experience.

The restaurant lived up to its reputation, and somehow, I felt at ease with him. Yet again, he went the carnivore route, guineafowl with a white wine reduction, while, true to form, I went with the vegetarian option, and a pomegranate quinoa salad with kale. The Chardonnay was excellent, but interestingly, Ryan limited himself to the wine and one glass at that. By the time the waitress brought the cheese and biscuits, we'd relaxed into each other's company, and the verbal sparring had stopped.

"Is it a cease-fire?" It was as though he'd read my mind.

"Were we at war, then?" I teased back.

"Only the eternal war of the sexes."

"That," I said with more cynicism than I had meant to show, "ceases only when the man has taken his prey."

"I will take your word on anything to do with praying," he joked, and I enjoyed the pun.

"And Allegra?" I queried, raising the name of his girlfriend.

"She may exemplify your maxim, Robin, but to be accurate, you'd have to add the prefix, *ex,* as that is her status."

"You or her?" I looked him in the eye. It was a direct question for once, and I signalled I was expecting a straight answer.

"You!" He smiled.

I hesitated, not quite knowing what to say. How he looked at me made me uncomfortable *and* excited; it was a bewildering mix.

Seeing that, he added, "If I want a chance with you, it would be unfair to lead Allegra on, and as she wasn't prepared to wait to see how rural affairs developed. We agreed to end it—amicably."

Now, I was genuinely unsure what to say. Of course, Ryan could be making it all up, how was I to know? But as he thought it worth going there, I could hardly question his good faith unless I wanted to signal that I was not interested… But was I?

"Don't tell me I have finally reduced you to silence?" His broad smile told me he was anything but sorry if that had been the case.

"I dare say there are many more fish in the sea," I parried back.

"My nets are cast your side of the boat, Robin."

"Are you sure you want to catch a lady vicar?"

"I didn't bring you here to say I don't want to see you again, so you can assume I do."

"I am flattered," I said, hesitating to go further.

After dinner, we moved to the lounge area, a space that was enveloped in warmth and comfort. The plush armchairs were inviting, and the low wooden tables added to the room's rustic charm. Another roaring fireplace cast a flickering light, making the exposed wooden beams above feel like a protective canopy. The soft, ambient lighting created an intimate atmosphere, and through the large windows, the moonlit countryside was dotted with clusters of flickering lights from distant homes.

As I sank into one of the armchairs, a wave of tranquillity washed over me. Gazing out at the serene landscape, I imagined days gone by when candles and lanterns had lit the night and families had huddled around the hearth to ward off the chill. The scene outside felt timeless, a peaceful reminder of simpler times.

Ryan, on the other hand, seemed to take it all in his stride. He casually stretched out in his chair, more focused on me than on the surroundings, using the cosy setting as just another backdrop to his charm. His presence was warm and steady, yet it was the lounge's gentle embrace and the picturesque view that truly soothed me.

This was a room to unwind, to sip warm drinks and share pleasant, quiet conversations, or curl up with a good book, snuggling under a comfy blanket. A deep sense of contentment filled me, the kind that only comes from being in a place that feels just right, with someone who, despite his nonchalance, seemed to understand that too.

I was not in the mood for coffee, so I chose some fennel tisane instead, while he, on the other hand, had his usual espresso.

As we settled into the easy chairs, he stretched out his hand. I did not pull mine away. His hand was cooler than mine and stronger; I liked the firmness. His eyes met mine.

"Let me get this out now before I regret it," Ryan whispered.

I must have looked confused; my eyebrows must certainly have been raised.

"You know what I would want, Robin, but I can wait until you are ready to deliver."

My cheeks flushed lightly, and instinctively I looked away—worse, I heard myself laugh, though I did not consciously do so. I forced myself to meet his eyes, and hold my chin up. My impression of the strong confident woman I wanted to be, not the shy girl I suddenly felt.

"I am an old-fashioned girl, Ryan, and if you want modern mores, I'm not the girl for you." I tried to keep my voice devoid of judgment but firm enough so that he knew my earnestness.

"You'd be surprised. I like that you are not modern. We have time," said he, with that blue ribbon smile.

"All the time in the world," I added.

"I hope," he said, squeezing my hand, "that it won't take that long. Would it be intrusive of me to ask if you are a virgin?"

My eyes flared at such a question; worse, I blushed violently. "Yes, it would." Scarlet cheeks, or not, I met his gaze.

"I'd win, though, if I place a bet on that horse."

"I think it may be time to go," I said, wanting to shift away from what was becoming an uncomfortable conversation.

"Of course," he said sweetly.

He paid yet again and helped me with my coat.

"I do like that beret, but I am afraid I lied earlier," he said with a tone I was unused to.

I began to ask how but discovered he was not averse to tangling with someone wearing a red beret as he pulled me to him and kissed me. Shivers shot through me. I tingled in places I didn't usually and found my lips opening. His tongue felt its way in, me on tiptoes. It was everything those novels said it should be.

His hand was on my bottom, and then, given the length of my skirt, it slid underneath, cupping my knickers. I don't know how long we stayed like that. My arms clung round his neck, and I was pulled into him, his hands on my bum. His body was so comfortingly warm; he smelt delicious. After what seemed an age upon age, we disengaged. He looked at me.

"A foretaste. You have a delicious arse."

As he pulled away, I was breathless, unsure what to do or even what I desired. But I knew what I did not want.

"Why, thank you, kind sir," I joked or at least I hoped it sounded lightly sarcastic as I got into the car, Ryan holding the door open for me yet again.

I had never felt this way before. I was in a daze as he drove me back, the lights and buildings swirling into a kaleidoscope of shapes and colours that nearly swept me away. So preoccupied was I when we came to my door, I did not recognise it. Lazily, as if in a dream, I unfastened my safety belt. He leaned over, and again our lips met. For a moment, I struggled with the feelings surging through me; my base desires threatened my resolve but I held firm.

"Thank you," I said, "that was..."

"That words fail you tells me more than you could say, Robin. Let me ring you tomorrow, and see whether by then words have come."

He kissed me once more.

Watching him drive off, I realised that I was facing a real challenge to my principles for the first time in my life. As I hung my beret up, I giggled to myself. It was all very well him tangling with a red beret wearer, but was I up to resisting?

And so it began, our extraordinary romance, unlike any I had ever known.

During the following months, I taught Ryan a lot about dating a vicar, or at least attempting to.

The challenge being, May, June, and July were the busiest months of the year for weddings, so the idea of a Saturday afternoon spent at the beach, one he often floated, was knocked on the head. Sunday, with seven churches to cover, even with help, was pretty exhausting, and by the time Monday came, I was pretty well flat out with fatigue. I thought it must have been relatively serious from *his* point of view, as he kept coming round. He was certainly persistent, that I had to give him.

As a consequence, we managed to only steal all to brief encounters, here and there, for a sandwich or tea. I was always thrilled to be with Ryan, and enjoyed each encounter thoroughly, but somehow I never felt completely at ease. I chalked it up to it all being so new. Dating was, after all, a novel experience for me. Of course, this was all in addition to phone calls, chatting about our days—he patiently listened, poor dear, as I chattered on about my various duties and their villages and churches, and my impressions of each. He always listened good naturedly.

My favourite of all the churches was Little Linstead. It had originated as a chapel of ease and miraculously survived congregations' steep decline since the 1960s. I suspected this was because it was on the Surtees estate, and his lordship liked having his own church, even if he and the family were not the most assiduous attenders. It felt like the orphan of our Deanery, as it got only one Communion service and one evensong a month.

I had always loved evensong, not the choral evensong so beloved of many Radio 3 listeners, but the plain-spoken evensong of the Book of Common Prayer. There may only have been myself, Miss Bennet and her companion, and Mrs. Rooke, but you could feel God was there too. As I gave the final blessing, I felt an air almost of elation.

Miss Bennet smiled as we shook hands. "You seem rather pleased, Miss Topham. I have to say, as you know, I was not in favour of ordaining women back in the nineties, but the proof of the pudding is in the eating, and Susan and yourself do us very well."

I thanked her in words, but surprisingly she reached out for a hug, and I returned it along with a broad smile. Her sentiment was not uncommon in this backwater. It was nice to hear, and as I disrobed back in the vestry, I reflected on how lucky I was.

One of the things I loved about Little Linstead was that I could walk it. I chose the footpath from the Old Rectory across the wheatfields straight to the Church. It was half an hour if I dawdled a little, and on this beautiful summer's evening, why wouldn't I? I loved the swoosh of my cassock against the wheat as I walked. God was in His Heaven, and all was right with the world. I stood and listened to the birds.

High overhead murmurations flew. The quietness enveloped me.

As I approached the wooden footbridge across the ditch, I became conscious of a noise from beyond the hedge.

Who on earth could be walking that way on a Sunday evening?

There was no barking dog, so that ruled out the usual suspects. The sun was low on the horizon and dazzled my eyes, so all I could see as I approached the bridge was a tall, imposing figure silhouetted by the light.

"Robin, finished early I see!" he exclaimed, his ever-present smile lighting up his face.

It was Ryan!

I was so overwhelmed, so much so, that I yielded to the cliché—and fell into his arms. For a moment, the world was as dead to me as I was to it; all that existed was the beating of our hearts. He held me for what seemed forever but it may have been all of five minutes. The warmth and the safety were infectious, and I felt for a moment as though all I wanted to do was to rest like this.

"Well, madam, this will never do," he joked, pulling away with every show of reluctance. "We need to get you back to the Old Rectory, where Cook has supper on the go."

As I had been anticipating a scratch supper of whatever was not too out of date in my fridge, this was indeed welcome news, and I held his hand tight as he guided me across the wheatfields to the Old Rectory.

It was warm and light enough for us to dine out. Ryan was all charm itself, and I began to relax.

The weather was perfect, the sky was uncharacteristically clear, and the evening pleasant. Ryan had on of his usuals—steak, roasted potatoes, and grilled asparagus, and a glass of some red from the cellar. For me, a simple spinach quiche with a glass of Vermentino. As was our habit, we talked of nothing and everything, all punctuated with laughter. Finally, the dishes cleared away, he had finished his coffee, and I had mine, and we just sat together for a few moments.

"Must you go back?" His fingers played with the rim of his empty cup, his head tilted to the side, a half-smile drawn across his face as his eyes met mine.

I knew what answer I would give but was more than tempted for a moment, perhaps *more* than a moment.

"You know the answer," I told him, finally drawing in a long breath while pushing my empty cup away as well.

"Can't blame a man for asking. You are so delicious, Robin. And, by the way, don't worry, I am a gentle soul." His smile changed from a half to a whole smile as he sat forward, his elbows on the table. "I am also persistent, my dear Robin, I never, ever give up."

His kiss as he dropped me off home took my breath away. This, I reflected as I stripped off my clericals, was getting to be like one of those books my mother used to read. I was not even sure I liked men, and I certainly hadn't been looking for one. Despite his comment about being *gentle*, but with his comment on being *persistent*, I could not ignore the growing sense of being a little like his prey.

Then the phone went. Who on earth?

"Robin here," I answered in a voice that showed my curiosity at such a late-hour call if not a minor annoyance.

"Is that the vicar?" The voice at the other end sounded anxious, and I detected an ever so slight accent.

I confirmed it was and asked how I could help.

"It's difficult," said the voice, "I need to talk about something confidential with someone who isn't the police."

"I would be happy to talk. Do you want to talk on the phone, or would face to face be better?" I responded; my personal cobwebs were instantly blown away as my vocation took complete control.

"I don't live far away; I can be with you in ten minutes," the voice added.

"Can I ask what it's about?" My alarms sounded, and I would not ignore them.

"Yes, yes, of course, it's about my employer's son." The previously strong but apprehensive voice became a hushed whisper, "Ryan Surtees."

The line went as silent as my heartbeat. The buzz of the broken line echoed through the room.

I was still in shock when I opened the door, but this was where professional training came into play. I was glad that I had not had too much to drink. As she entered, her eyes flicked about like a young rabbit afraid a hawk would appear from the shadows. I took her coat and ushered her into the study.

"Can I get you anything to drink?"

"If it is no trouble, I'd appreciate some tea."

Her accent, and the way she'd phrased the answer confirmed what I had intuited on the phone—she was Eastern European, from her appearance, Slavic. She had high cheekbones and delicate features, and she was taller than me and blonde. At a guess I'd have put her in her early twenties if that.

"Do you want to come to the kitchen while I make us a pot?"

She came with me.

"So," I said, breaking the ice before it began to form, "I'm Robin, and you are?"

"Irina," she replied. "I work at the Old Rectory; I came over on one of Mr Ryan's programmes."

As I prepared a pot, my questioning established that she had been in the country since Easter. She was Ukrainian.

As she sat, I noticed how *very* short her skirt was—and how attractive she was. I asked if she felt comfortable sharing her concerns with me and if she was sure she did not want someone else to be with us. She shook her head vigorously.

"Do you feel able to tell me what is concerning you?" I inquired, trying to remember my training in how to deal with people who came to you as Irina had. I must have succeeded as her fingers stopped fiddling with the hem of her skirt, her breath came slower and deeper while her shoulders eased, lowering from her ears, thus reminding me less of a terrified rabbit than when she'd arrived.

"It's Mr Ryan," she started slowly, her eyes on me, searching for my reaction.

"What is?" I asked, trying to keep the strain out of my voice. It occurred to me that I might not be the right person to hear this and that given my involvement with Ryan, I might indeed be the worst person for her to confide in, but Irina was ready to talk, so me it would have to be.

Irina's eyes looked about the room, everywhere but me, her cheeks flush down to the top of her breasts. "I don't want you thinking I am some kind of..." Irina paused, taking a breath before she spat out, "Some kind of slut."

She continued, "I like men, and I liked what Mr. Ryan, and I were doing at the start, and that's why I don't want to go to the police. It began with my consent, and if it is his word against mine, no one is going to believe a Ukrainian girl against a man in his position."

By now my heart was racing, and my stomach was doing gymnastics. It was all I could do to repress the urge to run to the bathroom and vomit. I could feel myself trembling. Was it really only a few hours since I had been in Ryan's arms?

"I don't know if you know about Mr Ryan's business?" Irina's voice was filled with apprehension.

I confirmed I knew something, knowing I was about to learn far more than I wanted.

"You know that he is a trustee— Is that the word, for a refugee charity?"

I nodded, I did know that, and liked him for it. I might have been dropped into the North Sea for the icy cold numbness that enveloped me.

"My family were displaced by the Russian invasion, and we were helped by his charity. I have been working for the charity for the last year and was invited over to help interpret at the recent conference. Mr. Ryan asked me to stay to help set up further meetings with the Russians."

I remembered my training. *Listen, let them tell their story in their way, at their pace, it's their story. Your job is to listen.* I topped up her cup, and mine, as she proceeded.

It had been, she said, after the second meeting with the Russians that *it* had happened. I wondered, idly, when that had been, but concentrated hard on her. The conference had finished late, and Mr. Ryan had booked them rooms *just in case.* He'd bought her dinner as a thank you and then one thing had led to another, leading them to a night of passion.

Yes, she's just his sort — young, pretty, and lively — but also vulnerable. The training had clearly taken, as I concentrated grimly, trying desperately not to gag.

It had, she said, all been 'good' until recently. Just over a month ago things had changed.

'Mr. Ryan' as she called him, had been courteous and not too pressing, but, as she put it, 'when he stopped spending time in London so much' his demands had escalated. It had come to a head on Friday last when two Russian guests had stayed at the house. Lord Surtees had been away, and Mr. Ryan had suggested she join them to 'help lighten the evening'. To her shock, at the end of the evening, when she'd been, as she admitted, rather drunk, he had offered her 'services' to the Russians.

"I tell him no, over and over. At first he tried to convince me," Irina choked back tears. "He stopped being kind, and turned hard, and cold. He scared me so. Then he said the most hateful thing, *You are bought and paid for, and you are my whore, so you'll fuck who, and when I tell you to.*" With that, she began to sob, her shoulders shaking as she pressed a fist to her mouth, trying to stifle the sound.

I wish I had been more kind. I only handed her tissues. My only defence was that his words, as she'd reported them, sent a wave of numbness through me.

You are bought and paid for, and you are my whore, so you'll fuck who, and when I tell you to? My mind was reeling, could this be true? Was this the Ryan that I'd thought I knew?

It took a few moments but finally Irina could go on. I made sure she was well supplied with tissues and I held her hand to comfort her. Every word of her story was a dagger to my heart.

So, feeling she had no choice, she had done as he'd told her. The following morning, Ryan had paid her an extra £1000 and had told her that she'd be expected to 'join the other girls in town' next week—that was tomorrow.

When she finished there was silence; me from the shock, her from exhaustion.

"What should I do?" Irina asked.

I had almost not heard the question, for I was too stunned to hear. That was an excellent question. It was also the question I was asking myself. I knew one big thing and said it at once.

"Irina, you must stay here tonight. You cannot go back to the Rectory; it is not safe."

"I don't want to go to the police, I don't trust them. They will take his side." The force of Irina's conviction struck me like a blow. I wish I could have said she was wrong, but I knew she was not. She began to cry, bordering on sobbing again.

I held her hand and stroked it. "I won't do that, Irina, as long as you stay with me. I know some people who can help you—and they are not the police and will respect your wishes."

Her tears slowed, and she looked at me with a glimmer of hope. I handed her a tissue to blow her nose into.

"These people, they are good, yes?" Her tone told me her trust had been shattered, and I had to start rebuilding it.

Her accent became more pronounced the more tired she became. I assured her that they were good people. To my relief, she agreed to stay. I sent her to shower while I made up the guest bed. I left an extra dressing gown on the bathroom door, telling her it was there, along with a spare nightdress.

She came down, freshly scrubbed and fragrant. I could see why Ryan had fallen for her; she had a gamin-like charm. Without her makeup, she looked much younger. She smiled, for the first time. "You are very kind to me, truly."

"I am a Christian, Irina, it's what we do. But I am also a woman, and my blood boils at what happened to you. I have a question, though. You mentioned 'other women' in London, what did you mean?"

I had a horrid idea what she was going to tell me, and part of me did not want to hear it. I'd thought I'd known Ryan. Yes, he was a bit pushy, rather full of himself, but he was also funny and, I had thought, a good man underneath the braggadocio. Now, this strange woman had come from nowhere to slap my face and turn my life upside down. Interestingly, it did not occur to me to question her bona fides. It was patently obvious that she was sincere—and terrified.

I had poured a small scotch and water for myself and asked if she wanted one; she nodded. As I poured, she answered my question. There were, she said, houses in London where refugee women were kept where men paid for sex. She was being sent to be with them. Mr. Ryan was driving down there first thing in the morning.

My mobile went. It was Ryan. I switched it off.

"It's okay," I explained, "just a friend, and I don't have time for that now."

The last thing she needed was to overhear me talking to Ryan. And perhaps more selfishly, I had no desire to hear his voice at that moment either.

My phone pinged. It was a text:

Exhausted you did I, darling? Off to L 2moro, xxx R

Two hours ago, I'd have responded enthusiastically, but then two hours ago, I'd have taken the call breathlessly. But two hours ago was before my private life had imploded.

I showed Irina to her room. I put her clothes into the washing machine, and I'd dry them later so she'd have them clean for the morning. As I took them, she touched my arm and looked at me with tears in her eyes.

"Thank you," she said, before embracing me. Her body flowed into me, like heated candle wax softened to matching a form — just as I felt my own tense up as formed wax cooled and hardened.

The contrast with the last hug I had experienced, the one with Ryan, brought tears to my eyes. I had felt safe in his arms, or at least thought I had, but if I were honest with myself, I was never as certain of my safety as I was sure of my desire for it. Irina felt she was safe with me. Now, as I left her, I thought to make sure that I did not let her down as I had been let down by Ryan.

As soon as I got back to my study, I phoned the hotline. It was manned all hours of the day and night, though I had feared that Sunday after ten might be a test too far—but they did not let me down.

"Clewer Trust, how can we help?"

I explained who I was and why I was calling. By sheer good fortune, the woman at the other end remembered meeting me a few years previously at the launch of the trust, which helped. She was pleased with my advice to Irina and suggested that they should send someone round to talk with her in the morning, though, given the time and where we were, it was more likely to be in the afternoon. She confirmed with me that Irina was safe and that I was in no danger. I was relieved.

The Clewer Trust was an organisation through which the Church worked to combat the evils of modern slavery. For the most part, my limited contacts since I had been in Suffolk had been to do with gangmasters and rural labourers, though I knew colleagues elsewhere who had dealt with cases like Irina's. All of that was easy enough, at one level. What was not easy at any level was what I was going to do about Ryan.

I suddenly felt physically sick. Feeling myself starting to shake, I ran to the bathroom and retched into the toilet until I could be sick no more. After flushing away the detritus, I brushed my teeth and used copious amounts of mouthwash; gosh, that took me back to my teenage years.

I settled myself and went to my home altar, lighting the beeswax candles. As I prayed the opening lines of Compline, it was with a sense of irony I spoke the words about 'a quiet night and a perfect end'.

I did not reply to his text.

Lying in my bed, as I chased sleep, I realised that some part of me had known. All the signs had been there; I'd just been too caught up to see them. My relationship with Ryan had not been one of *courting*, to use the old parlance, but of pursuit. I had enjoyed it, the thrill of it. But now I saw it for what it was; the *pursuit* was not one of an ardent lover seeking a relationship but one of a hunter. Now I had to face the fact that what I was to Ryan was nothing more than prey, like poor Irina, just another trophy for his collection. That thought led to unsettling dreams.

I woke with the sunrise, which at the time of the year meant just before five in the morning. As I drew my curtains, a solitary red sports car drove past—it was Ryan's car—he was on his way to London.

I said Morning Prayer then showered and dressed. Just after seven, the soft squeak of the old bed sounded, and the shuffling kiss of bare feet on the carpets filtered through from the spare bedroom. Irina tiptoed down the stairs, no doubt thinking I might still be asleep. She started when she first saw me. It was so sweet I smiled, a smile she returned.

"Breakfast?" I asked, trying to seem chipper, but probably failing miserably.

"Please, whatever you are having will do, thank you so much." Irina eyed me warily, like an abused animal watched a prospective caregiver, no doubt wondering if she would be betrayed again.

I prepared us both a bowl of cereal with plenty of fruit and a pot of herbal tea. As she tucked in, I told Irina what I had done and who the Clewer were. Her manor shifted, shoulders relaxed. It was then I knew that she clearly trusted me as she calmly accepted it all. I was glad it was my day off, though I doubted I'd be taking much rest.

As Irina showered, I phoned the churchwardens to tell them that something had cropped up and that I wouldn't be about for the rest of the day. I let them assume I had gone up to town. Then I phoned the archdeacon's office to fill them in on the situation.

While Irina showered, I ironed her skirt and blouse and found a fresh pair of tights for her.

"You are perfect hostess." She smiled, stripping off the dressing-gown, and asked me to help with her bra clasp.

I was a little taken aback, but happy to help. She was so beautiful, and her body was perfect. My hands were shaking, but I managed without a heart attack, still it was a close thing.

"What do you think?" she asked while giving a twirl.

My throat was dry, yet I found my voice and told her she looked just fine, then she went off to fix her make-up.

By the time she was back, I'd done the washing up and begun making the bread, my usual Monday morning routine. She watched, fascinated, and was delighted when I asked if she'd like to knead it. She told me it reminded her of home when she'd helped her mum; I told her that was why I delighted in doing it.

When we'd finished, I let it rise, and suggested we had some coffee. As we sat, Irina told me more about her life. Ryan's charity had provided her with support when she and her family had needed it, as well as a way out. Irina told me that she'd been aware that some of the aid workers had exploited the girls they'd been helping, but that she'd thought that as a worker for the charity, and with Ryan, she'd be safe. Then she asked the question I'd been dreading, "And do you know Mr. Ryan?"

There seemed no point in doing a St Peter and denying it, even though the cock had crowed many hours before. The question was how to say it? I decided to trust my instincts, and her, so told her the truth.

"Quite well. Indeed, until last night we were dating each other."

Her eyes widened, and her voice trembled ever so slightly. "And your telephone, it was him?"

I admitted it had been, and told her about the text.

"You, too, had sex with him?" she asked, her voice barely above a whisper, her eyes growing even wider as her face grew paler.

I thought she might bolt for the door, but she settled back again to listen to my tale.

She seemed somehow relieved when I explained the situation to her.

"But he is quite forceful and so handsome." She looked at me, intrigued, almost impishly. "Do you perhaps not like men as much as they like you?"

I explained to her that it was a question of morality. I did not believe in premarital sex; this was the doctrinal position, and I saw no reason to believe otherwise, and I lived it, so far. I did not think it necessary to go beyond this point into my deeper thoughts on the subject and how I wrestled with them. Nor how I had been sorely tempted by Ryan. I had not succumbed, and after her revelations, I could not imagine ever doing so now.

Her eyes widened momentarily with a flash of surprise or perhaps realisation, or was it recognition? She took a hasty gulp of coffee, then, put her cup down with a soft clink.

Leaning forward, she fixed me with a gaze, her voice soft and a half octave lower, in a conclusive tone. "I think maybe you do not like men as much as you think you should," she responded with the finality of a judge sending someone to hang.

I felt uneasy, wondering how to parry the questions.

"Do you, perhaps, prefer women?" She smiled the sweetest smile.

She reminded me, as I had subconsciously known she did, of Elena, who had been my best friend in the sixth form and with whom I had a sapphic affair. Quite innocent, but we had kissed and shared a bed, though to no great effect.

"You blush, Miss Robin. Am I perhaps in the ballpark?"

That was a good question. It was not one I wanted to answer.

Thank goodness for the phone, which rang at the right moment. It was the woman from the Clewer, Lynne, her voice tinged with a hint of frustration. She was in town, apparently lost, and wanted to know the way to Little Linstead, as her sat-nav seemed unable to find it, thus leading her astray and leaving me thankful for small mercies.

For Irina's sake, I was hopeful that this woman and The Clewer Initiative she represented would help us. Of course, I knew of the Clewer, but never in my worst nightmares had I ever thought I would need their assistance. I prayed Lynne had the resources and connections to protect Irina and hopefully help us deal with Ryan and whomever he was working with, for I doubted he could, or would, do such a horrid thing alone.

As I stood looking out of the window, I felt Irina's arms round me. I felt her breath on my neck. I let her pull me to her and we stood together for what seemed the longest while. Something had broken.

Lynne's arrival put an end to our embrace. Our conversation did little to settle anything.

"Luckily, Irina you are a recognised refugee, therefore, you have the right to stay in the UK and can work legally in any job. That is not true of asylum seekers who can't work unless they've been waiting for over a year for a decision, and even then, only in certain jobs," Lynne explained.

Irina's eyes widened. "But must I leave if I don't work?"

"No," Lynne answered. "But if you don't work, you'll need to rely on benefits, which might not cover all your needs."

Irina frowned. "But I need money. Ryan promised I could make a lot more money…if I did what he wanted. I need that money for my family."

A surge of anger rose within me. "Irina, what Ryan is doing is wrong and I suspect it's illegal as well. You shouldn't have to choose between your safety and supporting your family."

Lynne nodded. "Robin's right. If you refuse Ryan, he might sack you, and you'll have to rely on benefits. But we can help you find a safe place and the support you need. Our priority is your safety."

Irina's hands trembled. "I don't want my family to suffer because I am too proud to do what I must to help them."

I squeezed her hand. "Your family wouldn't want you in danger, and I can't imagine they would want you to sell yourself either. We'll find a way to support you and ensure you're safe."

Lynne added, "We'll support you. Our goal is to get you to a safe place away from Ryan and others like him."

Irina took a deep breath. "Okay. Let's do this. I don't want anyone else to go through what I did."

Determination and anger burned within me. Ryan had to be stopped, but right now, we had no solid evidence for the Trust or the police. "Lynne, if we find a safe house for Irina, will it complicate her status?"

Lynne sighed. "It might, but her safety comes first. We'll deal with bureaucratic hurdles later."

I must admit that I had hoped that Lynne might offer more hope and help than she had. I didn't know what I had expected; I had just expected more, somehow. To be fair, the Clewer were not fairy godmothers able to wave a wand and change a sow's ear into a Loui Vuitton original. They were part of the CoE structure and limited by power, money, and society to what was humanly possible.

The whole situation boiled and roiled in me; I am not a woman who angers easily, and such strong emotions unsettle me, not that I do not have them. I felt them now; it was just that I had to find a solution, or those emotions would turn inward, and I would feel helpless. Irina did not need me dancing about my bag, enjoying the music of my pity party. Irina needed a solution, for although my pity party might have a seat for one, Irina's had a potential cast of thousands, and I would be damned if I was going to sit by and allow Ryan to add more seats to that party.

I wanted to get Irina to safety, and although I might be able to do that by finding her another position, what was there to stop Ryan from replacing her with yet another vulnerable girl, or a string of them for that matter? Was there already a string? That thought made me nauseous.

How was I to stop Ryan?

I don't know from what well of wisdom or folly the idea came to me, whether from above or if born of the pit of sheer desperation. All I know is when the thought struck me, I felt a wave of peace flow over me as a pale of warm water, rinsing the suds from my hair, flowing down my body, warming my chilled skin to finally tickle my toes. I knew it might be dangerous, akin to suicide, if not handled properly, but somehow, I just knew I had to try.

Before I could overthink and possibly talk myself out of it, I said, "I have a suggestion."

"Lynne, this might sound insane, but bear with me. What if Irina and I make arrangements with Ryan for her to continue working with him?" I pause, the absurdity of the idea even striking me. "I know I'm not a solicitor, but it seems to me that, as things stand, we don't have anything concrete to go on—certainly nothing that he can't wriggle out of. Ideally, we need Ryan to incriminate himself. If not an outright confession, then at least some sort of admission or statement of complicity in the trafficking. Irina, how would you feel about that?"

"This is not a crime drama, Robin. Ryan isn't going to just say 'it's a fair cop' and then confess; he's no fool," Lynne replies, her voice tinged with frustration and concern, and more than a hint of sarcasm.

"Of course he's no fool, but he is arrogant, which is all the more reason to have someone close to him," I answer, glad she has made the point. "He will slip up and show his true colours. We need someone to either catch him out or at least keep a bell on him until we find something, or think of some other approach."

Irina's jaw drops slightly, her mouth agape. "Continue working with him? You mean... as a prostitute? But why?"

"No, Irina, not as a prostitute," I reassure her quickly. "Ryan doesn't need to know what your exact role is. We will need to be careful to avoid that, but having you close to him will be crucial. He need not know the specifics; he just needs to believe you're still involved."

I took a deep breath, feeling the weight of what I asked. "I know it sounds risky, but listen. Someone has to be close to Ryan; we need more solid evidence. At the moment, we have nothing substantial for the Trust or the police. Your account, while powerful, might not be enough on its own without additional proof. Is that about right, Lynne?"

Lynne looks at the floor, clearly conflicted and ashamed. "Yes."

"I don't know," Irina responded, her voice quivering, yet her gaze lingered on me a moment longer than seemed necessary—a clear window to her soul that hinted at something more, perhaps resolve or a silent assessment?

My heart went out to her, recognising the fear and trauma that gripped her, but another part of me stirred, sensing her underlying strength. Was she evaluating my courage, assessing whether I had the mettle to confront Ryan and bring him to justice? This unspoken question hovered between us, discernible only to those attuned to the quiet language of the soul.

Although I felt certain that Irina needed some sort of resolution with Ryan, I was asking too much of her, for my own reasons and closure.

Trusting in my convictions and placing myself once more into my Lord's hands, I felt a surge of determination that overcame my fears.

"It's alright, Irina," I assured her, taking her hands in mine to offer comfort whilst reinforcing my resolve. "I will handle this. Your help in setting things up will be crucial, but I am ready to take it from there."

Her eyes, alight with a measured intensity, briefly betrayed a flicker of approval before they welled with tears, which she swiftly dashed aside, restoring her composed façade.

"But, Robin, the risks are immense. You can't imagine what they are capable of," she countered, her voice a blend of fear and, I thought, perhaps an emerging respect for my resolve. Her caution served as a stark reminder of the dangers ahead, yet her gaze held a silent acknowledgement of the path I had chosen.

I couldn't shake the feeling that there was more to Irina than met the eye. Each layer of her story that unfolded seemed to suggest she was not merely a victim of circumstance, but perhaps there was more here than she would or even *could* tell me. It was a fleeting thought, one that was tucked away for later reflection.

Irina took a deep breath. "No, if you insist on doing this…"

She sat up straighter, her head held high. "I can't just slink away to hide in some halfway house while he continues to do this to some other girl. We can't allow him to get away with this," Irina's voice grew strong; she had returned to the determined woman I had so quickly come to admire. "What do you suggest?"

My mind was working at full pace; perhaps it was divine inspiration or simply desperation, but I outlined a plan, which I put to them both.

There were many moving parts, some simple, some difficult. First, it would depend on the archdiocese finding a temporary replacement for me for a day or so; luckily, that was where Lynne proved helpful. The Clewer could recommend someone, but I would have to sort that out with the Archdeacon's and pray for the sort of swiftness which never typically happened in the Church. Second, we needed the help of the police, and how that might be brought about was beyond me. When I mentioned the need for the police, I ran immediately into the first resistance to my plan.

"Hold on, ladies, let's not get ahead of ourselves," Lynne interjected.

Under other circumstances I might have laughed at her expression—another half inch and her eyebrows would have become her fringe. Her hands up with fingers wide waving back and forth over her face, as if to ward off an impending mishap. Her mouth silently opening and closing like a fish gasping for air, finally she gained her voice again.

"The Clewer isn't a political entity, Robin. We don't have the Home Secretary or the Director General of the Security Services on speed dial, for heaven's sake."

Lynne shook her head and collapsed into a seat, her gaze flitting between Irina and me. We both met her look squarely, Irina with her hands on her hips and her posture defiant, embodying the silent challenge of 'What do you mean, you can't help? We're the ones risking everything here'.

Lynne looked away, unable to meet Irina's eyes; she seemed to shrink, and then, in a few moments, looked up again.

"Alright," Lynne said in a whisper. "I know a couple of people who owe me a favour or two and *might* be able to put a flea in someone's ear, but you must know, Robin, that the authorities will not willingly slip a noose around their necks based on Irina's, or even your, word, especially given who is involved."

Lynne did not have to name his lordship for his presence to be felt.

"Then we must have irrefutable evidence," I said, looking from Lynne to Irina and back. "Can you be sure that the police will be where they must be if the need arises?"

Lynne did not answer but simply sighed and nodded in the affirmative. At this point, she seemed to make some silent decision, as if now she had crossed her own personal Rubicon and had become an active member of our little conspiracy to end Ryan's reign of terror.

Lynne admitted that in her work, she had occasion to meet certain people who would likely help, and gave us the contact number in London. She said meeting such people was an occupational hazard.

Lynne made a call, then nodded to me, and I called the archdeacon's. To my mild surprise, all was well underway even before I'd made the call, and the various pieces were falling into place.

I thanked Lynne, and she hugged both Irina and me, and then she packed to leave. "Be careful," was all she said before she turned to go.

Irina and I watched Lynne drive away then Irina turned to me. "Are we mad?"

I could not suppress a chuckle. "Possibly? No, I think probably, but we can't let this continue. Are you happy for me to phone Ryan now?"

It was her turn to nod.

I phoned. Ryan answered. This would be the test.

"Sorry, darling, I was so exhausted last night I couldn't get back. But there was also a problem." I had it on speaker so Irina could hear him ask what it was.

"There was a strange woman, Irina, who came to me last night with some cock and bull story. I've set her right; she apologised this morning and wants to return to work. She said she was supposed to be with you in town today, so I thought I'd come in with her because it's my day off. It would be an unexpected chance to see you."

Sometimes, my tendency to rattle off conversation at the pace of a machine gun was of immense help. Ryan could hardly decline such an offer, and must have had many questions yet scarcely knew where to start.

Sensing his hesitation, I replied in my cheeriest voice, "Don't worry, my darling, she told me what she'd done, and I told her that blaming it on you was silly. On balance, you didn't force her, and men, in the end, will be men." I hoped that I sounded believable; if so, either Ryan was a fool, or I was a gifted actress. But I played into his conceit; like many, his conceit was the lens through which he saw the world and all those within it — principally naïve women.

I glanced at Irina, and she was smiling, then opened her mouth and pretended to make herself gag with her fingers. I almost burst into laughter; it was a close thing.

His sigh of relief was audible to all and with that we knew he'd bought it. Why would he not? After all, I was a virginal clergywoman; what did I know of such things?

"You're a gem, Robin." I could almost hear the smug bastard smiling to himself.

"You see it correctly. If you want to bring her, I'll text the address, and perhaps you and I can have some fun later?"

I clicked off without answering, too cross to trust my voice. Irina guessed my mood; her hand covered mine, squeezing to reassure me it was all right. The truth be told, it wasn't and never would be. I had trusted Ryan, and he had played me. My emotions were a roiling cauldron of anger with Ryan but seasoned with rage at myself for being so gullible.

I wasn't sure if I wanted a good cry or to throw something—likely both.

I had always thought it a cliché that if a woman held out the promise of a bit of carnal pleasure, a man would swallow anything. Ryan certainly had taken the bait, hook, line and sinker, so perhaps the cliché was true.

I telephoned the Churchwardens to tell them that an emergency demanded my absence for the rest of the week, but that the diocese would be in touch.

I went with Irina back to the Old Rectory so she could pack a bag, and from there we took a taxi to the station.

As we settled on the train, she smiled at me nervously as we sat holding hands; soon, she leaned in and kissed my cheek. I glanced around to see if anyone was watching as I blushed, which of course caused me to blush more.

"Thank you, Robin. Do you think we can do this?" Irina asked, a mix of excitement and fear in her voice.

I nodded, kissing her back. Then, over cups of coffee, we planned our campaign. Much depended on whether Ryan believed me, but then, as he had no reason to suppose I didn't believe him, and as I was delivering the elusive Irina, why should he not believe that his naïve girlfriend was, as ever, being a good girl and helping out? The idea that I was working against him would not, I imagined, occur to him, and the only undercover work he would have in mind would be of a more literal nature.

For a moment, I felt overwhelmed. Quietly, I prayed for help. Literally, God knew I needed it.

Chapter 3

UNDERCOVER DISCOVERIES

The most direct route was to catch a taxi from Liverpool Street station to Greek Street near Soho, but we had a stop to make first. We hailed a cab and gave the address Lynne had provided. Luckily, it was close to our route. I told the cabbie to keep the meter running and that there would be a bit extra if he waited. Seeing Irina and me, he readily agreed.

"Tell me that it is going to be okay," she whispered.

For a fleeting moment, I felt *she* was reassuring me rather than asking for comfort. I smiled and said it would be, squeezing her hand as firmly as she held mine. "I doubt Ryan will do anything terribly wicked while I am there."

Her eyes showed she was not so sure, and honestly, neither was I, but I could hardly say that now, could I? I prayed that I was justified; after all, during our journey, she and I had gone through all the what-ifs we could think of, even the most horrible ones, discussing what might be done with each.

We had devised what we knew was an overly optimistic Plan A: drawing out the evening with a slow, leisurely meal, perhaps some drinks and dancing—anything to delay going to the room. But we also knew we would need to improvise a Plan B if things did not go well with Plan A. The difficulty was in devising one. The cab stopped in front of an unremarkable building nestled between a row of identical, dull façades. It was the kind of place one could pass by a hundred times without ever noticing. Lynne had mentioned we might need one or two pieces of kit, and this was where we would find them. Once we stopped, I reminded the cabbie to stay, that we would make it worth his time. He just nodded, and I doubted he would stay.

The flat was on the first floor. We knocked twice and the door opened.

We were met by two women you would forget in a small crowd. The first had jet-black hair and piercing black eyes, shorter and thinner, with an unremarkable but pleasant face. The other, taller and sturdier with dirty blonde hair, she had an equally ordinary face, though, rounder with plump cheeks than her companion, she exuded an equally no-nonsense air. They waved us into the apartment without a word, the tension thick enough to cut with a spoon.

I couldn't place the raven-haired woman's slight accent. In contrast, the blonde woman's was thicker and more distinct, and hinted Slavic, perhaps Russian or Ukrainian. Lynne certainly knew interesting people.

"This is Airtag keyring." The raven-haired woman took Irina's keys and moved them to the ornate ring. "At short distance we can track you. It is common to find such things, helpful with one's luggage."

They took her clutch and tucked a small black disk inside the lining. I found myself walking closer to see what was happening.

"We give you these in case they take your mobiles," she explained. "This is likely, but perhaps they will not."

I held out my own purse for them to make their changes.

"Ve do not need." The blonde only glanced at me, her accent the much thicker of the two. "She was first, will likely be first. She is also not British, not attract attention if she goes missing. You vould—be trouble. One tracker is explainable. Two? No."

The blonde continued, "That is GPS tracker; if they use detector, they vill find tag, it is short-range tracker, if they find, just say you had bag stolen recently, and the authorities suggested. It is reasonable."

I wondered whether Ryan would be so stupid; one device might be forgiven, but two? However, I could also see the logic. If someone expected to find something, they might overlook the second. After all, if one expects to find something one tends to stop once it is found. If they expected nothing at all, neither would likely be discovered.

Still, I could not shake the feeling that this was a bit ad hoc for my taste.

"Are there no better options?" I asked, hoping for something a bit more subtle.

"Ve are not the NSA or your MI6; ve do vith vat ve have," the tall blonde snapped.

The raven-haired woman put her hand on her companion's shoulder, and the two women shared a wordless exchange.

The raven-haired woman turned to us, taking a breath before she began speaking as if to a child, "There are more sophisticated tools, but if those were discovered, it would mean your lives. These are common enough. One may purchase both on Amazon or in tourist shops for pennies. We think it unlikely you will be searched closely, at least before your destination, so as not to raise your suspicion."

Given the oddity of the circumstances I had crafted, everything seemed reasonable at this point.

"Once you are at your destination, if found, it is not unreasonable for you to have them, and even if destroyed, the authorities vill be close by," the tall blonde woman finished their shared logic.

They then took our phones and installed the required apps to follow the trackers, as well as a modified app that allowed our phones to function as listening devices, capturing nearby conversations and storing recordings in a password-protected folder on the phone and in the cloud. Irina and I were not told the password.

They confirmed the apps were working and then showed us how to use them.

If I had let myself admit it, it was all a bit thrilling. However foolish, it was how I felt.

My nagging fear was that something would go wrong, and we would have to improvise. I knew little of such things but suspected that would not go well.

"One more thing. You were given a phone number," the raven-haired woman said while returning our phones. "There is an encrypted app called Signal on your phone, Robin. When you know the time and place, send the message to that number. Be sure of your information; such things are not flexible with sudden changes."

With that, we left to continue on our journey. Much to my surprise, the cab had waited; he must have been very eager for his reward, and I hoped I had the cash. I gave him the address and we were off. Glancing at my watch, I was shocked to note we had been only a quarter of an hour! I suddenly thought better of wearing this watch—it had been a gift from my mother, and I could not help wondering what choice words she would have for me with all this.

Irina held my hand tightly; her hand was shaking and a bit sweaty, or perhaps that was mine. I was frightened, excited, but frightened. I could not speak for Irina, however, the situation was what it was, neither of us wanted to be where we were. This was not a situation of our choosing, this was all on Ryan.

The rational part of me wondered, what on earth was I doing? This could be dangerous. Why was I putting us both in danger?

Honestly, this situation was as much about me as it was Irina. I wanted to assist Irina, yes, but I was furious with Ryan and myself.

I knew I might be able to rescue Irina, but what about the next girl? Could I live with myself if I did nothing? No, no, I couldn't. But why had I asked for Irina's help.

Staring out of the window as the city rolled past, I realised it was so she could begin to heal. In assisting me, I hoped she would regain some sense of agency — some control over her own life and decisions.

But deep down, I knew that was bollocks. The ugly truth was I wanted to unmask Ryan for my own reasons and I could not think of another way that did not involve Irina. I said a prayer asking for protection, especially on Irina. I would gladly take what would come to her, if it would protect her and somehow shield her from my desire to bring Ryan to justice.

I continued my navel-gazing as we travelled through one of the older but gentrified neighbourhoods. I wondered what happened to those displaced—it always seemed that the poor were moved on from what little they had.

We turned a corner and stopped, shaking me out of my meditations on life's injustices. We reached Greek Street in time. The building was an old, imposing Victorian affair with weathered well-maintained red brick and towering dark but modern windows—an odd blend of old and new.

I rang the bell, which made me jump, then I gave our names.

"Come right up," a voice instructed, clipped and precise, sending a shiver up my spine—whether it was fear or anticipation, I was not sure.

The door opened onto a flight of stairs, and we went straight up and found ourselves in a receptionist's office. A pleasant-looking young woman smiled at us and asked if we'd like a drink. She buzzed and told her boss we were here. Ryan opened the door and smiled broadly.

"Great to see you, Robin." And then with rather less warmth, "And you, Irina, glad you *finally* made it. Do come in. Fiona, bring me a coffee too."

His office was modern and spacious, the Victorian terrace seamlessly blending old charm with modern utility. The high ceilings and large windows let in an abundance of natural light, highlighting the sleek, minimalist furniture that contrasted with the ornate Victorian mouldings. It was odd that amidst the hurricane of events, I would find comfort in the architecture and decor. Yet, it was exactly these details to which I clung, desperate to anchor myself and quell the turbulent swarm of bees wreaking havoc in my tummy.

As I took a seat in one of the contemporary leather chairs, Iriana sat beside me.

Once Fiona had brought our coffees, it was Ryan who said, "Down to business."

"I take it, Robin, you are aware of the services Irina offers our clients?" He paused, his mouth slightly open, head tilted, eyes squarely on me. I sensed he was not so much searching as expecting. "It's regrettable, but she knows the culture with which we are dealing. The Russians expect sweeteners, and what she provides helps us materially. You could look on it as oiling the wheels."

From what Irina had already told me, I had deduced that this was his purpose, but I still had not worked out how I fitted in with Ryan's plans. Perhaps he assumed that I shared his patrician disdain for the lower orders and foreigners and thought, as he did, that they were just there to be used?

I knew full well that if he knew how I regarded the farrago of nonsense he'd just emitted, we should get nowhere, so I played the ingénue.

"I can't say I approve, *darling,*" I stuttered, my throat suddenly dry on the words, "but I know nothing about these things. And yes, I was a bit upset at the start, but as I said before, your explanation fits with what was said last night. It is just business, is it not? And as long as no one is harmed, and they are not are they, darling? And of course, if Irina is now happy, that will have to do."

Leaning back in his overstuffed leather chair, he crossed his arms, and his lips curled up in what might have otherwise been a smile, but did not look terribly friendly. He looked so smug, I had to fight not to vomit. I wanted to hurl something at him—preferably something heavy and blunt, but he turned to Irina.

"And I take it you are?" he asked; the condescension was thickly dripping. I wondered if it might stain the expensive carpet.

Irina, for her part, smiled, crossed her legs, and showed a generous expanse of shapely and remarkably toned thigh. If I had noticed, and I definitely had, Ryan most certainly had.

"Of course, sir, I am sorry I panicked. I hope you can forgive me," Irina replied with just enough thinly veiled yearning, mixed with just the right amount of uncertainty, to make me wonder how genuine she was.

I chose to hope that I had drastically underestimated her gifts as a thespian.

She crossed her legs again in such a slow and languid way that Ryan must have had a clear view. I followed his eyes. He had got, he thought, what he sought, and leaned back in his chair, content that the women in the room were both complying with his wishes and entirely under his control.

"Irina, I am glad you are here. I was not looking forward to having to postpone tonight's meeting with our clients. Here's the address, oh, and get yourself something nice to wear—you know their preferences. Fiona will give you the cash. You can spend the night at the hotel, and someone will meet you in the morning. All clear?"

I was struck by the change in his tone. Now he was getting what he wanted, he'd both relaxed and gone into dominant male mode. Seeing she was dismissed, Irina thanked him, and me, and left. As she shut the door, I suddenly, not for the first time, felt a frisson of fear. We had expected something like this, and Irina had said there would be other women involved, so it should be possible for a police raid to begin the process of rounding up the men—and tracing the women. She was content to take the risk, but now it was down to me.

He smiled broadly. "Look, Robin, I don't expect you to understand, but this is how business is done out there. Backs need scratching, palms greasing, and it all helps the girls. But I am afraid some of these foreign fillies don't have the pedigree and take fright easily."

I had to conceal both the anger his words provoked, *and* that I was indeed masking that rage; hence, I resorted to Irina's tactic. Anticipating the need, I had worn a short skirt and crossed my legs, feeling both nervous and awkward; there was no doubt that Irina would have done it much better. Fortunately, as it turned out, by his widened pupils and flushed cheeks, my gambit must have been successful. Some men could be so thick sometimes I wondered how they made it through the day.

"It's okay," I did my best to reassure him, "I know I don't understand,

and you know I don't approve, but what do I know?" I hoped my smile appeared genuine. I wasn't accustomed to intentionally misleading anyone, and the deliberate use of my sexuality as a blind was utterly foreign to me. I doubted I did it well; I was afraid it was much like a little girl who had got into her mum's closet trying to look all grown up.

He laughed. "You take it in excellent part, and I think you are owed a swanky dinner somewhere nice. Look, it's four o'clock now, why don't we meet at Maxim's at six for drinks?" Ryan asked in more of a command than an invitation.

"That's where Irina will be entertaining the clients, and I need to ensure they are happy. You and I can go on to a little club I know, and then…" He hesitated eyeing me up like a nicely trimmed lamb cutlet in the butcher-shop case. "Well, let's see. If you really need to get back, I'll pay for a cab. How's that grab you?"

I confirmed it 'grabbed' me just fine.

"I am so hoping," he added, "that finally, I shall be able to uncover the secret of those legs of yours. Fiona has some hospitality funding, and I think this calls for a new frock—see you soon, darling."

He leaned forward and kissed me. Somehow, I contrived not to shudder.

The die was cast.

As Ryan had suggested, I talked with Fiona. She explained that rooms had been booked at the Excelsior, which was across the road from Maxim's and just down the road from the club, so if I wanted to use the money to buy a 'frock', I could change at the hotel. She gave me the room number.

As I caught a cab to Oxford Street, I was quietly simmering. Looking at the tracking app, I saw that Irina was already close to our mutual destination. I had no intention of using his money to buy myself anything, but I had a suitable outfit in my bag, so I asked the driver to take me to the hotel. As I arrived, so did Irina. She smiled at me, and I returned it, feeling my own shoulders relax—odd that one notices the relaxation but not the tensing.

"So far, so good," Irina said, with a genuine smile. "So?"

As we checked in, I told her that Ryan had invited me to drinks with them, followed by dinner and a night of unbridled *passion* at his Club. I told her I thought we should be cautious in the room, as it might well be bugged. She nodded, adding that she would not be surprised if there were hidden cameras as well. *Great, that's all I need, someone perving on me changing.* We dumped our cases, and I suggested we grab some tea; once away we might reassess our campaign plan. We had about forty-five minutes, and to be honest, the less time we spent in the room, the better.

"I am not liking this, Robin," Irina said, her brow furrowing. "Why is he wanting you here? Why has he given money for clothes and a key to the room? Can I ask personal question?"

I nodded my assent. Her accent always thickened when she was nervous, and it made me wonder what she had to say.

"Are you virgin?" she asked, looking me in the eye as we walked.

I stumbled; I was so taken aback that my cheeks grew warm.

"Yes, I thought I'd told you," I replied, sure that I had, and annoyed that my virginity seemed to be a popular topic of discussion.

"You told me you hadn't with him, but I wasn't sure about, well others, men at least."

"No, Irina, as to that, save for a snog or two"—I glanced at her and lowered my voice—"I am a complete virgin."

Even as I was about to ask why she'd enquired, the acrid vapour of horrible suspicions began to gather in my mind, forming storm clouds. As they had yet to become rain, I kept my peace.

We found a little place for tea, ordered, and then chose a small, secluded table.

"Have you told our friends the time and place?" Irina asked while adding sugar and lemon to her tea. A habit I had not acquired.

"Goodness, it completely slipped my mind." I took out my phone, my hands shaking. This had been a great deal more thrilling, and much less unnerving, when it had all been hypothetical.

"I know the where; I have no idea of the when." I looked at Irina, who seemed to be doing mental arithmetic.

"A great deal will depend on the appetiser; they may be desiring to savour the main course." She looked at me as she sipped her tea. "I think your knights in shining armour must appear by ten o'clock, or they will be of no use at all."

I composed a quick message and sent it; the response was almost immediate—*Understood*

I sipped my tea and ate a biscuit; I was suddenly hungry. I took a breath or two, finally feeling a little relaxation, like in the quiet before the storm, and that allowed me to think. I thought a moment about the conversations of the day and noticed Irina was watching me, and I thought of her comments about a meal and then my virginity.

The distant sound of thunder in my mind belied the wonderful weather around us, as the gathering clouds of doubt warned of the coming storm. Then, with a stab of lightning and a crash of thunder, the first drops of horrifying realisation fell.

"Surely not!" I exclaimed, the blood draining from my face.

Irina leaned back in her chair, right arm casually laying across her lap, as her left hand lazily stirred her drink, but her eyes were locked on mine. For all the world, I felt like a slow-witted child, just realising that water occasionally falls from the sky. She must have read my mind.

"Why not? What can you do, complain that a Russian mafia boss screwed you after you dined with him in a dress bought with money from the entertainment budget? You do know what these bastards would pay for a real virgin, especially one with your looks and body?" Irina said with a calm detachment.

The truth was, I had no idea, but clearly, it had to be a good deal by implication.

I had always thought that phrase about your 'blood running cold' was an odd one, but at that moment I felt its full force; my veins filled with ice. I had messaged where we would be but had given them ten o'clock as the time; suddenly, as we approached five-thirty, that seemed too late and an age away. I was out of my depth.

Irina reached out and touched my hand, her touch sending yet another quake through me. When she did, the strangest thought: *So she thinks I am pretty and have a good body?* That thought thrilled me, I felt myself tingle. *Where in the world did that come from?*

"I doubt he intends to take you to the Club at all. I am betting he suggests we dine here; that would explain there being two rooms booked in the company's name. I propose we try to dine for as long as possible, and then, how about this…?" She leaned in and whispered to me, the makings of a plan, all while her hand now rested on my knee, making it all the more difficult to concentrate. Despite my brave thoughts and words earlier, I was ashamed to admit I was sorely tempted to panic and run screaming down the street, heels or no.

I listened and slowly calmed down. What she suggested was daring but might just work. After all, they would be in no hurry; they thought they had all night. Interestingly, my thoughts ran along those same tracks, and I could think of no objections to the scheme. We agreed on the new details of the improvised Plan B.

When we got back to the room, I tried to see if I could locate any hidden cameras, but couldn't see anything. Assuming they were there, I decided against showering and slipped on the dress as discreetly as I could, watching as Irina changed into her extremely fetching mini dress. I looked positively frumpy next to her. We helped each other with our make-up. I seldom wore any, so it was more a case of her helping me.

I found myself suddenly stopped just inside the hotel room door. I knew that once that door closed behind us, there was no going back. Right now, we still had the chance to turn aside, change back, take the lift and return home. Lynne could find somewhere for Irina. I could go back to my comfortable situation and pretend I knew nothing. I looked at Irina, and I had the uncomfortable feeling she knew what I was thinking but let me work it all out on my own. We stood there a few more moments, and suddenly in my mind it was like the room was filled with dozens of other young women who would take Irina's place if I did not do this. It was not the first time that this thought had crossed my mind, but now, now I could imagine their faces, all looking to me.

I took the handle and pulled open the door.

We had to have scrubbed up well, as I was aware we were attracting glances in the lounge as we waited. Ryan was on the dot of six.

"My darling, you look radiant. Love the frock—green so suits you. And, Irina, what can I say?" he said so earnestly he almost appeared sincere.

Gone was the formal Ryan of his office—his jacket was open, his tie was gone, and he was all smiles and hugs. I was growing to hate his smile.

"Darling," he said, half apologetically, "do you mind if we dine here? The other guests who were joining the two Russians have failed to show, and I don't want Irina here to have to deal with them all alone. Is that okay? I shall make it up to you, promise."

He looked and sounded so genuine that for a moment I almost believed him, but then I caught Irina's eye—we had been right. She was the appetiser, and I was the main course. Again, my tummy made a break for it. I managed to tamp it down. I had recently had a good deal of practice. Despite everything, a part of me still clung to the hope that he wouldn't do this to me, that there was something in him I could reach. I remembered our quiet walks, the tender moments, playing Poohsticks on the bridge, hoping against hope that there was still something salvageable in him, something good I could appeal to before it was too late.

I agreed with good grace, or at least as much as I could manage.

"You are a princess," he said. "I am lucky to have you."

Luck, I thought. *I shall be lucky to get out of this intact, with an excellent chance that it will only be partially so.*

Ryan bought us a round of drinks. I had left instructions at the bar to serve me the most dilute white wine spritzers known to womankind. We were taken to a very comfortable, secluded little nook, which I would have enjoyed in other circumstances.

While we were being seated, Irina glanced at me, her eyes wrinkled a bit, her head nodding toward our host. I had noticed it as well; Ryan's laugh was too loud, and too forced, as beads of sweat formed on his brow—unmistakable signs of his unusual, uncharacteristic anxiety. I had never seen him like this. It occurred to me that he was beyond nervous; he was afraid. Just as I began to wonder what was coming next, two Slavic-looking men in expensive suits followed the hostess to our little gathering.

Ryan nearly leapt to his feet at their approach; the source of his nervousness was apparent.

"Gregory and Boris, let me introduce you to Robin; you already know Irina."

"Enchanted to meet you," said the taller and brawnier of the two, who was Boris. He gave me the most predatory look I had ever experienced.

I didn't know how Irina could be so calm but told myself to follow her example. The shorter and thinner of the duo, Gregory, was equally polite but less predatory, at least in my direction.

After some light conversation, the lovely hostess, who was an inch or two shorter than I, even with her higher heels, came and collected us, taking our troop to the dining room. My appetite had quite vanished, but fortunately, Ryan was used to my eating habits and paid no attention. The wine kept coming, but I managed to prevent my glass being filled too often. Irina was the life and soul of the party, keeping the men amused with stories about how different life in rural Suffolk was from life in Ukraine. I managed to find something to say in response. However, as time passed, I became aware of tension building, as both the guests seemed to become restless.

After checking his large, expensive watch for the twentieth time, Boris finally asked Ryan, "When can we get down to business?"

Looking at his own watch and seeing the stage of the meal we had reached, he suggested that we should retire to our rooms and have dessert and wine sent up. The Russians readily agreed. I noted with horror that it was just eight o'clock. Irina suggested she needed the bathroom, and of course, she could not go unaccompanied—we women hunt in packs.

Once in the impenetrable fastness of the ladies, I sent a message with an updated time to Lynne's friends, but this time there was no response. That done, we quickly considered our options. One was to cut and run. It would achieve none of our objectives and create difficulties back home for me, but we should be safe for now. The other was to go through with it and take the risks. Irina reminded me of our contingency plan.

"I have another, but let's see if it's needed. I have asked for help if we get into trouble before the official cavalry arrives."

"Do tell?" Irina's eyebrows arched, leaning closer, as if to hear a whisper.

"Let's say that we virgins have a protector," I answered.

She blinked once, then twice, tilting her head, her eyebrows arched even higher this time, in utter disbelief.

"Faith, my darling Irina, the hope of things believed in but not seen," I responded; it is hard for people to have faith these days, and I was undoubtedly putting mine to the test.

"Whatever," she chuckled quietly. "I still prefer my plan. Look, if things start to go poorly, and I feel either of us is in danger, I will wave, and you will know to prepare for Plan B. We need a way to buy time until the police can get here, and our little improvisation might do just the trick. I know a thing or two about these sorts of men, trust me."

Irina moved close, then gently slid the back of her hand down my right cheek, her nails sparking a thrill under my skin.

I kept looking at this beautiful woman; I had some inkling of her horrid experiences. I wondered if her faith, if she ever had any, had been tested in her ordeal and if she had found it wanting. I prayed that if mine were so tested tonight, it would be sufficient.

By the time we had 'refreshed', the men were ready. Getting our coats, we crossed the hotel lobby. There was a tense silence in the lift. Gregory had already attached himself to Irina, his arms resting across her back, his hand on her hip, pulling her close as he stood at her side. I looked at Ryan; he was looking back at me. I could not read his expression.

I was such a fool; I'd thought this man cared for me.

"What's going on, darling?" I somehow managed to ask. I hoped the tone did not reflect my growing unease or that it might be interpreted as overly obvious concern for Irina.

"We'll just have a few drinks and then leave them with her," Ryan responded. The tension, particularly around his eyes, told me all I needed to know.

He led Irina and me to a different suite than we had been in earlier; I panicked a little but realised we still had the trackers. I noted the door and hoped I could text it unnoticed, but otherwise, I trusted the trackers would do their work.

Rather than the room we had changed in, this one was a suite, spacious and richly appointed, with a large sitting room and adjoining bedrooms, their doors wide open, revealing the beds beyond. The sight of them made me shiver and my knees weak.

As we took our coats off and settled, Ryan poured some wine. Gregory sat next to Irina and had his hand on her thigh. I did not need to feign the unease I expressed to Ryan.

"I think we should go, darling." I hoped my voice was as frosty as I felt toward these 'gentlemen'.

Boris eyed me, a sharp glint of desire in his gaze, then turned to Ryan.

Ryan turned to me. "Come on, don't be such a prude, Ro." Ryan's tone was a strange combination of confidently commanding and pleading.

I despised being called *Ro*. No one called me *Ro,* and certainly not more than once.

"I am sorry you feel that way, Ryan, but I *am* a prude, and I *am* going." I stood up, gathering my bag, making ready to leave.

Boris, seated next to Irina, shifted, his muscles tensing as if preparing to pounce. Irina reached out to calm him, but he pushed her arm away. The tension in the suite was suffocating, the silence heavy, every heartbeat echoing like a drum in my ears.

Ryan glanced at Boris, then at me, a sarcastic smirk spreading across his face; he did not move a muscle other than to swirl the ice in his drink. A chill ran down my spine and a cold sweat broke out on my skin.

Inside I raged. *So much for knights in shining armour.*

"Wait," Irina said, hands out with fingers spread wide to stop everyone. "Robin, we are all friends. Let's talk, shall we?"

This was Irina and my prearranged signal to let me know our Plan B was in effect, made necessary since the cavalry was still more than an hour away, assuming they arrived on time, or at all.

Ryan's shoulders visibly relaxed at the reprieve. He got to his feet, curiosity flickering in his eyes.

"What do you mean, Robin?" he asked, his voice tinged with a mix of confusion and anticipation.

Irina had disentangled herself from the octopus named Gregory, which was no mean feat.

"Look, can't you see darling Robin is nervous?" Irina said, all while trying to smooth her skirts. "Why don't you let me relax her and see if she still wants to go? Or are you in a rush? I had always thought Russians customarily savoured their pleasures, not rushed through them like pigs to the trough…"

The way she'd said 'rush' implied she was challenging their manhood in general, and I suspected endurance in particular. She busied herself with her phone, while the men looked at me like I was a fatted calf. I was no big lover of meat, and after that feeling I knew I would never willingly eat it again.

The small respite ended when gentle music suddenly began to fill the room. Normally, I would have thought it soothing and even sensual, but now I was not so sure. Irina turned to me, her eyes never leaving mine as she began to move with the music.

Wolfish grins spread across the faces of the two Russians. Ryan seemed amused but leaned forward, his face lit up with his excitement.

"Do I get a say in any of this?" I asked, my fists on my hips.

Ryan looked at me, his expression immolated what tattered wisps of caring I might have had for the man I'd thought he was, leaving only ash.

"Look, Ro, let me level with you." Ryan paused, seemingly trying to appear candid and even doing his best to be sympathetic; it was a poor facsimile.

I squared my shoulders, raising my chin defiantly.

Irina was moving between the Russians and Ryan and me; I suppose to block their advance, I was not sure, but she surely had their attention. Neither Boris nor Gregory seemed to notice anything but her.

"Go ahead, let's hear the truth if you are capable of it?" I asked again, stepping back as Ryan got closer, leaning over me.

Ryan's smile didn't reach his eyes as he leaned in closer.

"I thought it might be fun to… share the pleasure… so to speak, darling,

I didn't think you'd mind. You have a lot of lost time with men to make up," he whispered, the words dripping with a vileness that made my skin crawl.

My face must have mirrored the shock that jolted through me, my eyes wide and mouth agape in stupefied disbelief.

"You… you what? How dare you!" I almost choked; if he had come closer, I would have slapped him. "As to your views on fun… Oh, Ryan, you do have a way with words. Did you come up with that all by yourself, or did you have help from a sewer rat?" I shot back.

Ryan's face twisted in anger, but I held his gaze, refusing to back down.

Ryan sneered, leaning back slightly. "You think you're so clever, don't you? Always so righteous. Well, here's a dose of reality for you. You're nothing special, just another naïve virgin out of her depth."

I felt a surge of defiance. "And you're just a pathetic man hiding behind threats and manipulation. You're the one who's nothing, Ryan."

He stepped closer again, his voice a dangerous whisper. "We'll see who's nothing by the end of this night, won't we?"

I had foolishly held out hope that he would not betray what I'd thought we'd had. But now, looking at him, I felt a cold dread settle deep in my bones, an icy certainty that I had been terribly, irrevocably wrong.

A note of iron entered his voice, along with a slight sneer. "Ro, you asked if you got a choice, you do. You agree, or it happens anyway. Why not relax and enjoy it? Take up Irina's suggestion. I've seen the way you girls look at each other; I don't think you'd mind the experience." He stood there smiling arrogantly.

The look on his face made me ill; the ugliness in him was truly bottomless. How had I not seen it?

"So, let us both be clear, I either accept my fate or be raped by force, and Irina and I are to put on a little show for you three into the hat?" It was a stupid thing to say, and it might have gone very badly. I was angry and more than a bit frightened, but I wanted him to say it. To condemn himself with his own words, more than what had been said already.

But he didn't; he just stood there with a smug look that I would have scratched off his face if I had reached him.

The truth of why he had pursued me became painfully clear: it had never been about genuine affection or respect. Ryan had meticulously groomed me, seeing my innocence and trust as mere tools for manipulation and control. Unlike Irina, who was vulnerable and desperate, I was not without friends or connections; I was far from helpless. Yet, whether I gave myself to them willingly or was taken by force, to him, it meant the same. His sense of self-importance was heightened by my downfall. I was dangerous prey—I could bite back, I could scratch and leave a mark—but that only made my defeat all the more satisfying. I had never been a potential partner; in Ryan's world, there was room only for him. I was but a trophy, a conquest to elevate his twisted sense of power and satisfaction and feed his rapacious ego.

I looked at each man, one by one, and then finally at Irina.

I shook with rage, but managed to keep some semblance of control. I was killing time, but not enough. The Russians eyed me like a tiger eyed a goat staked as bait, their gaze sharp and unyielding. Beside me, Irina danced, her eyes wide, their silent plea shimmering. She knew these men surrounding us, understood the gravity of the situation all too well, and the fear in her glance spoke volumes about what they were capable of.

"You bastard!" I snarled at Ryan. "I will report this."

"Report what? You came back willingly enough, and it's your word against four others, including another woman. Best of luck with that." Ryan actually laughed, but it was as close an admission as I would likely get. "Listen, Ro, this is just business, I don't want you to get hurt, and you don't have to; just relax. Irina is good, she can warm you up. As I said, you are behind in the game, so best start catching up."

This was going where we had feared, and so I feigned an acceptance of my fate. I let a tear fall and wiped it away; looking at Irina, I saw a tear there, too. I longed to run to her; doing anything else felt futile. To delay any contact at all would endanger me certainly and possibly Irina. Perhaps we could draw out our 'entertainment' and stall long enough for the authorities to arrive.

I swallowed hard, feeling a lump in my throat. Taking a deep breath, I forced myself to speak, my voice wavering but determined.

"Well, if it is going to happen, I suppose this would help prepare me." The words felt like poison on my tongue, and I immediately cringed, ashamed of how hollow and loony that sounded. He could not possibly be so daft as to believe that tripe, could he?

Taking this as her cue, Irina, understanding our unspoken plan, moved to the centre of the room and intensified her dance. Her movements were slow, deliberate, each sway and turn drawing their attention. Her eyes, however, never left mine.

The delicate silk of her dress clung to her body, accentuating every curve, every line. I had been with her all evening and earlier had watched her put it on, but now, under the soft light and in this context, it transformed into something else entirely. The fabric seemed to shimmer, highlighting the grace of her movements. My pulse quickened, blood pounding through my veins, as the allure of the moment captured me completely.

Her dance was a masterclass in sensuality, a performance that would have left Salome herself in awe. The men watched in rapt silence, their eyes fixed on her every move, captivated by the elegance and charm she exuded. She danced not for them but for me, her gaze locking with mine and holding me captive in a world where only we existed.

On the fringes of my vision, the men were shifting in their seats, their trousers apparently growing uncomfortable. Gregory loosened his tie, while Boris ran a finger inside his collar. Their eyes were glued on Irina, panting like dogs, but Irina's focus was solely on me

My body betrayed me. My face flushed with heat, my cheeks undoubtedly turning a deep shade of crimson. I cursed my tendency to blush so easily. Why did I have to be so transparent?

Watching Irina, feeling the intensity of her gaze, I was moved and aroused in a way I had never been before. Her dance was a display of sensuality and power that touched my soul, igniting feelings that Ryan had never even approached. I wished I had worn a bra that might hide my obvious arousal, anything to feel more shielded, less vulnerable under her intense focus and the scrutiny of the others. The feeling of my heart racing, the warmth spreading through my body—it was as if she was casting a spell over me, and I was powerless to resist.

Despite the fear and tension, Irina's unwavering focus provided a strange comfort. Her eyes, filled with determination and a hint of something deeper, held mine, creating a silent bond of solidarity. In that moment, I knew we were in this together, and her strength became my own. Her presence was a beacon in the storm, grounding me and giving me the courage to face whatever was to come.

Irina's movements slowed, her dance coming to an end; she reached out her hand and I took it, she then turned to face the men. The atmosphere was electric, every heartbeat echoing in the charged silence.

"Shall I take her to the bedroom? You three can watch," Irina suggested, the melody of her voice weaving the last strands of a tantalising spell that was working even on me.

I knew her sultry proposal was designed to captivate and distract the men, providing me with a much-needed defence. But I would be lying if I said it didn't affect me as well; it most certainly did.

Ryan's eyes gleamed with predatory hunger, his nod slow and deliberate. "Good idea," he said, his voice dripping with a mix of anticipation and triumph.

The room felt like it was closing in on me, the walls pressing in as my heart pounded louder in my chest. I could feel the men's eyes on us, their lust palpable in the oppressive air. My hand in Irina's, I drew strength from her calm, unwavering gaze. We had to play this right, to buy time until the authorities arrived. I prayed our plan would work and we would come out of this unscathed.

Ryan grinned wolfishly. "Good girl, Ro, and you may even enjoy it." Ryan's smirk, sharp and mocking as it spread across his face, emphasised the scorn in his cold eyes. I wondered what I had ever seen in them. I nearly launched myself at him; my fists were clenched and my whole being was taut, but I forced myself to breathe. With his comment, my stomach tried to exit through my mouth yet again. Luckily, Irina had kept her wits.

Ryan's reaction stunned me. *Why am I surprised by him at this point? Does he really thinkg I am so sexually repressed that this would be appealing? Is he that deluded?*

Irina took my hand, and we went toward the bedroom. My legs barely worked, in my mind I thought of and my unsteadiness seemed to seal the deal with these bastards if their whispered comments were any judge.

I was trembling. This was ridiculous. How on earth had I convinced myself that I could play the role of undercover investigator? Irina squeezed my hand. We both seemed to know I had been a fool and had got us into this terrible mess.

We had at least an hour to kill before help arrived, and I remained nervous. Ryan had proven to be the pig I'd feared, our overly optimistic Plan A—that of drawing out the evening with a slow, leisurely meal—had been a spectacular failure. Now, we were relying entirely on our improvisational Plan B. For all the bravado I was trying to summon up, it was painfully clear that we were both in grave danger. What they could do to us could not be undone, and furious though I was with the abominable Ryan, I knew I could trust Irina; she had been right all along. One thing Ryan had got correct was that I was not altogether averse to being with Irina—I just wished for a bit of privacy. But privacy was not on offer—in fact, just the opposite. We were to have an audience of slavering dogs.

Standing by the bed, she pulled me to her and kissed me. Despite the circumstances, my body — and spirit — readily responded. Doing so more deeply and profoundly than any kiss with Ryan. I loved the softness of her lips against my own, and her scent aroused me like no other. It felt good, but more than that, it just felt *right*. As kisses went, Ryan's had been mere finger paintings to Irina's Mona Lisa.

I enthusiastically assented as we moved to stand by the bed together, willing my mind to shut out the loathsome audience.

Irina's fingers tightened in my hair, pulling me closer. "Robin," she whispered against my skin, her voice a soft caress. "Focus on me. Just us."

Her words calmed my frayed nerves, though they couldn't silence the internal battle. I nodded, unable to speak, and let her take control; it just felt so right. The kiss was demanding, insistent. I needed her, needed this connection. My left hand rested awkwardly on her back, feeling the smooth silk and delicate lace of her lingerie, while my right hand remained tangled in her hair. Through the thin layers of fabric, I could feel her heat, her every curve pressed against me.

We stumbled back onto the bed, our movements clumsy with desire. Irina guided me down gently, her presence a comforting reassurance. Her lips never left mine, and I clung to her as if she were my lifeline. Each kiss was deeper, more consuming, and I lost myself in the sensation. The feel of her against me, her scent surrounding me—it was intoxicating. It felt different, stronger than anything with Ryan, whose love had been a mirage hiding his all-consuming arrogance and selfishness.

Her hands cupped my face again, her thumbs stroking my cheeks as she kissed me. She pulled back slightly, her eyes searching mine. "Are you okay?" she asked softly, her breath mingling with mine.

I nodded, my voice barely a whisper. "Yes. I need this, Irina. I need you."

She smiled, a soft, understanding smile that made my heart swell. "I've got you, Robin. We'll be alright."

Her words were a promise, and I wanted to believe her. She kissed me again, slow and deep, and I let myself get lost in her. The fear and anxiety that had gnawed at me melted away, replaced by a growing sense of calm. Irina was here, and as long as we were together, I knew we could face anything.

We moved together, our bodies in sync. Each touch, each kiss reaffirmed our connection. I felt the intensity of her emotions, her determination to protect me. It mirrored my own, and I knew that no matter what happened, we would face it together. But the conflict within me raged on. Was I betraying my faith, or was I finding a truer part of myself? It felt confusing but also so right, so good.

Irina's kisses became more insistent, her hands exploring my body with a confidence that left me breathless. I responded in kind, my fingers tracing the lines of her back, feeling the tension and strength there. We were a tangle of limbs and passion, our movements growing more frenzied as the moments passed. It was a profound revelation, an awakening of unknown senses. I have never felt so connected with my inner self and my body.

The world outside our cocoon of intimacy faded further away. The men's lecherous gazes, their crude comments—they all seemed insignificant compared to the connection we shared. I felt invincible with Irina, as if together we could overcome any obstacle. Yet the voice of my faith continued to whisper, challenging the righteousness of my actions.

Her lips trailed down my neck, her tongue tracing a path of fire along my skin. She bit down gently, causing me to gasp and moan, the sensation both pleasurable and overwhelming. I arched into her touch, my body responding to her every move. Her hands slid under my dress, her fingers brushing against my bare skin, sending waves of pleasure through me. I gasped, the sensation overwhelming, and I clung to her, needing more, needing her. It was beyond anything I even imagined imagining.

As I surrendered to the moment, I realized how profound my feelings for Irina were. Unlike with Ryan, this connection was real, powerful, and deeply genuine. Her touch ignited a fire within me, an emotional and physical awakening that made me feel more alive than ever before. My body sang to Irina's touch, my breasts ached, my nipples screamed for Irina's lips. Ryan had never made me feel this way. With him, I had felt like prey, but somehow I knew Irina wanted to be my lover, and my body responded to her in ways it never had before.

"Robin," she whispered again, her voice steady and sure. "Just us."

And in that moment, it was. Just us.

But finally, Boris had had enough.

With a roar, he tore at his clothing, popping buttons, the sound of cloth tearing and seams ripping. The previously stylish high-end London suit was being reduced to rags as he tore it to strips himself, until he was finally revealed in all his revolting glory.

I had never shown much interest in the intricacies of the male form, but there was no denying the raw physicality of Boris. His muscles were well-defined, each one seeming to ripple under his skin with a life of its own, illuminated by the dim lighting of the room. Across his broad pectorals, well-executed tattoos of stars spread out like a constellation, there were other graphics I did not recognise and others I wish I did not. They drew the eye to the stark images inked below. On his abdomen, the most disturbing artwork revealed itself: nude women, bound and gagged, their forms twisted in inked terror. These images added a chilling layer to his already overwhelming presence.

Yet, it was not just the ink that drew the eye but also the monstrous enlargement of his endowment, a stark and intimidating presence that seemed to distort the very air around him. It was pointing directly at me; with each of his movements, it throbbed and moved as if on its own. As his shadow loomed over me, grotesquely magnified, a tide of fear surged within me, threatening to overwhelm my composed exterior. My heart pounded against my chest like a drum, my breaths quick and shallow, while Irina's steady grip on my arm was the only thing that kept me grounded amid my rising panic. This was the first time I had seen a nude man before, and I prayed I would never see another.

"Enough of this. I want her, Surtees, you gave your word. I paid well for her, she's mine. I want her now!" Boris's voice, rough, guttural, and feral.

Irina cried out as Boris thrust her away from me. Grabbing hold of my hair, he pulled my head up.

"Mine!" He was exultant in his victory.

I crossed myself...

Then it happened. There was no flash of light, nor song of heavenly choir, nor puff of bright and colourful magical smoke.

It just happened.

"What devilry is this?" Boris stepped back, releasing my hair, dumbfounded. In an instant, his arousal deflated, and to say deflated was an understatement; evaporated into nothing might be more accurate. The once menacing member now seemed positively mild mannered if not completely cowed. His fury was compounded by his humiliation.

Irina, at first speechless, her mouth open in shock, burst into giggles, then into uncontrolled laughter. Finally, she clambered over me, to put herself between Boris and me while remaining on the bed.

"What's up? Oh, sorry, I should have said what's not up! Oh my god it is so... tiny." She pointed, unable to resist the jab.

Now blind with rage, Boris lashed out with a powerful punch, his arm sweeping through the air like a barnyard gate in a storm. Irina easily ducked the blow and, with a swift and precise kick, struck Boris in the arse. The force of her kick, combined with his own momentum, sent him stumbling toward the bedside table.

His head smashed into the bedside table with a hollow thump, like a ripe melon dropping on cobblestones. Irina's body blocked my view, but the splash of thick blood staining the wall showed he was hurt, perhaps seriously. He stumbled into the adjacent wall only to collapse to the floor, apparently dazed.

To my horror, I saw over Irina, Boris's bloody hand reaching up to brace himself on the Queen Anne nightstand. He began to rise, trying to stand, but his weight was too much for the delicate legs. The nightstand splintered beneath him, and he collapsed again, pulling the lamp, phone, and clock down with it. The shattered wood and debris crashed on top of his already injured head, adding insult to injury. My curiosity got the better of me, and I moved to peak over Irina. The sight of blood mixing with the debris sent a chill down my spine, but I couldn't muster any compassion for him after what he had tried to do. Taking the opportunity, I moved down the bed, trying to make a break for safety—where that was I wasn't sure, but my baser instincts were driving me. A movement caught my eye stopping me instantly.

Frozen, I watched as Gregory, undaunted by Boris's fate, lunged forward; he, too, grabbed me. I shuddered as his fingers made contact, only as whispers on my skin, but it was enough. Then he cried out, making a sound I cannot describe, but it was filled with the very essence of agony and despair. He fell away, clutching at his groin, his eyes rolling back until only the whites were visible. His mouth opened in a wordless scream, gasping, with thick foam forming at the corners. He keened in agony.

Boris recovered somewhat, leaning against the wall and wiping away the blood that flowed from the gash on his brow. Finally, he climbed unsteadily to his knees and threw himself at me, arms outstretched, bloody fingers spread to strangle. However, the moment his fingertips brushed against me, his body went rigid, his eyes bulging. He clutched at his groin again, falling back in agony, his hands gripping his manhood, and his mouth wide in a soundless scream of pain.

I had done nothing. I wished I had, but I had not; whatever was happening was not my doing.

"Darling Robin, what the bloody hell! What the fuck are you doing?" Ryan shrieked, then he, too, leapt for me.

He grabbed my shoulders and then fell back as though electrocuted, his body wildly convulsing, flopping on the floor like a freshly landed fish.

Now on our knees on the bed, Irina embraced me. I think she was as terrified as she could be, but somehow I was not. I was comforting her now.

"Darling Robin, is it…?"

I was possessed of a cold fury. I nodded, unsteady but somehow supported. Irina's arm around me consoled me, and I felt another feminine presence, her gentle but protective arms embracing us both. The three men cowered, rolling and moaning helplessly on the floor, as I climbed off the bed and stood, Irina behind me now.

"Do you want more?" I felt invincible. I felt that if I stretched out my hand, lightning would shoot from my fingertips. I briefly considered testing it, but somehow knew the damage such action would do to my soul. Fortunately, my deliberations were cut short.

It was at that moment that the door flew open, and the cavalry arrived — finally.

I didn't know who was more amazed — Ryan and his Russians or the police. Whatever the latter had been expecting, two women in a state of partial undress with three helpless men on the floor moaning had certainly *not* been it.

"Sorry for the delay, ladies," the first of the officers said.

"Oh, don't worry," I said, pulling my dress back into a proper position, "we had other help."

I glanced at Irina, intending to help her dress as well, but she had things well in hand, moving at a languid pace that made her seem every bit as sensual in dressing as she had in removing her clothing. I have to admit, I marvelled at her skill.

"So I see," the officer laughed. "It makes these three easier to round up."

"My name is Detective Inspector Michael Harding." DI Harding reached to shake our hands. "Impressive bit of work there, ladies. Thank you for the tip and your assistance. These three sure are easy to round up."

He was right. The fight had gone entirely out of them.

"Cuff them and get them out of here," Harding instructed his men.

"Do you know who I am?" Ryan boomed.

"No, but I am sure you will have the opportunity to tell us, in an interrogation room," Harding responded with a smile. "Caution them and get them out of here."

As Ryan was escorted away, his calm façade shattered. He began thrashing against the officers, his face contorted with rage.

"These two slags are lying through their teeth!" he screamed, his voice cracking with hysteria. "They're whores, for God's sake! They set us up and attacked us! You're all fools if you believe a word they say! They're trying to ruin me! They are both lying cunts!"

One of the officers dragging him out, a burly man with a thick London accent, shook his head and muttered, "Bet your old man'd be proud now."

"Ryan, I think you'll find that my story will be believed," I responded, dismissing him from the room and my life.

"It will, miss," said DI Harding, turning to me. "We will need you to come down and give statements—but I think that even the Crown Prosecution Service couldn't screw this one up."

Harding wore a sympathetic smile. He was young and not particularly handsome, but he had gentle eyes, eyes that showed he had seen much, perhaps too much.

"Let's get you two checked over at A&E." Harding's tone was calm and authoritative, reassuring in its steadiness. "It is standard procedure to ensure you receive medical attention and that all necessary evidence is documented."

I glanced at Irina; her eyes were half-closed and her shoulders slumped. I was no better—my limbs felt heavy and my own eyelids drooped; the adrenaline had worn off, leaving us both utterly knackered.

"I don't think we need medical assistance, more than a good night's sleep would do for us, Detective Inspector," I responded while smiling, but I feared I looked as tired as I felt.

"I understand, but it's important to follow protocol," Harding responded. "You have both been through a traumatic experience, and we need to ensure your wellbeing and collect any potential evidence. I will escort you to the A&E, where you can be checked over, and we will take a brief statement there. Please come to the West End station tomorrow at 10 AM, and I will take your full statement then."

Harding turned and with a sweep of his arm, gestured to the door. "Oh, one more thing, this room and the other room are now part of the crime scene. The lab staff will be here shortly to process them, and they are off-limits. So gather what you need. Let's head to the lift."

I glanced at Irina and then around the room. "We need to gather our things," I said, but realised we had little with us and had brought everything from the earlier suite. "Luckily, we packed light." We quickly grabbed our belongings, ready to leave in moments.

As we descended, I was trying to think where we might stay the night. My flat was still being refitted from the previous tenants, and despite it being late tourist season, I worried that hotel rooms might be scarce at such short notice and so late at night. I was imagining Irina and I cuddled up in a box under a bridge with several fluffy pink puppies keeping us warm, when my impromptu standing nap was rudely interrupted by Harding's mobile chiming.

Harding grunted, then muttered, "Interesting."

I exchanged a blurry-eyed look with Irina. "Is everything all right, Detective Inspector?" I asked.

Harding showed us the text message. The message was cryptic:

password = liberation.

"I just received this. Does it mean anything to you?" he asked.

Irina's eyes widened. "Robin, might it be the password for the secure cloud storage? It might work on our phones."

I nodded. "Liberation, indeed," I said with a laugh. "Certainly our liberation from Ryan."

She quickly brightened, as if awakening from a long sleep, and rummaged through her bag. After finding her phone, she located the file, entered the password upon request, and instantly, a large audio phone appeared.

Irina hit play and, as clear as glass, the room conversation started playing, Ryan's voice clear as crystal and his demand I cooperate or else, from earlier in the evening. She smiled broadly at me. "There is more, lots more."

Harding nodded. "So, the recordings are in the cloud and can be accessed with this password, as well as on your mobiles? Outstanding, this just gets better and better."

Harding took our phones into evidence, promising, "I'll make sure to retrieve the recordings from both the cloud and the devices to ensure they are admissible. I promise to get these back to you by morning."

As we crossed the lobby, a small, officious figure with a nervous smile and overly formal mannerisms scurried up from hidden office to intercept us. His name tag read 'Mr. Collins'.

"Ladies. Detective Inspector," he began, wringing his hands. "I am terribly sorry for any inconvenience caused. I assure you, I knew nothing about any of this." His voice wavered, the words sounding hollow to me. Irina and I exchanged glances. I had thought Ryan seemed very familiar with this establishment and I doubted that our experiences tonight were a one off.

Mr. Collins looked like he might faint from worry, his eyes darting around as if seeking an escape. "Please, allow me to offer you our best suite as a gesture of our deepest apologies. Complimentary, of course, for as long as you need."

I glanced at Irina. We both looked at Harding and nodded slightly. Harding stepped in, his tone firm. "They'll accept your offer. We'll have officers stationed outside their room, and they'll have an escort to the station tomorrow."

Mr. Collins nodded vigorously, relieved. "Of course, Detective Inspector. Anything you need."

"Well, at least it looks like we have a bed for the night," I said, not caring at the moment if it was over nails as long as it was horizontal.

At University College Hospital, the staff, alerted by Harding's presence, quickly got us checked in. In a private examination room, a kind nurse offered us warm blankets and a cup of tea. Then a thorough if embarrassing examination, though uncomfortable, was reassuring. I flinched slightly as the doctor checked for bruises, but his gentle manner helped ease the tension.

After what felt like an eternity, the doctor gave us the all-clear. "You're both in good health, just a bit shaken," he said with a reassuring smile. "Rest and take it easy for the next few days."

Harding took our statements next. He was meticulous, ensuring every detail was captured accurately. His professionalism and patience shone through as he asked questions, listened intently, and took notes. The bright lights of the hospital seemed less harsh with his calm presence.

Then our gallant Harding escorted us back to the hotel. He paused at the entrance, turning to us with a sincere expression. "I'm going to have a little chat with His Lordship and the others now," he said, with just a hint of sarcasm. "I want to thank you both for your cooperation and bravery tonight. If you need anything, don't hesitate to contact me."

"Thank you, Detective Inspector, for everything," I said, genuinely appreciative. "Your assistance and kindness have meant a lot to us."

Irina nodded in agreement. "Yes, thank you."

Harding gave us a reassuring nod before heading off to do whatever Detective Inspectors do in such situations. Two uniformed officers accompanied us into the hotel, ensuring our safety.

Once we were in our new suite, which was more splendid than either we had seen yet. Honestly a bit overwhelmed at the opulent decor, I ran my hand over the rich furnishings.

"A girl could get used to this," I whispered, as Irina nodding enthusiastically, then started laughing.

That carried on awhile then I suppose we came back to earth. I looked at Irina and she in turn at me. Both of us smiled, a moment of shared relief and exhaustion. We checked our things and unpacked, finding all well, and appreciating the small comforts of the suite. The room was spacious and luxurious, a stark contrast to the chaos of the evening.

The manager, keen on keeping this as hush-hush as possible, had provided the best accommodations available. He had even included a complimentary bottle of champagne and room service on the house. After all, it would do him no good to have his establishment splashed all over the papers as being even remotely complicit in human trafficking, now would it?

We gave the outer room to the officers stationed as our protection and retired to the bedroom. The sense of security they provided was a welcome relief. As we closed the door behind us, the quiet of the room enveloped us, and we finally allowed ourselves to relax. The plush bedding and soft lighting created a peaceful atmosphere, a stark contrast to the turmoil we had faced. We gave each other privacy for a quick shower.

Wrapped in thick robes lying on the bed together, Irina and I found ourselves alone again. I was lost in thoughts when Irina broke the quiet. "You were right," she said, her voice just a whisper. "I should have had faith."

"It is easy for me. I have always had faith in Our Lady," I told her. "Always, from as early as I can remember, and I asked her to be my protection if all else failed."

"And she was," Irina said. Then she smiled. "But not against me."

Moving closer to her, I took her right hand in my left. Then I moved as close as I could be to her.

"Well." I smiled as invitingly as I knew how, then running the backs of my fingers along her jawline to entwine in her lovely hair, as I stepped closer, I said, "Maybe you are no threat—and maybe I welcomed you."

"Did you?" She looked at me wide-eyed, returning my smile.

I looked deep into her eyes, our noses almost touching.

"Well," she whispered, "perhaps we should discuss this further."

"I'd like that," I said, tilting my head for our lips to brush against each other. The touch of her lips was electric; I am certain I moaned. Someone was, and Irina was busy kissing me, so it must have been me.

Her touch ignited a fire within me, deeper than before, unlike anything before, as if my very soul was ablaze.

Every hair on my body tingled, the pounding of blood in my ears a thunderstorm, and I wanted her to continue. My breasts felt full, my nipples so hard they ached, desperate for her touch, screaming for it. I could feel the wetness between my legs, a deluge. My entire being begged for Irina to show me all the ways she could draw pleasure from my body, to make me hers and hers alone.

But I couldn't.

Perhaps I am a woman out of sync, a flower blooming in the wrong season, far from the garden where I would flourish, now struggling to find my place in a landscape that feels foreign.

Irina must have sensed my turmoil, for she pulled away just enough to hold my gaze.

"You want this, don't you?" she whispered.

Her voice soothed me, and I nodded as tears welled up.

"But you can't, can you?" her whisper caught in her throat.

I shook my head, and tears fell.

She kissed my tears away.

"Robin, I want you, you are beautiful and rare, and I desire you like I have never desired anyone." She kissed me again, her eyes held a mixture of longing and restraint. "But I would be crushed if there were any regrets between us. I will wait till there are none."

She held me while I wept, until sleep took me.

Chapter 4

NEW ROLES

In the quiet aftermath of Ryan Surtees' fall from grace, I found myself ensnared in a web of unintended consequences. Reflecting on this turbulent period, words like 'Rubicon', 'caesura', and 'watershed' seemed apt, marking irreversible points of no return in my life's narrative.

The irony was bitter – no good deed unpunished, as the saying went.

The first repercussion felt like the sharpest sting of injustice. Lord Surtees, Ryan's father, wielded his influence like a sceptre, and I, by mere geographical proximity to their estate, became an unwitting casualty. The powers that be cloaked their decision in a guise of concern for my *wellbeing*, and suggested that my departure from the Benefice would spare me further distress. Such '*kindness*' left me bereft of home and security, adrift in a sea of uncertainty.

One day, I'd been an indispensable pillar to the seven parishes, especially with Susan hospitalised; the next, I was suddenly expendable, my presence inconvenient. The church, in its infinite wisdom, had decided my fate, granting me paid leave as a hollow consolation while they deliberated on my next posting. And so, I found myself back in my London flat, a world away from the life I'd known, awaiting a decree from the bishop's advisers.

I couldn't shake the feeling of being marked, much like Cain in the Scriptures, for venturing beyond the confines of my expected role. Despite the accolades and the dubious honour of being dubbed the 'Ravishing Rev Robin' by the press, the duality of my situation weighed heavily on me. No one dared to broach the subject of Irina and me, their silence a loud testament to the judgment I felt.

Ah, Irina. Even she was taken from me. Her choice to return to Ukraine under the noble pretence of aiding war refugees served as a convenient veil for the church, a distraction from the brewing storm. The narrative was carefully crafted around me acting in collaboration with the authorities, ignoring Ryan's venomous accusations and the uncomfortable truths they harboured.

The unspoken rule of *don't ask, don't tell* permeated the air, a stifling blanket over the unsavoury details of the ordeal. I found myself wrestling with the secrets I hid, the truths I couldn't voice even as I wandered along the Thames path, lost in thought. The temptation to attribute my actions to sheer terror or adrenaline was there, yet I couldn't lie to myself. My connection with Irina, despite the looming presence of Ryan and his associates, was something I couldn't deny or bring myself to regret.

As I approached Teddington Bridge over the Thames, my mind wandered to the nature of self and whether one could ever truly escape their essence. Despite the ordeal, I remained, in the eyes of the world, untouched and pure, yet internally conflicted by desires deemed forbidden by my vocation. The church would have offered solace had I been a victim of Ryan's malice, but my consensual intimacy with Irina painted me in a different light, surrounded by metaphorical red flags.

The sad reality was that at this moment, the one person whose wisdom and support I desired most, was estranged from me. My mother lived not a five-minute walk from where I stood, but she might as well be on Mars for all that mattered. I forced my eyes to avoid that direction; it hurt too much. She would not see me regardless. Just two winters before, I had gone to her and tearfully confided my fears about my sexual uncertainty. She had not taken it well. Even her rejection did not stop a girl from longing for her Mama. There would be no comfort there. I was alone.

The church's silent stance on same-sex relationships among the clergy—a 'keep it under wraps' policy—left me in a limbo of sorts. Despite my aversion to helplines, which I had often recommended to others, my potential alignment with the lesbian community within the priesthood marked me as a hypocrite in my eyes.

So lost in my thoughtsreplaying every step along the way, every decision, every choice I had made that led me to that room with Irina and Ryan. Each seemed reasonable and inevitable at them moment I made them, and even now, upon reflection, they still made sense.

As to reflection, I had completely lost track of my movements. Looking around, I found I had crossed the river and having wandered, completely without thought, I found myself outside a sweet looking tea room. I thought I had been there once, long ago in what seemed a different life. It seemed my subconscious had more sense than I had, so in I went.

Reflecting over tea, I pondered the irony of my situation, now living a life as chaste as any nun's, rendering my internal turmoil moot.

My thirst satisfied, but my spirit not, I started my wanderings again. Afterall, what else had I to do? Thinking and walking were often my form of meditation when trying to work out a problem. I wondered if this one would see me to the moon.

Evensong at Holy Trinity provided a rare solace, a moment of peace amid the storm. The casual inquiries from Ted and Alice about my future only echoed the uncertainty that clouded my thoughts.

"Adsit omen," I whispered to myself—a plea for acceptance of whatever lay ahead.

My days of rest in the benefice, once filled with country walks and casual encounters with parishioners, seemed like a distant memory. I had always viewed my role as one of service, a notion reinforced by Susan Fletcher, my mentor, who'd taught me the true impact of ordaining women in the ministry. The shift from divinity as a calling to a career had eroded the foundational aspect of service in our faith; a trend I sought to counter through my own actions.

Since I was a conduit for God's Grace, confecting the Sacraments was not just my duty but my privilege. Yet, the expectation of being more than what I was, to emulate charismatic leaders, those Billy Graham wannabees, chafed against my understanding of my role, or at least the one my heart bade me to strive for. My reflections during those morning walks were a testament to my ongoing struggle with my identity and purpose within the Church.

It was while pondering that on my morning walk into Richmond down the Thames Path that my mobile went. Rummaging in my bag, I found the thing just in time to take it.

"Yes, Robin here. How can I help?"

"Robin, my name is Margaret. I am Bishop Summers' PA. Would you be free for a chat over the phone later today? I don't suppose there's any chance that you could pop into Lambeth Palace this afternoon is there?"

Jane Summers was one of the auxiliary bishops who helped the

Archbishop of Canterbury. That was either a good sign, or very bad one. Either way, I signalled my agreement to an afternoon meeting at three. It gave me time to get home, put my dog collar on and something more suitable than my sweatshirt and pants in which to meet a bishop.

I had always taken the view that being a woman and a priest did not mean one had to look dowdy. A slimline black dress, flared from the waist and just above the knee, with glossy black tights gave the image I was comfortable with. I was vain enough to enjoy some of the looks I got on the District Line from Richmond.

Being one of those women who would rather be an hour early than five minutes late—a girlhood trauma thanks to Mama who was a Tartar on punctuality—I gave myself a good amount of grace time, just in case, and I needed a walk to clear my head and calm my nerves before the meeting, so I decided to get off at Westminster and walk up to the Palace.

As Parliament was still in recess, Westminster was pretty quiet, though the police officers and barriers reminded me that dangers were always present. To my amazement, as I walked past the public entrance, my eyes met the gaze of one of the policewomen on duty. Her tall figure, beautiful face, and olive complexion were unmistakeable. The long, black hair cascading down her back was just as I remembered from our school days. Despite the uniform, her striking beauty—a mixture of Greek and English heritage, each blending to the advantage of the other—had matured as a fine wine would.

"Robin, Robin Topham?" The beautiful face with a familiar voice asked.

"Oh my, Elena, is it really you? Wow, you did your training then?" To say I was shocked would be a profound understatement.

"Are you allowed to say to a lady vicar that you look hot?" Elena's purr was anything but professional.

It made me blush. "You, are, Elena," I retorted, and was rewarded with a flicker in Elena's eyes.

We'd been friends at St Guthlac's, but had lost touch after the sixth form.

"Must be ten years, Robin. You here on business? Can't imagine it's for pleasure!"

I laughed, how very El, as she had always been known.

"Actually, El, I am off to the other palace up the road, Lambeth."

"I knock off here at six. If you're still in the area, fancy a drink?"

"Love to—let me text you."

"Sure, here's my number," she said. Suddenly her body language changed from the casual stance to almost stiff. "Thank you, madam, and yes, just along the road that way."

Another officer was walking over. I knew nothing about the rank of police officers, but it was clear by his gate and he was her superior and wanted everyone to know it. Funny, I once read that some people when given authority walk as if they have a 'stick up their arse' but until then I had never understood it. This man looked and acted as the thing had thorns as well.

"Thank you very much, constable, much appreciated," I played along.

"Hi, sarge, I was just directing the Reverend to Lambeth Palace," El addressed the man who stood stiff, as if it was his natural condition.

The police officer was a tall man who, if he was trying to look unamused, was succeeding spectacularly well.

"Well get on with it. Just because this is your last week here is no reason for slacking, constable."

"Of course, sir," El replied before discreetly winking at me.

Gosh, this was a nice coincidence. Maybe my luck was turning?

I had to admit that I felt a little bruised by recent events. If I were honest with myself, I'd enjoyed rural ministry and would like to have gone on with it. It was unfashionable, poorly paid and a lot of work, but it suited me. Working in the country felt like gardening. Your hands got dirty; it was hard work, but things grew, and the roots reached deep and endured. Work in the city, by comparison, felt like potted plants—pretty helpful but, in the end, temporary. However, in the end, the only view I could take was that God had other plans, so it was time to stop moping, end my personal pity party, pick up my purse, and get on with seeing what was next.

I got to Lambeth Palace in good time, and was shown into one of the waiting rooms. I'd been here a few times, always impressed, if not slightly oppressed, by the many Archbishops who gazed down from their flattering portraits.

"Rev. Topham, could you come through? Bishop Jane is free now."

I followed Margaret upstairs to her office, which reminded me of my old tutor's at Queen's.

Bishop Jane was a tall, but slight woman, in her fifties, shortish grey hair, well-styled, and she smiled in what looked like a benign way.

"Coffee, Robin?" Jane queried.

"Pleased, white, decaff, please," I responded, feeling a bit nervous.

She asked Margaret to get us one each, then gestured to me to sit down.

"First, can I say, Robin, how sorry I am about what happened, but I hope you understand that your Bishop and Susan both thought it was for the best, given your local circumstances."

"I do understand, but thank you for the apology. But would I be right in thinking that's not why I am here?"

She smiled as the coffees were served, offering me a biscuit with it.

"You'd be spot on, Robin. I have a new posting for you if you want to take it."

My eyes widened in genuine curiosity; Jane just smiled.

"Your work in Suffolk helped unmask a network which brings Eastern European women here for sex trafficking, and we have been, along with social services, establishing shelters for these women. We want to appoint a chaplain to those homes, and we want you to be it. By *we*, I mean the Archbishop and myself."

"Golly," I said, my stomach more than a little aflutter, "I did not even know he knew I existed!"

"He was told of your work, and he and I agree that given your unusual experience, you may be the right woman for the job."

I noted how carefully Jane had referred to *my experiences.* I held my breath but she did not make it an issue, or make it sound sordid; I could have kissed her for it.

"Where would it be based?"

"Well, you could go back to Suffolk, to the coast at Felixstowe. We have homes there and in Lowestoft, as well as some women settled in the community where you could help the local clergy. You'd report directly to me though. What do you think?" Jane asked. If I read her right, she was sure of me already.

I was taken aback. I had thought my little adventure had gained me a permanent black mark on the record, but it seemed not, unless this was their way of putting me into the sidings.

"There's an old rectory we are having refurbished in Lowestoft, near the mission, that would be suitable. Will you take it?"

This was the only offer on the table, so I assumed it was this, or wait until something came up.

"I should like to try, if you feel this is somewhere I could help." I was no negotiator, and if I could help I would.

"One question, if I may, Robin?"

"Of course, Bishop," I answered a bit defensively, wondering if there was a 'but' in all this.

"Oh do call me Jane, Robin. Reading between the lines of the report of the case from the Intelligence Services, I note that you stayed with, was it Irina, afterwards. I know the church operates a 'don't ask, don't tell' line on such matters, but in confidence, I want to know, are you gay?"

Oh gosh! Well, there it was on the table. She was my Bishop, she had asked me a straight question, she deserved as straight an answer as I could give.

"I think I am," I responded.

A smile flitted across her lips, but her head tilted, a subtle knitting of her brows.

"You think? Robin, are you not sure?" When she said it out loud, it did sound a bit silly.

Cheeks burning, I looked away. *How could someone not be sure about that?*

"Not really. Irina was the first time I had had sex with *anyone*. I have been attracted to men, but, well, to be honest, I don't think I am going to go there." I found myself responding more openly than I had initially intended.

"Thank you for being so honest, Robin. It's okay, I am also gay, and the reason I asked is that there is a network of gay women in the church, and I have a feeling it might help you if you ever need to talk."

Had there been a feather in the offing, you could have knocked me down flat with it.

"Thank you, Jane, for trusting me with that."

"I know how hard it can be, Robin. My generation was the first to benefit from the Church agreeing to ordain women. I hope your generation might be the first to benefit from a more liberal attitude to gay people."

I was suddenly overwhelmed, a small tear forming in each of my eyes. It felt such a relief. I took out my handkerchief to dab them away.

"It's alright, Robin, let them flow. It can be such a relief to tell someone. Please feel free to talk to me whenever you need."

"Thank you, Jane, but well, is it safe to put me into a ministry with vulnerable women?" If I was going to be open, I might as well be fully candid.

"Put it this way, Robin. You don't strike me as a predator, and you do have a manner which will help put these women at ease. Tell me, with Irina, who took the initiative?"

"She did, Jane." Again, more honest than I had intended, but again it felt good.

Her smile was subtle, almost imperceptible. There was something in her gaze, too—a brief, appraising look that flickered across her face before it smoothed into neutrality. I found myself wondering what thoughts lay behind that serene expression. Was there a hint of understanding, perhaps even a shared curiosity lurking there? Or was I reading too much into a simple smile? Shaking off the thought, I continued, trying not to let my own assumptions colour the conversation further.

"As I thought. Look, Robin, these girls have all been used and abused by men—putting a male vicar in there would not work. Let's see how you do. Oh, one final question?"

"Yes, Jane." I could not believe how relaxed I found myself with a woman I had just met. She certainly had a gift.

"Is there a woman in your life at the moment?"

"No, so no impediment to my giving all my time to this ministry."

"Good. Now, drink up your coffee, and let's talk a little about what you will be doing."

A massive sense of relief washed over me.

From my training, I knew that confession was good for the soul, but I had not realised how much I'd needed to tell someone about this. Secular friends thought it mad; nowadays, who cared? Well, as I would say to them, the Church did. My Bishop now knew, and what was more, she sympathised.

We discussed the practicalities of the new position, and Jane told me the paperwork would be with me on the morrow. They wanted me to start at the end of the month, but if I wanted to start earlier, that could be sorted. I asked if I could have a day or so to make up my mind—a favour granted with a smile. She arranged for me to see my friends at the Clewer Trust, which dealt with modern slavery. Lynne would be delighted to see me I was sure. The events with Ryan had been a shock, but Lynne had come up trumps, which I was happy for. This new role would certainly mean more contact with the trust that was for sure. I hoped it would work out as smoothly but as they say, you can't dip your toe into the same river twice.

"What were you planning for lunch, Robin?" Jane's question shattered my reverie, abruptly snapping me back to the present.

"I had no plans, Jane. I am meeting a friend after she finishes working, but that apart, I had no plans except to see what I could scour from the bookstalls along South Bank," I responded, completely uncertain where I stood with this woman.

"In which case, let me treat you to lunch here," Jane replied; her warm smile and genuine enthusiasm were infectious.

Whatever I had been expecting, it had not been such kindness.

We walked a short distance to a place she knew, and were quickly seated at her usual table.

. Overcoming my nervousness, I managed to order a salad and some mineral water.

Jane regaled me with stories from her early days in ministry, not least about how hard it had been being one of the first women priests.

"So there was just no way I was ever going to mention my sexuality. Besides, Robin, back then attitudes were much worse. There was a law against teaching children about gayness, and oddly or not, the AIDS pandemic made things worse. There was no point trying to tell anyone that the only couple guaranteed never to get AIDS was two lesbians."

I liked her sense of humour, and appreciated her forthrightness with me. It felt special.

I told her more about what had happened with Ryan Surtees and the Russians, and she listened with rapt attention.

"I may have been naïve, Jane, but Our Lady saved the day," I replied, feeling uncomfortable with praise I did not think I deserved.

Jane softly smiled, recognising my discomfort at taking credit where I did not think it was my due.

"She has that habit. Would you like to join me in praying the Rosary after lunch?" Jane asked, making me feel oh so much better.

I accepted, which was how we ended up in her private chapel praying together. We prayed for my ministry at the end, and she thanked me.

"The pleasure was mine, Jane," I responded, feeling my cheeks redden, unsure why.

"I think, for the first few months, Robin, perhaps a personal briefing would be useful; what do you say? I'll throw in lunch," she asked, smiling.

I was unsure, but even with my naiveté, I was pretty sure I heard something was on offer, certainly more than just a professional meeting.

"A deal!" I said, grinning from ear to ear, before I leaned in and kissed her cheeks.

That still gave me time to scour the South Bank bookstalls for anything of interest, not that my library needed *more* books; it was an outlandish exaggeration that my bookshelves had once threatened to unionise, but I so love the atmosphere anyplace where books might be found.

I sat and had a coffee, reading through a collection of George Herbert's poems; now there was a gift I wished I had. There was something luxurious about just sitting there and watching the world go by, and all human life seemed to be there.

My phone pinged, just after five—it was Elena suggesting we meet up at the King's Arms. I texted back that I could be there in fifteen minutes, as I was on the South Bank. She texted back saying that she'd be happy to come over, and did I fancy eating. As I had nothing else to do, I texted back my location, and ordered myself a mineral water.

About ten minutes later, I saw Elena, now out of uniform, and waved at her; she waved back.

Her Greek ancestry showed, from that jet black hair and olive-coloured eyes to her slightly dark skin; she was even more beautiful than I remembered. It had been a decade, and it had been kind to her. Her white dress set off her skin perfectly, and showed just enough cleavage and leg to attract attention, but not so much as to invite it.

"What would you like to drink, Robin?" she asked. Her happiness was evident in the way her brilliant smile illuminated her face.

"Well, if we're eating, why not get a bottle of white?" I asked, trying not to appear overly taken with her, but likely as not, failing utterly. Even though my quick pulse would have told the tail had she felt for it. Some part of me hoped she would.

"Great idea," she said, going inside to order.

It was a calm, warm, late summer evening, perfect for sitting out of doors, sipping wine, and catching up with an old friend.

Elena had, she said, gone straight into the police force after finishing her sociology degree. She enjoyed the job, and had been based at Westminster for the last two years.

"So where next?" I asked. I could not help but wonder at her protestations of enjoyment; some part of me wondered at that, given her younger self might have thought such a situation rather dull.

"Border Agency," she said, "working to make the Government's policies actually work."

"Sounds like a big promotion. You must be happy," I responded, remembering she'd always been an ambitious dreamer.

"It is, and I am," she beamed and raised her glass in a salute that I returned.

"Where will you be based?" I asked, sipping the wine, which was rather good, but using the moment to glance at her legs, which were tastefully crossed yet still on display. A skill I had never acquired but which, thankfully, was not often required of a reverend.

"They're sending me to East Anglia. What about you? Who knew vicars could be so attractive?"

"Are you flirting with me, Elena Pandelides?"

"Too right I am," she responded with a playful smile. "Between girlfriends at the moment, and it isn't every day you bump into your first love."

"Was I that?" I asked, a bit taken aback but delighted still. My cheeks heated; I never would have thought I was *her* first love, though she was undoubtedly mine. A part of me had believed she was rather out of my league.

"You were the first girl I went to bed with, love, so that has to count." She casually tossed her hair and there was *that* smile again. "So, are you based here? What was Lambeth all about?"

"I was in Suffolk, but something happened which made that untenable, and for the past few months I've been kicking my heels," I responded, hoping my tone did not match my mood.

"Nice heels they are too. I didn't know vicars were allowed to wear high heels?" she asked, looking a bit higher than my heels.

I hoped I did not blush, at least not too much. "Oh these things, had them for ages, and I don't count them as high!" I responded. They were perhaps a bit higher than someone might expect, but they were reasonably comfortable, and besides, they set off my calves. Just because I was a reverend did not equate to being a frump.

"Now, you intrigue me. So, what was the Lambeth thing about?" she asked again, nothing if not dogged, just as I remembered her.

As I spoke, her eyes widened, a spark of interest igniting. Her lips parted slightly, an unmistakable sign of her attention.

"Lowestoft? I'll be based in Ipswich, covering the coastal areas— Hey, maybe we could meet up? Unless your girlfriend objects. Or did you decide guys were your thing?"

I told her that there had been a man, but that it had gone nowhere, and then found myself spilling the beans about the whole Ryan thing. She listened with rapt attention.

"Fuck, Robin, the things you vicars get up to! Are you and Irina still a thing?" Her tone made it clear that she hoped the answer was no.

"Alas, no, she went back to Ukraine to help there," I responded, hoping my voice did not give away how her parting made me feel; although our time had been brief, I did miss Irina terribly.

"You up for a meal?" Elena inquired again.

"Why not? I'd be dining for one at home."

We ordered one of the specials, and chatted about old times, old friends, and what we'd been doing since. Catching up with her was a genuine pleasure. The long summer evening allowed us to sit out until after nine o'clock. The Thames was lit up with passing boats, South Bank humming with people. It felt good to be here in El's company.

"One for the road?" El asked.

"Why not. I'll have a grappa," I replied.

"Good idea. Let me get them."

Perhaps it was the effect of the drink, or a long day, but I was beginning to feel a little tired, and it would take me at least an hour to get back home—indeed at this time of night, more like two.

El came back with the drinks. "I took the liberty of paying; hope you don't mind?" she said.

"That was sweet of you, let me next time."

"Deal"—El gave me her seductive smile—"you'd like a next time?"

I said I would, realising that I *really* would. As things moved on, there was a comfort in harking back to a more settled time. Even as my thoughts turned in this direction, I noticed that El's foot was playing with mine. Could she, too, want old times?

"You look tired, Robin. How long will it take you to get back home?"

"I'm in Teddington, so at least an hour and a half at this time of night."

"I'm in Clapham, and we could be there in half an hour by cab. Fancy spending the night?"

It was tempting; I was *very* tempted.

Seeing my hesitation, El added, "I shan't jump you, Robin. You can sleep on the couch, or we can do what we did at school."

What we had done at school was spend a night together, kissing and cuddling, but going no further. Neither of us had seemingly the slightest idea of what we ought to have done next, oh so long ago. But now we were older, and more experienced, and I could not imagine that a night with El would be chaste.

"I would love to, El, but I am trying to work some things out," I answered, not without more than a bit of regret. I was still a bit confused and didn't want my turmoil to ruin what might be a budding relationship.

"Well, I am in Suffolk next month, so maybe our next dinner date could be there?" El responded, her eyes brightening with anticipation. That seemed a good way of postponing answering the question of whether I wanted to have sex with El, so I agreed.

Our goodbye kiss indicated her mood—and mine. I had not expected to be kissed on the mouth, but didn't object to it. I had not expected her hand to find its way under my skirt, and did object to it—if not immediately.

"It would be lovely to get to know you properly, Robin," El said, again with that smile, and colour in her cheeks.

"Yes, it would," I responded, with more than a bit of my own flush, trying to put my kit back to rights.

All the way back to Teddington I pondered what had just happened.

At one level it was as clear as daylight. El fancied me and wanted to have sex. I fancied El, but it was not me to want instant intimacy. I'd long ago accepted that was the way I was. Recently, I had told Irina that I didn't believe in premarital sex; as a matter of doctrine, I did not think premarital sex was healthy, and the prevalence of STIs made promiscuous sex dangerous at the least. However, I had found, as countless others had before me, that living that doctrine faithfully was much more challenging than I'd ever imagined. The night with Irina was proof of that; I chalked it up to emotional release as much as anything.

The truth was I was ambivalent and deeply conflicted on the subject.

When preachers went on, during the rare occasions they ventured into the subject at all, about premarital sex being sinful, it caused me some vexation. For ages, and indeed even now in some quarters, the whole idea of lesbian sex was considered sinful. There were two logical reactions to that—celibacy, which was not me, or ignoring it and going ahead anyway, which was also not me. The net result was a messy Robin compromise, rather like the position taken by my Church on the issue—no wonder I was an Anglican!

Recent events had proven that I was far more attracted to women than any man. Women, of course, did not carry with them the risk of pregnancy, so the practical reasons which had dictated the moral code, did not apply. That, I thought, was a frightfully pragmatic view, but there it was, and I was not going to pretend otherwise. Some people had the gift of celibacy, and while I respected that, I had begun to realise that I did not share that vocation. Despite valuing celibacy and my desire to remain faithful to my beliefs, my experience with Irina had left me conflicted—a struggle I was still grappling with. I liked Elena, and if, on closer association, I wanted to go there, then I would. But would that, I wonder, have implications for my future? Besides, I could not get past that it was all so rushed.

I began to see why Bishop Jane kept quiet. Maybe that lesbian network she'd mentioned would help?

I walked the short distance from the station to home, and caught up with my emails. The job offer was there. I replied accepting it. A few moments later I got a text from Bishop Jane:

'I am glad that you accepted, J xxx'

Three kisses from the Bishop?

I dismissed it. Surely I was overthinking their significance, something I have *never* been accused of. After all, Jane and I had only just met. I decided my over investment in their meaning, must have been the after effect of the wine and Elena.

I lay in bed that night, excited about so many things I could not sleep. Then, at about midnight, I thought of something rolling around the back of my head, but only now, in the quiet of the night, did it come to the fore. Jane had mentioned reading reports from the Intelligence Services; as I fell asleep something was there, but I could not grasp it just out of reach. That brought up my thoughts about Irina and her sudden departure and work in Ukraine, and how that had so fortuitously come about. Those thoughts rolled around, chasing each other, like cats with a ball of string, till finally the clatter settled and I found some semblance of sleep.

In the morning, I looked around my flat in London, the place I had returned to since the whole Ryan mess. Despite its familiarity, it no longer felt like home. I needed a change, a fresh start, and a new horizon to sweep away any lingering regrets. With this resolve, I contacted the estate agent to let them know the flat would soon be available to rent, and began preparing for my new future.

Chapter 5

REV. ROBIN SAVES

It felt good to be back in Suffolk, even if Lowestoft seemed a million miles away from my rural ministry. The rectory, newly refurbished, offered a sanctuary of comfort amidst the surrounding chaos. The building stood at the edge of the town centre, an area that had seen better days. The streets were lined with old hotels, many of which had been converted into hostels for those down on their luck or places where women in unfeasibly short skirts plied their trade at all hours. My new 'parish' was like no other.

Inside, the rectory was a stark contrast to its surroundings. The walls were painted a soothing cream, and the wooden floors gleamed with polish. The sitting room was cosy, with a well-worn leather sofa and a bookshelf overflowing with theological texts and novels. A large bay window let in the afternoon light, casting a warm glow over the room. The kitchen, though small, was immaculate, with gleaming countertops and a collection of mismatched mugs hanging from hooks above the sink. I thought I would enjoy living there. I set myself about moving in. It did not take me long—I am not a great one for *things*, with my greatest weakness being clothes and shoes, but those weren't arriving until tomorrow so I was traveling light.

One of our hostels, called the Retreat, was ten minutes' walk from the Rectory, and it was the first place I chose to visit so off I went.

Straightaway, it was clear to me that I had a choice—or rather, if I was to do the job I had been sent to do properly, I had no choice. The area was bad enough during the daylight hours, but after dark it took on a threatening air, with gangs of men roaming the streets, and youths hanging around every street corner; it was not a place for a woman to be out on her own. And yet, if I were to do my job, I would need to walk those streets whenever I was needed.

The Retreat was a modest yet welcoming building tucked away on a quiet side street. The exterior was unassuming, with weathered bricks and a simple sign indicating its purpose. However, stepping inside, I was immediately struck by the warmth and care that had gone into making it a haven for those in need.

"Ah, Mother Robin, how nice to finally meet you. I am Miriam. I manage the Retreat and two other hostels in the town. Can I get you a coffee?" With that she turned, and continued on chattering as she walked. She struck me as sweet and more than a bit nervous. I followed her.

The entrance hall was painted in soft, calming colours, and the floors were covered with sturdy but comfortable rugs that muffled the sound of footsteps. A bulletin board by the door was filled with flyers for local services, community events, and motivational quotes, offering both practical information and a sense of hope.

"Mother, what do you like in your coffee?" She stood in the door way with a tray filled with all the things one might want anywhere near your coffee, and many I would never have imagined. She went through the hall to and I followed, not a clue where we were going.

It turned out to be the common room, which was the heart of the hostel, furnished with a mix of donated sofas and armchairs, arranged to encourage conversation and camaraderie. A large, well-worn coffee table in the centre held magazines, books, and a few board games. On one side of the room, a small kitchenette provided the basics: a kettle, a toaster, and a selection of teas and biscuits, always available for those who needed a moment of comfort when the main kitchen was closed, which apparently was never with Miriam around.

The walls were adorned with cheerful artwork, much of it created by the women themselves, reflecting their diverse backgrounds and shared experiences. Large windows let in plenty of natural light during the day, while in the evenings, soft lamps and fairy lights would create a cosy, inviting atmosphere.

Miriam was a stout woman in her early forties with dyed brown hair, hiding the grey, and what my own Mama would have called a '*bustling manner*'. I liked her from the start. She was open-hearted, cheerful, and clearly driven by a need to serve others. She told me about the women in the hostel. Every one of them was a refugee from Ukraine, though most had arrived unofficially via traffickers.

"I fear, Mother, that some of them still work for their old employers. We can't watch them twenty-four-seven, though we can, and do, enforce a nine o'clock curfew."

I knew that some women priests liked being called 'Mother', the counterpart, of course, to men being called '*Father*'; but I was not fond of it.

"Oh, Miriam, do call me Robin," I said cheerfully, in the hope that she would stop making me look around every time she said the word *Mother*! I honestly wasn't sure she heard, for she just kept forging on.

"We hold an assembly every morning at eight, and it would be wonderful if you could lead us in prayers. Many of the girls are, or were, Catholics, and I think it would steady them to have something religious to start their day."

We sat and chatted a little longer. "Would you like a look around?"

I was in mid sip but nodded the affirmative. And with that, we were off, most of the rest of the rooms were much like the common room, meant to emphasise comfort and reassure safety. My office and connected study was just off the main door, and would offer some privacy when needed. It was just as warm and inviting as the rest. I looked forward to spending time there.

Upstairs, the bedrooms were simple but clean and private, each with a single bed, a small wardrobe, and a nightstand. Fresh linens and warm blankets were provided, and the women were encouraged to personalise their spaces with photos and personal items. The bathrooms, though shared, were kept meticulously clean, with plenty of hot water and a selection of toiletries available.

Throughout the hostel, there was a palpable sense of community and support. The staff, including Miriam, were always present, ready to lend a listening ear or a helping hand. The women, though many had come from difficult and traumatic circumstances, found solace in each other's company and the safe, nurturing environment that the hostel provided.

I toured the other three hostels, and before long, it was beginning to feel as though we were a real little community. I only realised how much so after Morning Prayer at the Retreat a few days after I had arrived. Although the Morning Prayer Assembly was voluntary, ten out of the fourteen women came, and I soon got to know them. I made time for each of them to tell their story, and, promised where necessary, to work with Miriam and her small team to help them with Immigration. After Morning Prayer, Darnya, one of our residents, asked to see me.

Darnya was the sort of woman you noticed. She was a natural blonde, with an enviable figure, and she carried herself with an air of confidence.

"What can I do for you, Darnya?" I asked, smiling, trying my best to be welcoming as I knew how.

"Well, it is more what some of us have done for you, Miss Robin." She returned my smile but still seemed unsure.

We went to my office and sat down. Her long legs in that short skirt naturally attracted my attention.

"You are a good woman, Miss Robin. It is not everyone who would spend time with us. I think Miriam will have told you some of us still do sex work." Darnya's straightforward approach cut through the usual fluff; she laid bare the facts without a trace of discomfort, either hers or yours.

"Yes," I replied, looking at Darnya and not being in the slightest bit surprised.

"Some of us work for a man called Dimitri who runs several brothels. He is not a bad sort, and he likes to keep things peaceful, so Yana and I had a word with him, and he has put out the word to his men. Anyone caught bothering you when you are about God's work will be beaten. I think, Miss Robin, the streets will be safe for you. He would like to meet you, though, if that would be acceptable?" Again, matter-of-factly. Her calm was as unsettling as it was unexpected. She spoke with the casualness of someone commenting on the weather, all while discussing something as serious as protection from a local crime lord.

I must admit it took me a moment or two to come to grips with that particular revelation, and I could not help but wonder whether some price had had to be paid for this boon. I hoped for her sake it was not too high.

It would have seemed ungrateful to have said no, and, after all, we were taught that no one was without the chance of redemption, so I agreed to a meeting. I received a message from Darnya asking if three o'clock at one of the cafés off the promenade would suit me. I texted back saying it would.

Perhaps it said something unfortunate about me, but Dimitri was not at all what I had been expecting. I'd had Ryan's associates in mind, men who looked thuggish and rather scary. Dimitri was none of those things. In fact, when he waved me over to his table, I actually looked around to see who he was waving to!

As I crossed the distance, he stood, buttoning his jacket as he did. His suit was perfectly tailored, of the finest quality, silk but not too shiny, certainly from the best in London, although I guessed his shoes were Italian, also top drawer. In any other setting, I might have thought him a corporate type, perhaps a financier. However, I knew all too well where and who made him his money.

As I approached, he held out his hand. "You must be Robin? I am Dimitri," he said, smiling and shaking my hand firmly. "Can I get you tea and scones? That would be suitably English, would it not?"

He drew out my chair for me as I laughed, and agreed, "As long as there was some jam and cream."

That, in turn, made him chuckle. He then returned to his seat, his back to the low wall that separated the café from the adjacent alley.

"Thank you for seeing me. I wanted to meet the woman who is taking such trouble with my women. I am also interested that you have not forbidden them to work for me. Surely that is condoning sin?" His eyes showed he was intelligent, but I thought there was an edge there, an iron grip under manicured nails.

I nodded, and thanked the waitress as the cream tea arrived.

"It is recognising their right to choose. From what they have told me, they do this because they want to. I have known women forced to do this, and Darnya and those who have stayed with you are not, I think, being forced," I responded, holding his gaze, hoping my fluttery tummy did not show through.

He nodded and, looking earnestly at me, went on, "Whatever happened at the start, they are not now. We pay them well, give them health checks, and ensure they are looked after." Dimitri paused and leaned over the table. "Any man who hurts them will not do so again."

Leaning back in his chair, almost posing with a self-satisfied air, he smiled and gestured with his hand, palm up, fingers splayed as if he were reaching out to me for understanding. "We also, as Darnya will have told you, try to keep the streets safe. Your police do not seem to be interested in this part of town."

"That almost sounds like you think you are doing good, Dimitri," I responded, not taking the bait of his being some sort of self-styled Robin Hood.

"I would say we do less harm than others. The Albanians over by the harbour are an example of what could happen here," he replied, rationalisation clearly evident.

I had heard nothing good about the Albanian gangs in that area, who did seem to fit the stereotype.

"So, you are the lesser of two evils?" I asked, trying to keep my tone light. I did not wish to accidentally make an enemy here; Dimitri could make my work easier or impossible.

"You could put it that way. You have met Darnya, do you think we could force her?"

"Oh, I am sure there are ways of forcing even the Darnyas of this world, but if you are asking whether I think you are forcing her? No, I don't." Again, meeting his gaze. I needed his respect.

"I wanted to ask you something." His elbows were on the table this time, fingers laced as if in prayer.

"Go ahead," I responded, sipping my coffee, only glancing at my cup then meeting his eyes.

"I think it does the girls good to have a mother confessor. They are used to it from home. Would you be willing to hear their confessions?"

For the second time, Dimitri had surprised me. I knew I'd have to seek permission from the bishop, and told Dimitri so.

"You do know they are supposed to repent of their sins and amend their lives. What would you do if they did?" I asked, probing a little deeper, determined to see just how deep his *magnanimity* went.

"Give them the money we have saved from their earnings and let them go. There are plenty more fish in the sea, Robin." He leaned forward again, the artifice falling away; now, he was being upfront. "Nature has given women the same card to play; some by nature, a higher value true. Most, when hunger bites, will play that card to survive. It is the way of the world."

He leaned back again and, with a shrug, added, "I am simply the dealer."

Alas, that I knew was the truth.

"There is a confessional at St Mark's, and if I am allowed, I will use it between midday and two o'clock on a Monday." I did want to help these girls not only spiritually but also literally; if I could only help one, the rest would be worth the discomfort.

"Thank you, Robin. Here, let me warm your cup." He poured, and I watched; perhaps my experience with Ryan made me leary, but I observed.

We got around to my asking him how on earth he became involved in this business.

"I defy your stereotype do I, Reverend Robin?" Again, he was lounging a bit, grinning back at me.

"You do," I responded, playing with my cup.

"I did a degree in Business at the LSE, went back to Russia and worked there, and then worked in Ukraine—came here when Putin invaded, and through a friend of a friend, got into this."

There was, I was sure, something he was not saying, but I did not intend to press him. Dimitri and I parted, and after refusing his offer for a lift, I started walking. I needed the chance to think, and I did so all the way back. His words seemed reasonable, but I couldn't shake the feeling of unease.

Reflecting on the meeting later, before phoning the bishop, I felt ambivalent. Was I being played? At some level, yes. He presented as a *nice* man, who professed to *care* about his *employees*, who were prostitutes, and who were protected by his thugs from worse thugs. But didn't all abusers, when challenged, declare they *cared* about their victims? And as to his protecting these women, was that anything more than preserving the value of his assets? Even if he was the lesser of two evils, he was an *evil.*

Bishop Jane agreed in principle to my bargain with Dimitri, if not to the spirit of it.

"Robin, I'm glad you rang. It is a perplexing one. As you told him, confession is meant to be followed by amendment of life, and that is not happening. At that level, the question of whether you should do it has an easy resolution—no. But if I ask the question what harm will it do to the women to be able to talk to you in confidence, I find none—for them. My worry is for you, Robin. What happens if they confess something criminal?"

I couldn't help but wonder if she was really just worried for me, or perhaps herself too? After all, there was as much danger for her as me, conceivably more. I sighed, disappointed with myself—the whole business with Ryan had made me paranoid.

"What happens is what always happens, Jane. The confession is sacred, and I cannot reveal its secrets. But in the event of something criminal, there are aways of indicating to the authorities that they ought to be looking at someone or something."

"Sophistry, Robin, but a good and acceptable answer. My question to you is, can you cope with all this?"

"All what?" The jaded voice in my left ear counselled toward the belief she was anxious for herself. However, my gentle and hopeful right ear voice whispered; at worst, she questioned my ability to adapt, or perhaps she was concerned I might be tempted or *seduced* into something awful? If it were the latter, then her concern was for me after all, which made me feel good.

"Robin, you are a celibate young woman with sexual desires, and you will be hearing confessions from and working with sex workers. Are we asking too much of you?" Jane inquired, but something in her voice caught my attention; what caused my senses to be alert? I was not sure, not yet, anyway. However, it was clear that Jane had not yet apprehended my sense of determination once I set my mind to something.

Mama had once said, '*Robin, your will is like an oak root; it digs deep, bites hard, and never lets go, even when it should.*' Sometimes, I wondered if she'd meant it as a compliment.

"Time alone will tell." At that moment, I was less concerned about the titillation aspects of the confession than I was about the helplessness of not being able to change the trajectory of these women's lives.

"What I would ask, Robin, is that at our meetings, we discuss this, and if you have any problems, phone or text me at once. Agreed?" Her genuine desire to be helpful warmed my heart.

Of course I agreed. I greatly appreciated Jane's concern. If I was asked at what moment the seeds of my affection for Jane were sown, it would have been this one golden moment when I first felt that Jane might genuinely care for me, both emotionally and romantically. This moment paralleled Scripture as to those seeds, and only time would tell whether those seeds fell on good soil or among thorns.

So it began.

Not all the women came to confession, and not all those who came, came every week, but most did come.

Their sins were the usual ones of the flesh, and I gave them the usual penances as well as the absolution which adjured them to go and sin no more. But like the rest of us, they invariably returned to confess the same old sins. Was it wrong of me to hear their confessions? Only if it was wrong of me to hear other confessions. We all desire to amend our lives, but we all fail. Perhaps they did not mean to amend their lives, but possibly that made them more honest than the rest of us?

There were no conflicts of interest. Prostitution itself wasn't illegal in the UK. Their sins were, in some senses, more straightforward than others. They sold their bodies. They regretted it. But they did not seek alternative employment, mainly because nothing else offered them anything like the money they already earned.

My reports to Bishop Jane were received with satisfaction, and she told me that it seemed as though I was coping well.

In a sense, I was; in another, I was bewildered. Sometimes, Jane was so warm; other times, she was matter-of-fact. I had a growing sense that I wanted more from Bishop Jane than my superior's pat on the head. Although I was honest enough to admit I was very gratified with the ego strokes she gave me on my performance.

Jesus was known as a friend to sinners, and it's likely that some of his followers, by the strict standards of the time, were women of easy virtue. In that spirit, I embraced my role, aiding those who felt solace in confessing their sins. While the work differed vastly from parish ministry, with parishioners unlike those in rural Suffolk, I saw them all as children of God, deserving of equal care and love. The challenges of loving and serving them only reinforced my commitment to demonstrate God's love, aligning with what Ministry is truly about—not my desires, but God's.

Jane had pointed out the irony of my situation well. As a single woman among sex workers, I found myself reflecting on the need for balance—a middle ground between their world and mine.

Such were my reflections that cool late August morning when, as had become my habit, I walked along the prom to watch the sunrise. As the easternmost town in the UK, the sun rose here earlier than anywhere else. I was not a great believer in jogging, although I did occasionally, but I preferred to take a daily walk along the beach, praying and meditating as I did my ten thousand steps. I wished I had put leggings on rather than shorts, but if I walked fast enough, I'd warm up.

I was listening to the Rosary on my phone and following, which explained my slowness; well, that, and the fact I was hardly expecting to see anything at that hour. My mind had, as ever, wandered, and I was trying to get it back to the meditative prayer when my eyes caught a commotion in the sea.

I strained to look and immediately dialled the emergency number. There were people in the water. I rushed down to the beach, to find two men staggering, soaked, and gasping for breath. They were speaking a language I could not understand. But what I could understand was that there were others in the water.

I rushed in, and swam out a little to a clutch of women; they kept breaking the surface, then screamed for help, only to sink again. The water was frigid, and I knew they had little time before hypothermia would take them. Although the cold cut to the bone, my body was filled with adrenaline, and at that moment I barely felt the chill; I was desperate to get to the floundering women. I helped two to the shallows before, my heart pounding in my chest and my ears, diving back in to help a couple more.

Nearby, the two men who had earlier dragged themselves onto the beach lay there idly, offering no help as I struggled with the latest victims. They joined their companions, speaking quickly, among themselves in an unfamiliar language, evidently detached from the crisis unfolding only yards away. I took only a moment, hands on my knees, gasping to catch my breath when finally the water cleared my ears, and I could hear clearly again.

Sirens wailed in the distance. As I glanced back, the two men were running, the cowardly bastards, leaving the four women huddled on the beach, shivering in the cool mist. The hysterical pleas for help drifted over the lapping of the surf. Near exhaustion and with the creeping cold finally beginning to seep into my awareness, I forced myself to continue. Ignoring my waning strength and the screaming of tired muscles, I threw myself into the surf and swam out, searching for the source of the cries. Nearly beyond my capacity, I finally found her still struggling against the currents. With the very last of my energy, I pulled us both back to the safety of the shore. Praise God that by this time, the blinking lights had reached the beach, and police officers were putting emergency blankets on the huddled women.

My temporary companion held onto me, and we collapsed on the beach, totally spent. Finally, I rolled onto my back as an officer approached us.

"You the one who called it in?" A tall police officer looked at me; once upon a time, I might have thought him handsome, but I was off men for the foreseeable future.

"Yes," I spluttered, barely able to form the words. "There could be others out there."

"Right," was all he said, and with that, staring out into the surf, he unabashedly stripped down to his underwear and went diving in. Luckily, search and rescue helicopters with searchlights cut through the gloom to illuminate the roiling surf as rescue divers joined the search.

He pulled two more nearly drowned women out but could find no trace of their boat.

By this time, the ambulances had turned up, and a paramedic offered me some foil sheeting and something purporting to be coffee; well, it was hot, and it was wet. It's only redeeming qualities.

"Robin!"

I turned to hear a familiar voice.

"Elena!" I genuinely was shocked to see her and revived more than a little. I did not have the time to think by what providence she was here, but regardless I was thankful for it.

"It's okay, Sarge," she said to the tall officer, also now clad in foil to keep him warm. "This is the Rev Robin Topham, an old school friend."

"Well, Robin," he said, "you just saved these women's lives. We'd been tracking a boat, but lost it about half an hour ago, and God knows what would have happened if you hadn't happened to be here."

"Well," I said, "God had other plans for them."

"Sarge, she should know," Elena laughed; he laughed with her.

"Right, Robin, you'd better come with us to the hospital and get yourself checked out. Then we'd like to take a statement." The *sarge* seemed to be in much better shape than I was; whilst I was trying to get my breathing under control, he looked ready for another 1500 metres.

"Lead on, Macduff," I replied, still winded but able to walk. The adrenaline had worn off completely by this point.

"How on earth did you know my name?" he asked, his eyes widened in surprise.

"Serendipity?" I replied, feeling exhaustion overtaking me; seeing that he was not amused, I sighed. "Macduff is a character in Shakespeare's *Macbeth*. It is commonly misquoted; the actual line is 'Lay on, Macduff' from Act 5, Scene 8," I answered, giggling, so exhausted that I was giddy.

Elena's lips curled into a mischievous grin, her eyes sparkling with amusement as she tried to suppress a chuckle.

I last remember hearing Elena's voice, saying, "You can't get anything over on her, Guv."

The ride was comfortable. As I leant on Elena, her perfume was as I remembered, but perhaps I was just choosing to remember that way. Eventually, we must have got to the hospital, as I was gently carried in.

The medics pronounced Macduff and me fit and undamaged by our early morning swim and provided hospital scrubs to replace our wet gear. There, I learned that Macduff was, in fact, Detective Sergeant Daniel Macduff, and my Elena was now a Detective Constable, on loan from the Border Force, reporting to DS Macduff. He and Elena took a brief statement then and there, but asked me to come down to the station for a full interview when I had dressed.

Darnya, whom I had called, brought some clothes for me, and I was just preparing to leave when I got a call—it was from Dimitri.

"I hear you have been doing early morning swimming, Robin." His voice all but danced with amusement, and I couldn't help but feel a bit more than a prick of annoyance.

"I have," I replied, wondering what this call was about and having a disquieting suspicion.

"I have some information about those people which I am willing to share with you. I can't go to the police myself for obvious reasons, but I would like to help." The way he said it made me imagine him, feet up on the desk, casually admiring his latest manicure.

"Thank you, Dimitri," I said, hoping he was honestly attempting to assist my mission, but doubting it.

"Meet you at eleven for morning coffee if you have nothing better to do?" Dimitri's voice breezed through the phone, light and unconcerned. I found myself puzzling over the real reason behind his casual invitation. What was he really up to?

"Well, as I have to go to the police station sometime this morning, can we make it ten, as I can then give them the information you give me?"

"See you at our usual then."

I was just about to put my phone in my bag when it went again.

"Robin, what's this I see on the news?" It was Jane's voice all but crackling with tension, every word taut with urgency.

"The news?" I said, with the naïveté born of the fact I rarely bothered with the thing and had no television. But Bishop Jane did, and was trying to find out what was going on.

"It says, 'Woman vicar walks on water to save'. What happened?" Jane's voice carried an unfamiliar tone that unsettled me, though I couldn't quite say why or even how.

I told her a less dramatic version of the events.

"This isn't to do with your women is it, Robin?" Jane asked.

My women? Was that the root of her odd tone? I hoped not, for if it was, I was afraid I might have overestimated Bishop Jane. I wanted to be wrong and that my respect, indeed admiration for Jane, was not misplaced.

"Quite the opposite. Their pimp is going to tell me who did this. I am off to the police soon," I replied, still wondering what was going on behind this conversation.

"Well, Robin, thank goodness you are safe. Well done, my dear!" Jane responded, and she sounded genuine.

Perhaps my concern was misplaced, but if I were being honest with myself, the whole situation was insane. After all, I had just been out for a walk and then all this? I honestly couldn't blame Jane for her concern. It certainly warmed my heart that she *was* concerned for me, not just any of her flock, but for me. Her praise made me beam, and I knew it was because of her. I had to have been smiling all the way to get checked out.

I realised what Jane had been talking about when I reached the hospital entrance. A TV crew and some journalists were lying in wait. My first reaction was to wish my hair did not look so messy and that Darnya could have picked something more flattering than the summer dress with the yellow flower pattern.

How vain was I!

"Rev Topham, can you tell us what happened?" A journalist thrust a microphone in my face.

Best get it over with. I took a deep breath before explaining what I had seen and done, then went on my way.

I saw Dimitri at the coffee house at ten. Something was amiss. Instead of his usual impeccably tailored suit and gleaming shoes, his shirt was slightly wrinkled and his tie was not perfect. More than that, his hair, which was normally perfection, seem just shy of its usual order. As he caught sight of me, his expression swiftly shifted—he adopted his usual suave manner. Watching him scramble to put on his accustomed façade, I couldn't help but feel a twinge of satisfaction at his momentary vulnerability.

"Pain au chocolat with your cappuccino?" Dimitri asked, a grin, which I could only describe as *sly*, curled at the corners of his mouth, as he leaned back in his chair with an air of self-assured ease.

"You look like that sort of girl." His eyes twinkled with a hint of amusement, clearly enjoying the presumption.

"Oh," I replied, smiling as disarmingly as possible. Before adding, "And what sort of girl is that?"

"The sort of girl who has that style," he parried, again the smile which, with each appearance, lost more of its charm.

"Why, thank you, kind sir," I chuckled as he went to order for me.

"You must tell me about your adventure," he began.

So, yet again, I told him.

"That was brave. Did the police catch the two men?" Dimitri asked, assiduously observing his drink.

"No, they seem to have escaped into thin air," I replied, carefully observing his reactions while trying not to be seen doing so.

"They'll be with Mehmet and the Albanians down in the centre of the town," he said. "They were smuggling girls in to challenge our supremacy. I can tell you where they will be if that will help."

I smiled, taking a bite of the pain au chocolat the waitress had brought.

"It will help you," I replied, stating the obvious, undermining his competitors while appearing to be the white knight helping the downtrodden girls.

"Yes, it will, but it will also aid your authorities, will it not? What happens to the girls?"

"Well, they will be accorded temporary asylum. As it happens, one group of girls moved from one of our homes, so we can probably put them up there."

"And then?" he asked, trying his best to seem calm, but not quite successfully.

"Then, well I am assuming some of them may decide to vanish into the community." I suspected I knew where he was headed with this; I hoped he would prove me wrong.

"We would look after any such," he said, feigning nonchalance.

"Dimitri, you expect me to recommend you to them?" I held my breath.

"No, just not to stand in their way. And, of course, if you can help them as you do the others?"

And there it was.

"You know I am conflicted over this, Dimitri?"

"Ah," he said, the smile disappearing, "because you can't associate yourself with whores? Didn't Jesus?"

The café, I thought, was no place to get into a discussion on the mistakes made by Pope Gregory over the Marys in the Bible, and in any event, he was not being totally unfair.

"It's not that. It's that it would be better if they really repented."

"And did what?" he asked, his voice quickening, a sharp glance darting my way as he drummed his fingers on the table.

"Well, you are not exactly Mother Theresa, are you Dimitri?"

That seemed to restore his good humour as his laugh attracted the attention of others.

"A fair point, and anyway, thank you, Robin. Will you be taking confessions later?"

"I shall." I smiled, happy to have averted an argument. I knew Dimitri was playing me, but it was the women who mattered.

It had turned into a pleasant morning, so after coffee, I took a little stroll before returning home. A crowd of people and vans filled my street, and I wondered what on earth was going on. As I got closer, I realised it was the press and TV crews.

Three of them dashed up to me when they caught sight of me.

"Robin, Robin, can you tell us what you saw?" they all shouted at once; it was impossible to tell which had asked.

The questions piled in, but were all along that line.

Oh goodness, I thought, I really wasn't dressed for the media, but I did my best to answer the questions. As I got to the door, thinking I was done, a journalist buttonholed me.

"Robin, I'm from the *Daily Mail*, could you do me an interview? We'll donate a fee to a charity of your choice," a young journalist asked, catching his breath as he spoke. His eyes, wide and hopeful, darted between mine and the notebook in his hands. He had an open and friendly face, not the cynical expression I had become accustomed to in the press. It was clear he knew just what strings to pull with his mention of charity, my Achilles heel.

The second part of that sentence cancelled out my instinctive reaction of 'no' to the first part, so I invited him into the house.

Over yet even more coffee and biscuits, I recounted what had happened and, once the reporter had finally gone, I went about preparing for confession.

It was with a sense of shock, then, that walking past one of the shops on the high street, I saw myself on screen. That was compounded by the billboards at the newsagent's: '*Red Robin Rescues Refugees!*' Someone liked their alliteration.

Confession, or to give it its proper name, the Sacrament of Reconciliation, was always a draining process. What the women poured out seemed to pass through me, and I always prayed afterwards for them, and myself. By now, it was the usual confessions of sins of the flesh, followed by the usual absolutions. I took some time after finishing today's confession in the confessional to pray for all of us, waiting to see if anyone else came in, and had just convinced myself that I was indeed done for the day when the confessional door creaked open, interrupting the silence of the church.

There was a brief quiet then a hesitant shuffle of footsteps before the soft hiss of fabric against the wooden seat on the other side of the curtain. A soft exhale, just audible—it was so soft that it made the stillness I had been enjoying seem overpowering, almost oppressive. I hoped she would speak if nothing else than to relieve me of the burden of the silence.

"I am here to confess something." It was a young woman's voice, but not one I was familiar with. "But not in the way you think. You can't trust the police you are working with; they have an informant there who tells them everything. I don't know who it is, but there is such an informant, believe me or not. I am taking a risk telling you, but they allow us to have confession, and this is my only chance."

With that, the door's ancient hinges sounded, followed by a click as the door shut, leaving a whisper of relief that seemed to linger in the air like a hint of perfume.

This 'confession' left me bewildered. I was assuming 'they' were the Albanians, who were behind the trafficked women I had saved earlier. But why did I think that? Because Dimitri had told me? But could I trust him? Honestly I doubted I could, but what was his game, what would he gain?

For the second time, I put in a call to Bishop Jane, telling her what I had been told.

"That is a dilemma, Robin. Is there anyone there you think you can trust?"

"My old schoolfriend Elena is with the Border Force. I have known her since we started school together, so I think she will be okay."

"Well, take care. I shall have a word with a friend in Whitehall. I'll let you know what she says. Would you be free to move our monthly meeting forward to this coming Monday?"

"That would be good, yes, by all means." I was all anticipation.

"Good, thank you. See you then, darling."

It hit me as I put the phone down. Had the bishop really just called me 'darling'? My cheeks burned, and instantly I realised I had never heard a more beautiful word.

Chapter 6

CENTRE OF ATTENTION

I found myself a minor celebrity, which was every bit as awful as they said.

It had been a slow news day, so the interview appeared on the national news, while the story in the *Daily Mail* prompted others to phone me. In the end, I asked Miriam, who ran the Retreat, to tell people I was busy.

I had only done what any decent person would have done; if that made me a hero, then there were millions of those; I was simply no longer in the unsung category.

"Mother Robin," Miriam asked; her concern was unmistakable, but there was also a hint of confusion in her voice. "Shouldn't we be trying to save these women from the wicked trade they are involved in?"

"Yes, and we are," was my only response; I tried not to sound condescending but to help her see the narrow path I was trying to walk.

"But why do you hear their confessions?" Miriam responded, this time with more confusion than judgement. "I thought that people who confessed had to, what's the phrase, *amend their lives*, and try to live a better life after."

"They do," I confirmed, not bothering to try to stop Miriam calling me 'Mother Robin', realising I would have to suffer through whatever made her comfortable. "But think for a moment, if I stopped being an outlet for them, what would happen?"

"Maybe they would reflect on their evil deeds and reform?" Miriam postulated, but in her question, she revealed a commonly held perception that these women had chosen the path of their own free will.

"In an ideal world, but what about in this one?" I answered her question with one of my own, hopeful that she might wonder why I had asked it in response to hers.

"But as Christians we have a duty to redeem them," Miriam responded.

In some ways Miriam brought my own Mama to mind. Mama and Miriam seemed to see the world in the same rigid way. Mama would have approved of Miriam, especially since the latter would have made sure the house ran like a clock and the tea would always be served exactly on time. Neither were terrible women; I thought both had good hearts. It was just that there were few shades of grey in either of their views.

"We are all sinners, Miriam," I gently reminded her, trying to avoid scolding. "God, the only just judge, redeems. We are called to love our neighbour as we love ourselves. These women get enough judgement from others, all of it adverse. If I can help them, I must; it is what I am called to do. It is what *we* are called to do."

"Oh, Mother Robin, you are a good woman, too good for this world. You don't know such women and what they are like." Miriam took this moment to make her exit, to go on making the trains run on time.

I let it go.

Miriam had done what we all did at times, the self-justifying rationalisation. At first, she had seen the women as victims, then moved on to calling their actions *evil,* therefore ending in blaming them. But of course, while not identifying with such women herself, she might have had a point.

I wondered on some level if, by making that rationalisation, she inoculated herself from believing that she might have had to make the same choices if she'd been in the same situation. She might see herself in them if she continued to view them as victims. If, however, they were somehow complicit or even directly at fault, then she could believe herself able, as a *moral woman*, to void their fate and thus not feel their helplessness.

Perhaps I was a bit naïve. I was an upper middle-class woman from a good background with the social capital that went with all that. It was easy to judge others who had none of those advantages. I was not stupid. Nor was I blind. But I had talked with these women, and while one or two, like Darnya, had clearly decided that, on balance, this life offered them more than the alternatives, most of them felt trapped. They used drugs, although I thought it likely to self-medicate the despair of feeling trapped. Unfortunately, drug use formed its own cage. They needed money to support their habit. Prostituting themselves was the most straightforward option. But, of course, through that choice, they were being exploited.

It was a vicious circle. These vulnerable women had been led into this life by their pimps. But until, and unless, they could see a viable alternative, a meaningful ray of hope which was something I could try to help with, they would remain where they were. I could go into *saviour* mode and work with the agencies to try to pull them out, but the evidence suggested that unless the decision to leave was owned by them, they would slip back, and in this town, a waiting Dimitri was the lesser of two evils. That, as I told Bishop Jane at our Monday meeting, did not mean I thought that what Dimitri did was not evil.

Jane smiled at me. Against my better judgement—after all, Bishop Jane was my direct superior—I felt a thrill at her smile. Unlike Ryan, her smile reached her eyes; it was genuine, and I adored it.

"I see your dilemma, Robin, I really do. But what worries me is the idea that someone in the Border Force is aiding and abetting all of this. I talked with my contact in the Home Office and discreet enquiries are being made. You might expect some contact soon I am told."

As to what sort of *contact*, Jane could not tell me that, as she did not know.

Jane was happy with the reports on the mission. All of my three Rescue Houses were, she said, doing a good job, and, happily, the number of women opting out of prostitution was increasing.

"I am told that some of the women have said that your non-judgemental attitude has helped them. Two said that they felt they could not carry on confessing and going back to their old ways." Again, leaning back casually, Jane smiled as she sipped her tea.

I was also becoming relaxed with her, which was a welcome change from the tension of my previous situation.

"If that was the Spirit moving in their hearts, it is to our Lord, not me, that the credit is due," I responded, more than a little embarrassed that I should receive praise for doing my duty as I thought our Lord would have wanted.

"True, Robin, but he has only your hands to work with and your mouth through which to speak, so take credit. This mission is still somewhat controversial, and there are many, perhaps a large majority, who would take Miriam's point of view," Jane gently scolded me, setting down her cup. "By the way, she says you are wonderful."

"Bless her"—I could not help smiling myself—"she is a good woman, and I could not do what I do without her and my little group of helpers."

"You're a good team leader, Robin, and I am hopeful that the success will aid in defusing some of the criticism. Your early morning swim helped that cause along splendidly."

"Oh, Jane, it is much exaggerated." My cheeks were warm enough to boil the North Sea; I had to have been pink to my breastbone.

"I am sure." Again, she was smiling, her eyes twinkling, but something in her voice implied more.

I noticed a look in her eyes, a look that I was not at all familiar with, it seemed to border on hunger but that would be too harsh—I suppose the closest word would be desire... Regardless it left me a little tongue-tied—certainly not a state I was overly familiar with, nor one I particularly enjoyed.

"Sorry, Robin, I was distracted by the idea of you in your swimwear." Her voice was at least half an octave lower than earlier; it made me a little giddy.

Jane let the words lie there. I am embarrassed to say I think I stopped breathing altogether.

"So, lunch?" She sat up, as if the previous moment had not occurred.

"Please," I said, leaving the words where they lay. Luckily, my heart and lungs resumed their services again.

Get a hold of yourself, Robin; what is the matter with you? I knew I was behaving like a lovestruck schoolgirl. A stage I thought I had outgrown.

The bistro Jane chose was a short walk along Embankment, and offered a view of the Thames whilst we dined. I wanted to hold her hand, but we were within sight of Lambeth Palace, and the chances of someone working there seeing us holding hands was too great to take.

We ordered from the 'light bites' menu. I was not a great one for lunch, and the anxiety I was feeling reduced my appetite still further, so I ordered pea soup with fresh bread, while Jane ordered a ravioli; somehow the content of the meal was not important.

Jane spoke to me of her anxieties about the whole *Living in Love and Faith* or LLF process.

"There are some who will not give an inch, and others who will not accept anything less than full equality with straights. I find myself in a squeezed middle."

Banishing the thought that I should dearly love to have squeezed more than her middle, I offered my thoughts. "It is harder for you, Jane, being a Bishop. But I cannot see why the Church cannot do what it usually does, and find a middle way that no one wants but everyone accepts in order to stay together."

"You make it sound like a bad marriage."

"Maybe so," I said, "but it is the least worst of the options on the table.

"I am uneasy," Jane admitted with a deep sigh, which seemed to speak of something deeper than she was revealing. "All my career I have had to conceal my sexuality, but unless called to celibacy, I have never seen how lying or concealing something can be worse than being honest and open. But to be honest would risk ruin."

My heart went out to her. I touched her hand to squeeze it. She looked at me. The depth of sadness in her eyes spoke to my soul. Trying to lighten the mood, I essayed a joke, "Well, Jesus had his last supper, Jane, and we have had our first lunch. I do hope our aftermath is happier."

"I wish… " she started. She did not need to finish, the squeeze back on my hand spoke volumes into the silence as our eyes locked.

So, back it went to LLF…

For some years the Church had been encouraging an open discussion, called *Living in Love and Faith* about how it should behave towards gay people, especially gay clergy. Anything short of the usual Anglican genius for fudging would already have broken the Church. As it was, traditional conservatives thought that even considering blessing gay couples went a chasm too far. Gay rights activists thought the Church had gone nowhere near far enough. The former ignored the feelings of millions, whilst the latter ignored Canon Law and the views of millions of others. I felt for the archbishops; damned if they did; damned if they didn't. I was glad I was a humble vicar.

"The Archbishop is in a dilemma, Robin. What would you do?"

"He is, and what I do is thank God I am not an archbishop - or to be honest, even a bishop."

"Ah," Jane sighed from the heart. "A wish I have often had."

I could not help but feel for her. "I am sorry not to be of more use, Jane, but for me, the Spirit is the same one of love that I show to the prostitutes."

"You think lesbians are like prostitutes?"

"I think that in the eyes of the Church hierarchy and many parishioners, that is the case. That does not mean I agree, it simply means that as I refrain from judging the one, I do the same with the other. I know there are differences, big ones, but in the eyes of many Christians, a woman with my feelings is as big a sinner as a prostitute."

Jane looked at me, searchingly. "You know, I believe you. But then you have never been a prostitute; you have been a lesbian."

"True," I said, sighing.

"Is the past tense correct?" Jane asked.

"In the sense that I am celibate, yes, in the sense that I am attracted to women, no."

"Do you have a girlfriend, Robin?"

Jane's hand felt so warm. My heart beat faster, not quite pounding, but it was close, and given its previous quick pace that was astonishing. Her eyes met mine.

"Do I?" I smiled at her, leaving so many words unspoken, hoping Jane's heart would know what I meant.

"I am sure, my dear, that you could easily acquire one, so much easier in your later twenties than twenty years on," Jane responded softly, her eyes moving down at our clasped hands.

There was a note of sadness in her voice which I found unbearable.

"It depends," I said, despairing of anything meaningful to say.

Was she really coming on to me? Part of me wondered if my eagerness and inexperience caused me to misread her meaning as more than kindness, but the better part knew my instincts were correct. She *was* indeed, at the very least, interested.

"On what?" she asked, finally meeting my eyes again.

There was a tone in Jane's voice I did not recognise. I wished I had some experience on which to draw, but I might as well have wished for the moon.

"On circumstances and, yes, Canon Law in our case," I replied, trying not to blush but by the heat of my cheeks, failing miserably.

"Our case?" she asked, her left eyebrow arched up along with the tone of her voice. She smiled suddenly, her laugh lines creasing, making her look even more beautiful.

"Robin, either you are blind, or you don't want to see," Jane continued to laugh; it was a lovely sound like the ringing of silver bells.

"It's, well, it's just..." I tried to find the words, but it was another awful moment when words failed me.

"That you aren't gay? That I am not your type? That you don't feel anything?" Jane's laughter faltered. Her smile faded slightly and she glanced down, her fingers nervously twisting a strand of her lovely hair.

I was so flustered that all I could do was blurt out what was in my head, seldom a good idea, as like most of us, I was better when I had time to process what my brain spun out. "No, no and no!"

The laugh lines deepened. Jane was so stunning at that moment. Her almost white hair framed that smile, and her eyes seemed lit up like the sky at dawn. For most, greying hair made them look old, but not with Jane. With her colouring, the shape of her face and the brilliance of her eyes, the gleam of her hair was not the dull grey of decay bearing the wear of long years but was a mane of iridescent silver gleaming with wisdom, life, and vitality.

She did not look beautiful; she was beauty itself. How had I not seen it properly before?

Her hand touched mine.

"Is this all too much, too soon?" Jane's voice had become almost maternal, but her eyes smouldered with decidedly non-maternal thoughts.

"Yes," I answered too quickly. "And no," I added more slowly, going with this sudden *speak your mind* fashion I had recently adopted.

"Yes, it's too much and no, not too soon?"

There was almost an impishness in that smile. Jane softly squeezed my hand; I thought she was trying to reassure me. My cheeks coloured, and I was reassured.

"Would it be better to continue this after lunch?" Jane asked ,her voice dropped in tenor; the husky tone definitely suited.

"I hope we are not going to break Canon Law?" My throat desiccated, and the words caught.

"That forbids marriage, darling, which would, perhaps, be too much and too soon, to quote someone I have fallen in love with." A smiling Jane brushed an imaginary stray hair from my forehead before she took my chin in her hand to lift my eyes to hers.

She said it! Wait, did she say it? I think I heard her say it. My thoughts were swirling. I was close to hyperventilating.

My head did an *oh my goodness!* thing. I know it's not the most articulate way of putting it, but that reflects where my mind was at that moment. The words *love* and *fallen*, in the same sentence, directed at me? No one had ever said that to me, not in this way.

I giggled! I just bloody well giggled, feeling nervous and emotionally naked.

"You have a nice giggle, darling. Would you like to take a stroll? I have nothing except you in the diary for the next two hours," Jane added, the smile and joy of my reaction shown in her eyes.

So we did just that. On a cool late summer's afternoon, we strolled down to Westminster Bridge and talked, and talked.

Jane could hardly have been sweeter or more considerate.

"We need to take care. Usually, I would report to my immediate superior that I was involved romantically with one of my priests to avoid any perceived conflict of interests so that any appraisals, for example, would not be done by me. But since, officially, the Church disapproves of us, I can't do that. But I will make sure that one of the Archdeacons deals with you. I shall say that as your mission is special, that would be better. She will understand," Jane went on, almost absentmindedly; I did not interrupt.

"Is the 'she' one of those in the network you mentioned?" I asked, still trying to get my intellect to engage.

"She is, and you should not worry. But I hate that we cannot be open," Jane responded, her undimmed smile still making me giddy.

We both agreed that it was ridiculous. In what other walk of life would two professional women have to hide their love for each other?

"Maybe," I said, "that is one of the reasons I can't find it in me to condemn or judge the sex workers. So many of those who would condemn them, would also condemn us as sinners, despite the fact that there are almost no passages in Scripture condemning lesbianism."

"Robin, you are a sweetheart, please never change. Let me deal with the traditionalists."

That seemed just fine to me. But as we walked to South Bank, we still had not addressed the question that had been floating around my head and, I assumed her head too. As though she were clairvoyant, Jane then broke the silence.

"Can you stay for a night or two soon?"

"Yours?"

"Yes, mine, though I should visit you soon."

"You are not worried?"

"No, the staff are loyal, and it is not like we will be parading it."

I felt a sense of relief, followed by one of anxiety. Jane noticed.

"I am taking it from what you have told me that you do not have a great deal of experience in these matters?" she asked.

"Apart from Irina, no, and that was simply a couple of nights," I responded.

"Don't be anxious, darling, I shall help you explore. It will be fun."

I thought of that look on her face all the way home. I also thought, longingly, of the kiss on the lips we had shared as we parted. I was in a state of shock. Bishop Jane was saying she loved me? Me! How on earth could that be? What should I do? How would it work? In fact, I was so preoccupied with my own thoughts that when I changed trains at Ipswich, I did not spot Elena until she virtually bumped into me.

"Robin, you were a million miles away. Thinking of those modelling contracts then?"

I blinked, feeling disoriented and trying to process her words. "What?"

"Oh, you missed the tabloid pics of you on the beach in your wet shorts and tee-shirt then?"

The words "oh my goodness", formed on my lips.

Elena pulled the paper from her bag, and there I was, Miss Wet Tee-shirt of the day, complete with apparent nipples and the headline, "Rev Robin bathes the day."

"Wish I looked that good coming out of the sea, darling." Elena grinned. "You catching the Lowestoft train?"

"Yes, just coming back from seeing my boss."

"Had she seen the pics then?"

"Not when I left," I said, wondering what Jane would make of them, and while I was wondering. "Who on earth took that picture?"

"I'd guess one of the bystanders," Elena answered. No doubt seeing how shaken I was, she threw me a rescue line, "Here, let's grab a drink, there'll be nothing on the train."

Luckily for me, clad in my clericals, complete with a sensible skirt, I was just about unrecognisable as the woman on the beach in the picture, which was a relief.

Elena seemed eager to talk as we got to the train.

"I was talking to members of the team, Robin. They say you have an 'in' with the boss, Dimitri."

"Is he the boss?" I asked.

"Seems to be. What can you tell me about him?" Elena asked.

I told her what I could.

"I'm a bit amazed, to be frank, Robin, that you, a vicar, are so accepting of all this."

"That's like saying you're amazed that I acknowledge the weather. Of course, I'd love it if there was no need for these women to do what they do, but two things: what are they going to do if not this; and given it exists, would you rather exile these women to the margins and condemn them, or extend God's love to them?" Again, I responded to yet another woman seemingly willing to cast other *women* aside for the sin of avoiding drowning by grasping the only flotsam they could reach.

"You're very forgiving, but you ought to see what goes on with these girls, Robin. What happened to the men who were with the girls?" Elena sounded almost as surprised by my compassion as I was at her seeming lack of it.

"They got away," I responded flatly.

"Could you identify them? Would it be worth you talking with a police sketch artist?"

"To be honest," I laughed, "one thuggish man looks much like another."

"So you know it is the Albanians who are bringing these women in?"

"So Dimitri says," I replied.

After that, she changed the topic, moving on to the differences between where she had been working in London and Suffolk.

"It's like something lost in time, really. All those big sea front hotels, are now either empty or used to house prossies or refugees. It's a good thing you're there to help. Social Services seem over-stretched."

I agreed that they were.

We talked about the past, and then suddenly she said, "I'm going to be in town for this week, you fancy meeting up for a drink?"

"That would be nice," I said, meaning it.

"Okay, fancy Wednesday night?"

"Great," I said.

The train was just coming into the station. As was my habit, I waited to let others off; Elena lingered with me.

"I was told that you listen to the women in confession, is that right?"

"I do," I said, adding swiftly, "but I can't reveal what they tell me."

"Not to anyone?" she asked.

"Not to anyone," I confirmed.

If I had thought that the 'celebrity moment' would be just that, a *moment*, I was wrong.

Nigel, the rector of St Mark's, commented on it when I met him for a coffee before taking confessions there.

"There's been a lot of comment, Robin, and I am afraid that some folks think it unfortunate."

I tried to reason with him, but I could see it was to no avail. To some people it was more scandalous that I had been photographed in a wet tee-shirt than it would have been to have let those women drown, and it was clear that I would have to live with it.

I left him to marinate in his sanctimony.

Darnya also felt the need to comment. "You know, Robin, you have a nice pair of breasts there."

As we were walking back to the Refuge, that rather took me by surprise, and I said so.

"Well, Robin, I may fuck men for money, but I fuck other women for pleasure." She winked at me.

"I am attached already," I said.

"To another woman, I bet!"

I blushed. "How did you know?"

"My—how do you put it—gaydar, is good. You are an attractive woman, Robin, and I sense you are lonely. I should be happy to brighten your evening—you are a good friend to us all, and it would be nice to be able to give something back."

Her hand brushed mine. I assured her that, flattered though I was, I should not be taking her up on the offer.

I needed to hear a friendly voice so I phoned Jane.

"My darling, stop worrying, it will die down. Now, how are you fixed for a little time together?"

She seemed sure; I hoped she was right; I feared she was optimistic.

One thing about our vocation was that the idea of a weekend away was impossible—Sunday was our busiest day, but with a bit of diary juggling, we found a Monday and Tuesday at the end of the month.

Part of me regretted the delay; part of me did not.

I had *almost* digested the fact that Jane wanted to be with me, but if I were honest with myself, I was having trouble with what might come next. Jane was, obviously, experienced in matters of love, and, to put it mildly, I was not. Except for my brief affair with Irina, I was entirely lacking, which made me worry about how on earth I'd satisfy Jane.

I was not even sure what I wanted sexually. From what the women told me, their men wanted quick satisfaction, which seemed to them something of a blessing. As more than one had said: 'gets it over with quickly'. But that was not how I felt. I wanted to feel Jane's body against mine; I craved that sort of intimacy. I knew something of the practicalities of lesbian love making from Irina, and I had enjoyed helping her to orgasm, and her helping me to the same climax. But somehow that mattered much less than the intimacy; it was that I craved. But of course that was the difference wasn't it? The women were providing a service, not sharing intimacy with someone they loved.

It was, I pondered, precisely that which was lacking from what the women told me in confession. They were engaged in a financial transaction—the quicker it was over, the better. But I knew from the tone in their voices that they, too, wanted more. One had talked about how a man simply wanted to talk with her and hold her. It was, she'd confessed, harder on her emotionally than the men who just wanted to use her to sate their sexual desires. This interaction was a simulacrum of what she herself wanted with the *right man*, or perhaps it was the sadness of these men who had to pay for the most basic of human companionship that affected her. My own confusion about how I had been so fooled by Ryan, and whether I could ever really trust someone again, added to the doubt around what I actually wanted from a relationship too. Hearing the confessions took its toll on me. But when it was over, although emotionally exhausted, I felt a sense of having been of use to them.

It was in that mood that I met Elena at the Green Dragon. She was sitting outside in the beer garden and smiled when she saw me.

"I thought you might like some wine, so I ordered a bottle and two glasses. You look preoccupied, what's up?" Elena's smile never dimmed.

I told her what Nigel had said. She listened quietly, not interrupting.

"Well, if it is any consolation, my male colleagues agreed with me, you look hot in those pics."

"Thanks, I suppose," I responded, thinking it would be a little churlish not to thank her, but feeling a little weirded out at the idea of men perving over me.

"So," she asked, as we clinked our wine glasses in a toast to 'pastures new', "have you met anyone out in this wilderness—apart from your ladies of the night?"

I told her about Darnya's suggestion, which made her laugh.

"Well, if you aren't taking her up on it, put in a word for me, I'm getting a bit desperate. Don't suppose you're free?"

I was relieved she had brought up what could have been the elephant in the room.

"No, no I am not. In fact, I have just started seeing someone." I tried to be tactful, as much as I liked Elena, I could be honest and say I was not interested in more than her friendship.

"A woman, I assume?" she probed on.

"You assume right," I responded, feeling a smile on my lips.

"How in the bloody hell did you manage that in this one-horse town?" Elena laughed.

"Oh I didn't, she's in London." I was smiling more broadly myself, but I did wonder at her assumptions.

"Yeah, my last lives there, but I'd prefer to find someone closer to home. I'm guessing that as a vicar, you wouldn't be wanting to cheat on your squeeze?" Her eyebrow raised as if to reinforce her suggestion, especially when combined with her impish grin.

"You'd be right," I told her.

I was relieved to have that out of the way, and it was typical of Elena that, having established that we were going to remain firmly in the 'friend zone', she chatted away happily, until her mobile buzzed.

"Sorry, Robin, I have to take this."

I took another sip of wine. The evening air was growing colder. There were those first hints of the chill that presaged autumn; I shivered, wondering whether we should go inside for an after-dinner drink.

How odd it was, I reflected, that Jane, Darnya and Elena should all have come on to me in the same week. Given our history, had Elena made her suggestion the previous week, I might well have responded favourably; there was no denying I was attracted to her. She was every bit as attractive as she was so long ago. In truth, if anything, her experience and confidence made her more so.

I was still pondering such matters when Elena came back.

"Sorry, darling, it's work, I shall have to love and leave you. Let me give you something for the meal."

"It's fine, darling," I said, "you can pay next time."

"Glad that there will be a next time." She smiled, kissing me on both cheeks.

I decided I'd have another drink and then go.

It had been a pleasant evening, the sort of thing I'd needed. I was conscious that all work and no play could indeed make Jill a dull girl. I finished my drink and headed for home.

The lights of the docks dotted the horizon, providing a picturesque backdrop to the view along the sea front. I realised that if I walked much further, I'd be into the area frequented by the prostitutes, so decided to take the back route. I wrapped my shawl around me. It was getting cool.

As my eyes adjusted, I thought to myself that the red-light district had to be spreading, as I saw a man and a woman kissing urgently down one of the alleys. I crept along, sticking to the shadows so as not to disturb them. They also moved, and it was with a shock that I recognised the woman as a streetlight lit up her face—it was Elena. She didn't seem to notice me, but I had clearly seen her, and the man.

It was Dimitri!

Chapter 7

ROBIN INVESTIGATES

I was shaken by what I had seen.

Only a few days earlier I had been told by one of the working girls that the traffickers had a *mole* in the police force. My thoughts had been focussed on the *Albanians*, but thinking back, that was because Dimitri had said they were the ones responsible for the women whom I had saved from the sea. And yet, had not every one of those ended up with Dimitri's outfit? Then I remembered how keen Elena had been to know if I could identify the two traffickers who had escaped from the beach. The inevitable question posed itself. Was I being played? Of course I was, but by whom, and to what end? And then there was the coincidence of Darnya and Elena both coming onto me.

I was not a great believer in coincidences. If, and of course it was still *if*, the women were being trafficked by Dimitri's organisation, then most things would slot into place. He would want to know whether I could identify his men, and who better to get that out of me than a policewoman with whom I was friendly? If she could get more than *friendly*, it would help him discover what else I knew, especially if Darnya's offer had been designed for the same purpose. Worse, if I had yielded to either — I would be compromised.

I felt myself shaking as I got to the house; and it was not the cool night air.

I had a restless night. I could have been wrong. Elena had been kissing Dimitri in that alley, that was undeniable. But the meaning of it? Well, that was open to interpretation. Because of my current preoccupations, I had given the encounter connotations which fitted together; but was I being too suspicious?

I tried to attach other meanings. Perhaps Elena was undercover? Jane had told me that I would be contacted by someone, could that person be Elena herself? I had never mentioned Elena to Jane, so there was no reason she would have thought that I would already have known the person.

The morning caught me by surprise - the inevitable result of a disturbed sleep. Pondering it all over breakfast brought no ideas.

At the Church, I did my morning prayer, with the usual sparse attendance, but just as I was putting my clericals away, someone came in. I looked up, and instantly my heart leaped—a wave of surprise and sheer delight washed over me. My eyes widened and the corners of my mouth curled into an uncontrollable smile as I realised—it was Irina!

"Robin, they said I would find you here. How are you?" Irina was smiling; I'd always thought she had a lovely smile. I was starting to think I had a thing for smiles.

I had last seen her a few days after Ryan Surtees had been arrested, after we'd spent a couple of wonderful days together in the hotel suite. The flashes of memory set my cheeks to alight.

"Irina, how wonderful!" To say I was a bit shocked would have been an understatement.

"Were you not warned?" Her voice showed more than a bit of apprehension.

So, I thought, that was what Jane had meant. The Ukrainians had sent Irina. So, what was her role now? This shock brought to mind the assessing look she had given me what felt like centuries ago. I had thought it might be her trying to determine if I were to be trusted, now I wondered even more. Was this role new or had it been hers before she had taken me to bed? Was she too playing me? I shook myself, to focus on the here and now, leaving those thoughts for the dark hours of the night.

"I was just told someone would be coming, but not who," I replied, wondering now about my previous assumption and its implications for Elena.

"Well, I hope I don't come as an unpleasant surprise?" Irina's smile dimmed slightly, and I thought I saw a glint of tears in her eyes.

I realised she had to have heard some note in my voice that reflected my sudden doubts, and I knew instantly I had to wipe those doubts away. I forced as bright a smile to my lips as I could—it was not difficult as I was very fond of Irina.

"Nonsense, I am so happy to see you." Rushing to her, I took her in my arms, and kissed her cheeks before pulling back to look into her eyes. I was smiling so hard my cheeks hurt. "It is just that they gave me no information as to the who, leaving me to guess, and I might have guessed wrong, but let's not talk about that now. There will be time later, right now let's go grab a coffee, my caffeine level is low."

"We can't have that," Irina laughed, her doubts seemed to melt away. "I know how you are about coffee and how you are without it."

We went to the Sweet Peace on the sea front, which gave us a good view, and over cappuccinos and pain au chocolat, we got down to business.

"We know that the Russians have a business in trafficking Ukrainian girls taken from their homes. Some of the Russian commanders have arrangements with criminal gangs to do that. Mind you, you could characterise the Russian Government itself as a criminal gang. We think they will use existing networks, and your east coast here will be the preferred landing ground. There is too much activity in the Channel, whereas out here, as long as the boats don't capsize, and a glamorous vicar does not rescue people, no one really notices."

"But the women we picked up were not forced." I voiced my thoughts.

"No, they would not have been, but we think it was a dry run for the real thing. That would be why they have been trying to determine whether you could identify the men concerned," Irina retorted.

That made sense, but then I thought, how on earth did Irina know that? So I asked her.

"Our allies have intercepted their texts and calls, and it is clear that they are agitated. You may have been asked by someone called Darnya."

"I was. But I am told by sources close to the Home Office that they have a mole in the police helping them," I responded, trying to repress my doubts.

"Yes, I was told that. Do you have any suspicions of who it might be? Has anyone from the police been asking the same questions as Darnya?" she asked, her piercing eyes focused on me so intensely I wondered if she could see my soul, and my doubts.

Would it be too awful of me to mention Elena? That would be sure to get her into trouble with the authorities, and all I had to go on was that I had seen her. But then I had seen her kissing Dimitri. It was easy to accuse myself of jumping to conclusions. So I decided to jump to none and simply tell the truth.

"Yes, my old friend from school, Elena, asked me." I made an effort to be nonchalant, but it was hopeless.

"She's an old friend? You can trust her?" Irina implied that I shouldn't.

"I think so, or rather, I thought so until last night." I wrestled with my doubts, realising that the Elena I once knew might not be the woman I now know.

Irina's eyes bore into me—it was like having an x-ray. I took a deep breath and told her what I had seen.

"She was kissing him?" she responded, her voice neutral, so neutral it was unnerving. Her tone frightened me.

"She was," my only response, just above a whisper. I studied my cup; I could not meet her eyes.

"That's not good," she said, stating the obvious in an attempt not to offend me. "Do you think she is the, how do you call it in English, the mole?"

"She could be, but I know Elena and find that hard to believe." Perhaps it was misplaced loyalty but I felt the need to defend my school crush. "I can't imagine the Elena I knew… but it might be possible."

"We shall perhaps sit on that and see." Irina observed me closely; she had to have felt my apprehension.

"So," I asked, "what are your plans?"

"Oh well, I am not here officially until later, and then I shall be going to see Dimitri!"

My eyes widened in shock, and a quick breath escaped me. Across from me, she caught my gaze, a subtle recognition lighting up her face as she noticed my reaction. "It is called 'undercover,' darling. For most of the past six months, I have been working with the Ukrainian end of this operation as a minder for the girls," Irina answered matter-of-factly.

"You mean you are a Madam?" I asked. it was difficult to make my mouth work I was so surprised given what we had both been through with Ryan.

"I suppose so. The Russians are worried about the welfare of the girls; they are worthless to them, sick or dead. But, my friend, they seem very concerned about the slow erosion of numbers, for which they blame you," Irina replied with a smirk, but I sensed a note of concern, and perhaps even a bit of respect.

My cheeks reddened again. "Well," I said, somewhat indignantly, and with no small amount of pride at my results, "it was Dimitri who asked me to get involved."

"Yes, but I think they may have underestimated you, darling. Back home, where all the priests are men, neither an Orthodox nor a Catholic priest would have reacted to them as you did. I think they were expecting you to condemn them, not reassure and certainly not rescue them." She openly smiled at me. I was certain now—she was proud of me.

I took her comment as a compliment and treasured it.

In that moment, her words provided a momentary justification for my work, a fleeting vindication. The need to justify my actions sprang from a flawed paradigm. I had seen my work through the world's lens, where sex workers were viewed merely as victims. They were acted upon by their 'saviours' in a manner not entirely different from their 'clients', ultimately denying them their agency and autonomy.

My instincts, however, had guided me down a more pastoral path. The absolution of their sins was not merely to 'save' them but to empower them. By listening, not judging, nor lecturing, I helped them find their own path out of darkness—their own agency. God had reached out to them through my voice, and some had indeed heard Him. I was humbled.

I smiled and thanked Irina.

"When you are working there, I will need to see you too." I made sure I had a smirk of my own.

"I was rather hoping you'd say that, as that is precisely where I will be able to pass on information to the authorities—the confessional is sacred even to the Dimitris of this world. But what about Elena?" Irina responded, but the mention of Elena caused me to take a breath and let it out in a sigh.

"Can we, for now, go with my instincts? I don't *think* she is the source, but I will try to find out more."

"I'll go with that," Irina said. "But now, I'd better make myself scarce, don't want to be seen with you just yet."

At that, she squeezed my hand. "I loved our time together, and if you are ever at a loose end..."

She let the words lie, and again my cheeks warmed. At this rate, I would save a pile on rouge.

What, I wondered, was this? Was I giving off some strange lesbian aura telling attractive women I was available? I should, I knew, have told her about Jane, but some instinct said not to. It was not cowardice, just something which said not to.

I spent the rest of the morning catching up with emails, when I was not pondering what I was doing here. My mood was lifted by what Irina had told me. I emailed Jane to inform her.

I went to the Retreat for lunch, where Miriam told me that one of the *girls* as she called them, wanted to see me. I said I'd grab a sandwich in my office and asked her to get the woman concerned.

I was just about to unwrap my sandwich when a small, light-haired woman ventured, shyly, through the door. My first impression was that she seemed very young, with an almost elfin beauty. Her blonde hair was in a ponytail, and the red and white check mini dress she wore added to my first impression.

"Is okay to talk now, miss?" The young girl's voice was little more than a frightened whisper.

"It is. Please call me Robin. Can I get you something to eat or drink?" I said smiling, hoping to reassure her.

"Is okay, miss, sorry, Robin. I am Marta, thank you for seeing me." Her tone was a little more confident.

"How can I help?" I continued eye contact; her eyes were lovely and expressive. I saw fear. I showed her in to my office, checked that the hall was clear, then closed and locked the door.

She was still nervous. I remembered her voice from the confessional. I felt for her. I asked her to tell me what was bothering her.

"I am sorry, miss, that I still am being whore, but these men, they have my passport and if I don't, they could hurt my sister back home, and my mother. But it makes me sad, miss, and now I hear something which is bad, and I need to tell."

"You are taking a risk, Marta. I'd be happy to wait till confession on Thursday."

"It not keep, miss. I overhear one of the men telling Darnya to be ready for new girls tomorrow. He say they are from Russia—our women captured by Russians and sold. Can you help, miss?"

No wonder Marta was shaking. I thought I might start trembling myself.

This mapped onto what Irina had been saying, but gave us both a day and a probable place.

"These women, Marta, you're sure they are being brought to Dimitri's?"

"Yes, miss, that is what I heard, is why I tell you. They will be moved on once they are here, so it is not time to wait," Marta replied, her voice firmer in its conviction.

"Thank you, Marta, thank you. Do you think anyone saw you come here?" My fears for this young girl bloomed like flowers with an awful stench.

"I say I come to ask for help with medicine, miss. I on my period, I say so, and men, you know what they like when you talk about such matters." She smiled, quite happy with herself at this deception, one that women had used for millennia.

I could imagine. It was courageous of Marta, and I did say that if she was worried, I could make arrangements to keep her safe, but she declined, saying that if she vanished, her family would suffer.

I arranged for Miriam to provide her with the requisites to back up her story, and then phoned the emergency number I had been given with for the Border Force to tell them what I had been told.

The next day, my nerves were on edge. I had just finished evening prayer and was taking my vestments off when my phone buzzed; it was Elena.

"Robin, I will be in Felixstowe later, would you be free for a drink, or perhaps a bite to eat?"

As I was, I said so, agreeing to meet her at the Green Man at seven.

I had not heard from Elena all week, and now, when I had been told that more women were about to be landed here, Elena wanted to see me. Of course, as she was with the Border Force, she would be coming, so perhaps I was being paranoid?

I put on my striped cotton top and a mid-calf length skirt with heels before throwing on my beret at the last minute. Smart, I thought, but not too obviously sexy. Was I wanting to attract Elena, or did I just want to challenge the myth that women clergy were dowdy figures? A bit of both, I thought to myself as the chill night air embraced me.

Elena was already in the pub, so I shared a bottle of wine with her, and we ordered supper.

Once we were seated, she asked how I was, and then, after we had run through the pleasantries, she told me, "I'm here on operational business. I'll be at the police house tonight, and I can't be later because I'm up early."

"Oh," I said, trying to sound surprised. "Do you know why?"

"No, the top brass has been very cagey about this one. Do you have any idea?"

"I'm afraid my top brass"—I pointed up, while smirking—"is as tight-lipped as yours."

"Okay, well I'll let you know when I know. How are your girls? Saved any brands from the burning?"

"One or two," I said. "When I saw Dimitri, he seemed to accept that as collateral damage."

"I'd have thought you'd want to save them all," Elena spoke with some earnestness.

"God saves," I replied, smiling. "All I do is plant the seed. Where it sprouts is up to him."

"So, you have met Dimitri?" Elena asked, picking up the cue I had rather hoped she might. "What's he like?"

"Have you not met him?" I asked, feigning an innocence that really ought to have earned me a nomination for best actress in a supporting role.

"No, I have yet to have the pleasure. What did you think of him?" Elena was remarkable herself; she gave no sign of lying that I could see, a rival for my Oscar.

I told her what I thought, namely that he seemed better than the alternatives but was still a bad man in an evil trade.

"Some girls like bad boys," Elena said, which seemed both apropos and a bit daring. Was she trying to communicate with me? There was something in her look, and the way she had blurted that out made me wonder. So I went there.

"Do you?"

"I've dated a few, Robin, we can't all be good girls like you." Elena smiled back, but I did not feel warmth in the smile.

There was something in that look, but I let it go, wanting to see where this might yet lead.

"Goes with the territory," I joked, softly chuckling.

"Have you really never, Robin? You're an attractive woman."

"If you mean been with a man, then no, but thanks for the compliment."

"You don't know what you're missing. Strap-ons are one thing, but a warm hard cock driving in and pulsing inside you is quite another!"

Yet again my cheeks warmed, and I could feel the heat rising under my skin..

"I shall take your word for that, darling," I said, trying to make light of it. It was evident that Elena was bisexual, possibly with significant experience of both sexes.

She grinned. There was something in the grin that was more than mischievous, but I was still unsure what it was.

"Sorry, I should not have said that." Elena recovered herself, and momentarily, I saw the girl I knew.

She shouldn't, of course, but being me, I told her not to worry. Quite why I was incapable of just saying that she should indeed not have said it, I would never understand. It was, no doubt, something to do with not wanting to offend anyone. But then again, I thought, why shouldn't she say it? We were friends, and it was what she truly believed; I was confident it was what most thought. She was simply conveying her experiences to a friend, experiences I chose not to share.

"One for the road?" she asked.

"Sure," I replied.

"I'm sorry if I upset you, Robin. I thought you might be bi, like me. I am sorry if I was rude."

"I've never been with a man, so honestly, I just don't know."

At that point her phone buzzed. "I have to take this," she said.

Her eyebrows knitted together and her mouth set in a tight line as she turned back to me.

When it ended, scooping up her things, she turned to me. "Come with me, Robin, something's happened."

"What?" I said, grabbing our coats.

"A woman was found dead not far from one of your hostels." Her tone was matter-of-fact, lacking any empathy. It chilled me. "They don't know who it is, you might."

My heart sank. I'd known deep down that something like this might happen; prostitution was inherently dangerous.

It took us only minutes to get to the scene. I looked down. It was Marta. A sob broke from my lips. I muttered a quick prayer and made the sign of the Cross.

"You know her?" Detective Sargeant Macduff looked at me, his eyes searching yet swirling with questions.

"She is called Marta. I saw her earlier today on a personal matter," I responded, trying to keep my mind focused; it was the best I could do for Marta.

"Can you tell us anything that might help?" he asked, his eyes sharpened.

My mind was spinning, as was my stomach. Marta had been so full of life only a little while ago, and now there she was lying cold and dead on the ground at my feet. Her eyes stared up at me as if to accuse me of failing her. I felt ill; I did not wish to desecrate her, but I was certain I would vomit if I did not leave.

"Can we please do this someplace else? I feel sick." I tightly covered my mouth, clutching at my stomach and moved away, trying to control my gag reflex. *I should have done something; why didn't I do something?*

"Of course," he said, the hardness around his eyes softening, his voice now low and gentle. "Elena, can you stay here with the regular police and go to the hospital with the..."

I knew what he'd been about to say. My head snapped up to look at him, and my eyes narrowed into slits. My temper flared as hot as my hair was red.

Macduff coughed, clearing his throat. "With Marta. I'd like to know the time of death as soon as possible."

Elena looked at him, then me. "I'd rather stay with you two," Elena said. She gave a small, understanding nod, her expression softening as she spoke, but she did not touch me. I wished she had—I could have used a hug.

"Elena, this is a murder inquiry now. You know procedure, chain of custody. I know you are worried about Robin, but I will take her back to the station for a statement. She will be fine." He left no other option.

Reluctantly, Elena agreed. She nodded at me, let her fingers brush over mine, before whispering, "I am so sorry."

Neither Macduff nor I spoke as we drove to the station; the drive seemed to take forever. I told him, and him alone, what Marta had told me. His eyes went wide, and his lip twitched in what I suspected was Macduff's version of shock.

"That..." he said, his voice low, as if to himself as his eyes scanned the warn table. "That would explain a lot."

"What would?" I asked, hoping for some meaning to all this tragedy.

"She was dumped there after they killed her, but there are signs she was tortured," he answered softly, not looking at me.

"Dear God," I gasped, and my stomach tried to escape through my mouth again. I swallowed it back down. "So that means they know you know about the trafficked women?"

"Yes, but how did they know she had been to see you?" MacDuff asked, again his eyes on me. If there had been any doubt in my mind that I was a suspect, that doubt was gone.

"It would have been easy enough for someone who saw her to have reported back, and I'd guess they had put one and one together." I ignored his gaze as I thought out loud.

Macduff's eyes narrowed slightly as he studied me, a flicker of suspicion crossing his features.

"There's something you're not telling me, Miss Topham. I've been doing this job long enough to tell. Look, if it was told to you in the confidence of the confessional, I understand, but you've seen the lengths these people will go to; do you really want to hinder our investigation? Don't you think you owe that to this dead girl to help catch her killers?" His voice carried a distinct edge, making it clear that my evasion had not gone unnoticed.

"First, Sergeant Macduff," I responded, my voice a little harder than necessary, but I needed to make the point. "It is Reverend Topham, and, as the title implies, if it was something from the confessional, there is no way I would tell you what it was, but no, this is something more circumstantial."

"It wouldn't be something to do with Elena, would it?" he asked in a way that told me he knew more than he was saying.

"What makes you say that?" I asked, my voice quavering. I was playing for time and more than a little surprised.

"The way you looked at her when you identified the body. Come on, out with it?" He softened his tone, but his eyes were no less firm in their gaze.

"It may be nothing," I began, feeling very much like the beetle squirming under the stare of the entomologist before the pinning.

"Let me decide that, Miss Topham." The edge was back in his voice again.

"Well, the other evening when Elena and I dined, she was called away." I took a breath to steady my nerves. "On my way home, I took a different route than usual and happened upon a couple in the shadows…"

DS Macduff listened carefully, but leaned in, his brows furrowed and fingers drumming on the table—a clear sign of his discomfort mirroring my own. *In for a penny, as they say,* I thought. I was not sure whether to pray that Elena was involved or not. If she was involved in the trafficking, she might have to face the consequences, but what if she was innocent? I might very well end her career by revealing her. I prayed I was doing the right thing.

"I saw a woman kissing a man." I paused momentarily. "I saw Elena kissing a man."

"Who?" he asked directly.

I had gone this far. There was no turning back now. I took another deep breath. "It looked like Dimitri," I replied softly, trying to find someplace to look. They needed a sweep up; a good dusting was also required.

"Looked like?" Macduff would not let me wiggle out.

"Yes, I could not be absolutely sure, but it did look like him," I trailed off in a whisper.

"I see," he said.

I knew in that instant what I had just done. It was not hypothetical anymore; Elena's career was over before it had begun, even if she were innocent. The mere accusation of such a relationship was enough to paint her as a risk; even before Marta's death, such a lapse of judgment could not be tolerated. I prayed for Elena despite her possible guilt; I still cared for her.

The silence that settled was an oppressive one. The sound of our breathing and the hum of lights above our heads were the only sounds.

"And you did not think of telling us?" Macduff's voice had lost all its previous kindness.

"I did not know what to think," I answered, suddenly only too aware of how inadequate an answer that was.

"Well," Macduff said, his voice rising with each word, "I suppose that to a virginal vicar there may be a perfectly innocent explanation, but I am damned if I can think of one! Robin, what the hell were you thinking?"

Not liking his tone, I responded with some heat, "I was thinking that you and others might immediately constitute yourself a hanging jury," I replied. "Furthermore, Detective Sergeant Macduff, the condition of my virginity is not a topic for discussion and is none of your business. Nor does it have any bearing on your investigation, but the fact that you so cavalierly think that it is a suitable topic certainly does justify my concerns about your objectivity in this matter, don't you think?"

"Oh come on!" he said. Where before his face was a bit pink, it was now red, and the veins in his neck were no longer invisible.

I was bordering on Hulk anger myself.

"One of my officers is seen snogging one of the leaders of the criminal gang, and you think that there could be an innocent explanation?" His hand slapped the shabby table in front of him.

"I didn't say that," I responded just as hotly, slamming my palm down to match his. "I said that you might immediately jump to the conclusion that Elena was not to be trusted; it's clear I was correct on that point as well."

"Well, what the fuck else am I to think?" he responded, as a dog with a bone. He ran his fingers through his hair, causing it to lift almost like a cockscomb, with his face as red. We were both losing our tempers. I hate it when I do, even more when others do. I have never been good with raised voices and lost tempers, from a girl up till now. They make me desperate to run away and hide, but I would not be bullied, either. I had had enough of that from men long ago.

"That," I said sharply, "on your part, would require an ability to reflect, the very thing that I was trying to do. Apart from anything else, if she *is* involved with them, surely you want to be able to use that to your advantage, something that would be blown by you reporting her!"

"The Elena I remember is ambitious, driven, and very intelligent." I took a deep breath. "Perhaps she thought she might gain some information or leverage from this relationship to your mutual advantage. Her career is very important to her, I believe that."

"You know her; you have worked closely with her. Do you really think she would so easily throw her career away?" I was a bit cross and must have looked a sight as he stepped back. My fists were grinding into my hips, and my head tilted and thrust out toward him. I leaned in, trying to make my point. "I think she is trying to make a name for herself and is willing to throw the dice to do it; I just hope she doesn't get herself killed."

Macduff stopped in mid-thought. I could see that I had brought him up short, and now he was making an effort.

"Sorry, sorry, I should not have sworn, and maybe, just maybe you have a point. Did Elena know that Marta came to see you?"

"No, as far as I knew, no one did," I responded, hoping that, for Elena's sake, she had nothing to do with Marta's death.

"Okay, okay, look, you're right; if she is involved, best we keep an eye on her. Would you help me with that?" Macduff seemed to have mastered himself again—it took a while but he calmed down, as I did too.

I was grateful for that; being angry or around angry people leaves me feeling wrung out. He had to have sensed how I felt as his tone changed; he took a deep breath and looked up to the heavens. I wondered if he was seeing it as I did.

"We have to be careful. She might be on the side of the angels, but even if she isn't, there might be others who are definitely not and they might react badly to her being found out. She could be in real danger either way. I will have to keep this close to the vest." Macduff sighed. "Let's keep it to ourselves until we are sure; I will keep my eyes open. You do the same." He then gave me a weak smile.

"You can trust your virginal vicar to do that?" I joked, returning his smile, yet still feeling drained from his earlier show of pique.

"Okay, sure, look, can we start again?" He rolled his eyes and threw up his hands.

"Always," I laughed. "And I'm not saying she is not involved, just that we can't be sure."

"Well, we can be sure this lot will stop at nothing." He tossed back.

"Look," I said, "I know you think I am naïve, and you may be right, but if we start quarrelling, we shall get nowhere, agreed?"

"Robin, if I can call you that, I'm sorry, I was a complete ass. Let's reset and cooperate. We are still assuming there will be some sort of landing tomorrow. How about a morning review of the beach? I must admit, your last outing made quite the splash," he said, the tension from his earlier anger visibly draining from his body as he leaned in, just outside my personal space, relaxing as if he had just had a massage, his eyes twinkling with a playful smile.

I know I should have been cross with him, but he was so genuinely trying to extend an olive branch, sure with the delicacy of a randy teen boy, but I was certain it was genuine.

"I see." I smiled at him. "Virginal vicars in wet tee-shirts are your thing then?"

"They could be." Macduff's eyes twinkled with mischief as he let out a genuine laugh. The sound mingled with the distant cry of seagulls. I couldn't help but laugh too, the tension between us dissipating like the morning mist, leaving the air clear and fresh.

Later that evening, just as I was about to settle in for the night, my mobile buzzed.

It was Macduff. Tension gripped me as I answered, wondering if there had been any new developments.

"Robin, it's Macduff. I'm sorry to call so late, but I wanted to update you on the beach surveillance plan for tomorrow," he began, his voice tinged with frustration.

"What's going on?" I asked, feeling a knot form in my stomach.

"I had a discussion with the higher-ups. They've refused my request for overnight surveillance," he explained.

"But what if the smugglers still go ahead? Or go early? What on earth have you to lose?" I asked, struggling to keep my voice even, my hand gripping the mobile so hard I thought it might break, all while desperately trying not to cry in frustration.

"I know, I know," he sighed. "But they're firm on this. Budget cuts have us spread too thin. There's just not enough manpower to go around now, let alone sitting waiting for something to happen. Look, I'm upset too, but we'll have to find another way. The truth is, they are more than likely right, all in all, it is unlikely information hasn't been leaked that'll have stopped them from wanting to risk it."

I took a deep breath, trying to process the news. He hadn't said it in so many words, but I know the meaning. They thought Marta would have compromised this opportunity. "Alright, Mac. I understand. Thanks for letting me know. But I think you are all wrong, I think Marta took her secrets to the grave."

"I know you do, Robin, I wish I was as sure as you, but your instincts are not proof. Stay safe, Robin. We'll get another chance," he said before ringing off.

I stared at the blank screen of my mobile for a moment, feeling an agonising mix of frustration and determination. I still believed Marta might have held out, even with what he'd said about her weak heart and the torture she'd endured. I was certain we wouldn't get another chance if we didn't act now. But there's no persuading a man in power when all you have to go on is what they would call 'women's instinct'.

Chapter 8

EARLY MORNING BEACHCOMBING

I doubted that I would have rested well anyway but after Mac's call, to sleep would have felt like a betrayal of the sacrifice I believed Marta had made. I sat in my study, praying and thinking about all the pieces of the puzzle. As the sky began to lighten, around five o'clock, I donned my leggings, tracksuit top, and running shoes, carefully packing my mobile. Just before leaving, I ensured I had Mac on quick dial.

The cool mid-September air had in it more than a foretaste of the coming autumn. The horizon was dark still, a thin streak of yellow light hidden behind the clouds of night. The only sound was the lapping of the waves as they pushed up the shore, clawing back the sand and shingle.

What was I doing? I had no idea whether they were coming, and no clue as to where. I had not even considered the matter of what to do if I was right. But all I could do was to follow my instinct. If the capsized tug had been a trial run, then, I reasoned, they'd try the same route. The weather was calmer, making a landing much safer.

I took myself down to the deserted beach, the night air cool against my skin. My feet sank slightly into the soft sand, and I was glad I had worn tennis shoes for this expedition.

Nestling in the lee of one of the overturned skiffs, I relished the indescribable freshness of the sea air, which contrasted harshly with the artificial chemical smell of the still drying paint. I had to be careful in my hiding place—I wanted to watch and see, not ruin my clothes.

The freshly painted keels of the fishing boats faced the stars in neat rows. The sheer number of boats made it easy to hide, and from any distance, my flaming red hair would blend seamlessly with their paint. I felt a sense of safety there, concealed by the darkness and the sandy camouflage.

It was a time for prayer, so I went through the office of morning prayer, which I knew by heart.

"Blessed are you, creator of all,
to you be praise and glory forever.
As your dawn renews the face of the earth,
bringing light and life to all creation..."

But even as I offered thanks for a new day, two flashes of light appeared on the misty horizon. As I was wondering if I had imagined it, the lights flashed again. I turned and looked behind me at the reflection of a light. I was in the right place at the right time; but what on earth could I do?

I reached for my phone to call Macduff, trying as best I could to cover the light of the screen, but before I could dial—*Snap!*

Startled at the sound behind me, it was as if I were turned to stone, forgetting entirely about my call. I focused my eyes on the direction I thought the sound came from, will them to pierce the darkness. I saw nothing, and since the sound had been so faint, and since I was so on edge, I thought I had imagined it until it was followed by a whisper.

"Shite." A voice I knew well; it was Elena, who immediately ducked down beside me.

"You took a bloody risk; what the hell do you think you are doing?"

I couldn't see the anger on her face, but her voice was filled to the brim.

"I had to follow my instincts. But what are *you* doing here?" I responded. My doubts were probably as evident as Elena's anger, but I hoped not as obvious.

She gasped, took a deeper breath, and let it out slowly, then in a low, exhausted voice said, "Look, I know you saw me snogging Dimitri, but it's the price you pay for being a double agent." Her voice hinted at desperation; she might have been the best actress on earth, or she needed me to believe her.

I looked into the blackness that I thought must be where her face was hidden. I wished I could see her eyes.

I read a good deal, perhaps more than was good for me. I remembered reading that double agents lived a tortured existence; they lied and fed lies to those who trusted them until they themselves no longer knew the difference. Worse, when they finally reached their breaking point and were forced to tell the truth, they were such practised liars that the truth seems more impossible to believe than their lies. Leaving them empty and desperate to be believed; the trouble was, *only they* knew if they'd reached the point of honesty.

Was Elena at that point? Could Elena, the girl I'd shared whispered dreams with under the garden stars, really be caught in such a tangled web?

"Double agent?" I asked, sincerely wanting to believe her and to find something of the girl I'd once known. The Elena who had laughed and dreamed with me, the girl whose aspirations and dreams soared as high as the stars themselves.

"Yes, Dimitri's mob gets information from me, but only the information that we want them to have, nothing serious. In return, I get intel we can use. But as to why am I here? I know you, Reverend Robin, you are a dog with a bone, you were never going to let this go, so I followed you, to protect you if I could."

Elena seemed earnest, but still something was nagging at me.

"I was going to call Macduff." I unlocked my mobile to make the call.

"Let me call him. Now we know something is happening, we need all the help we can get," Elena urged, looking pensive as she glanced out to sea, while fiddling with her mobile. Elena stared closely at her phone and she swore.

"Bloody hell, no signal," she said, showing it to me, no bars. Mostly out of reflex, I decided to try my own, but found I had no signal either.

"What should we do?" I asked. To this point, I had no clear plan; I just had a desire to do *something*.

"Watch and wait. I can find out where they are being taken," she said, lifting her phone's camera for a clear view. "Let me capture this to prove we were not making it up."

"Wouldn't it be better for me to do so? If it is needed in evidence and comes from you, you'll be compromised. If I take it, well, I will just tell the truth, that I was sure Marta was right." Hunkering down behind the boats, I hoped I could block the screen's light from the sea and the land. I looked at my battered phone, which was far from the newest model but serviceable.

"Besides, undoubtedly, my camera is likely better; after all, you being a civil servant and me being a highly paid vicar." I glanced up at her just then.

In the muted light of her phone, Elena smiled. She looked so like the girl I knew.

"We'll make a policewoman of you yet, Robin." Her smile broadened, as she looked into the gloom over the sea.

She had the most beautiful profile, and I had always loved her smile.

So, as the first light of dawn began to edge across the vast horizon, we watched as a lone fishing trawler came closer. It would fit in nicely with the rest of the small fleet anchored nearby; but this trawler's catch was female. Their voices carried across the water to my ears.

The slow-moving boat beached itself, a dangerous manoeuvre given the rocky shore. Three men slid quietly into the hip deep frigid water, then ordered the women to follow. The men gathered the dozen women, now clutching each other, and waved them on. The women moved together like a centipede bracketed by their keepers. Thus, two of the three men dragged the women to shore while the apparent leader turned back and ordered the boat away. Its motor rumbled to life, pulling off the beach, and quickly turned, thundering off into the night at full throttle, unconcerned if its erstwhile cargo were discovered.

The women were shivering. Whichever idiot had thought that short dresses and bare legs were ideal wear for an early morning boat ride, ought to have tried it himself.

I was grateful that Elena was there; there was comfort in numbers. I pushed my doubts deeper down as we hunkered behind the hulls.

How capricious fate was. These women were as much casualties of war as were the men who were killed fighting on the front line, but what sort of government allowed its soldiers to rape women and then sell them into prostitution? But had that not, historically, always been the case? Look what had happened to Adromache, the widow of Hector of Troy, who had been enslaved as a concubine to the man who had killed her son. Women suffered in ways that even male soldiers could not be expected to comprehend. Civilisation was a thin veneer covering the surface of a seething pit of primal drives. We had always been men's prizes, at the mercy of those with the most power. We told ourselves things had improved; now rape, as an action of war, was supposed to be an international war crime, but how did you prosecute such a crime against a dictator who not only sanctioned it but might well tacitly encourage it? Perhaps we had not come as far as we liked to tell ourselves.

Elena and I watched as the girls were loaded into a van. I longed to do something, but for the present, all I could do was observe and pray that providence would provide a way.

"I will give you the pleasure of telling Macduff, I must be off. You'll protect my cover?" Elena asked.

"I shall, but you must tell me where they are being held, in return," I promised, I had no right to ask this, but I wanted the information. Something was amiss, and I wanted to know what—at least, I told myself I did.

She hugged me; it felt good to have her so close. I rested my chin on her shoulder and held her tight.

"Thanks. It's important this remains secret. As soon as I know, I will tell you." She pulled free, looked me in the eye, and then turned away.

I watched her go; I could not shake the feeling that some younger, more naïve part of me went with her. Now she was gone, and it occurred to me, *Why was she here at all, and if she thought there was a leak back to Dimitri who was she going to report too?*

She had not interfered with my observation, but how had she helped? Then another thought struck me, *Was she here to keep me from acting?* After all, what could I have done more than I did? The men might have reacted poorly if I'd done something foolish, like bursting into their little beach party. At the very least, I might well have been beaten, perhaps severely, or even killed. I was sure they had killed Marta. But *any* of those outcomes would have attracted attention that would have been bad for business. However, with Elena present, I had allowed her to suggest a course of action that had been passive and safe for me, her, *and* the smugglers. I did not like where my thoughts were leading, not at all, but in truth, her story was at least plausible.

Regardless, I needed to ring Macduff.

The dawn was breaking over the North Sea, painting the sky with hues of crimson and gold. The first light of day cast a warm glow on the gently rippling waves, turning them into a sea of liquid fire. As the sun climbed higher, it bathed the coastline in a soft, amber light, making the sands shimmer like grains of gold. The gentle surf, unusual for the season, rolled in, and early morning dog walkers ambled along the beach where the women had been rounded up only a few minutes earlier.

Taking a deep breath, I savoured the growing warmth of the rays, my eyes closed as the sea breeze washed over me. I gingerly walked up the beach toward the sea wall, as I braced myself for the call I knew I had to make. Finally, I took out my mobile, and discovered it had a weak signal, then listening to the buzzing tone, dreading the connection and conversation. A groggy male voice answered.

"What the bloody hell!" Macduff sounded cross. "You do know it is only half-five in the bloody morning?"

"I do, and I also know that ten minutes ago those women you were so *sure* were not going to be landing were landed here. I captured it on my phone. Let me send you a picture or two."

"Bloody hell! Where did they go?" Macduff was fully awake now. The sounds of his rustling and banging about filtered through the line, and what I suspected was the jingling of a trouser belt. Then, the sound of a dull thump.

"Damn!" Macduff shouted in my ear; I held the mobile away too late. "How did that get there?"

I tried hard not to snicker, wondering what he had tripped over. I knew it was awful of me, but I somewhat enjoyed his discomfort; given he had been complicit in ignoring my concerns about the women, it seemed a small amount of what others might call karma.

"I think I know where they were taken, but let me check," I said, playing for time. "I could hardly tackle them myself, could I?"

"I know, I know," he said before falling back on more expletives.

I suspected he was angry because he, and his superiors, had made a judgement call, but the wrong one. I wondered how much of his anger stemmed from being mistaken or proven wrong by a woman and a non-police officer, into the stew.

I waited, and as I had expected, within fifteen minutes, a police car arrived. I motioned to them.

"You're Robin, yes?"

"I am," I said, "and you can still see the footprints where the women were landed."

As they sealed off the beach, I could not but wonder at the folly of it all. If they had listened, they could have been here, intercepted the women, and could have achieved something! Now? Well, now they were *doing their job*, examining the stable door after the horse had long bolted. Budget cuts, I understand, they are endemic, but would it have been too much to have a single car or something? Anything?

It was then that a nasty thought crossed my mind. *Maybe he didn't want a car here? Elena said there was a leak, and a lot of money sloshing around…*

The sound of a car shattered the maelstrom of my dark thoughts; it was Macduff.

He used the car's rearview to adjust his tie before stepping out but it was still askew. He walked toward me, tucking his shirt into his trousers, then running his fingers through his hair, still leaving it dishevelled, his eyes darting about, taking it all in as he walked toward me.

"Robin, can you come with me to the station to make a statement?" Macduff asked.

"I can, but that might delay my discovering where the women are being held. Can you give me an hour?" Taking rather too much pleasure in his discomfort, I realised some part of me was a bit cross with him.

"Okay, but can you let me have the video you said you had?" he asked, looking down, shuffling his feet and rubbing the back of his neck.

"Sure," I said, sending it to him.

He only nodded when he received it.

The presence of the police had brought a small crowd of onlookers and, of course, an inevitable journalist from the local press. "Rev Topham," she started. "No swimming this time? What's going on?"

"As you can see, I still have my top on, and the police will have to tell you the rest." I turned to walk away.

"Can I try to catch you later," she said, then started following, her heels digging into the sand, allowing me to get a few feet away.

Then I thought better of running away and stopped to wait for her. "Okay, I'll be at the Retreat, so why not come by? You could even do something about what we are doing to help the women."

"Yes," she responded with, I thought, less than full-throated enthusiasm. I presumed that doing good did not sell as many copies as graphically describing the world's sins.

I trotted back to the Rectory, trying to get at least a modicum of exercise. My mobile buzzed. It was Elena.

"Robin, tell me, if I told you to stay out of this, would you? Someone is dead already, please just drop it. Let Mac and I handle it." Elena's voice was quick and sharp, the tension evident. I chalked it up to all the excitement of the investigation.

I did not respond, but kept my tongue.

"You are not going to drop it are you?" Elena's voice softened, heavy with resignation.

"You know me better than that, El," I responded. There was a sigh on the other end, a sigh of defeat.

"They are in the old seaman's mission at the back of the quay. You've got about half an hour," Elena ended the call before I could respond.

"Thanks," I said, to the dead line, then reversed my jog and only just caught Macduff. I told him the news.

"How do you know?" Macduff asked; his tone convinced me he was unsure of me.

"I just do," I said, slightly annoyed by his attitude. "Either believe me or not."

He gave me one of his sideways looks but reported back to base.

"Would you be willing to talk with the girls," he asked in a neutral tone. "If we can retrieve them?"

Part of me wanted to tell him not to refer to them as *girls*. Wasn't it bad enough that they were denied agency without being stripped of their adulthood as well?

"Of course," I said, as usual taking the route of politeness. Direct confrontation was neither in my nature nor my education. Further, I doubted my objection would achieve my goal or be understood.

"Well, hop in, and we'll give you a ride," Macduff suggested, emphasising his offer by reaching across the car to open the passenger door, all while fighting the driver's seat belt. He looked so ridiculous that I had to cover my face to hide my stifled laughter.

He gave me what I took to be a flirtatious look, and it hit me for the first time that Macduff was attracted to me; that was all I needed. Smiling, I slid into the proffered seat, closing the door behind me. I found his flirtations thrilling and not something I was used to as a rule.

I thought it perhaps unwise for the police to have their sirens blaring as we approached the mission, and I stood and watched as Macduff and his officers approached the heavy wooden door; its once dark wood faded with the years. In response to a hard rap on the door, it was opened by a young woman. I could not hear what was being said, but it was clear that she was denying whatever Macduff was speaking to her. He pushed past her, and the other men went in.

He and his officers were out of sight for several minutes, creating an interminable wait, and I could not stay in the car as he'd instructed me. I got out, leaning against the car, my fear rising. What if I had been misinformed, either accidentally or intentionally?

It might have been *accidental* because of miscommunication or misheard whispers — all well and good. But what if it had been *intentional*? I wish I could banish the growing fear in my mind, but I couldn't. I was becoming suspicious of shadows.

Finally, after what seemed like a lifetime, he came out and beckoned me over.

"What's up?" I asked, my voice belying my nervousness.

"You'll see," he responded.

His voice and expression revealed nothing to me. Which did not reassure me.

We went into the hall, which was tastefully decorated, not expensive but not tacky either. There were trestle tables on which breakfast plates were laid, and around which a dozen or so women were sitting.

The hall was old, at least two, if not three, centuries, which actually made it one of the rather newer vintage buildings of the area. Stained wood abounded, and with walls painted a traditional mix of grey-tinted navy blue, it gave the room a nautical ambience, which was helped by the paintings of ships with pennants flying and white sails billowing. There was a large stone fireplace burning to drive off the damp and chill the women were undoubtedly feeling. Of course, I liked the room for where there was not a door, window, or painting of an elegant schooner, there were book shelves with I knew not what sorts of books. An amused looking Dimitri was talking with a policeman. When he saw me, he came over.

"Robin, good to see you." He certainly seemed sincere, but I couldn't be sure whether he was. "I was going to get in touch. As I was telling the sergeant, these women are fleeing from Ukraine and will be applying for asylum. We found them on the beach after a tip off from an informant."

"Well," said Macduff, "they are illegals and, as such, should not be here."

"That is up to you, Detective Sergeant, my understanding is that your Government is sympathetic to the plight of refugees from Ukraine." Dimitri certainly thought he had the winning hand, that was certain.

"These are not bloody refugees—you are trafficking them!" Macduff's voice had risen half an octave, and his volume matched.

"Detective Sergeant, I am shocked." Dimitri had an expression that bordered on a smirk as he folded his arms and leaned back against his chair.

He seemed all too nonchalant for my taste. I wanted to take him by the ear and shake him.

"I am simply trying to help women fleeing persecution. I am hurt by your allegations. Feel free to ask any of the women."

The look Macduff gave him would have burnt the paint off the walls.

"Oh, we shall. But in the meantime, you are under arrest on suspicion of human trafficking."

"Anticipating you might be this narrow-minded, DS Macduff, my lawyer will join us at the station. But what will you do with all these women? Deny them breakfast after their ordeal?"

Macduff's face flushed, and his jaw tightened. His hands clenched at his sides, and his eyes blazed with barely suppressed anger.

I stepped in, trying to diffuse the situation. "Detective Sergeant, why don't you leave me here with the women and a couple of your policewomen, and I can try to fix up somewhere for them to stay locally?" I tried to sound as innocent as Dimitri was pretending.

"Good idea! Bless you, Robin." Dimitri smiled; the smile held less charm for me now, more of a predator showing its teeth. "We can have a hostel arranged for them, but I am happy to go with what the ladies want."

To look at him, butter would not have melted in his mouth. Did he really expect anyone to believe him? But then that did not matter, he had his story worked out, and unless Macduff could tie him to the trafficking, at most, he was guilty of finding a group of refugees on the beach and providing them with accommodation.

As if sent by heaven, the smell of fresh coffee washed over us, and my stomach growled loud enough to cause a twitter of laughter among the women. I felt myself blush.

"I am sorry, with all the excitement, I completely forgot breakfast," I stammered, putting my hand to my dissatisfied tummy.

"Don't you worry, dear, you sit, and I will find something," the cook responded, smiling broadly at being able to be helpful. "Would you like some eggs and toast? Or some ham; I am sure we have some leftover ham…" She scurried off to a new series of subdued laughter from the women.

She was back in moments with a platter ladened with more than I would eat in a week. It was loaded with steaming hot sliced ham, sausage, bacon, and a heaped pile of scrambled eggs, with fried potatoes and sauteed mushrooms. She put this down and before anyone could squeak, she was gone again. About this time, three of the women followed her in and then one returned with an equally heavily ladened platter with all manner of sliced and stewed fruits, and even different yoghurts. Only a few moments passed, and a platter with smoked salmon and kippers as well as cold cuts and a variety of cheeses came through. Finally, they all returned with hot pitchers of coffee, hot chocolate and tea, along with sugar, honey, and sweet cream. It was a feast and one that would have taken some time to prepare.

"My, my, Dimitri, it seems that this little party was anticipated," I said, smiling sweetly at our host.

Dimitri's hand twitched slightly as he adjusted his collar. He cleared his throat and continued, "I sometimes host some of the girls here, as well as my men. This was prepared for them, but by coincidence, these young ladies were rescued and brought here. Giving them food and shelter is the least a good citizen might do for those in such a situation."

"Well, thank you, Dimitri. Now, why don't you and the other men bugger off so we ladies can have a nice bite to eat in peace? There's a good boy." I tilted my head slightly and flashed him a sweet smile.

They didn't like it, but as the women twittered in amusement, the men beat a hasty, if less than entirely dignified, retreat.

Whatever the source, the interruption broke the tension in the room and the ice between the women and me. As we settled around the table, I could see the women's expressions soften slightly, their initial wariness giving way to cautious curiosity. They whispered among themselves, casting furtive glances my way.

But although they were more accepting, they were not terribly forthcoming. I could sense the heavy weight of uncertainty still hanging over them. Every smile was tinged with a shadow of anxiety, every laugh a bit to forced, as if they were waiting for a bell to sound or a shoe to drop.

Dimitri's shadow certainly loomed large. His presence, even in his absence, was felt. He seemed to cast a pall over the room, each women's eyes frequently glancing to the door as if they expected him to burst in at any moment and crush the fragile sense of safety I was trying to build.

I made small talk with them, but it was clear that they were frightened and not likely to do anything which would bring the wrath of Dimitri down on them. I asked about their journey, their homes and hometowns, anything to draw them out, but their responses were either clipped and guarded; some only responded with tears. They all spoke in hushed tones, their gazes dropping to their plates whenever the conversation veered too close to their supposed host.

We chatted for a while longer and laughed a little. They seemed to grow more at ease, still none volunteered much; and their eyes no longer checking the door, they were constantly darting around them like caged animals, uncertain of whom to trust. It hurt so much. I wanted to hug them and promise them it would be okay, but I could not lie.

I stayed till the room grew quiet, but not until it was uncomfortable.

Finally I wished them well, and promised to return as all asked me too. When I left them, the officers saw me back home.

Back at the Rectory, I showered and while the cleansing water washed over me, I burst into tears. Had Marta died for nothing? That horrible fear would not leave me. We had caught Dimitri, and yet there seemed nothing that he could be charged for. I cried and held myself until the water ran cold. Finally I got out, dried and dressed in an informal cassock—my grey one with the fitted waist and knee-length skirt—along with my best dog collar. While dressing, I reflected that although tears would not bring Marta back, they needed to be shed. She had died trying to save others and deserved nothing less than to be mourned, and I would mourn her.

I called Macduff and told him I would be happy to talk to the women privately, so I walked down to the station—the weather was beautiful for this time of year. I needed the walk to clear my mind; Marta's sacrifice would not leave me.

I had half-expected them to show me to a drab interview room, but they gave me access to one of the better offices; it even had a window and a view of the nicer parts of our little town. I sat and waited.

The first woman was one I had sat next to in the hall table. Her eyes widened as she took a step back, clearly shocked by my appearance.

"You are not police? You are priest?" The shock at that revelation was written all over her. I was sure she hadn't had a single cavity in her life, for her smile gave me a view of her teeth that surely only I and her dentist had ever shared. It took her only a second or two to recover and move to the chair opposite me.

"Yes." I smiled, taking hold of her hand. "And yes."

"You hear confession? You not say what I tell you?" Her eyebrows furrowed, eyes intently on mine.

"Yes, and yes again," I replied, still smiling, finally letting go of her hand.

"Okay, I am Anna and I sinned. I have done bad things, and I seek forgiveness." Her voice was firm but nearly cracked with emotion; I could feel how desperate and burdened she was. "You will not tell police?"

“Anna, the confessional is inviolable.” I kept my eyes focused on hers. ”What you tell me you tell God, and in return I am his instrument of absolution.”

“It nice to have woman priest. You shall understand.” Anna flicked away a tear, trying to ignore that she had shed it.

“I shall listen,” I promised.

For the next twenty minutes she poured out a story as old as time.

Her village had been captured by the Russians. She had been raped and brutalised many times, so many they all became a blur, and she had become numb. Finally, she’d been sold on by her captors. She, and other women, had been transported here and they knew what fate awaited them.

“So, why do you not tell our police and seek their protection?” I asked although I suspected the answer.

“I have sisters back there, and they will be harmed if I not work. If I betray them, they will kill me, you not know how brutal these men are.” Anna was so matter-of-fact it was chilling.

Judging by the fear in her eyes, I could only guess.

I gave her a suitable penance and absolution. I had known few who needed it less and desired it more.

“So, you will go to the hostel they are providing?” I asked, trying to gauge her mood.

“I have no alternative,” she responded, putting away her things.

“Will you do one thing for me?” I asked, trying to engage her help without pushing too hard.

“If I can?” she said, but her eyes narrowed, scrutinising me.

“Will you tell the other women that if they wish to confess, I will hear them?”

She agreed, and was as good as her word.

One by one, the women came to me, often shaking and ashamed. Others, though contrite, their heads were held high.

Those confessions were the hardest ones I had ever heard. I wept with some of them, comforted where I could, and absolved them of sins which they had not committed of their own volition. Everyone had her own horror story. Each woman had made the same choice as Anna for much the same reason. It was clear that months of brutalisation had left these women frightened, damaged and vulnerable.

Later that morning, I got a call.

Macduff offered me lunch, as it was nearly one o'clock before the last of the women entered and the attending officers told me that there were no more to see. I texted Miriam so she could cancel my appointments. Then a young policewoman took me to Macduff's desk.

Lunch turned out to be a sandwich with a bottle of water. At his desk, no less!

"Last of the big spenders," I joked, smiling as I saluted him with my bottle, wondering if all civil service chairs were as uncomfortable—my bottom was still sore from the one I had spent the morning in. I would need the walk back and a soak to work out the kinks, a nice massage would be lovely. I absentmindedly wondered if Irina might be busy.

"Sorry, we have so much going on with this, it's lunch at the desk," Macduff apologised while trying to wipe a bit of mustard from his previously stained tie.

"A thoroughly uncivilised habit, Mac, and I hope you won't repeat it." I tried to smile without soiling my own blouse.

Macduff laughed; he had a nice laugh.

"All we got from them was the same story as Dimitri told us. How about you?" he asked between sips of water.

"Well as they talked under the rule of the confessional, I can't tell you specifics, but you are right if you think they are too terrified to speak out and you think they have been trafficked. For the rest, to be honest, you can guess, but it won't be as bad as the reality," I responded as honestly as I could.

"So, there is nothing we can do to Dimitri, his smart London lawyer was clear that the most we could charge him with was not reporting the landing, and that would go nowhere." Macduff softly snorted; his distaste with this particular *smart* lawyer was evident.

"You can't do anything to him. But perhaps we are thinking about this in the wrong way?" I responded primarily to myself, but I was thinking aloud.

He looked at me. "Go on then, Einstein." Macduff moved forward with interest, elbows on his desk.

Ignoring the sarcasm, I replied, "What options do we have regarding the women while they apply for asylum?"

"Dimitri says he has a hostel for them," Macduff responded flatly, his tone belying his genuine opinion.

"Oh, I am sure," I commented with thinly veiled sarcasm, then shifted to feigned innocence, "But I am guessing it would need to be approved by the authorities. What would happen if it was found to be unsuitable?"

"We'd have to… Hey, are you planning something?" Macduff's lips curled into a conspiratorial grin.

"We can't nail Dimitri, but we can jinx his hostel, and my Retreat is losing a dozen women this week who are being moved on. And, of course, I already have permission to house asylum seekers, soooo." My own elbows on the table, fingers forming a steeple, I matched his naughty smile.

He whistled. "You're not just a pretty face, are you?" Again, his smile.

"Well, I got a degree in theology and a doctorate, so no!" I returned his smile. "But thank you for the compliment."

"That's bloody brilliant. If they are staying with you and there is a curfew, he can't prostitute them." Macduff's hands were behind his head as he leaned back in his chair, back to the office window.

"Glad you like the idea." I wiped my fingers clean and finished my water.

"I do. Let me get onto making sure that the dive he wants to keep them in is not approved?" Macduff was unquestioningly enjoying this; I wondered if he would stop smiling by supper.

I was weary when I left the station, but I felt satisfied. I needed a lie down and a change.

On the walk back to the Retreat, I turned everything over in my mind wondering about Elena and her role in all this, and what to do about the women who had arrived, and what might be done with those that would follow them.

When I stepped through the door, I was greeted immediately by Miriam, as excited as a puppy. She was just a bit too long in the tooth to hop up and down, but was full of curiosity about what I'd been up to, her words flying like a machine gun. She reassured me that she had rescheduled my few appointments, adding that a journalist had been very persistent.

After a shower and a change of clothes, I phoned Jane, having established a suitable time by text.

"Darling Robin, I heard from my source at the Home Office. They will not allow the traffickers to host the women. You can look after them at the Retreat?" Her words were supportive, but I thought I noted a hint of concern in her tone.

"Yes, my love, I can." I tried to reassure her and sound as confident as I was uncertain. It was, after all, a tremendous leap of faith, but what else could I do? I had to do something, didn't I!

I informed her of most of what had happened, leaving out the detail about Elena. I did tell her about Irina.

"Ah, your former lover, she is back?"

I thought I heard a hint of emotion in her voice; I hoped it was not jealousy, or worse, that I might have somehow hurt her. I was still uncertain about what relationship she wanted with me and, more importantly, what I desired with her.

"Yes, working undercover with the traffickers," I volunteered on impulse, then immediately regretted the revelation. I hoped it would not endanger Irina somehow. A slip of a lip and all that.

"Well, I am sure it is nice for you to be with her again." Her voice had hardened, and I felt its chill.

There were times when the only word that would do to describe me was *foolish*, and then times when stupid fitted better. This was one of those times. Her tone only reinforced for me my earlier concern that Jane thought that this might have an effect on us, whatever *us* was. Now, I had no choice but to sit down somewhere with a cup of tea and figure out my part of this.

"Jane, my love, it was a fling, and no more. We need time together," I responded.

This was no lie. Of course, I cared for Irina, but my heart doubted there could ever be a relationship there. We were paired by circumstance, not design, and although I was attracted to Irina, we were just too different — but with Jane? I hoped something *could* develop, and I prayed she would give us the space to become an *us*.

"We do, darling, and I promise we shall get it soon. I think a pastoral visit up your way is needed."

Her voice softened, and I let my unintentionally held breath out slowly.

"Now that is one visitation to which I shall be looking forward," I responded with a soft giggle.

We chatted a bit longer before she had to go. I thought she was reluctant, which as wicked as it sounds, I was happy with.

I got down to some work, having rather neglected the upcoming Deanery Synod. I'd never make a church bureaucrat, there was something about an agenda and a meeting that made me realise I needed to file my nails or watch paint dry, anything rather than attend to item eight. But it was an excellent penitential discipline, so I did it, feeling a sense of relief when I had put it all to bed.

Just as I had finished that chore, there was a ring at the door. I was surprised to find myself peeking to see who it was. It was Macduff, but when had I started checking?

"May I come in?" He was all pleasantry, but I doubted this was purely a friendly visit.

"Yes, of course. I was about to grab a coffee, care to join me?" I asked, moving aside and holding the door.

"Sure," Macduff said as he stepped past me.

I made us both a coffee and joined him in the small sitting room. It was cosy now with both of us.

"I wanted to thank you for your help this morning, and the idea about the residences. Their premises have been declared unsuitable, and I am told that you have the space. Can we move them in tomorrow?" Macduff was trying to be expressionless, but his eyes were sparkling. I was sure he was enjoying all this drama; honestly, for my part, I found it all exhausting.

"Sure, of course. I will see to each and make sure they know they will be protected, as far as possible."

"Good," Macduff replied, taking a moment. "Look, I was a bit of an idiot earlier. Buy you dinner one night to make up for it?"

"That would be nice," I said, thinking to myself that the last man who had bought me dinner was Ryan just before he'd tried to betray me to the Russians. Perhaps this might be a pleasant way to supplant that awful memory or soften its edges by replacing a wicked man's betrayal with a good one's gallantry.

We chatted a moment longer, arranged a time for the women to come over to the Retreat, and Macduff left. Closing the door behind him, I'd half hoped he'd suggest this evening for dinner, but I was exhausted after the day's events. I decided to take myself down to the local pub. They had a good cook, and I looked forward to a decent evening meal I didn't have to wash up after, and the walk would do no harm.

"Hi, Rev, good to see you again. Your usual?"

I have found that when the barmaid knows you by sight and by your *usual*, it is a sign that you are a regular. I smiled. I quite liked being a *regular*. Too many priests stood aside from their communities, thinking being aloof made them pious and thus more effective, but I did not believe the shepherd should avoid her sheep.

I ordered the calamari salad and a glass of Chablis, and took myself to a table in the corner to indulge in some people watching.

Tabetha, the waitress, brought me my food and wished me bon appétit. I enjoyed spoiling myself, and was just about to signal for another Chablis when a familiar figure came over to me - it was Dimitri.

"Might I get you a drink, Robin?" he said, all smiles, his teeth reminding me of fangs the more I saw them.

"How kind," I said, all sweetness and light. There was no point being hostile, I'd find out precisely nothing that way. I was willing to gamble he did not intend to drug me, at least not at this moment. It was a terrible gamble after Ryan, and my intuition told me he was capable of it, but only when he was confident he needed to, and there were no unfriendly witnesses.

He went to the bar and came back with another Chablis, and a pint of lager for himself.

"To what do I owe the pleasure?" I asked, tipping the glass to my lips but only sipping. I was not confident of my bet.

"I am told that the women we rescued this morning are to be housed with you?" he replied, his smile less bright.

Smiling sweetly, I answered, "Oddly, that was not how the police described your role. They seemed to think you were trafficking them."

"Robin," he said, with a tone of something masquerading as regret in his voice, "how cynical your police are. I want to help those women."

"The way you have helped the others?" I asked, returning to the remains of my meal, although with less appetite.

"Did any of them say that they were not happy to be helped by me?" His smile had changed to a smirk, thinking he scored a point.

"Should they have?" I parried his thrust.

"I would have thought not, but only you can know that," he responded, focusing on his glass.

"None accused you of anything, Dimitri, but you know the police," I said, blocking his advance.

"I do, Robin, and I hope that I can be of assistance with the women." He drove forward but overstepped and was now off balance.

"I should appreciate that. What had you in mind?" I parried again, trying to find advantage.

"Well, I have a new associate, a Ukrainian woman called Irina. She would like to be able to talk to the women and act as a liaison between you and me. A nice, what is your English phrase, *threesome*, is it not?" Again, the broad, toothy, hungry smile.

It gave me the shivers. I must have coloured up.

"Was that what they call inappropriate, Robin? You must excuse me, a man in my line of business sometimes forgets himself, especially in the presence of a beautiful lady." He saluted me with his glass and smiled again. I wondered if his lips went together at all.

Okay, I thought to myself, *this is a record.* In the last forty-eight hours, Elena, Irina, Jane, Macduff and now Dimitri, had all indicated some level of desire for me. Was it environmental or hormonal? Or was it simply that Jane Austen had got it wrong? Maybe it was a universally accepted fact that a single woman in possession of a modest fortune and good looks was in need of a partner?

"Why, thank you, kind sir," I replied, with more smoothness than I had thought I possessed, and, to judge by his smile, it had worked. Golly, was it that easy? Flutter your eyelashes at them and a man would eat out of your hand - if that was not a bit of a physical stretch? I felt oddly empowered. Then I thought of Marta, and pulled myself together.

"I should be happy to meet this Irina, and to work with her to help," I responded with as little reaction as I could muster.

"Thank you, Robin, I appreciate it." He seemed like he was making ready to leave, his glass nearly drained.

I smiled and let him squeeze my hand.

"There is," I said, "just one thing I ought to pass on, as I did not quite understand it."

"Please do," he said.

"One of the women confided something about their worrying about relatives back home." Side step, arm tense.

"I am sure they must worry," he said, shrugging and glancing at his nails, "that is understandable."

"It is," I said, "but the bit I did not quite grasp was that she added that if anything happened to those relatives, the blackmail would not work any longer. Puzzling, don't you think?" Thrusting home.

From his eyes, I could see he did not quite know what to make of what I had just said.

It was obviously out of the question for a nice girl like me to be passing on a threat, let alone a warning to leave the women's relatives alone or else, and I had, after all, confessed to being puzzled. I liked the uncertainty in his eyes. Point and match.

"It is, it is, but I shall make sure Irina knows," he responded, trying to seem confident.

"Thank you, Dimitri. Now, alas, I must find my bed."

"Alone?" he said, again with a rakish smile. He had to have had great success with it in the past.

"For tonight," I said, wanting him to suppose there might be a chance he would get into my panties. That might keep him malleable.

Gosh, I thought to myself as I walked home, *I am turning into some kind of femme fatale!*

Chapter 9

PHOTOS AND DECISIONS

The following day was *busy*, to put it mildly.

After Morning Prayer, attended by the usual handful of older ladies, I returned to the Retreat to work with Miriam and the others getting things in order.

"Robin, you don't need to help with the rooms, that's what we are here for," Miriam said, sounding a little put out as I brought in the new bedding.

I smiled at her. Like so many who helped us, she had an exalted view of the role of the priest. In truth, one I struggled with.

"Jesus washed the feet of his disciples, Miriam, I think he would not mind me helping change the bedding!" I said softly. In truth, being on a pedestal was in many ways a prison, doing something was so much better than watching others do for you.

From the look on her face, she thought I was a strange one. Her reaction put a soft smile on my lips.

By coffee break time, we had things more or less shipshape, so, in a change from the usual rather pallid coffee Miriam served, I ordered in from the café down the road along with some pastries. The Last Supper it wasn't, but fellowship is to be found where you find it. It was, I thought, important to make it clear to those kind enough to help that they were appreciated. I had seen too many churches where the vicar seemed to take it for granted that others would help; I wanted them to know they were valued.

"Are these the women the police found yesterday, Robin?" Jean asked.

Jean was in her early fifties, her husband had left her a few years back, and she found in the church a comfort and support; she was what one might call a stalwart - except that sounded rather patronising. She was a good woman and she liked to help others; what more could God want?

"Yes, they are," I responded evenly, not making eye contact lest she see it as a challenge, I was not sure where she was leading with her question, so I chose to keep my response neutral.

"Are they prostitutes, Miss Robin?" chipped in Maureen, a grey-haired woman in her sixties.

I repressed a sigh; I supposed deep down, I'd known this question was coming. I put my cup down, feeling my back straightened and my shoulders square; I needed to confront this issue directly.

Softly, I responded, "They were captured, raped and brutalised by Russian soldiers, Maureen, and we want to help them recover and then find their self-worth again. I believe it is our duty to them and our Lord."

I thought it best to be precise. Church communities tended, by their nature, to be female and slightly censorious about sexual activities outside of marriage. I wondered sometimes how they would react if they knew that I was gay? How odd, I thought. In what other sphere of modern life would one have to wonder that? There were times… but then there were still substantial numbers who did not think that women should even be priests, so I should be thankful, I guessed, if only for small mercies.

"That is awful," Jean said, "men can be such beasts."

That produced a general murmur of agreement and an animated discussion with examples of male behaviour which supported the initial comment. I chose not to add my own opinion, given my experience was mixed at best, but more so that I felt unqualified to add to the conversation.

I forbore to ask the ladies why, in that case, they were all, or all had been, married. Gossip had a dynamic of its own, and I knew that most of them would, of course, exempt their own man from the general condemnation. The thought crossed my mind as to whether this was the time that I should come out, but then Maureen interrupted that train.

"I don't know, ladies, here we are all trashing men, what will the Reverend think of us? Ignore us, miss; most men are nice." Maureen smiled in a way that showed she thought the conversation had been too much.

I could hear the unspoken question hovering on her lips.

"Do you have a boyfriend in London, Miss Robin?" Miriam chipped in, expectation written across her face.

The looks of the surrounding women told me that there had been speculation.

"No, no," I answered a little too quickly. "Single and available," I joked, feeling decidedly uncomfortable but hoping it did not show.

Later, I kicked myself for not saying anything. But why should I have? Honestly, what business was my sex life of theirs? But still, I felt like a coward.

The police vans turned up as promised at noon, bringing the women with them. We had everything prepared, and we had collected clothes for them. We laid on a welcome lunch, and they seemed to visibly relax. I was able to assure them, collectively and individually, that they would be safe if they stayed with us. I advised them to be careful.

As they returned to their rooms to settle in, my phone buzzed. It was Irina.

"Robin, can I come round later to see the women?" She sounded chipper, and I had to admit my heart raced a bit with her voice.

"Yes, see you about four perhaps?" I responded, controlling my breath so I did not embarrass myself too much.

"Okay, see you then," she responded; I could almost hear her smile.

I gathered the women together, the old guard of the village, and announced there would be a special prayer meeting at three. I hoped they would all attend, and to my delight, they all turned up. It was a simple Book of Common Prayer evening prayer service, but it met our needs. I needed to rest back on the rock of tradition. The old familiar language soothed my soul and seemed to speak to them.

Afterwards, over afternoon tea, I talked with them about what they could and could not do under their asylum-seeker status, explaining that they could not do paid work but would be paid by the state a basic sum to allow them to live on. We all agreed it was rather silly, that they would be paid for not working. It was at that point Irina came in. I introduced her. I could see the worried look in the eyes of the women.

"Irina is here to make sure that lines of communication remain open to your families, and to ensure that the men who say they rescued you do not try to break the law by encouraging you to take paid work." I tried to reassure while explaining as little as possible and thus raising possible questions that I did not want to answer.

I must say that Irina gave an admirable performance at looking shocked at my revelation.

Anna, who I had noticed was a sort of unofficial leader of the group, clearly grasped what was being said.

"So, you are saying, Miss Robin, that anyone who attempts to find us paid employment as sex workers would be breaking the law." Her head tilted, looking at me, then Irina and back again.

"That is precisely what I am saying. Prostitution is not illegal, but anyone paying you to work as one would be breaking the law. You will, of course, Irina, be taking that news back to Dimitri?" The tone of my voice emphasised that was precisely what I desired all of them to tell Dimitri.

"Of course, Reverend Topham." She did an excellent job of being seemingly shocked at the news, and even a bit uncomfortable at the *revelation* that her *boss* would be unable to use their *services*. I hoped it would provide Irina enough cover. "I will certainly let him know the situation. I know he will have some *concerns* but the law is the law. Now, ladies, I need to see each of you to get details of your relatives so I can let them know where you are." I allowed Irina to take control of the group for this purpose.

I was speaking to Irina, but I wanted all the women to hear so that it would get back to Dimitri unambiguously.

"These women are under my protection and being observed by the police; whoever attempts to induce these women to violate the terms of their asylum-seeker status or attempts to use these women in Dimitri's brothels, well then Dimitri will find himself under arrest." My tone was emphatic.

To my delight, Irina reported back the following day that Dimitri was furious at being thwarted, but had decided to cut his losses. But somehow, I knew this would not be the end of it; I suspected he would want his pound of flesh.

At supper with Anna and the women that evening, she raised the question, if they could not work, what could they do.

"Well," I said, "volunteer work is not forbidden, and will stand you in good stead if you get asylum. What skills do you have?"

The conversation started as a trickle, each woman admitting one skill or another. Soon, they were all chattering as if a damn had been broken. At first, it seemed odd, and I wondered at it, but then abruptly, I realised the meaning of this simple conversation and felt like weeping. This was the first conversation about mundane, simple things these women may have had in weeks, if not months. They were more than their bodies, and they might again be able to cook, clean, and sew with no other demands than what they *chose* to share.

It transpired that there were a variety of skills, including an accountant, but for the most part, they were practical - so we were able to offer the locals help with their gardens, cleaning, cooking, and childcare.

"Can I suggest," I said, "that we form a volunteer corps? This town has many poor people, many lonely ones, and many needing help. If we can help, then it will win support for you."

"Are we allowed to do these things, Miss Robin?" asked a young woman I had not yet met.

"As long as we receive no money, yes," I answered, trying to remember her face to ask her name.

"But how will people even know we are here?" This time, it was Anna.

"Leave that to me." Smiling, I felt a thrill run through me as if something in my heart knew I was doing what I was meant to do. Now I that I had decided to take this on, I had to find a way to do it. I rolled several ideas around trying to avoid the most obvious. I took more than one walk and might have worn out my shoes, but finally I realised the simplest solution was also the best one.

I made arrangements with the journalist, Hattie Miller, who had been so anxious about visiting with me. She loved the angle with the asylum seekers volunteering to help around the village, and thought it would be juicy. She was so eager I think she was already wondering what she should wear to whatever awards dinner she was hoping to attend.

"That's a wonderful idea, Miss Topham," Hattie said. Her enthusiasm, I thought, was a bit artificial, but I would take it just the same.

"It's about being a community," I said, "and getting away from the ghastly idea that people fleeing persecution are somehow a burden on us. We should want to help them, and God knows, there are enough people here who need help too, those who have been left behind by the state."

The result was an excellent piece in the local paper, which was picked up by one of the nationals and by the regional television:

'Rev Robin Rides to the Rescue!'

I told Bishop Jane what we were doing, and she was delighted.

"Sounds like a pastoral visit is needed, my darling. Well done, you!" Jane's enthusiasm was infectious.

"Well, I'd be delighted to welcome you." I could not have helped smiling if I had tried.

I had hoped that this would help with the process of acceptance of the refugees, and though, in the broader sense, it did, I could not help noticing that Miriam, and one of two of the other women, especially Maureen and Jean, seemed rather cold in their attitude when I went in the following morning.

As I had to work closely with Miriam, I would have preferred to let it ride, at least until after our Tuesday *mingle*, where a few of the Ukrainian women would be helping us with some of our older congregation members and their friends. Still, I thought I'd better find out what was up.

My phone buzzed, and a photo of Jane's smiling face appeared on my screen.

"Excuse me, Miriam," I said, and went into the vestry to take the call.

"Robin, thank God!" Jane's voice sounded breathless and upset.

"What is it?" I responded, her tone causing my words to catch in my throat.

"I am sending a photo—you will see what it is," Jane responded, her voice sounded on the edge of panic.

And there it was—a picture of Irina and I kissing outside the hotel where we had stayed during the Surtees saga. It was a full, open-mouthed kiss, leaving little, if any room for ambiguity. It was a kiss between two lovers, passionate and heartfelt.

"This was sent to me this morning, anonymously, with a message saying: 'Robin Topham is a lesbian predator. This will go to the newspapers unless you stop her interfering.' We need to talk, darling." Her voice seemed strained as if she was trying to hold back an emotion, anger perhaps, but at what? The photo's contents or its delivery and import?

"That explains something," I sighed, then took a deep breath and let it out slowly.

"What?" Jane asked, her frustration becoming evident; whether with me or the circumstances, I could not guess.

"When did you get it?" My mind was leafing through the exact times of my most recent conversations concerning the women in my care.

"This morning, but I was in a meeting until just now," she responded less cross but clearly a bit confused.

"Miriam has been off with me this morning. I'm guessing, but I don't think I'd be wrong to attribute it to that," I responded, not wanting to follow my mind's path but seeing no other trail to pursue.

"Let me take some advice, darling, talk soon," Jane responded, then rung off without another word.

I returned to the kitchen, where Miriam instructed the Ukrainians about their duties.

"We need to talk, Miriam." My usual calm demeanour was showing some wear.

She looked at me.

"Vestry, now!" I did not shout, well, not too loudly, but I managed not to stomp my foot.

I was proud that I did not *run*, but I did not waste steps either; Miriam was scurrying in after me, wiping her hands on her apron. Her face showed genuine apprehension. Seeing that, I took another deep breath to calm myself. "Miriam, did you receive a photo of me with another woman this morning?" I asked as calmly as I was capable.

She looked shocked. "I'd rather not talk about it," she responded, looking everywhere in the room but up into my eyes.

"I do not think that is an option. Show me." I was firm in my request, holding out my hand.

She did. They were the same pictures as the ones sent to Jane.

"Are you one of them?" Miriam asked, her voice sounding genuinely worried like a mother might when she was afraid her beloved daughter was in trouble, hoping against her fears, terrified of the answer. I had heard that tone before.

"If by 'one of them', you mean am I a lesbian? I honestly don't know. Irina and I had a brief relationship before I came here, but in so far as it is anyone's business, I am celibate. Why do you suppose these were sent to you?" My voice was even and firm, as firm as my true feelings of resolve.

"I don't know," she blustered. "Someone wants us to know the truth about you."

"Someone who also sent these to Bishop Summers with a message that these would go to the press unless she stopped me interfering. Does that sound like someone who wants to be helpful, or like one of the Russian thugs trying to intimidate me?"

I was unusually direct and more than a little cross. That seemed to take her aback; after all, to ask that question was also to answer it.

"The Russians, but, but, Mother Robin, it is against God's holy law to lie with a woman," Miriam responded, confident of her biblical footing.

"As it is to lie with a man before marriage, Miriam, so before we start examining the mote in my eye, shall we look at the beams in the eyes of every woman who has had sex before marriage? After all, there is more about that in Scripture than there is about women lying with women," I responded with more than a bit of heat.

Miriam stepped back, hand covering her mouth, surprised at my words.

I had meant my words to be general, knowing most women surrendered themselves to their lovers long before they had worn a ring. From her reaction, I suspected Miriam was one of those; having struck a nerve, I chose to make this a teachable moment.

"I want you to think about that for the rest of the day, examine your conscience and then we shall sit down and talk."

With that, she knew she was dismissed and left me to think.

I had not meant to mount such an offensive, but the fact was that I was humiliated and upset; how dare someone try to use Irina to discredit me? But where in hell had those pictures come from?

Time, I thought, for a word with Macduff, but first, I needed to talk with Irina and with Jane.

I left Miriam to ponder what I had said. I texted Jane to see if she was free, then Irina to call me as soon as she could, and finally, Macduff to say that I had a few questions for him.

An answer from Jane came there none, but Macduff phoned by return.

"What is it, that sounded urgent?" He sounded genuinely concerned; it was touching.

"It is, can we meet soon? I have some questions only you can answer." I sounded a bit breathless even to my own ears.

"Well, I was about to have lunch at the Green Man. If you fancy a bite, see you there!" he responded, and it was a genuine restaurant, not his desk.

I did, indeed, fancy getting away from the atmosphere in the church, so I took him up on his offer; it was only a few minutes' walk. The fresh air and sunshine were superb; both washed over me and cleansed me of the melancholy I had not realised I'd been feeling.

"I thought a glass of Chablis might be welcome?" Macduff handed me a glass of my favourite nectar.

"It would, thanks." Taking my glass, then thinking of food as my tummy betrayed me again, we chuckled at that.

"Sounds like we need to feed you up, lovely Robin." He gave me another patented smile.

Oddly, I enjoyed his appreciation, but not as much as I appreciated it with Irina or Jane. With them, it was so different, so primal. With him, it was simply pleasant and flattering.

We ordered some sandwiches and settled in a corner seat.

I showed him what Jane had sent. Macduff raised his eyebrow, his mouth parted slightly as he looked at me—that was as closed to jaw-dropping shock as I had seen with the man. "I don't know what to say. Where did these come from?" he asked, with a mixture of surprise and, I sensed, growing concern.

"I am guessing from our Russian friends. But the question is more precise—what sort of camera took these? I ask because there was a CCTV camera across the road from the hotel, and I think it came from there. Who has access to CCTV cameras?"

"We do," he said. "They are designed to help us; thousands of them are in the network."

"Would a civilian have such access?" I asked, my heart pounding in my chest, silently praying — *yes*.

"It's very unlikely. I can get colleagues in the Met to check. When was this?" Macduff asked, taking out his notebook and pen.

"It was right after the operation to take down Ryan Surtees," I said, "and the police were all over the place for a couple of days."

"Are you…?" he asked, sounding worried, reflecting my fears.

"Thinking that these came from the police mole?" I responded in melancholy. "Yes, I am, and I fear that there is only one person who was with the Met then and is here now."

"You're thinking it is Elena?" he responded, his face drained of colour.

"Well, I doubt it is anyone else, alas," I said, my voice choked with sadness.

Thankfully, our food arrived, and its appearance gave me time to martial myself.

"Does this get you into trouble with your bosses?" he asked as we ate.

"It could," I said. Finally, having lost my appetite, I pushed my sandwich away. My heart was breaking for Elena; I wondered what might have caused her to become involved. But even amid my grief, I suddenly remembered Marta. My anger replaced grief. If my suspicions were correct, Elena had to answer for her actions.

"However, I want to go on the offensive," I said; I had to fight not just for me but for my women.

"How?" he asked, his eyes brightening and his posture straightening with hope.

"Wait and see." Smiling, I enjoyed teasing him more than I should have.

"Can I ask?" Macduff looked at me as if he was trying to find a way to avoid offending while discovering what he wanted to know.

"What? Am I a lesbian?" I asked, taking a final sip of my wine.

With a vengeance, the colour returned to his face. "Not, erm, that it is any of my business." He stumbled through his words.

"I see," I said, "so your taking an interest in me was entirely altruistic?"

"Well, no, but, well I don't... erm... want to pry." Macduff shifted in his seat, avoiding my eyes, his face reddening.

"It's okay," I said, "we're friends, and I do, as it happens, have a girlfriend, but as to whether that means I am gay, who knows?"

He squeezed my hand. "I can't believe these bastards have tried this on you." His eyes softened, filled with genuine concern.

"I suspect I am lucky they have only done this. Think what happened to Marta," I responded, thinking of that sweet girl.

"But why?" he asked.

"Why? I'd guess these people had invested a lot in these women and are furious that I have out-thought them. Someone, probably Elena, has fed them these pictures in an attempt to get me out of the way."

"I am really sorry, Robin, let me get onto this. Can you send me those pictures?" He took out his phone, perhaps a little too eagerly; I could not help but needle him.

"I shall," I said, obliging with a smirk, "but no gawping at them!"

"No, miss," he laughed.

We hugged like friends, with lots of air between us. Then, we parted with wishes of a good and safe day.

I was on my way back from the pub when my phone buzzed. Again, Jane's photo filled my screen, and I answered.

"My love, I have had a word with the Archbishop, who is furious, but advises caution." Her voice was firm and a little distant in tone.

"What does that mean?" I asked.

"No idea, my love, I suspect he wants it to go away." Her tone told me she more than suspected.

"It isn't going to," I said, "but I have an idea. I will not tell you, darling, because you need plausible deniability."

"Robin, are you…?" Jane tried to interject.

"Going to do something unwise? You bet. These swine are not going to stop me." Trying hard to keep a check on my temper was a close thing.

"That's my Robin." I could almost hear her smile; I missed seeing it more than on just my phone.

I was not sure of my cards, but I would be damned if I was not going to play them to the end.

I phoned Hattie—the journalist with whom I had spoken earlier and who had managed to get both her stories about me into the nationals.

"Hi, Robin, what can I do?" She sounded pensive but curious.

"I may have a story for you—a big one. Could you meet me for coffee at the usual place this afternoon?" I asked, thinking she would crawl over broken glass to get there.

"Sure, you've been good to me, so see you at three, okay?" She was eager now.

The usual place was a café on the sea front, and there, punctual as ever, was Hattie. As usual, I was a little late.

She'd already bought me a cappuccino, so we got down to business. I thought for a moment before taking it, realising how paranoid I was becoming, knowing it was not without reason.

I showed her the photos and the text that was with them.

"Fuck! Sorry, pardon my French, Robin. This is dynamite! What do you want me to do? Try to prevent it getting out if they pass it on to the press? I will do what I can, but you know what journos are like—piranhas." She smiled in a way that made me smile in return.

"The opposite. I want you to publish it, along with the story that the Russian mafia are trying to destroy me because I have, twice now, prevented them from exploiting vulnerable women."

Hattie looked at me, her expression a mix of shock and disbelief.

"But… but, Robin, forget what I said about journos, we are not all like that. I'd love to help." She leaned over, and her fingers took my hand.

"Hattie, the best way you can help is by publishing this and destroying their leverage. It would look pretty bad for the Church to discipline me for kissing another woman just because the Russian mafia were trying to put pressure on me."

"But if they do, Robin? What will it mean for you?" It was sweet; she seemed genuinely concerned.

"Hattie, you saw Anna and the others. Together we are trying to build back their self-respect and self-reliance. I am asking them to be strong; I have to show the same strength."

"What about your bishop, how does he feel about this?" she asked, making the assumption most would.

"He," I responded, "is a she, and she told me not to do anything mad."

"And you ignored that?" Her eyes widened and her mouth dropped open in astonishment.

It was a reasonable response; I was putting my whole career on the line. Everything I had worked so hard for.

"No, I have my own definition of mad. Mad would be to let these beasts blackmail me into silence and allow them access to the women they have tried to exploit and already abused. In that scenario, my career does not matter. I am a pastor, a good shepherd; if I must sacrifice something, even myself, so be it."

Hattie squeezed my hand. "If you are really sure, Robin. Let me get back to the office. I promise it will be our lead, and I'll get onto the *Daily Mail*, which I think will also want to go with it. But, Robin, I have to ask. Are you sure?" Her brow furrowed, her eyes searching mine.

I was, and although I felt distinctly wobbly as I walked away, I was sustained by that inner voice which was the Spirit guiding me. This I had to do. I was not some knight on a white horse rescuing these women, I was a fellow sinner working with them to make something good come out of evil. That mattered. As for the rest, well a Church that would discipline me for those pictures after knowing why they had been sent — then that was a Church I was not sure I wanted to be part of. I did not think it would do that to me, but I had to do what I was doing. There I would stand; I could do no other.

I got back to the Retreat just as Miriam was closing up.

When she finished, she stood before me quietly for several seconds. I watched her, wondering whether she was working up the courage to ask to leave my service. She was moving weight back and forth, from foot to foot, like a little girl who needed the loo.

"Mother Robin, I am sorry." Miriam was close to tears.

"For what?" I was not trying to shame her, but for forgiveness to be meaningful, one had to be honest about one's transgressions.

"For being such a bigot," she choked out. "My opinion is what it is, but I should not have spoken to you like that."

I smiled, but I restrained myself from shaking my head. I supposed it was the best I could hope for, at least for now.

"Opinions are something we all have, Miriam, and I'd never judge you for yours. All I ask is the same." I considered hugging her, but I thought better of it.

"What's going to happen?" She let out a breath she seemed to have been holding and her shoulders relaxed. She naturally wanted to know what was next.

"If you get tomorrow's Daily Press, you will see," I responded to her question with a confidence I was surprised I felt. It occurred to me that this might be a narrow sliver sort of dark giddiness that soldiers felt on the eve of battle. As horrible as things might be in the future, waiting for it to happen was almost worse than having done with it.

I saw her shake her head as she walked away.

Had I lost her? Had I lost others? Well, if so, then if this ended my career in the Church, perhaps that would be just as well. I was resigned. I left myself in God's hands; after all, that was where my future belonged.

I texted and then phoned Jane. I told her what I had done.

"Darling, that was terribly brave of you." Her voice hinted at tentativeness but was earnest.

"Is that like in the civil service, my love, where the Minister gets told he is *courageous* when proposing to do something ridiculous?"

"A bit, darling, but I mean it, you are being brave. I have made sure that if the journalists want a quote or two, there are members of our organisation who will support you." Her tone reminded me of a CEO reading a statement once an employee had been caught being naughty on company time.

"And you, Jane?" I managed to get the question out without my throat closing up.

"Darling, you know that at this point I can't," she replied candidly, a true politician. "I won't condemn you, but I can't come out in support until I see how the land lies."

She was right, no doubt, but why did I feel so utterly alone?

My evening prayer was long and anguished, but as I came to the end of Compline, a kind of peace descended on me.

I should not judge Jane. I was not in her shoes. I even smiled, thinking how *nice* those shoes and associated ankles happened to be. Sighing, I realised I did not have to carry her burdens. I had to trust in her and her love, hard though it was when what I wanted was her to defend me to the hilt. But this had been my decision; I had made it alone. I would bear the consequences.

I woke early, opened the curtains to see a beautiful clear dawn, and prayed.

Only then did I go online, and the first headline that hit me on the BBC news was:

'Lesbian vicar blackmailed by the Mob: see the Daily Mail *for the full story.'*

I clicked on the *Daily Mail.*

'A kiss to die for? Rev Robin's rendezvous with the Mob, by Hattie Miller.'

And there, on the local news site, the same stories were writ large.

My least favourite headline was The Sun's:

'Randy Rev Robin's Russian Romp!'

How would I ever come back from a headline like that?

My phone buzzed. It was going to be one of those days.

Chapter 10

TRUTH AND CONSEQUENCES

It was Irina on the phone. I had tipped her off to what I had done—if they had connected her with me and Surtees, then Dimitri's mob knew who she was, and she needed to get out of there. Macduff had come to the rescue.

"Thanks darling, I'm safe now. When do you think they realised?" she replied, sounding far calmer than I felt.

How could she be so calm? After all, there had already been one death in all this.

"My guess? It is when they saw the pictures, which was why I texted you," I answered, trying to be as calm as she was.

"But where did the picture come from?" I could hear her concern, which I shared; I swallowed hard.

"I have a theory, but I have another few calls coming in, and one of them I have to take. Catch you later."

"Sure, and thanks, Robin, I owe you," she responded uncertainly but tried to reassure me.

The first call was Jane. I prayed she was well and hoped she saw the danger.

"Darling, are you okay?" Bless her, her first words were reassuring, trying to see how *I* fared.

"The deluge has just started," I said, "and I have not even finished my breakfast. How are things at your end?"

"You'll see if you turn on your TV in about fifteen minutes. Just know I have your back, my darling."

Relief flooded through me. Whatever the day might bring, I had not lost Jane. That feeling really pushed home what I was already realising. However little I wanted anyone to pigeonhole me; I was a lesbian. I loved Jane, and that she was standing by me meant the world.

The next call was from the BBC, who wanted to interview me for their news programme, which I agreed to do. They said they'd send a car, and if I could go to their Ipswich studio, they'd have me on for eight o'clock.

I turned the phone off; I wanted some privacy so I could shower, and fix myself up. I was not going on the news looking like I had just got out of bed.

I put the TV on while I towelled myself dry. I caught the interview with Jane.

"Bishop Summers, as the Rev Topham's bishop, what do you make of the headlines? Do you support her? What is your view on the fact she is gay?"

Jane met the interviewer's gaze steadily, her expression composed, her voice even. Not bland or lifeless in defeat, but the voice of a woman who knew how to use it like a rapier, effective in attack and defence, both precise and deadly.

"Can we disentangle that? One of my clergy was threatened by the Russian mob with being outed unless she ceased her efforts to help the women they were abusing. The first thing to say is that anyone in the media who concentrates on her sexual orientation is, in fact, helping the Russian abusers. Let me ask you, does that sit comfortably with you?" Jane leaned forward, pressing her point with her body.

The interviewer, who was female, looked taken aback, moving away slightly, before recovering herself.

"We just report the news," she spluttered, trying to hide her discomfort.

"I see," Jane said, "so the headlines concentrating on her sexuality and not the blackmail are, you think, in your considered opinion, fair and balanced?"

"We don't write the headlines?" she tried to retorted.

"Of course you do; they do not appear on the page by themselves, as if by magic?" Jane pressed the point. "Is it just an accident that you were chosen for this interview instead of a man? Or was it not for the titillation factor of the sex? Much more exciting than dealing with the politically thorny issue of women being trafficked to force them to be sex workers, and the implications of that?

"Maybe not, but do you really think headlines about '*Randy Rev's Russian Romp*', are either fair or balanced?" Jane asked.

The interviewer squirmed but did not answer.

"News outlets choose their headlines." Jane's index finger poked the desk with each word. "If I were writing the story, it would be that one of my clergy has defied a threat to ruin her career in order to help abused women." Jane was full of fire, and it showed. "For me, as a Christian, that is the story. You are always quick to report abuse in the Church, which is understandable, but perhaps in this instance, you might consider not denigrating the victims, Reverand Topham and the women she is aiding. After all, you would not want to look like a hypocrite, would you?"

"Thank you, Bishop Summers. That is all we have time for now, but there will be more later in our programme." The presenter turned to the camera; she could not hide how little she appreciated being taught a lesson by a polite instructor.

My heart swelled. Jane had stood up for me in public. I loved the way she'd avoided answering their questions, and made the effort to change the emphasis of the reporting. That was, I decided, what I should do.

The BBC car arrived just after seven o'clock. I thought it would take the best part of an hour to get to Ipswich, but I did not consider that the man might be a retired Formula One driver.

While we sped along, shattering every speed limit and lane shift after lane shift, sending me sliding back and forth within the safety belt, I took several more calls to distract myself.

Macduff was brilliant. He wanted me to know Irina was safe, and asked how I was bearing up. I told him.

"You must have a million calls coming in, Robin, so we'll talk later." His voice was firm and confident, much as I imagined a knight in armour would. "We have your back, please don't worry. I have a car outside the Retreat, and we will have a presence at each of the three hostels."

Whoever had said all men were bastards was wrong—Mac was solid gold. But the Russians were ruthless, and they were hardly going to appreciate the storm I had helped them unleash on themselves.

The next call, just as we came close, was from an unknown number. I briefly considered not picking up but did, pressing record as I did so.

"Hypocritical bitch! You better call the police off, or you will not like what happens next." The voice sounded like a cheap robot, so strange that at any other time, I might have laughed. I certainly didn't this time.

"I can't call anyone off, and fuck you!" I spat back before ringing off.

Shaking and on the edge of tears, I sounded braver than I felt.

My hands trembling, I texted Mac with the news and the link to the call. Then, I took several deep breaths to steady myself. Suddenly feeling better, I remembered something I had read long ago: '*Bravery is doing the right thing even when you are scared to do it*'.

At the studio, it was straight into makeup. The artist looked at me, frowned for a moment, then added a little powder, blended here and there, worked on my eyeliner and mascara, and then stepped back and told me I looked beautiful and there was little more that she could do than nature had done, then wished me luck.

I was unsure exactly what she meant, but I had no time to think about it because I would be seated next to the presenter within ten minutes of walking in the door. This was clearly their major interview of the moment.

Next was to get *mic'd up,* as they called it, which was also a bit uncomfortable. A man I had never seen in my life suddenly walked up behind me and, without a word, pulled my skirt hem back and inserted a chilly metal clip down the small of my back.

"Can we have your blazer off, please?" he asked matter-of-factly, expecting me to undress myself partially. "We need your wire to go down your back, then clip to your jacket lapel, assuming you will wear it? With the hot lights, the air is very chilly on set, and we certainly would not want you poking out on camera, would we?"

I chose to let it go; I had been doing much of that lately.

With my clothes back on and put back together, I was led to the gallows and sat an arm's length from a woman I had seen many times but only on a screen.

The presenter was precisely what you might have expected. Tall and blonde, pretty enough but not what I might call beautiful. She glanced at me, and then her brows knitted, and her lips pressed into a thin line, which was not in her favour.

She suddenly turned to me. "Before we start, may I call you Robin, or would you prefer Reverend Topham," she asked with a tone that implied she would choke out the full title; I opted for the less formal option.

"Robin will be fine." Smiling, trying to be friendly. For a moment, I wondered if the smile might have been misunderstood as she was decidedly uncomfortable and began furtively glancing around.

I could hear a woman speaking into her earpiece, and the presenter turned to me. "Ready? We go live in five seconds." Then she turned back to the camera while I tried to remember to breathe.

"We have with us, the Reverend Robin Topham who has made all the news headlines this morning. Thank you for agreeing to talk with us, Robin. Can I ask how you feel?" the woman asked, suddenly all sweetness. It occurred to me that I could not remember the woman's name for the life of me.

"To be honest, as though the sky has fallen in on me," I responded, perhaps a bit too honestly.

"Can I ask if you were *out*, before this?" She went straight for the titillation, just as Jane's interviewer had.

Following Jane's example, I was forced to change the terms of the discussion.

"You can," I said, "but if I had been, the Russians could hardly have used pictures of me kissing another woman as blackmail, could they?"

"So, you are gay?" A hint of a smirk appeared on her face, or was it a hidden smile?

I fixed her with a stare. "As my bishop pointed out earlier on your programme, you can concentrate on the salacious, or you can concentrate on the women with whom I am working to rebuild their shattered lives. Would you like me to explain? I promise I will come back to your question," I responded, my voice as smooth and calm as possible.

She nodded. I knew we had limited time, so I had to be brief.

I outlined what had happened to the women, how we had taken them from under the noses of their traffickers, and the threats they had received.

"Your viewers might also like to hear my most recent call," I said, turning my phone on to release the recording I had made.

The effect on my interviewer was priceless. The woman's eyes widened to the point I worried the orbs would pop out and bounce on the table.

"That is horrifying," she gasped; her presenter's mask had not just slipped, it had fallen completely off.

"This is what we are dealing with. Last week these people killed a heroic young woman whose only offence was telling us about the trafficking, and having failed at blackmail, they threatened to do the same to me. The Ukrainian women are working with me in Felixstowe to help those in our community who need it. You don't need to be a genius to determine who is doing God's work."

"And you, Robin, how will this affect you?" The presenter's voice was lower and softer; I would never know whether this was for effect or a genuine concern for my welfare, but I hoped the latter.

"It is not going to stop me doing God's work," I responded more assertively than I felt.

"You said you would be willing to answer my earlier question. Are you gay?"

I looked at her. It was just something they could not let go. Honestly, did it matter?

"It's a question I have been asking myself for years. If I ask, *what is gay?* People will think that I am avoiding answering because I am ashamed. So, I will answer it. Yes, I am attracted to women."

"But am I gay?" I took a moment to think. "No, but I am in the early stages with a woman I love."

"Rev Robin, thank you." She smiled and returned to the camera.

When the cameras stopped recording, I began unhooking my clip-on microphone. She leaned in close to me and whispered, her eyes darting around to see who might be listening, "Bloody sorry for that question, but that was what they wanted." It was clear she meant what she'd said with that look of unvoiced shame in her eyes that would not meet mine, and her cheeks were dusted pink.

"It's okay, I get it," I replied.

"Thanks—and best of luck." She shook my hand, and I felt something in her palm. I kept it there until I could slip out and look in peace.

I stuffed the paper in my pocket, then after happily divesting myself of the silly microphone package, its wires and the like, I handed it to the tech, hoping to never see another. I hated the loathsome things—the battery dug into my back, the wire alternately tickled and itched—sometimes both—and the nasty thing they called a 'pickup' clipped to my collar was constantly scraping on something, making the most horrendous sounds when I moved even in itch. I had no idea how these people put up with them. I just wanted to get home and get into a bath; I needed a good soak and scrub after this.

By the time I got out to the waiting car, there were photographers and journalists there. I let one stop me.

"How are you feeling?" an eager man asked, his phone in his hand recording me.

"Exhausted and it is only eight-thirty," I said, honestly.

"Anything you'd like to say to us, Robin?" Another voice I couldn't identify in the crowd.

"Yes, come to Felixstowe. See what the women are doing to defy the Russian mafia, and make the swine who tried to blackmail me pay for it. It would not take an investigative team long to find the bastards."

With that, I bade them farewell and got into the car; my phone was buzzing, so I turned it off. I remembered the scrap of paper, just a name, *Susan* and two phone numbers, one marked with a *W* and another with a *P*, signed with a heart. A heart? Was she thirteen?

Whether it was the ironic invitation or the sudden release of pressure having come out to the whole world, I started laughing, and once I started, I could not stop. The driver's nervous glances in the mirror only exacerbated a laughing fit. Once my throat hurt, my cheeks were streaked in tears, and I could not catch my breath, I calmed myself and then watched the city roll by until sleep took me.

Back at the Retreat, it looked peaceful, inviting and restful, save for the squad car parked outside. I knew Mac had stationed officers to keep us safe; it was nice to feel protected.

I went straight in.

To my amazement, the Ukrainian women were all there and applauded me when I went in.

"Thank you, Miss Robin, from the bottom of our hearts," Anna said with a broad smile, and I thought there was a hint of a tear, but the nods and smiles meant it was a shared sentiment.

My little welcome home party of hugs and thanks fed my heart and spirit; I felt love from these women who had been through so much. My efforts and sacrifice seem so small compared to what they had endured. Their love was refreshing and they gave me the strength I needed. But all good things had to end, and so did this meeting.

I left them to themselves and moved off for a few minutes in my study.

I had not noticed my shadow until Miriam asked how I was. I told her.

"Are you doing the confessions later as usual?" Miriam asked, her tone sounded concerned. As a mother might, knowing her only daughter was about to take her first skydiving lesson.

"I am," I said, refusing to be intimidated.

"Are you sure that is wise?" Miriam asked, again the voice showing motherly worry but also a hint of respect.

"No, I am not," I responded, for I honestly wasn't, "but I believe I have a duty to help those women too. A duty that supersedes my safety."

"Should I telephone the Russians to see if they expect you?"

"You can do better, Miriam, you can tell them to get Dimitri to phone me."

Miriam scurried off to make her calls, which left me alone, but only for a moment.

Anna came straight in. "Irina has been onto me. So, she was working with you and the authorities?" she asked, with a bit of heat.

I wondered if she was upset she had not been told.

"She was, but as you will know, she is safe now. It's a shame she was exposed as it was useful having someone on the inside there," I responded, being completely honest with Anna. She deserved it.

"Well, Robin, for whatever it is worth"—Anna stood up straight and squared her shoulders—"we support you."

"Thank you, Anna. We will not be bullied," I said firmly and meant every word; I was tired of being bullied and hiding who I was.

"Will you lose your job, Robin?"

I thought Anna's concern touching, given what she has been through.

"I have no idea," I replied, with an involuntary shrug, "but if I do, it is in a worthy cause."

I was well aware that at this early stage it was easy to get carried away on a tide of adrenaline, but there would be a reaction. The '*Randy Rev*' headline was out there and would haunt me forever. But it was not the opinion of the world which mattered.

Miriam came back in; her lips pressed tightly into a fine line, her eyes lost in thought.

"They did not seem happy, Mother Robin. The man I spoke to said that Dimitri was surprised you wanted to speak with him. He said he would phone you this morning before twelve."

It was already nearly half past eleven, so I made my excuses to Miriam and made a call.

"Robin?"

I heard the familiar voice on the line; I knew this would be difficult, but hearing her voice made it so painful.

"Elena," I responded, trying to control my emotions.

"I saw this morning's news." Elena's voice was tentative, even uncertain, for Elena an unfamiliar tone.

"I know," I responded, finding I could speak, painful though it was.

"You know what?" Elena's voice was weak and filled with fear.

"Where those photographs came from," I replied flatly, as devoid of emotion as I could make it.

There was a silence at the other end. I could only hear Elena breathing; it was fast and ragged. I was sure she was trying to control her own emotions.

"You don't understand..." she finally responded, her voice breaking slightly but becoming more confident.

"I understand that you, an old friend whom I trusted, gave those photos to Dimitri who used them to try to blackmail me." I made it a statement, not open to dispute. Part of me hoped she would give me something to hold onto, to understand her betrayal.

Sounding utterly defeated, she responded, "I had no choice."

"What do you mean?" I would not let her give me excuses; I wanted to know the truth. No matter how ugly.

"I mean, that bastard Dimitri is blackmailing me too. I mentioned to him that you had been involved in the Surtees case, and I am ashamed to say I spoke of the photos."

I did not speak, nor did Elena—the only sound was the tic and tock of the mantle clock. I let the silence fill the room. I am very comfortable with silences.

"Robin, it was just pillow talk; the photo was of a beautiful moment, and I was jealous of her. You know I have always been attracted to you; you must know that," she continued.

"I thought nothing of it, but he remembered and told me that unless I gave them to him, he would send compromising photos of me to the press. I am sorry, I had no choice; it was you or me." She went silent, save for ragged breathing.

I gave her credit for not lying to me. It still hurt, but at least she was honest.

"You must hate me?" Her voice was small and sad, like the young woman I'd once known.

I was angry, hurt, and disappointed, but I also felt in my heart that part of my vocation was forgiveness and, if possible, redemption.

"Well, at the moment, you are not top of my Christmas card list. The question is what are we going to do about it?" I tried to keep my temper in control.

"I presume you are going to report me and that my career is over. I'll be lucky to avoid jail. Do you know what they do to policewomen in jail?"

Now I heard genuine fear, not for her career but for herself.

"I can't begin to imagine. Mac knows it was you, though he has no actual proof. You are still in good odour with Dimitri, yes?" I was trying to find some way back for her, if I could, to make something from this mess.

"He is bloody furious with you. He said I was a *good girl* and wasn't to know that you'd pull what he called a 'stunt like this'. He wants revenge, it is his way." Elena seemed genuinely concerned for me but I had lost so much faith in Elena, I was not sure if I believed even that.

"Does he know that I know you were the source of the photos?" I asked, hopeful I could help her.

"No, he just thinks you refused to be blackmailed, which again, is a first for him." I thought I heard a note of admiration in her voice.

I decided to offer Elena a lifeline. "There is still a chance to redeem yourself, Elena."

"What can I do? I'll do anything." Elena grabbed hold and hung on for dear life.

"First, tell me the truth, are you really undercover?" I asked, praying she was.

"Yes, but I was not supposed to go as far with him as to have sex and get myself recorded doing kinky stuff." Elena's voice betrayed her humiliation.

"Okay. Given what you know of him, you think he will revenge himself on me? If so, how?" I probed.

She had confessed her sin, but now I needed to know how much danger I was in and, more importantly, my flock.

"He's a sexual sadist. If I had to guess, he, or one of his goons will look for a chance to assault you. Perhaps more than one. Robin, he is a savage; you don't want..." Elena's voice failed her.

A chill ran through me. That was, of course, very likely, and short of a twenty-four-hour police guard seven days a week, it was hard to see how to avoid the danger. So, I thought, what did one do with dangers one could not avoid and decided to face it.

"Okay. Elena, how about you becoming the bait?" I asked, allowing her to purchase some of her lost honour.

"What do you mean?" Elena responded.

I could hear the fear in Elena and repressed sympathy.

"Elena, I presume you told him we had been an item at school?" I asked, knowing in my heart she had.

"Yes, I did," Elena responded quietly.

"Have you said anything else about us?" I asked.

"Yes, I thought you still fancied me, and I certainly fancy you," Elena admitted, and I was sure she was being honest. I had seen it in her eyes during our meetings, or she was the best actress in the world.

"Good." I smiled to myself. "What about we arrange a date night, going back to yours after dinner?"

"Why not? Will that get me out of trouble?" Elena responded with a flicker of hope.

"If it lands them Dimitri, I think we might be able to make a case that the photo was the price you had to pay to stay undercover; thin, but plausible."

I hoped I was right; I hoped for Elena. I was confident I was right. I had learned something of political manoeuvres at Mama's knee, and I suspected the politics of the Church were not much different from those of the police. As long as those in charge came out smelling of roses, allowances might be made for those who made it happen.

"I'll do it then!" Elena was excited enough to jump through the phone. Her tone again reminded me of the Elena of old, as we schemed to get ourselves out of trouble we—usually I—had got ourselves deeply into; it made me sad and smile simultaneously.

"That'll put you back on my Christmas list." Smiling more, I did want to help her.

"You know I do fancy you, Robin," Elena said with renewed confidence.

"I guessed, and were I not involved elsewhere, I'd be interested too."

It was a white lie. After what Elena had done, I could never trust her. Indeed, could I trust her on this? It was my only way out. I'd tell Mac about it.

Just as I ended the call with Elena, Dimitri's name appeared on the screen. I took the call.

"Are you really thinking you'd be welcome here?" Dimitri nearly spat through the phone.

"And good afternoon to you, too," I said, hoping my smirk translated. "And why should I not?"

"Because you have cost me a great deal of money, and my bosses back in Moscow are not pleased with me."

"I can't tell you how upset that makes me," I commented, "because I'd be lying if I did."

"You fucking beetch! You just stay out of my premises and away from my whores. If you don't, you vont like what vill happen to you." He was furious; his accent becoming thick enough that I could barely make out his words.

"What, are you saying you feel threatened by a woman? Poor thing!" I responded to his venom.

"Fuck you!" he screamed followed by random tones indicating he was struggling to end the call.

I found I was trembling. What I needed more than anything temporal was a hug, so I sat, took out my Rosary and prayed. Calm came to me. I thanked God. I was strong in Him, not in my own feeble strength.

Miriam reminded me of my lack of physical strength when she came to see how I was. "It's lunch time, Mother Robin, and I'm not sure what you've had to eat today."

Concern filled her eyes. In a strange way that reassured me. I was still shaken from her reaction to my admission about my sexuality. It hit me then, again, that I was being pigeonholed. But perhaps I was just gay? I did not have time for that sort of self-reflection. Things needed doing.

"I've brought you a sandwich, Mother Robin. Anna and the others would like you to join them."

So I did. There was a deep fellowship in that room derived from the fact that we were all women and all under threat. I could only imagine what Anna and the others had suffered, though I had a good idea through their confessions. But between hearing what happened to others and fearing what *might* happen, there is a gulf as wide as the suffering is deep. Empathy takes you part of the way. Fear takes you further down that path, far enough never to want to go further.

I noticed Anna was looking at me whenever I glanced in her direction. I wondered if I had mustard on my collar with her eyes were locked on me; it was not a glance or brief meeting of our eyes, she was staring. When I got up to help with the washing up, she joined me.

"I am sorry this has come upon you because of us, Miss Robin. Can we help?" she asked so innocently.

"Your love and sympathy help me, Anna," I responded with a smile, for it was so true.

"You know they will want to hurt you?" Her voice was low and steady, the shadows in her eyes speaking of her firsthand experience with these men's depravity.

"I know, as they do you. Why do they do it?" I asked honestly, seeking insight. She had far more familiarity with men in general and these in particular.

"They are that sort of men, Miss Robin. They take us, they use us, and we are not human to them. We are little better than animals."

Her matter-of-fact statement sent a shiver up my spine, thinking of how close I'd come to discovering how little I was valued in that kind of man's eyes.

"It is the dark side of our nature. God tells us we are fallen beings, Anna," I responded while wiping a bowl.

"Can I ask a question, Miss Robin?" Anna asked.

"Of course." I put my soapy hand on hers, squeezed it, and smiled warmly.

I became concerned when Anna became quiet and had a far-off look. I had heard it described as the thousand-yard stare; she certainly had it.

"Anna, you can tell me anything, I promise," I said softly, putting my sopping arms around her, hugging her close.

"I don't remember much about the day… the day… they came to our village," she started softly, "all I can think about, all I can remember is what they did, what I did."

"When the soldiers took me by force, I had several orgasms. Does that mean I wanted it, that I am a whore as they said? Why else would I do that?"

I nearly burst into tears. Was this what had been bothering her?

"Anna, if I tickle you, you will laugh whether you are amused or not, yes?" I asked, looking into her eyes.

"Yes, of course."

"It's a purely physical reaction to a physical phenomenon, an involuntary response to stimuli." I kept her eyes locked on mine. "That was what happened to you when they forced you, Anna. Your mind shuts down, and your body's physical reactions took over. You are not the first woman to find that. Nor will you be the last, I am afraid."

She stared off into the distance, her brow furrowed and her fingers tapping rhythmically on the table. Then I added, "Would you like to talk to a trained counsellor about it? I know it is hard for you and the others, and I have held back from suggesting it, but if you would like to?"

"But we cannot pay, Miss Robin." Her hope lit her face, but it clouded over with her despair at being poor.

"The Church has trained counsellors in our ranks, and I can arrange something," I replied, trying to stoke that light of hope again.

"Thank you, miss; so it does not mean I liked what those men did?"

"No, it most certainly does not. It means you survived, and that is what matters."

"I am worried they might do that to you, Miss Robin."

"So am I," I admitted, "but well…"

I stopped. A coin dropped.

"Would you like to help me?"

"In any way we can, Miss Robin." Anna sat up straighter, looking determined.

I held her hand and thanked her. "I shall let you know," I responded, wondering if it might work.

I phoned Mac and told him part of what had happened.

"So the bastard threatened you? We have a guard on you." He sounded so angry and protective; honestly, it was lovely.

"You can't do that twenty-four-seven," I said.

"We can arrest the bastard," he added, confirming my suspicion, budgets were budgets, after all.

"For what? It is 'she said', 'he said'. But I do have an idea. You know we think Elena let him have those photos?" I asked, knowing he did.

"I do, but we have no actual proof."

"But she does have an inside track with Dimitri, which has given me an idea." I could not help but smile.

I outlined my thinking.

"Robin, that's bloody dangerous, using yourself as bait. What if something goes wrong?"

"That's a risk I am going to have to take." Sounding more confident than I felt.

"So when?" he asked; his mental gears turning.

"I will let you know."

I wished there was another way. But this was the dark road demanded by my work, and I had to have faith that the Light would prevail over the dark.

Chapter 11

ROBIN IN DANGER

Lunch had buoyed me up, though I was well aware that the adrenaline would go and leave me flat. As it was getting on towards three thirty, I thought it might be time to escape the drama and go over to St Mark's to help with evensong.

I noticed the odd look or three as I walked there, but that was nothing compared to my reception in church.

Father Richard was waiting for me; even from a distance, his furrowed brow and hands clasped tightly in front of him revealed his pensive mood. "Robin, I think it best that for now, you stay away from St Mark's. I have had a dozen or so complaints from members of the congregation."

"What sort of complaints?" I asked, keeping my voice steady, determined not to make things easy for him.

"Those headlines have upset people, Robin. We are a very traditional parish, and I have been reminded several times that the church regards homosexuality as sinful. Some have said they will not come to church while you are serving. I am sorry, but I can't be the cause of a scandal."

I sighed, realising I'd been right. The great world did not give a damn what I did in bed or with whom!

If only I was actually doing something with someone in bed! I thought the irony was rich.

But St Mark's? Or, more particularly, some of its congregation members certainly seemed to care and appeared to care a great deal.

"So, I am to be tried, judged and found guilty with no hearing? How very Christian of you. Even Pilate gave Jesus more than that." I tried mightily to keep the sarcasm to a minimum.

"I am sorry, Robin," he continued flatly, ignoring my remarks. "For many, it has been a stretch to accommodate women priests and bishops. They can't accept sin, and you can't deny that the Church does not recognise gay relationships as licit."

And there he went, with the weasel words. I was on the verge of reminding him that the *Living in Faith* process was still being discussed by the church and that the lines were less clearly drawn than he had pretended, but I stopped myself. I couldn't argue people out of their prejudice, especially when I was on the verge of losing my temper; so I chose to back off.

"I don't want a discussion, Richard." Mastering my temper, frustration, and humiliation. "I shall cause no problems."

"Thank you for understanding," he said, his shoulders relaxing, as he released the breath he'd been holding.

Whether I liked it or not, I disliked it intensely. I had become an exemplar of the argument consuming both my Church and the Catholic Church. It seemed especially unfair to be judged on the basis of two photographs of my kissing Irina; but such was life.

I could, of course, have said that I was celibate at the moment, and indeed had been for most of my adult life, but that would have sounded as though I was making excuses and had something to hide. I hated it, but since I could do nothing about it, I decided to leave it to one side. More urgent matters pressed.

I started back toward *home*, for home, it had become. I needed the comfort of friends and a cup of tea.

About halfway back to the Rectory, I passed a small copse of trees and flowers surrounded by a low wall. Honestly, I had not noticed it before. I did not know why it had been created or who was taking such care of it; I suspected it was the local garden club. The surrounding buildings largely sheltered it from the harshest gales. It was lovingly, carefully kept and tended, a tiny hint of the greater world ruled by nature and nature's God. It seemed so peaceful; it made me *feel* at peace.

As I stood there, I felt the buzz and heard my phone chirp. Elena's number flashed up on the screen. Taking a breath, I picked up without a word.

"Hi there. Dimitri is furious. I told him that we had a date for Friday night and would be going back to mine for some fun. He seemed to like the idea and asked me for a key to my apartment."

She sounded excited while surprisingly relaxed, much more than I felt; perhaps she thrived on this. It occurred to me that she might be addicted to the danger, the adrenaline rush. I had heard of such people, but until now, I had not thought I had met one.

"Good. Leave the rest to me," I responded, trying to sound calm, wondering if I had succeeded.

"Does Macduff know?" Her tone changed from anticipation to concern, tinged with fear.

"He suspects, but I do not think he will report you if this lands him the arrest he needs. If we succeed, you will both be heroes, but next time, Elena, no more cutting corners." I didn't give her a chance to respond and rung off. I didn't want to hear her excuses or apologies.

Suddenly, the street seemed lonely, and I felt a chill. I turned and walked a little more briskly home, leaving the little garden to the night.

I spoke with Jane that evening.

"I have been getting calls and emails all day, darling. Some very supportive, others calling on me to discipline you." There was a note that had not been there before; it sounded off and out of tune.

"I am sorry, Jane, I should have told you," I apologised; I had been so involved in my own thoughts I had not even considered what she might be hearing.

"If you had, I would have been guilty of putting you in the firing line," she responded.

"Where does this leave us, Jane?" I was afraid I already knew the answer, but I needed her to say it, to hear it in her words and voice.

"I still want to explore with you, but we may have to cool it a bit." Her tone was hesitant; something unsaid was hiding in the growing shadows between us.

My heart sank like a stone. Of course, I understood. She had been got at, been coerced. She was a bishop, she worked at Lambeth, and a public relationship with me would put a spotlight on her. There would be repercussions. I could not ask that of her. I would not ask that of her. But how ironic, I was getting flack for being gay, and the only woman I was interested in was cooling what was already a pretty tepid relationship.

They said God did not send us trials beyond our strength. Perhaps. But

I prayed for the strength to carry this burden. I wished her well, and told her she was in my prayers, although I didn't say I loved her. Still, I did, and likely always would. I don't stop loving easily, and never understood how one could.

I was not stupid enough to believe that Dimitri would wait for Friday night. I knew I was at risk, and I was grateful for the squad car posted outside the Rectory. Even so, their presence was a bit of a trial for me.

All those stimuli were rolled up in my protectors, from uniforms to cars. Of course, I valued and appreciated them, but they still worked me.

The news was worse; I could not bear to listen, though my phone updates told me that I was at the centre of a media storm.

That was confirmed when I logged into my emails to find interview requests from several journalists. I replied no to each, except to the reporter from the *Church Times*. I was determined to use this to say little about gay women to the Church but focus on the plight of the women whom I was helping. I felt emphatically that this was not a story about me.

Irina, who rang over breakfast, disagreed.

"The tabloids are all running it, pictures of you in your wet tee-shirt are prominent, as were your nipples." Seemingly, she could not repress a giggle. For my part, I wish she had; the photo was humiliating enough. "What was it the old woman said? If you looked like the back of a bus, you'd be okay, but you don't."

I sighed; I could not refute the reality or the reasons for it—sex sold, and naughty sex sold better. Apparently, I was the complete package, ready-made to move papers and magazines. We chatted a while longer about the situation and what might be done; after my conversation with Jane, it was good to hear Irina's voice.

On my way to the Retreat, I stopped off at the newsagents. Roly, the shopkeeper, looked at me.

"Well, lass, you are front page in a lot of the papers. Are you all right?" His tone was light and genial as always, but his brows were drawn down with genuine concern.

"Here today and gone tomorrow," I said, with far more optimism than I felt.

We had the first outings for our corps, with a schedule that included visits to the elderly, some shopping expeditions for them, and some housework. It seemed all so simple at first blush.

I have heard it said that we English could be standoffish people and villagers, more so, being unwilling to accept outsiders until some time had passed. Perhaps that was true in some circumstances, but the village elderly and isolated were so thankful for the company of my charges that most accepted them immediately; they simply beamed with gratitude. For their part, each of my flock took to helping like the proverbial duck to water, even going so far as to attentively pour over photo albums of long-dead English family members and listen to stories of children and grandchildren who had long since moved away. Tea was served over and over, without a single refusal, regardless of how meagre the offerings might have been; all were accepted with gratitude as if it were a feast.

Hours passed, chores completed, and finally, as the afternoon moved toward evening, we turned toward our mutual refuge. All chattering like birds on the wing, me chief among them.

My heart was soaring with all the good we had done; I was happy beyond what I had felt in days. I felt as if I were flying.

Until we walked by St Mark's, and my feet returned to the ground.

I found my voice stilled till we returned to the rectory.

Anna and the others were beaming, their cheeks rosy with joy, all with how the day had gone and how successful their efforts had been.

"This is what we want." Anna's smile would not dim; she was the happiest I had seen her. "Miss Robin, to thank your country for giving us refuge, and to give something back."

I could not help but smile with her; what were my little problems compared to theirs and helping them find a place in the world.

"Part of the essence of the Christian message, Anna. Love God, and love your neighbour as yourself; on these two hang all the law and prophets," I responded, feeling those words afresh.

How very complicated we had managed to make that simple message. If we loved one another, as God loved us, that was enough; God, literally, knew how hard even that was.

Could I feel love for Dimitri? He had had Marta killed; whether he'd intended her death or not, he was responsible. He had abused and blackmailed Elena and had tried to blackmail me; he had threatened me, even to kill me. How could I love him? Yet that was what God demanded. Perhaps if he turned from his sins and repented? Fat chance of that!

We all spent a quiet evening, I watched them chatting and discussing their experiences, laughing and enjoying each other's company. I must admit that it was a balm to my heart, the conversation with Jane the only dark cloud and these women who had suffered so much yet found such joy and healing in simply helping others? Who was I to mope and dance around my purse in my own personal pity party.

Snap out of it Robin! This is not your first heartbreak, nor will it likely be the last!

Finally, it was late, and I took myself off to bed, leaving them to continue their celebration.

The next morning dawned as clear and bright as the one before, holding the same promise as the first day of our mutual adventure. I prayed that our luck and blessings would hold as the weather had.

I plunged myself into the day. As it was all still new, I went with the team, introduced them to those we were there to help, and lost myself in the camaraderie of female friendship.

Interestingly, although the local women—many of whom were not regular church attendees or were actually agnostic—were all older, not one commented adversely on what had been on the news about me. Edna, one of the oldest and a northern lady of firm views, expressed them over a 'pot of tea' with scones, her preferred setting for sharing her opinions.

"I don't think it's any of their business, vicar. You're a pretty lass, and who you want to snog is your business—whoever it is, is a lucky girl!" she said, sitting beside me, patting me with her wrinkled yet firm hand.

There was nothing to be said to that except "Thank you," which I duly did. As I was to learn, the strongest, indeed almost the only, criticism of me came from fellow Christians. Was it, I wondered, any surprise that people thought we were a censorious lot?

It was a busy afternoon. I was able to leave the women with those they were helping, which meant I could get round the whole complex where most of them lived. It was satisfying to see how the younger and older women soon got on, talking with each other over cups of tea. It was so easy to forget, in the business of our society, how many older people, especially women, suffered from loneliness. Some of my charges had asked: *How can just visiting people help?* But after that afternoon, the question was never asked again.

Perhaps it was that sense of satisfaction or just the busyness of the late afternoon, but I forgot the sense of danger I had felt earlier. Assuming the women, including Anna, had returned to the Retreat, I left the complex and began to make my way back on my own.

I was so happy, my heels barely touched the uneven cobblestones. The air was cool, carrying the scent of salt and seaweed. Shadows lengthened as the evening approached, casting an eerie gloom over the narrow streets. Despite my joy, a sense of unease began to creep in, gnawing at the edges of my happiness.

Two scruffy men were leaning against a fence across the road. They looked like labourers, with dirty clothes and unshaven faces. One was larger and stockier, the other thin and wiry. I couldn't recall seeing them before, or anyone loitering there for that matter. Their eyes followed me closely, and a chill ran down my spine. I quickened my steps, my heartbeat echoing the click-clack of my heels.

My unease turned to fear when I realised they were following me. Their footsteps matched mine, speeding up or slowing down as I did. The larger man's heavy boots thudded against the ground, while the thinner man's footsteps were lighter, almost like a patter. I was so afraid, my heart pounding in my chest, my mouth dry with fear. I made for where the squad car had been stationed earlier, my pace increasing with each step.

Rushing faster now, I heard their footsteps behind me but not closing in. My breath hitched as I turned the corner to where the car usually was in front of the Retreat—my heart sank. It was gone! Panic surged through me, icy and paralyzing. I nearly broke into a run but feared I might fall and break my ankle. Curse my addiction to heels! I couldn't lead these men to the women in the Retreat.

I couldn't endanger them. Desperation clawed at me as I decided to make for the Rectory and its safety, leaving the women in the Retreat secure. I had a choice: keep to the road or take my usual shortcut through an alley that ran between buildings but emptied close to my door. The alley was part of a maze of connecting pathways, so I headed swiftly down there, hoping my knowledge of the labyrinth might yet save me.

Their footsteps grew louder, closer. My breaths came in short, sharp gasps. I was tempted to glance behind me, but fear held my gaze forward. My steps quickened, my breath coming faster. The sound of their pursuit did not relent. Their presence was oppressive and unyielding. Every nerve in my body screamed for me to run. I knew it was my imagination, but the hairs on my neck stood on end as if I could feel their hot and sticky breath. Any moment now, I expected their greasy hands to grab me, pulling me into the darkness. Every instinct screamed at me to reach safety before it was too late.

I risked a look behind me. Their faces twisted with predatory glee; they believed they had me. It was only as I passed the crossroads where the paths met that I saw something else, or rather someone else. It was Irina, and she was not alone.

"Quick, in here," Irina whispered.

I turned. Not only Irina but also Anna and the others were coming out of the shadows. As I turned again, the look on the men's faces was priceless—yes, a cliché, but sometimes they're spot on—as they faced fourteen angry women, some carrying iron bars, others thick branches or pieces of lumber, all held high and ready to strike without mercy. Their earlier confidence, the predatory glee that twisted their features, vanished in an instant. Their eyes widened, their mouths agape, as if frozen in place by the sheer force of the women's rage.

The larger man's mouth hung open in a silent gasp, his piercing blue eyes, separated by a nose showing evidence of repeated fractures, now dull and lifeless. His weathered complexion had turned an unhealthy pale, reminding me of a troll caught in the daylight.

The smaller thinner man's coal-black eyes, previously sharp and restless, were now wide and slack with terror. His angry, jagged scar of mottled flesh snaked across his face like a mountain chain, the pull of the scar drawing his lip up in a ghastly impression of a false smile. His features brought to mind a goblin, twisted and fearful. Both men were pale and wide-eyed, their terror palpable in the dim light.

"Are you sure you want to attack me?" I said, trying to hide the trembling in my voice.

"What you saying? We just walking," The Troll said, tripping over his words, his thick Russian accent evident as well as the fear on his face. For a moment, he stumbled over his lies and bluster, exposed in the light for what he truly was.

The Goblin, even with The Troll by his side, seemed equally terrified, unable to mask his fear. It was now obvious, even to men as witless as these, that they were not going to get anywhere that evening, so of course they pretended that they were out for a lovely evening walk.

"Well," said Irina, "if you and your lover don't go now, you will not be walking for quite a while."

"If ever!" came another voice; I was uncertain whose.

The look on Irina's face caused even me to shiver.

With suppressed fury on their faces, they turned tail and fled, starting off walking briskly and then bolting—the sounds of their feet that had so frightened me earlier, now made me laugh.

I burst into tears immediately, and threw my arms open, embracing Irina and Anna and finding myself surrounded by the biggest group hug I had ever experienced. From having just felt in mortal peril, I now felt not only safe, but surrounded by love. It was wonderful until my knees buckled, and they caught me before I hit the pavers.

As we walked back together, Irina said, "I was keeping watch and saw the police car leave. That's when I texted Anna."

Anna chimed in, "We quickly gathered everyone. We knew you were not at the Retreat, so that left only the Rectory. We left a few people there to cover both ends and waited here, leaving only a lookout to text us if you took a different path."

Irina smiled and added, "Besides, Robin, this is the only place along your path that would be suitable for an ambush. The rest is too well lit and easily observed."

I nodded, understanding now why I had felt the instinct to carry on. Their preparation and familiarity with my habits had guided me to safety. I was shaken, but immensely relieved. A massive wave of exhaustion passed over me, but I was sustained by the camaraderie of my protectors. Cast your bread upon the waters… I had helped them; they were now helping me.

As I approached the Retreat, I spotted Mac pacing near the entrance, his hands clenching and unclenching at his sides. His eyes darted around, scanning the area with a furrowed brow. When he saw me, he stopped abruptly. Tension filled his shoulders and his chest was rising and falling rapidly. I had never seen him so upset before.

"What happened, Robin? I got a text saying you might be in trouble." The concern in his voice warmed my heart; he was a good man. I had to remember there was at least one good man during those dark night hours when I thought ill of all of them.

"I was going to ask what happened to your car?" I wanted him to know I appreciated their efforts, but was a bit disappointed since I had expected them to be here.

"They got a call saying that you were staying till late and the car could return later," he responded quietly.

Again, I'd caught Mac by surprise, his eyes wide, and mouth open in a silent 'o'—he was startled that I'd asked.

"Well, not from me they didn't," I answered, more than a little tired and a touch cross, and I could not help wondering who sent the text to him, not one of the women, nor Irina or Anna, they would have said.

I told him what had happened, all the details, leaving nothing out.

"Heads will bloody roll!" His face was pink; whether it was from anger or embarrassment that they had been so easily fooled, I could not tell.

"I am not sure, in the circumstances, that's going to be of any use, Mac." I found myself sighing again; I had done that a great deal lately.

"You're too kind, Robin. But I will tell them all that, from now on, short of a message from me, they stay on your tail." He was so insistent; it was sweet. But I knew it was not practical.

"Thank you, but this is not sustainable. I fear the only way out is the one I *want* to take." I was emphatic, almost stomping my foot.

Mac's brows furrowed, clearly he was doubtful, but he finally nodded; as much as he hated it, he knew I was right.

I went to bed exhausted; not even night prayer calmed me. What was going to happen? Even if we did manage to trap Dimitri, there would be others. Jane was cooling on me. My reputation was, to put it mildly, *compromised* by my notoriety. Could you have a priest associated with a sex scandal? All these and other anxieties crowded in on me. Eventually, sleep claimed me and the black night swirling with the spectres and shadows of my fears engulfed me.

Chapter 12

ANNA MAKES A MOVE

The morning came too soon.

For one brief, blissful moment, before full consciousness struck, I felt fine; then not. It all flooded back, making me nauseated. I dreaded to think what the morning press would bring, let alone what my emails and texts would reveal. Beneath all of it was the pain of the loss of Jane. It was not so much her words about *cooling it*, as what they represented which made me feel sick and empty.

Was it too judgemental of me to contrast her caution with my lack of it? One might argue I was too harsh since, in refusing to be blackmailed, I had taken a risk. But I had done so because it was the right thing to do. I had refused to bow to pressure, or to equivocate. In all honesty, I had plenty to equivocate about. I was not sure that I was attracted to women exclusively, but I was for the most part, and to have talked thus in public would have sounded as though there was something shameful in being gay. So, I had spoken out, or at least not turned away from it, if I had not wholly embraced being gay, just yet. My reward? Notoriety, criticism and, in some quarters, ostracisation.

In the end, the consequences were, at the very least, question marks about my future in the Church, which was, of course, why Jane wished to *cool things*. It would hardly do for one of the senior bishops of the Church to be in a relationship with the *Randy Rev Robin*. Had I remained an obscure young vicar, that might have been accommodated; quiet weekends together, discreet liaisons, all might have escaped notice. But that had gone, and it was not coming back. Perhaps what hurt, and what I did not want to admit, was her career mattered more to her than *we* did.

Sighing, I prayed for a while. There were times when I wondered why I bothered; it felt like talking to myself, but this was not one of them. Heavy of heart when I'd begun, a feeling of shalom descending. A peace that I desperately needed.

Feeling lighter, I showered, breakfasted, and resolved to face the day. Was that dark skirt too short? I had nice legs, and I wanted to give them an airing. It was not as though I was known as the model of priestly modesty. The black stockings and suspenders were a deliberated provocation, but again, why not? The skirt was long enough to preserve my modesty, and I felt as though I wanted to say to the world that I was not hiding from it. That I would not hide under a basket nor be intimidated.

It was with a spring in my steps that I went out to say morning prayer at the Retreat, where Anna and the other women were all waiting for me. In the prayers, I added one of thanks for their friendship and support, and coffee afterwards was a cheerful affair as we shared out the jobs that needed to be done. I insisted that no one went alone, which prompted Anna to say firmly, "That goes for you too, Miss Robin." She had me at that, how could I refuse after yesterday?

We went round to the complex to talk with the concierge about what else we could do to help. It was a small community of thirty women who lived independently but with communal areas which alleviated the loneliness. Claire, the concierge told us how delighted her charges had been at our arrival, and how much of a difference it had made to them. We drew up a rota and a list of ways in which we could help. Then we visited the communal lounge and spent time listening to some of the women.

There was a fascination in listening to their lives, and a sense of sadness that their gifts and experience was being wasted; a healthy society would surely want to treasure such women? They, in turn, loved listening to Anna's account of her life in Ukraine, and some of them spoke movingly about their own memories of being little girls in the immediate post war era. It was as though they and Anna united over the memories of the ruined streets and bombed-out houses. There was a bond in shared suffering. It all made me rather ashamed of my own waking thoughts. Did I really expect to act boldly and suffer nothing for it? And what, in any case, was my suffering compared to the stories I had just been privileged to hear? That shook me out of my self-pity. If people wanted to label me, let them. I could do nothing about it—except to be who God had made me. There, of course, was the rub. But did it even make sense that I had to accept a label?

By the time we'd finished in the lounge, it was time to celebrate with a service of thanksgiving and fellowship. I had come to find such informal services went down well with those who were either unfamiliar with church, or uneasy about it. I asked Anna to help me. As always, she was eager and, afterwards, as I packed my things away, she asked me why I had done that as she was not, she said, a *believer.*

"Well," I said, "God believes in you, and he loves you, as he loves all his creatures, so what could be wrong with helping me to help bring fellowship to the women here?"

"You are a curious creature, Robin, not at all like the priests in my own land. I am sure you must have more important things to do than this, and yet you have spent time helping us, and these lonely old women, and for what? In the effort you may have wounded your career, and you have risked your life." She turned herself to face me directly.

"I just do not understand." Anna, her head shaking slowly, looked at me in vague confusion.

I smiled at her, noting, in passing, that this was the first time she had not referred to me as 'Miss Robin'.

I paused briefly, as if to catch a fleeting thought, then found the words that rested in my heart. "Anna, I love God because he first loved me, and I love you and these women because through my love for you, I reflect that love back at him. That's why we are here, to take that gift of love he gave us, and through loving others, we give our love back to him. If that love, or the act of loving others, costs me my career or even my life, then so be it. I cannot tell God you are not worthy of his love or mine. If he thinks I am worthy, then certainly you are too."

"Thank you, thank you, Robin. You bring me and the others hope in a world where we had lost it. After what happened to us, we thought all was lost. The counsellors you have arranged for us talk it through, but somehow, you live it." Anna had her arms around me, and I needed that so much.

That was it. The tears came to my eyes. I am British; we don't cry, especially with strangers, much less in public. But my tears would not be denied; the harder I tried, the more came.

I felt arms around me; Anna held me while stroking my hair and soothing me. It felt good. I could not remember the last time I had been held. I had to have stiffened slightly, but as she only hugged me tighter, I finally relaxed; no, I melted into her embrace.

"Oh, Robin, when was the last time someone held you?" Anna's voice was so gentle, it amazed me.

In time, I managed to straighten myself up, my nose running. I was so embarrassed and dug in my purse for a handkerchief; thank goodness my mother had taught me well. Anna did not seem to notice. I could not lie to this gentle soul and confessed that I could hardly remember.

"Thank you, Anna, that felt good," I stammered while trying to dry my eyes.

"You have taught me the need to connect with others, Robin." Anna held my shoulders in her gentle grasp. "And you have taught me that theory needs to be put into practice."

I felt her hand leave my shoulder and then tip my chin to look directly into her eyes as she continued.

"You really helped me with what you said about my rape. Would it be an awful thing to say that hugging you made me feel aroused for the first time since then?" Anna's cheeks were lightly flushed.

"No, it would be honest of you," I answered; it was true. We were not almighty concerning our physical reactions.

"But I am not gay, Robin," Anna answered, her voice tinged with uncertainty as she avoided my gaze.

"Does arousal have to depend on a label either you or others place on it?"

"No, I guess not. Like the tickling, it is a response, yes?"

I nodded in agreement and smiled. "Yes, exactly."

"I have to ask, and forgive me if it is not right to do so, did you enjoy?" she asked, and I thought I detected a note of hope.

"Yes," I admitted, then realising how emotionally vulnerable Anna was, I added, "but I was glad that we stopped where we did."

Her shoulders slumped, and her eyes dropped to the floor. My heart broke for her.

"Does that mean you would not like… if I wanted… to go further and explore?" she asked.

We were so close I could feel her trembling.

"No, Anna," I said, noticing her smile returning, "it simply means now is not the time or place. A lot has happened, and I need a little time, and I think you do too, but I promise I will take all the hugs you wish to share."

Anna's eyes sparkled with mischief and there was a suggestive but playful grip spreading across her face. It made me tingle.

"Good!" she said and took my hand; it was time to go on.

As we walked back to the Retreat, I was acutely aware of Mac's men following us closely, their presence a constant reminder that he was taking no more chances.

We gathered with the rest of the team for a debrief. What struck me most was how the experience of helping others had rekindled the spirits of the Ukrainian women. Just a week ago, their faces had been shadowed with fear and exhaustion, but now they were lit with a newfound vitality. Their smiles were genuine, and their laughter came easily—a stark contrast to the haunted looks they had worn when they'd first arrived.

During the day, they had been serving the community, bringing warmth and cheer to old, lonely women. I'd watched as they listened patiently to stories of bygone days, their eyes twinkling with empathy and understanding. The transformation was palpable; they moved with a purpose, their gestures more animated, their conversations filled with enthusiasm.

The night before, these women had faced down a group of thugs trying to harm me. They had stood their ground with a fierce determination, their courage unwavering. The same women who had once been victims of human trafficking now confronted their former oppressors with unyielding resolve, their strength a testament to their resilience. Though it was just a skirmish and not the final victory over their traffickers, the act of saving me had lifted their spirits immensely. The elation in their eyes, the tight embraces they shared, and the tears of relief and joy—they had reclaimed a piece of their power and dignity. It was as if a heavy burden had been lifted from their shoulders, allowing them to stand taller and breathe easier.

The positivity they exuded was almost tangible, filling the room with an infectious energy. It wasn't just a change in demeanour; it was a revival of the spirit. These women had rediscovered their sense of self-worth and purpose, and it radiated from them, touching everyone around.

Anna spoke afterward, her voice trembling with emotion, "I am going to ask Robin to pray with us all. I know not all of us are Christians, but I don't know about you, but I feel this is a special moment. I feel so close to you all." She flicked away a tear and took a deep breath, her lips pressed tightly together as she fought to maintain her composure.

The universal acclaim was a chorus of "*Yes*" in both English and Ukrainian.

So, I did something I thought I could not do, which was to pray extempore. I was very much a liturgical priest. I liked the certainty of it; the familiar words soothed me, and knowing that generations had been here before me was a comfort. For me, extempore prayer was for others, the more evangelical side of the Church, but to my surprise, the words came. Indeed, they tumbled out, and the women joined in, asking for help for their families, country, and themselves.

"Heavenly Father," I began, my voice trembling slightly but growing stronger with each word, "we gather in Thy holy name, assured of Thy presence among us, for where two or three are gathered in Thy name, there art Thou in the midst."

I glanced around the circle, seeing eyes closed in concentration, tears slipping down cheeks, hands gripping each other tightly.

"We give Thee thanks for Thy abiding love and protection, and for bringing these women to this haven of peace, blessing us with their fellowship and love."

Heads nodded in agreement, some whispering "*Amen*", their faces softening as they let the words wash over them.

"Forgive them, O Lord, for all they have borne, the heavy burdens they carry, and the deep wounds inflicted upon them. We thank Thee for Thy boundless blessings, those given and those yet to come. Grant us the faith to forgive, the strength to seek freedom, and the grace to meet all that lies ahead with Thy boundless love."

A woman beside me sobbed quietly, her shoulders shaking as another gently rubbed her back, offering silent comfort. The weight of their past seemed to lift slightly with each word.

"We thank Thee for the gifts bestowed upon each of these women, and we pray that their lives may be a beacon of Thy hope and light to others. May their hearts overflow with the love and healing that only Thou canst provide."

Faces lifted towards the heavens, eyes shining with a mixture of hope and lingering pain, as if the prayer itself was washing away some of their burdens.

"Send forth Thy holy angels to guard their families, encircle them with Thy divine protection. Bless the soldiers who stand watch, shielding their loved ones from harm. Send Thy warrior angels before them, scattering their enemies like chaff before the wind. Gather those who are lost and bring them safely home. Bless them with peace and prosperity, heal their wounds, and restore their land until Thy Son returns and wipes away every tear."

The room was filled with a tangible sense of unity and peace, the air thick with shared sorrow and collective strength.

"In Jesus' holy and eternal name, we pray. Amen."

As we stood there, looking into each other's eyes, the women began to voice their own prayers, their words blending with mine in a chorus of hope and faith. In that circle, praying and holding hands, I felt an overwhelming closeness to God, more profound than I had ever experienced. The world might have called them refugees and whores, but I knew they were a blessing.

Miriam had joined in, and as the women returned to their rooms, she moved close, taking my hand and looking up at me, her eyes brimming with tears.

"Thank you, Mother, I had no idea it could be like this," she said, her voice thick with emotion.

"If it's any comfort, nor had I," I responded, blushing; I was more than a little overwhelmed myself.

We both stood there, savouring the moment until, ever so slowly, it passed to become a cherished memory, Miriam's accustomed stoicism and efficiency coming to the fore.

"That lady from the *Church Times* said she'd phone you about four; is that okay with you? I was not sure, but thought you could always fob her off."

Miriam did not seem sanguine about this reporter or the interview; I was sure she was trying to protect me; oddly, it felt nice to be protected.

"No, let her through," I responded, hoping against my experience that it would not be a complete hash.

The conversation went well. Unlike the journalists from the mainstream media, she was actively interested in what I was doing, and in how what had happened was impacting me and the local church.

I chose my words carefully, emphasising that what was happening was a group effort. The women were giving something valuable back to the community which had offered them refuge. I invited her to come to see what was happening. As for me and the local church, well that was something she would have to take up with others. For my part, I was busy getting on with what I was doing. We arranged that she would come up from London on Friday.

Friday was now looming large in my mind. I was usually a 'take each day as it comes' sort of woman, but suddenly, I just wanted Wednesday night and Thursday to vanish.

I sat alone in my office; I supposed I should have been working, trying to put together something resembling a report to Jane. The thought of her, well, it left me cold and lonely.

The river of my reflections kept returning to how things were turning out. I wondered if I had made different choices, how things would have been different, and whether they might have been better or worse. Each step along the way seemed to make sense, even *guided.* I couldn't repress a chuckle at myself, given how that thought grated against my orderly nature. I am faithful, but I was not given to the common belief that miracles are an everyday thing. I didn't believe the Lord's visage appears in toast. But I could not escape at least the appearance of a guiding hand, given how fortuitous events had been. How many sticky ends had I avoided? How often had someone been in the right place and time to save me? And what of poor Marta? Not for the first time, I wished I had kept Marta with me; perhaps that tragedy might have been avoided. Always, my thoughts drifted back to that brave young woman who had only been trying to do what was right. Why save me and not her? Still, with all the joy I had experienced earlier, I felt more than a bit of anguish and tears threatened me.

Then, the knock on the door broke my ruminations. It was Anna.

I looked at her, and she at me. In her eyes was a fire I had seen before but not often; it was one of desire bordering on hunger. Strangely, I was not afraid. She came closer. I stood still, waiting. Our lips met as she pulled me to her. Her hands glided down my back. The sudden, unaccustomed sensation started my body tingling. The trail of her fingertips was electric. I pushed against her. Her hands slid up my skirt, and she broke the kiss. Moving up to my right ear, she blew hot breath into it, and my body shivered from head to toe.

"Stockings, how sexy," she whispered, then smiled, before gripping my bottom with her right hand and pushing her tongue against my lips.

I parted them. Her tongue glided over my teeth as she pressed me back against the desk, her hands hiking my skirt up and opening my legs as she intensified her kissing.

"Robin, I want you, I want you so badly." Low half-moans flowed through her whispers.

I nodded; the urgency of her passion was emphatically communicating itself to me, and I felt a quiver, as well as a dampness down below. Her tongue explored mine, and I certainly wanted to *explore* further. She stopped, pulling back till only just the tips of our breasts brushed each other. This slight contact seemed so much more erotic, and she looked into my eyes.

"I don't want to rush you, Robin, though I feel selfish enough to." Her voice was breathless and so much lower in timbre that it sent a shiver along my spine, but *up* this time.

Not wholly trusting my words, only smiling, I took a breath before attempting an answer. "Well, delayed gratification can have its benefits," I said, not precisely sure that I agreed with what I was saying.

Later, I wondered what might have happened had I not called *time.*

I was surprised by two things: the strength of her passion, and my reaction.

Anna had verged on the aggressive; not, I supposed, altogether surprising in someone whose last sexual experience had been one where force had been used against her. She wanted to regain a sense of control, and I had felt that — *strongly.*

More profoundly, it had been my own reaction that surprised me. Even with my initial unease, I had felt myself going along with her, if not becoming an active participant. My panties gave evidence to this, and would undoubtedly need a change. If I could hazard a guess as to what had got into Anna, I was not sure that I could have done the same with myself. I was at a loss as to why her vigorous advance had affected me; it was a wholly new and unsettling experience. I was relieved that instinct had called a halt, but anxious about where it had left things between Anna and myself.

I was coming to the conclusion that I was no good at relationships, at least sexual ones. The evidence was all too clear.

Irina and I had enjoyed a weekend of pleasure, but she had been gentle and further had shown no desire to follow up. Jane, on the other hand, had taken her own time to make a pass at me, but the pursuit had been glacial; and now, well, in the face of the media storm, she had effectively withdrawn. Elena had said she'd wanted to resume our brief affair, but had promptly betrayed me. Now Anna; who seemed to want to work out some of her trauma through me.

The only thing all of this had in common was *me*.

Even as such thoughts passed through my head, sleep came and took me through troubled dreams into Thursday.

I checked my phone. Nothing from Jane, not a surprise but a disappointment; hope springs eternal, I supposed. The media storm had moved on, as some television presenter had been caught doing something he ought not to have been doing. After breakfast, I went to the Retreat to do morning prayer, from which Anna was a notable absentee. I spent an hour with Miriam going through various bits of administration, none of which managed to grab my full attention; but Miriam was kind enough to understand.

Anna was there after lunch when the corps assembled. On our menu was parish visiting and going out into the wider community to those whom we knew needed help.

As members of the team peeled off together, Anna approached me. "Are you cross with me, Robin?" She seemed pensive, even ashamed, and it saddened me; it was not what I wanted.

"No, but perhaps we could talk? I'll come with you to Mrs Elmira's. It's not a long walk, and my escort can keep an eye on me." I smiled at her reassuringly and cupped both her hands in mine, trying to soothe her.

We assigned tasks and sent out our little groups by twos and sometimes fours. Soon, it was just Anna and I walking through the village.

"What happened, Anna?" I chose not to look at her lest she feel challenged. The weather was going to be lovely today.

"I got, how do you say, carried away? I wanted you that bad." She whispered the final words while glancing about us for listeners. I could not help a little smile.

"It felt aggressive," I responded, leaving the statement as a fact rather than an accusation or question.

"Yes, I did not mean it so, but the desire simply took me." Anna stopped under the shade of an ancient oat, turning me gently to face her. "Some women like aggressive. Look at me, I had climax while being violated."

Turning back to the path, we began strolling again. The tension in her shoulders had eased, and there was a lightness in her step. She smiled more easily now, a far cry from the haunted woman I had washed dishes with just days before. So, my guess had been accurate; she was working out her feelings about what had happened to her, and as her next sexual partner, I had been the recipient. I suspected she had achieved something of a détante with her inner demons.

"We discussed that, Anna," I reminded her, keeping my voice even with as much compassion as I could muster while trying not to expose more of my inner turmoil than necessary.

"I am sorry to have upset you, but I thought you liked it." She glanced down, her shoulders drooping and her face flushed with embarrassment, which was not my aim. She put her finger directly on the heart of what had been making me anxious, and we had come to it far sooner than I would have liked. Truthfully, I had no reasonable answer, and Anna deserved one.

"It felt too much, too soon, Anna," I said, "but I can understand why you thought that."

"You can?" Anna sniffled, just holding back tears, her voice trembling. "I can't."

"Look, let's have dinner later, discuss it then." I desperately wanted to hug her, but thought that would just complicate things.

She was clearly blaming herself for my internal confusion; I did not want her to bear a burden she did not deserve.

"You still want to see me?" Anna asked, sounding as she must have as a young girl.

"Of course I do, Anna." We were too close to Mrs Elmira's for this discussion. "But let's wait until we're somewhere more comfortable, maybe over a cup of tea."

We arrived at Mrs. Elmira's front door, and I knocked gently. She was a widow in her late seventies who, until recently, had been active in the church. A diagnosis of osteoarthritis and a long wait for an operation had changed all that, more or less confining her to her home. As the door creaked open, Mrs. Elmira's face lit up.

"Hello, Mrs. Elmira," I said warmly. "It's Robin and Anna."

She smiled, her eyes brightening with genuine delight. "Come in, come in."

We stepped inside, and her home, though modest, was filled with light and warmth. I had arranged with Fr. Richard to organise home visits from her friends, and now from members of my corps. Sometimes, just being there was sufficient, and since my arrival, Mrs. Elmira's spirits had noticeably risen. We were offered the inevitable *pot of tea*, with me doing the honours to spare her the pain of walking. She and Anna soon got into a conversation about Ukraine and the war. Her pain was assuaged for the moment, with the pleasure of companionship soothing her spirit. It amused me that Fr. Richard, great opponent of the idea of women priests that he was, was happy enough for me to fulfil a *woman's role*. In my view it was part of the pastoral ministry of *any* priest, but it came easier, perhaps, to a woman.

We were down to spend an hour, but stayed for another half an hour as Mrs Elmira and Anna got on so well. You could see, for a moment, how she must have been and looked fifty years earlier, a lifetime ago. And now, well, on the bright side, instead of isolation in her pain, she had some companionship. I asked if she'd like me to bring her communion on Sunday, but being from a low church charismatic background, she said not to bother.

"When you're here, I know God is. God bless you, vicar!"

She smiled in a way that touched my soul; perhaps she was right, since *where two or three gather, God is there.* I made a mental note to stop by to give her communion anyway, her faith deserved it.

I thanked her and took her shopping list, promising that one of the team would be back tomorrow. I checked that she had her medicines and confirmed she was taking them properly. I also asked if there was anything else we could do for her.

Some might have wondered whether a priest could not find more profitable uses for her time, but I was not one of them, nor was Anna. After all, was not a shepherd to care for all her sheep?

"She was so pleased to see us." On our walk back, Anna was buoyant and beautiful again. "If this is *your* Christ, Robin, I could believe again."

Her sincerity brought tears to my eyes; I could not speak as I held her hand and squeezed it.

Back at base, I caught up with the afternoon's emails and Miriam's various queries.

"Oh, that nice policeman rang, wanted you to ring back." Miriam's tone made me chuckle; she clearly thought a lot of Mac.

I rang him. He answered straight away and thanked me for getting back to him.

"There's been some movement at Dimitri's, and he's given my men the slip. Don't worry, we are still guarding you, but I wanted you to know."

I could tell he was concerned but trying hard not to show it.

"Thanks, Mac," I responded when something occurred to me. "I think I have an idea; let me investigate."

I phoned Elena. Her line rang and rang; I was about to end the call when she answered, sounding out of breath.

"Sorry, I was in the bathroom and left my phone here. What is it?"

I doubted that the walk from the bathroom to wherever she had left the phone would have left even Mrs Elmira out of breath, but I pretended to believe her.

"We still on for dinner tomorrow?" I asked, wondering if I might be eligible for an Academy Award.

"Yes, yes, of course," Elena answered, panting harder than ever before. I shuddered to think why.

"Any sign of Dimitri, or will he let himself in while we are out?" I asked.

In the background, I thought I heard the sound of faint rhythmic sound of flesh meeting flesh, followed by someone being quietly hushed.

"Yes, yes, Robin, I am looking forward to it; I'll see you here at seven tomorrow, okay?" Elena responded, sounding more in control of herself.

That confirmed it in my eyes. Elena had not answered my question and had responded to one I had not asked—which, of course, she would have had to have done if he was already there, but unable to hear. I was sorely tempted to do something to spare myself the wait, but quite what, I was unsure, so turned my mind onto the evening and supper with Anna.

I thought I ought to shower. As I stood there in the shower, comfortingly hot water flowing over me, I found myself thinking of Anna and how she had made me feel, but I shook myself and dismissed the thoughts which came to me and let the water wash away the cares of the day.

I chose a pair of lacy black panties with a matching bra. Over this, I decided to wear a black balloon-sleeve midi dress with a red heart print and a sash at the front—effortlessly elegant and with just the right amount of sexy if I chose to employ it. The weather was still warm enough to go bare-legged, and I thought my red stilettos would give me the right match and uplift. Was I dressing for a date? Lord, I had so little practice. I felt confident but also a tad foolish. Taking my shawl and red beret, I left for the restaurant. I noticed the looks from my protection detail, one of the men even gave me a big grin and a thumbs up. *Well,* I thought, *someone approves.*

I walked; they followed. I was of more than half a mind to turn and run the other way but somehow my shoes refused to listen and like a wayward horse, they took me to the restaurant. The cute little woman who greeted me, knew immediately what table I should be seated at and I followed her. When I saw Anna I nearly fainted.

Her solid lace white top scarcely concealed the absence of a bra, and it went well with her red and black plaid skater skirt; I was not the only one who had dressed up. My cheeks warmed a little.

As I approached the table and the server held the chair out for me, Anna's eyes travelled slowly from my heels to my face, a small smile playing on her lips. Her open appraisal made my cheeks flush with warmth.

"You look beautiful, Robin." Anna was smiling after taking my measure, which added to my blush.

"Thank you, I love that top, so pretty." I was honest; she was lovely and wore her outfit well.

"You don't think it shows too much?" she whispered, checking herself.

"Only if you get close." I grinned, moving a little closer.

"Any time you like." She smiled, her shoulders loosening as a gentle sigh escaped her lips. We ordered and shared a bottle of Chablis.

"I am sorry about earlier," she said.

Anna's brows furrowed in frustration as she paused, glancing away and biting her lip.

Seeing her struggle, I decided to help. "I know, and I suspect I did not help much, but I'd like to talk it through with you," I responded as soothingly as possible.

As we ate, Anna opened up as far as she could. I listened attentively, letting her talk, only asking questions where it seemed warranted.

"I know what you said about the orgasm, but it's like I need to tell myself that is not who I am. I can be in charge, not passive, not just accepting." Anna wasn't looking at me; it was almost as if she were alone, speaking to herself in the dark hours of the night, trying to talk her fears away.

"How were you before; if that is not too personal?" I asked softly, trying to coax her out more—the actual Anna, not the one she thought she needed to be to deal with her guilt.

"I ought to say that although I have been with men." She grasped my hand. "Not a lot, mind you, I wasn't; what is the word? A *povia*, a slut? But I had my share of interest."

She blushed as she struggled with what she wanted to say; I sipped my wine, giving her space to find her words.

"Since my … my village was attacked and what came after … I must say, I spent much time thinking about what I prefer." She stopped and took a large swallow of wine; I doubted she even tasted it. "I had a few times with women and enjoyed them, but I felt conflicted and worried that I was doing something wrong."

She paused momentarily, then looked me in the eyes before continuing, "But now I can say I prefer women; I enjoy more—much more. But generally, there, I have taken lead where that was wanted. It's just that since…" She paused for a moment. "Since what happened, I want to take the lead to prove that I am not going to be used, just a thing to be used."

I smiled, asking, "But what does that mean to you? What would show that you are not going to be used?"

"With you, I wanted to take control, Robin. I wanted to show you who I am—a strong woman, not a victim." At that moment, fierceness overcame her eyes and a hint of tears.

That, I thought, took us to the heart of the matter. However, it did not answer my questions about how I should react if I wanted to have a relationship with Anna.

"Do you think I am too damaged, Robin?" Her voice was small; the hurting little girl inside Anna showed herself again.

"No," I whispered, squeezing her hand. "But it's important that you face up to it, as you are. If you simply give in to impulses, it is *them*, not *you* who is in charge. You exchange one master for another. What is it *you* want? Just sex? That is what the Russians wanted you for? Is that the *real* Anna, to want to have another just for sex?"

"I have done that," she said with a sigh then continued, "and enjoyed it. Sometimes I just need to have sex, sometimes I want more. How about you?"

I was happier in the pastoral role, listening, gently guiding, and showing her that she was being listened to; I was less happy to be the object of her questions. I thought honesty was the best policy.

I tried to answer, buying time by pouring us both a second glass of Chablis and commenting on how well they had done the poached salmon.

"I'm not very experienced," I admitted, blushing a little. Not for the first time, I wondered how everyone around me found it so easy to explore their sexuality without a second thought. In school, one of my teachers had told me I overthought everything, but it felt like so many people didn't think at all. I knew I was reasonably attractive; the world insisted on repeatedly showing me that. Yet, shouldn't relationships be more than mere sexual combustibility? *What a funny species we can be!* Had I been very experienced,

I should have been at pains to protest that I was not promiscuous, just as Anna had earlier, the apology serving to emphasise that I was not some kind of slut. Yet here I was, also apologising for being inexperienced.

"That"—Anna grinned impishly, running her finger along the rim of her glass—"can be rectified."

I smiled back, feeling that same tingle. My jaw dropped, and my face flushed with delight at the idea. The thought that this beautiful woman, Anna, wanted to help me rectify my dearth of loves was flattering, to say the least. I met her eyes, and we both ended up covering our mouths, trying to stifle our laughter. The confused looks from other patrons only made us laugh harder, tears forming in the corners of my eyes.

It took us a moment; the tension was broken, and I took Anna's hand in mine. It felt good to laugh, but that was not all she needed. She needed more from me, and I had to be open with her.

"I can't see sex as being divorced from other feelings," I admitted. "I need a connection at a deeper level. Call me romantic and unrealistic, but I don't want just to have sex."

"Is that to do with being religious?" Anna asked me, her eyes earnest in her desire to understand.

Anna was asking all the right questions, but I had no idea whether my answers would be what she wanted to hear. In the end, that did not matter; what did was telling her my thoughts as honestly as I could unvarnished.

"Maybe. Love is the deepest expression of our connection with another person. We let them into us in unguarded ways, we open ourselves intimately. I don't want to do that unless I can feel that connection. As you know, I love being with others; you see, that is a part of my ministry. God made us to be with others, and there are many levels to that. For me, sex is one of the deeper ones—it is part of a real relationship where it adds depth to something more," I finished and waited.

"You are a romantic, Robin, but I like that." She gave me the warmest smile that I could remember receiving.

"You do?" I responded, releasing my breath; realising I'd been holding it.

"Yes," she said; instead of my hands laying across the back of hers as they had this whole evening, she turned her palms up to grasp mine. "I think you are very sweet. Thank you for being so open. Thank you for letting me in."

Maybe that was the problem, I thought—my self-imposed isolation, with its strict rules and consequential chastity. But was it worth changing? I decided I'd rather stay as I was than compromise.

We both decided to skip dessert and as I asked for the bill, the question arose: *What next*?

Chapter 13

THE TRAP IS SPRUNG

Our 'date' was over; at least the dinner was.

Anna had been delightful and continued to be. It had been a lovely evening; and we had certainly been blessed for weather as we left the restaurant. I could not remember the last time I'd had a date, then I realised it must have been with that bastard Ryan.

Has it really been so long? I wondered to myself, thinking for a moment as we settled up. Those lunches with Elena and Irina had just been meetings with munchies, kind of like with Jane. This realisation made me a bit melancholy, only adding to my growing convictions that whatever other gifts I might have had, relationships did not seem to be one of them. I decided to derail that particular train of thought and focus on *this moment* with Anna.

We held hands as we walked back. I wondered what Anna was thinking. It occurred to me that might be my problem. Why was I leaving her to make a move? *I really was rubbish at this.*

I turned to her. Taking a breath to calm my nerves, I realised that she really did have lovely eyes.

"Anna, I have to be honest with you, I don't think I am the right woman for you at this stage." I managed to get the words out between my teeth and round my recalcitrant tongue.

She smiled softly, her lovely eyes showing relief. I had made the right decision.

"Thank you, Robin, I was afraid of hurting you. But can we still be friends, please?" Anna's eyes were hopeful. She was holding her breath, just as I had been.

I truly wanted to keep her as a friend and in my life. However, she still had to work through her issues, and I wasn't the right person for that. If I tried, it would indeed be the blind leading the blind.

"Anna, always, and I hope you find someone who will fulfil all your needs. But, remember what we spoke of?"

"I shall." She smiled, kissing me goodnight as we reached hers. I watched her go in. She waved and smiled before closing the door behind her, and I waited for the sound of the latch. I knew the staff would lock up tight now.

I walked back to mine, slowly, too slowly I thought for my shadows. Poor things, being on body guard detail for me had to be the highlight of their careers. As I reached my door, I fumbled for my keys, then putting the light on, I noticed it.

There was something on the doormat. Gingerly I opened the packet. To my surprise, it contained a pair of panties, and to my growing horror, I could see they were stained with blood. There was a note:

'This is what happens to whores who defy us. You are next, bitch!'

The note did not have to be signed.

As usual, my stomach revolted as I nearly vomited but managed to control myself.

What to do now?

Mac would want to know; my hands shook when I took out my phone. Luckily, my minders had to have noticed something as one of them approached me; I recognised him as the one who'd approved of my dress earlier.

"Are you alright, Reverand Topham?" he asked tentatively as he approached.

I could not speak; I only held up the stained knickers.

"Dear Lord, don't move." He ran back to the car, only to return moments later with an evidence bag. "Put them in here."

I placed them into the bag the officer held for me.

"Where were you? I was told I would be watched." My voice was sharper than it might otherwise have been, but not as sharp as I had cause for.

"You have been, miss, my partner, Henry here—he kept watch looking after you. While I stayed to keep watch here," the first keeper said.

"That's right, Reverand." A second keeper—one I knew as my first keeper's partner.

I looked at the man; my shadow for the night now had a name, at least a first name – Henry. Henry looked to be in his mid-forties, with sturdy build and a little more than my height, I guessed 5 foot 10 in stocking feet. He had short-cropped sandy-blonde hair, with a hint of grey starting at the temples, his square jaw giving a no-nonsense appearance. His blue eyes, showed a warmth, not the coldness one might expect from long service with the police.

"Tom stayed to watch the house and look in on the Retreat when he could," Henry added, giving his partner a name and thus completing the set.

And I could now see where the fault lay. Although they were not far apart, the Rectory and Retreat were out of sight of each other. To check the Retreat, Tom would have had to leave his post at the Rectory. With me being with Anna under Henry's watchful eye, it was logical that at least some of the time the Rectory would be unguarded, or the Retreat would; it was unavoidable.

"When Henry told me you were on your way back, I thought I would nip down to the pub, right down the way from the Retreat, to use the loo, and grab a couple sandwiches and some coffee. I wasn't gone five minutes, Rev, honest." Tom filled in his part of our little saga; he was a younger man, early thirties I guessed, taller than either Henry or I, over six feet I thought, lean and athletic. His curly dark brown hair was neatly trimmed, his brown eyes were sharp, and attentive; I guessed little got past them, if the object of interest were visible that is.

Henry glanced down, shuffling his feet, while Tom's cheeks flushed as he avoided eye contact with me, both looking like young boys caught with their fingers in the cookie jar.

I only nodded; well Tom and Henry were human, after all. Obviously, I was being watched by more than just the police.

No doubt looking for a way out from under my gaze, Henry lifted the clear, resealable evidence bag, the tamper-evident seal and detailed label catching the light. It was completely illogical but somehow seeing that bag, with all the clinical information ready to be taken down, made finding those panties so much worse and more real.

"I will exhibit this in; I am sure the lab will be able to do something with it. Please tell me what happened." Henry took out his little book and listened to my story.

I started from the beginning, feeling foolish for touching the knickers thus disturbing the evidence, but he made noises that my reaction was completely natural. He took careful notes and asked a few simple questions; he had followed me most of the night, so he knew my evening.

"Henry, Tom, thank you, I know this can not be what you would like to be doing right now but thank you."

Henry returned to the car, leaving me to my fears.

"Rev, may I please check through yours, to make sure it is safe?" Tom asked, his face tight and his lips pulled taut.

Tom went in, followed by me, I waited with the door open where Henry could see me, while Tom checked through the Rectory. Finally, he returned, pronouncing it undisturbed and wished me good night.

I went in, locked my door, then went through the entire place, checking every door and window. Finally, still fully clothed, I flopped down on my bed; the slight buzz of wine and Anna's good company had been replaced by real fear. I suddenly felt exhausted and caught up in the situation.

I shook with the horror of it. The message wasn't telling me anything new, but to see my fears visualised like that was another thing. It was, I realised, one reason for pulling back from Anna. That sense of the violence which she had suffered had, to be frank, scared me. I realised, suddenly, that my body's reaction to her forcefulness was just what I had been telling her about her orgasms when she'd been violated. I knew the theory. Now, I realised, I knew it in a new, real way.

I also now better understood her own self-disgust, as I felt it with myself. I had imagined that getting that aroused was a sign of some fault in me; but it had been a physical reaction.

Still shaking, I sat and pondered. Maybe Mac was right? Look what had happened when I had tried the same gambit with Ryan. It had almost gone wrong, and only Divine intervention had saved me. Was it wise to keep tempting Fate?

I knew I could not trust Elena, and yet I was going to her apartment. Dimitri had the key. He might be there when I got there. How long would Mac and his men wait? That might be long enough for him to do me some harm. What if Elena was actively helping him, not just pretending? I assumed she had kept this from him, but what if she had not?

At the thought of Mac, I suddenly realised I had yet to text him; I fumbled around to find my phone just in time to have it start buzzing — *unknown caller.*

"Robin here," I tentatively answered.

"It's Darnya. Thank God I caught you. Are you going round to Elena's tomorrow night?"

"I am," I confirmed, wondering how many knew of those plans. Deepening my fears that things were off the rails already.

"Dimitri knows the police are watching you. At dinner, Elena will slip something into your drink, which will mean an ambulance will be called. It won't be a real one; it will be Dimitri's men." Darnya was whispering, her voice tinged with fear and conviction in equal measure.

I did not like to ask how she knew; I was just extraordinarily grateful that she had told me.

"I know I work for Dimitri, but you have been so kind to us all. I overheard him earlier. I could not let any harm come to you." She sounded as she might in confession, ashamed at her situation but desperate to make things right.

"God bless you, Darnya, God bless you." It was heartfelt on my part.

Since that night behind the boats, my unease about Elena had simmered, lurking like a ghost in the shadows of my mind. A ghost whispering incessantly, warning me that something was amiss. I'd battled this ghost, burying it beneath layers of denial, yet that ghost refused to be silenced. Now, with Darnya's revelations, like a relentless tide, my ghost had breached every defence, scouring my façade of denial. Maybe it was Ryan's betrayal that made it possible for me to finally consider the possibility. I didn't know, but it felt like I had lost something, something dear to me.

Acknowledging the truth became inevitable; my gut had sensed a tear in the fabric of what I believed about Elena. Despite our early years of camaraderie and my lingering affection, doubt clouded my understanding of her.

Before I had thought Elena was yet another of Dimitri's victims, someone whom out of love, I had thrown a lifeline and had thought she had grabbed onto it in order to save her from the flood that threatened to engulf her. But now? Now I had to face the reality that Elena might not be a victim, or even an active participant but much worse—Dimitri's willing partner.

Did I ever honestly know her? For a moment, my brow furrowed and knitted together in a frown.

In stark contrast stood Darnya. Our acquaintance was brief, yet the same intuition that cautioned me against Elena nudged me towards trusting Darnya. This dichotomy left me adrift.

Heartbroken, I finally texted Mac, outlining the events and the warning, but worse, confirming his initial suspicions following the infernal kiss.

After night prayer, I settled into the first deep sleep I'd had for a while. Whether it was the sleep of the just or due to the wine and emotional exhaustion, who could tell? In the early hours, I was woken by my phone buzzing as it danced across the bedside table.

It was Mac; I took another breath to clear my mind before answering. I was surprised at how awake I was, given everything.

"Just got your text. Bastard! How do you want to play it?"

I could hear him dressing; this was becoming a habit; at least he did not stub his toe, but I did hear a woman's sleepy voice in the background, which *was* new.

"Mac, do you have company?" I asked, unable to hide the smile in my voice.

"Yeah, sort of, hold on a moment," he replied.

He was gone more than a moment, and hearing distant voices, I felt uncomfortable and considered ringing off, when I heard a door open and close, then he returned.

"Sorry for the delay. It's my ex. She's moving to Australia, so this was a kind of goodbye."

"Oh," was my brilliant reply, suddenly feeling uncomfortable and unsure how to address it. "I see."

There was a brief pause before he continued, "Anyway, back to business. What's the plan?"

"We need to lure him out," I said, my voice steady despite the anxiety bubbling beneath the surface.

"And you think you can be the bait?" Mac's tone was laced with concern. "Robin, I'm not happy about this."

"I know, Mac, but we don't have another solution right now," I replied firmly. "We need to catch Dimitri in a way he can't wriggle out of, and maybe Elena will come clean before it's too late."

He sighed heavily. "Alright. We'll adjust the plan, but be careful. I can't lose you to this, the paperwork would be murder."

I could not repress a chuckle. He joined me, though his was decidedly forced.

"Thanks, Mac. And, um, I hope everything goes well with your ex," I said awkwardly, wanting to acknowledge it but unsure what else to say.

"Thanks, but it's been over for a while. She left months ago, and she's moving to have a new start." He paused. "It's not easy being with a copper."

"I am sorry," I said, honestly there is really nothing else to say in those situations.

"Don't be," Mac replied.

I suspected he was trying to be more chipper than he felt.

"It was for the best, and I hope she will be happy there. As for you, you be careful, alright?"

"Of course," was all I said before I rang off, then glanced at my phone for the time.

It was still early; Mac had called exactly at half five in the morning. I could not help but grin.

"Well done, Mac, turnabout is fair play." I proceeded to drag myself out of bed.

After showering and breakfasting, I went down to the office at the Retreat to get some paperwork done before Miriam arrived. Amazing the way the 'paperless office' produced so much paper, almost as amazing as my utter detestation of administration, the closest thing to perdition I ever hoped to see.

I prepared myself for the reporter from the *Church Times*. I had asked Anna and the members of the corps to meet us at ten thirty, so that gave me time to brief her. Maddie, as she'd asked me to call her, was in her early thirties, slim, rather elegant, and she seemed genuinely interested in what we were doing.

"You must be tired of the press; I'm amazed you agreed to see me." Maddie was trying, I could tell.

I explained that what I was tired of was jaded media tropes about sexy vicars and *Randy Revs*, which simply objectified me and marginalised what was really going on. I told her something about Dimitri and the background.

"But, Robin, if I may, does that mean you are still in danger?" She seemed genuinely concerned, which touched me.

"Yes, that's what I really did not get with the BBC and the other *journalists*. There's a story here about the Russian mafia killing and trafficking women, and all they wanted to focus on was my tits." I could not believe I had said something so vulgar; mother would have gone white, but it needed to be told in a way that the readers would hear it.

She laughed, causing me to chuckle as well; it felt good to laugh even a little.

"I promise that I will write a real story." Maddie made more notes.

"That was why I agreed to see you." I smiled, crossing my legs. I caught her glancing at my legs, smiling a little more.

"I have a thought; why not take a quick go round so you can see and meet some of the women here." I stood, leaving her little choice but to follow my lead and agree.

I took her to the Retreat, where she met Anna and the others, and spoke to them about what they were doing. I had arranged that she would go out with us to talk to some of our clients to get their perspectives.

It was, in so many ways, just what I needed to take my mind off what was going to happen later. It also reminded me of why I was doing what I was doing.

I'd arranged to take Maddie for lunch at a nearby pub, where we were able to settle back and relax a little.

"Robin, what you're doing here is so countercultural. You're not only welcoming refugees, but also helping brutalised women regain their self-respect, and you're reaching out to the marginalised in our own communities," Maddie continued, leaving me curious as to her point and objective.

I was unsure if she was asking a question or making a statement. Perhaps it was just her editorial opinion of our work. It can be hard to tell when an interview ends.

"Isn't that rather the point of following Jesus," I replied, smiling. "Is that not just what he commands us to do—love one another. Faith without works is dead, Maddie."

"Can I use that as a direct quotation?" She was already writing while she asked.

"Please, Maddie. And now, I am sure you want to ask about the church and the personal angle, so fire away. I'll trust you to report it fairly," I responded, taking a breath and a not too small sip of wine.

"Thank you, I did not want to pry, but our readers will be interested in how the church is treating you."

"I'll choose my words carefully. My Bishop, Jane Summers, is very supportive, and I am grateful for that, but I am very aware that her hands are, to some extent, tied by the wider controversy over the place of gay people in the church." I tried my best to be generous but neutral with Jane; she deserved both.

I told her how the vicar at St Mark's had reacted. I was honest, if less generous, and I was frank about how I felt about that.

"It divides along predictable lines. Conservative and traditionalist elements disapprove both of women priests in general, and of lesbian ones in particular," I responded with the lay of the land as I saw it.

"But the church is trying to find a way forward here, so why the hurry?" From the look on her face, we both knew it was a rhetorical question.

"That need is created by those who want to stigmatise women like me. How much hurt must we endure from those who say they believe that God is love? It is so easy to say *wait*, when it costs you nothing."

"Can I ask a personal question?" She put down her notepad and pen, but her phone continued to record.

"If it is whether I am in a lesbian relationship at the moment, the answer is no, I am not. What I would say, though, is that if I had a boyfriend and I was sleeping with him, would those criticising me continue to do so? After all, premarital sex is also forbidden by Scripture, and much more explicitly than lesbian relationships."

"That's a good point," Maddie conceded. "I'd not thought of it that way. How hypocritical is that?"

"My point precisely," I added, to emphasise it. "There is something deeply hypocritical about criticising a celibate lesbian when you would not do so for a woman engaged in lots of premarital sex. The church needs to sort itself out on this issue, not just with gay people, but with sex in general. It seems okay to allow sex outside marriage for heterosexuals, despite what Scripture says, but then it insists that two women sleeping together in a loving relationship is the most dreadful thing imaginable and deeply sinful."

"Robin, that's just great, thank you so much. I've got so much there."

I almost told Maddie about the imminent changes in store for Dimitri, but I thought better of it. Instead, I opted to keep my cards close to my chest.

"Maddie, I might have something more for you soon. Could I talk with you tomorrow?" If all went well, I would do my best to give the woman a scoop.

"Sure, I'm actually staying with my mum in Norwich for the weekend, so I could even pop over here." She added, packing her things up.

"Good, it will be worth it," I responded, getting myself together as well.

We parted as firm friends. I liked her. I had no idea whether her editor would allow her to tell the whole story, but was sure she'd do her best.

Just after Maddie had left, my phone buzzed. It was Elena.

"Robin, could we meet at the pub? I think you can guess why. As

Dimitri has the key to here, he may be here when you arrive, and I think it might be nice to have a drink and something to eat first," she asked. I could almost hear her holding her breath.

"Sure, makes sense to me, El. Shall we meet around seven?" I responded, trying to keep emotion out of my voice.

"I shall see you then!" Elena actually sounded elated and relieved.

There it was, the Judas kiss. I had wondered how she was going to do it. I had not doubted Darnya's story for a moment, but here was conclusive proof.

My heart hurt; I could barely breathe for what seemed an eternity.

I had tried; I was sure I had. For the love of youth, now gone, I had given Elena every chance to save herself, but at each fork, she had taken the wrong path. Now she had formed the noose and put it around her own neck; I could do nothing more for her.

I phoned Mac and told him.

"You still want to stick with your plan then?" he asked, but we both knew the answer.

"Unless you have a better one?" I sighed, knowing he had only one other option, and it was hopeless.

"We could just arrest the bastard, and Elena too." It was his one card, and it was not a good one.

"And what proof do we have?" I replied.

"Okay, but I don't like you being used as bait, Robin. I would never forgive myself if any harm came to you." He sounded so sincere and desperate for an alternative. It made me smile; he was such a sweet man.

"Thanks, Mac, you've had my back all week, and I can't tell you how much I appreciate that," I said, knowing it was not beyond possible that I might never speak with him again if things went sour.

"Do you ever dine with men, or is it girls only?" he asked.

I thought I misheard. "Are you asking me out to dinner?" The sound of my incredulity must have been thick.

"I'd like to buy you dinner. Friends only, of course, no ulterior motives, except I like your company," he stumbled through his response, sounding so shy I could not help but smile.

"Why, Mac, you're a perfect gentleman, when this is all over, I'd love it." I was smiling again, for he had cheered me up a bit after Elena's betrayal. I needed it.

"Thanks, Robin. Best of luck!"

I rung off, just before Miriam came in with some new paperwork crisis or another.

She and I dealt with the day's emails and some queries, and I said that she could go home early.

"Why do I have the feeling something is afoot?" Miriam's brow furrowed, and she bit her lip in worry. I had an immediate flash of her in a different age, asking if she should carry her revolver. I did not let on; she would have made an excellent Dr Watson, faithful if, occasionally frustrated with her wayward Rev Holmes.

"Something is always afoot with me," I laughed, realising the humour in our choice of words. The moment crystallised for me how I cared for and appreciated Miriam. She had been a rock through all, if a little slippery at times for my footing.

"So I see," she replied, sounding worried. "But please, Robin, take care."

I was touched, not only by her caring, but by her calling me *Robin*, for the first time. It felt like some barrier had come down. I thanked her and said, "See you on Sunday."

I then had a word with Anna, who said that she would be glad to do what she could to assist. And so, as far as was in my power, the plan was set. It was a gamble, no doubt, all in and dependent on a dice roll.

What I really wanted on that suddenly lonely Friday afternoon was a call from Jane, but none came. I did not know what to say to her, and feared that if I did call her, then I might say something I'd live to regret. I still had feelings for her, and she was, after all, my boss. That side of things had always concerned me, but I had never thought that we would ever find ourselves in this situation.

I shrugged. *Funny how the world turns.*

I understood; of course I did. I had not lied to Maddie; I had just not told her the *whole* of the truth. Me being the *Randy Rev* put Jane in an impossible position. Being romantically connected with me would destroy her with her role under the Archbishop. I knew it. Of course, I didn't like it, but I knew it. I couldn't drag her into a controversy that could split or destroy the Church. I couldn't, and I wouldn't. Great Romantic that I was, I was bound to feel wistful that Jane would not give up all that for me, but even to fantasise such was to see how ridiculous I was being. Our relationship, such as it was, was hardly in the foothills, let alone at base camp. I was being spoiled and silly. Time to pull myself together. Put on my big girl knickers and do what had to be done.

I went back to the Rectory and dressed as Elena would expect for an evening out.

I went for a wine-red Hatton top that came mid-thigh with a built-in bra; suitably elegant with a touch of sexy, and it went with the red high heels. I did my hair, some make up, and was ready—almost. I texted Anna and Mac to tell them I was going.

I got to the pub. Elena looked pretty stunning in the red equivalent of the little black dress.

"Robin, you look wonderful!" She hugged me and actually kissed my cheek, the irony.

"So do you, Elena. Shall we have a drink and then go through to dine?" I asked, keeping my eyes open.

"Yes, let's." She seemed overly chipper, very un-Elena; she had to be nervous.

We were both attracting appreciative glances, something which pleased me. Whether I enjoyed the *company* of men, at least in my mind, had been decided, but that did not mean I did not appreciate being admired by them.

It was hard to believe that Elena was going to betray me. She looked so beautiful, so caring. What an actress. It made me wonder if I had ever really known the *real* Elena.

The waitress brought our drinks. We'd ordered a bottle of Chablis, and Elena poured one each. I excused myself and went to the bathroom. I got a text from Anna saying Elena had dropped something into my wine. Another chill ran down my spine as I read the message, along with a tear on my cheek. I still had held out hope.

"A toast?" Elena suggested, lifting her glass just as I sat down.

"Robin, how are you, and who is this gorgeous creature with you?" A familiar voice asked from behind Elena.

"Anna!" I exclaimed. "Lovely to see you. This is an old friend, Elena."

"Such a beautiful dress. Can I see how it fits? Give us a twirl!" Anna could be so persuasive and forceful; I could hear in her voice that she would allow nothing else but Elena's acquiescence.

Elena glanced at me, then slowly stood up and gave a hesitant twirl, her discomfort evident despite her attempt at grace.

"How is it on the bum, can you turn?" Anna was giving me every opportunity, as Elena obeyed.

The moment she did, I swapped the glasses.

"Perfect. Thank you so much. If Robin does not carry you off, she has my number." Anna smiled and gave me an air kiss; I never took my eyes off the wine glasses.

We both giggled as Anna walked away; the sway of her hips was… exhilarating.

"I think she fancies you," I teased. "So, that toast."

"The future!" Elena lifted her glass to me.

We clicked glasses and drank. I almost felt bad, but steeled my heart.

She did this to herself, I repeated the thought over and over again.

A few minutes later, Elena began to look disorientated.

"Are you okay?" I asked innocently, reaching out to steady her, then gently helped her sit.

She slumped in her chair.

"Could you call an ambulance, my friend has fainted."

They did, and within minutes two men in uniform came in. They looked at me.

"That's Robin," I confirmed.

"Ve take her from here," one said, the other giving her breasts a good grope while pretending he was assisting her into the well-worn wheel chair, before covering her with a blanket.

The moment they left, I texted Mac. It was obvious that Dimitri would not come himself, but would have me delivered somewhere where I could be taught my lesson. I had taken the chance that his thugs would not know what I looked like—and had been right. The idea was for Mac to follow the fake ambulance.

I threw down some money and dashed out to the waiting unmarked police car, cursing my decision to wear heels. This time, Henry was driving, and we were off, tyres squealing even before the door was closed, leaving me sliding about as I fumbled with the seatbelt.

The police tracked Mac and the others to one of Dimitri's seedy hotels. It seemed I had just got the buckle to click when I had to undo it and get out to follow Mac and his men to the door. We had been delayed by traffic, as we were not using marked cars, but airborne observers had been able to keep the ambulance in sight.

We had arrived only moments after Mac had, but minutes after, *the* ambulance.

"Wow, you look good, Robin!" Mac exclaimed; it was ironic, given he wore a bulletproof vest, as did many of those with him. I had not thought they would come armed, but that was obviously how seriously they took Dimitri and his men.

"Thank you, kind sir!" I responded, and would have curtseyed if I hadn't been so frightened. I stepped forward as if to follow.

He said nothing but glanced around at the other officers, who suddenly found other things to pay attention to besides us.

"Robin, I'm bending a dozen regs letting you even be here, but this might end badly, and if it does, well, you might be needed. But stay in the back, out of the way, and if this goes pear-shaped, get out, do you understand?" Mac's face made it clear he meant every word.

For once, I kept my gob shut and didn't argue.

He and the rest pretended I was invisible and carried on.

"Right, break the door down; we have probable cause," Mac whispered loudly.

The team nodded. The two burly men with the bright red ram moved into position. The larger of the two took up a spot on the left, while the other prepared to enter once the door was knocked aside.

The man on the right tilted his head to the left, from where I watched, his blue helmet making him look like an overgrown dog trying to understand something confusing. Then, without a word, he held up a hand to stop the man with the battering ram.

He reached for the doorknob with his gloved hand, turned it, and found it locked. But when he pushed, the door opened just a bit. Both helmets shook as they looked back at us, large smiles plastered on their faces.

"Well, someone left the door ajar!" one of them whispered. "Very considerate of them."

I must remember to thank Dimitri, I thought. Unfortunately, poor Mac looked a bit disappointed, like a small boy told he couldn't bash the walls with a hammer.

In we all went: armed police leading the way, followed by the two large men with the battering ram, then Mac, and finally little old me, trying not to turn an ankle in the dilapidated hall with its filthy carpet.

Raised voices from upstairs reached my ears as we all climbed the stairs, one after another, like a human centipede.

"Are you bastards mad? This is not the right woman!" Dimitri's voice was distinct, as was his accent. The paper-thin walls muffling nothing.

"But the other beetch said this vas!" Another voice, which sounded like the faux-ambulance driver, his accent thick enough to cut with a spoon.

"Idiots!" Dimitri proclaimed the obvious.

Mac shouted, "Armed Police!"

Just then the two burly men bashed the door open. As the rest rushing in, I chose to wait in the hall.

What followed was a good deal of commotion and words in Russian that I doubted I wanted to translate.

Peaking around the door jam, all I could see were men's backs and one struggling on the floor.

"They were right, you know," I said, as Mac was putting handcuffs on a prostrate Dimitri. "I did."

Mac *helped* Dimitri to his feet and was not very gentle about it.

"It was just the wrong *her*," I said as sweetly as I could, tilting my head to the side smiling.

For the first time that I had known him, Dimitri was at a loss for words.

Mac seized the opportunity. "You are under arrest for attempted kidnapping. I am sure other charges will follow in due course." Mac looked as happy as a boy with a new pony. "I have been so looking forward to this. You do not have to say anything. But it may harm your defence..."

I continued to smile, and how was Dimitri? Well, he seemed a bit put out. His hands were tightly bound and the two very large officers were assisting him in standing upright on his tip toes.

The look of fury on Dimitri's face was beyond value. Beet red, his jaw clenched and unclenched till I thought his teeth would crack, and his eyes were ablaze with unbridled fury. It truly priceless and certainly worthy of posterity so I snapped a couple photos for momentos. I probably shouldn't have but I did.

"You won't get away with this!" Dimitri shouted, spit flying in all directions dribbling down the corners of his mouth.

"That was what you said last time," I said, "but this time you are the one who will not get away."

Mac nodded to his men, and Dimitri and the rest were not so gently removed. By the sound of it, they hit every doorjam and corner at least once, poor things.

Once they'd been dragged out of earshot, Mac turned to me and, with an inscrutable look, asked me something I didn't quite process.

Finally, he asked me again, "She is in a bad way, medical is on its way. I owe you, Robin. For Dimitri, for Marta, all of it. We wouldn't be here without you. I might regret this, but I'll give you a few minutes with Elena until the ambulance gets here. Maybe you can work out what happened to her. Alright with you?"

It then occurred to me that he was hoping I might be able to gain information that he might not. Elena might be a turncoat, but she was still a trained police officer and would use the system to her advantage. Mac knew that she and I had a history and had once been very close. I suspected he thought I might be able to get more from her unofficially than he would be, certainly once she had been cautioned. He was using me, and I understood that.

It was then I saw Elena. I nearly rushed to her to comfort her, but then I realised that she'd intended this for me, or if she had not intended it, I was sure Dimitri had. Still for love of youth, and as a decent human being, my heart went out to her and I had to know the why of it, and do what I could for her.

She was tied to a chair, her lovely dress ruined, torn from neckline to nearly her waist. Her breasts were completely on show, both marked with nail scratches and darkening black and blue finger marks. Her nipples were bruised and puffy from several minutes of rough treatment that had to have bordered on brutal. That could have been me sitting there, tied to a chair, so exposed and brutalised. She only vaguely resembled my Elena, the beautiful woman I had always known.

I suspected Dimitri's thugs had had orders to go no further than groping the woman they brought back. It spoke volumes about Dimitri that the woman he had taken as a lover had been treated so, yet his only anger had been that it wasn't me.

Undoubtedly, the thug who'd got in the back with her had started the *fun* when the van door had been closed.

"I am assuming the drug will wear off soon," I said. "After all, Dimitri would not want to wait too long before teaching me my place. Mac, just give me a few minutes. I need to understand what happened to her; maybe there is some reason…" I just had to know, in order to put paid on this whole sad affair.

"I should take her in now, but so far, trusting you has paid off… fifteen minutes… at most, Robin." He glanced at Elena, a momentary flash of sadness and pity in his eyes vanishing just as quickly.

"Besides, they say confession is good for the soul," Mac said, one final look at Elena, the expression on his face making my blood run cold. At the door, Mac glanced over his shoulder toward us, then drew the door almost closed.

He seemed to know I needed some closure, which was true. Not to mention that anything I could get from Elena would help them; if not in her prosecution, perhaps her redemption, and certainly in shutting down the smugglers once and for all. *If* she would speak, and *if* I could share it, that was.

I dropped my bag, set my phone to record, and put it down as close to her as I could, then I went to the sink. I found a plastic-wrapped flannel, unwrapped it, and drew some cold water before going back to dab Elena's bleeding lip. I moved the second chair, the only other furniture besides the bed, to sit in front of her. I made no move to untie her.

Watching the sleeping El, a hurricane of emotions washed over me. She was the first girl I had kissed; she was a policewoman and a Judas. I struggled to cope but knew what had to be done.

I started dabbing her split lip and wiping away some of the blood that was blocking her nose so she could breathe. It must have hurt because she began to rouse, groaning, just moving her head, eyes still closed.

"Oh fuck, what happened? Dimitri, where am I?" Elena's eyes opened slowly, then shot wide. "Robin? Where am I? What am I doing here? Where is Dimitri?" She tried to move, realised she was bound. "Why am I tied up? Robin! We have to get out of here; they will kill us."

She began thrashing about trying to get release, but found it was hopeless. Dimitri's men might have been fools, but they knew how to tie a helpless woman.

"Who will kill us, Elena?" I asked, dabbing a little more blood that had found its way to her right ear.

"Dimitri. He was so angry with you," Elena started crying.

It hurt me to hear it, but I had to be strong.

"I am sorry, Robin. I didn't want to do it, but they made me." Elena was whining.

I have always hated whining in children, and cannot abide it in adults.

"Explain, Elena, how did they make you?" I continued to clean her, wiping the blood away, not looking into her eyes.

"Dimitri blackmailed me," Elena protested; she was sobbing now, almost beyond understanding.

"How is he blackmailing you, Elena?" I asked, trying to sound calm.

Her lip was split enough that I thought it might need stitches. I dabbed it, and she sucked the water out of the flannel, blood and all. I dipped it and let her suck some more. I allowed her to cry for a while, but we did not have much time, and I knew she would do plenty of crying later.

"Elena, how was he blackmailing you?" I took her bound hands; not releasing them from the bonds, just holding them.

"When I first joined the Met, they were trying to get someone into a Russian tea room in London; they thought it was a gambling cover." Elena was just getting control of her crying. "I was a fresh face, no one knew me so the Sarge thought I was perfect. I was there for over six months, waiting at tables and listening. Well, one day, Sarge got anxious because we were not progressing. He pulled me aside and told me to dig deeper, *do whatever it took.* He looked me in the eye, Robin and said it twice, *do whatever it takes* to get the dirt on the kingpin. *Whatever it took*, or he would send me to traffic. That would end my career before it started. I had no choice, Robin, I had no choice. The way the Sarge looked at me like I was meat, Robin, I had no choice."

She started crying again. I almost held her, but I didn't, I couldn't, not yet anyway. I simply nodded and wiped her brow.

"Is this Sarge the same one who came up to us when we met in front of the Palace?" I asked, guessing the answer already.

She nodded. "Yes, that's him." Her nose wrinkled as if she smelled something terrible; given the state of the room, she did not want for choices, but I knew what stank to her at that moment.

"Well, I let the guy, who we thought was the kingpin, Yuri Orlov, take me to bed." Elena could not meet my eyes. "Two days later, a well-dressed bloke shows up, and I am told to talk to him."

"Dimitri?" I looked at her.

She just nodded and started crying again. "He said they knew I was a police officer, they had always known. He showed me photos and said if I didn't do what they wanted, they would ruin me," Elena started sobbing again.

We only had a few minutes left; I didn't have time for this.

"Elena, what happened." I was sharper than I might have been otherwise. "Tell me what happened now, and stop blubbering."

She took a shuddering breath and calmed herself. "Please, Robin, untie me; my hands are numb."

"In a minute. Now answer me." My voice had a hardness that shocked her, her eyes opening wide. It certainly shocked me.

"He said all I had to do was bring them information, nothing serious, mostly just family stuff; it wouldn't harm anyone. I told you at the beach, remember?" Elena pleaded with me to believe her.

Honestly, I didn't know what to believe anymore.

"They gave me all I needed to take down Yuri, who was running not only gambling through the tea room but using their food vans to move drugs. It was a huge bust; I got a promotion," she went on, almost sounding proud, reliving the moment.

She was looking at me, desperate for understanding.

"That was just the beginning, wasn't it?" I asked, starting to loosen the bindings so blood could get to her fingers but leaving her ankles tied.

"How did you know?" she asked, genuinely surprised.

"They were grooming you, Elena, using your ambition and your beauty to get what they wanted." I rubbed her fingertips to get the blood flowing; her fingers were stiff and cold.

"They gave me information about different gangs, some horrible people, Robin." She was sounding more desperate than I'd thought possible.

"So they fed you what you needed to bring in busts, and you gave what you thought was useless information in return? Is that about it?" I kept rubbing her fingers gently between mine.

"Exactly. It was harmless; stuff that I heard, stuff in reports, it wasn't under the official's secrets act or anything." Elena leaned forward, trying to catch my eye. "You have to believe me, Robin, please."

"Oh, I believe that you thought it was useless, but somehow, I am certain it was not." I had a bad feeling about that information and how it would have been used, but that was for later. "What did Dimitri have planned for me, and how did you enter into it?"

"They wanted me to," she whispered, unable to meet my eyes. "To get you so that they could take photos. They knew that the Church would move you if you were exposed. They just want to operate, not hurt anyone, because that causes too much trouble."

"Tell that to Marta," I almost spat, my voice trembling with anger.

"That was an accident; they didn't know she had a bad heart," Elena returned to pleading again.

"Oh, I see; she just wasn't up to the torture they wanted to inflict; how inconsiderate of her to die on them." I was starting to really become hot.

"I wouldn't let them hurt you; I would love you properly this time, remember? Like we promised when we were at school? They would have what they needed, to put a bell on you, don't you see? You help them with the women, and they need you under control. That's all! Then we would be together, like before, at school, we could start again, I could start again." Elena was beyond the edge of hysterics and was in tears. "I was to come with you in the ambulance, to protect you. Robin, I would have protected you, I *have* been protecting you! I sent the text to Mac, when I found out about the attack on you. I had the jammer with me on the beach so you could not call him and get yourself hurt. I promise I was protecting you… I was protecting you…"

She dissolved into uncontrollable sobs, and I doubted I would get much more from her tonight.

I found myself looking at Elena, wondering how she could possibly be so deluded.

Rustling sounded from out in the hall; we were out of time. Mac and a couple of medics entered the room, rousing Elena from her crying. As a trapped animal's would, Elena's eyes searched mine for some way out. I knew at some point in the future, I would offer her my hand again; I could hear the words of scripture. I would forgive her seventy-seven times, but not just yet—not tonight.

"I will come to see you in the hospital, but Elena, you need to make a full and free confession about everything, even your sarge; he should not have put you in that position; it was wrong."

I held her cheeks as the med techs worked removing her bindings. "Elena, listen to me. You must do this to have any hope for the future. You do this, and you will be free. I will help you however I can."

Mac pushed me aside gently, then faced Elena who looked up with the face of a beaten puppy.

"Elena, you are arrested for aiding and abetting a criminal conspiracy. I have no doubt other charges will follow." Mac went through the caution, but of course, it was a formality; Elena knew it by heart.

I kissed her forehead, and the techs helped Elena stand; before they took her, she kept telling me she would have protected me. The funny thing is I think she believed it, even with Marta and all the evidence to the contrary. I knew she would have tried.

"Are you alright?" Mac asked the magic words, as his arms encircled me.

I had not even noticed him move up next to me. I found myself melting into his strong arms before I broke down sobbing. I don't know how long we stood there, with him holding me tight, making sure I felt safe. Wrapped in his strength, *making* me feel protected, I could see how a girl could get used to it.

Eventually Mac had to let me go. Holding me at arm's length, he dipped his head to look directly into my eyes. "Do you still want to go with her to the hospital?" Mac asked.

I shook my head no. I took a deep breath to answer the question he was too much of a gentleman to ask.

"She confessed, told me everything," I responded, feeling disgusted and awful. I opted not to tell him about the recording, not just yet, anyway. "I will give you the details. You probably can't use it, but you can encourage her to give a full confession in exchange for protection; she might be more forthcoming. She wants to talk, but please let her sleep tonight. I think she will be willing to talk tomorrow. Let me know if she doesn't, and I will speak with her again."

"I heard most of it. An awful business that, and I suspect heads will roll; she should not have been put into that situation in the first place." He shook his head, and sighed, "I think it broke her, somehow, but that is not for me to say."

He let me go but was not done talking. I could only guess he felt he needed some sort of good to come of it all.

"Unfortunately, I can't wait, she will be more forthcoming now, at least to get some sort of statement. I can only hold her for 24 hours, so I have to go to the hospital."

"We have rounded up the rest of Dimitri's crew and have taken Darnya and the women into protective custody. Shame that your beautiful dress has not had an evening worthy of it. My offer of dinner stands." He was smiling now, although I thought it a sad one.

I sensed he was just being kind, and suspected he had to get back to Elena, not to mention Dimitri and his ilk. It broke my heart; this victory had cost us both… well at least it had cost me.

"Thanks, Mac, I will take you up on it someday, but right now I ought to get back to the Retreat. Anna will be worried sick." Besides, my ankles were killing me. What sadist invented heels, and why are we women so masochistic as to wear them?

"Happy to offer you a lift." His smile seemed more enthusiastic now.

"I would rather we celebrate with a walk back along the prom, but my feet think the lift would be nice," I laughed, too emotionally exhausted to refuse. I was feeling light-hearted for the first time in weeks.

We both knew that Elena's deceit would be a scandal for the force, but he would get credit for her exposure, and Dimitri's arrest would be a feather in his cap. Things were coming up trumps for him, but I was still worried about my women, and even for Elena. Despite everything, I knew I would be praying for her for a very long time.

Still, the shadow was lifting, not only from me, but from the women who had come here seeking refuge. I was happy to work with Darnya and the others to see what we could do about helping them now that the horrible brothel was closed. But at that moment, I just wanted to breathe and suck in the night air.

We silently walked to his car, and then drove, remaining quiet. It had seemed like such a long distance driving from the restaurant to the hotel, but apparently Dimitri's men had been taking the long route for reasons of their own. With the Retreat just within sight, my mobile buzzed. It was Anna.

"Robin, are you alright?" Her voice sounded strained, almost dry, like wind in fallen leaves. "I waited till the police cars went by, then the ambulance…" Her voice caught, choking back tears.

I could hear the click of her heels as she paced.

Then I felt like a complete cad; here I was so caught up with Elena that poor Anna had been stewing, worried about me.

"I am alright," I softened my voice, pouring in as much sympathy as I could muster. "You are so sweet to worry about me." Then a flash of realisation—at the Retreat she would not have seen any of what she had described. "Where are you?"

"I waited at the restaurant. I didn't know what else to do." Anna's breathing seemed to slow, except for the occasional gasp, trying valiantly to control herself.

I felt awful, but I could not help but laugh; we had only just passed the place a few minutes before.

"Mac, Anna is still at the restaurant…" I didn't have to finish the sentence as Mac turned the car around.

"Stay where you are; we will collect you," I answered, murmuring more *sorrys*.

She agreed, and we rang off.

Mac had heard enough; there was no need to elaborate further. We parked a little way off, as it was a popular place, requiring a brief walk. Along the way, I paused at the small garden memorial. It appeared different in the evening yet retained its soothing peace. It seemed to draw out a confession from me.

"It was not easy to pretend to be that harsh, that uncaring, but I do not think she would ever have admitted her involvement without it," I said, feeling more of the tension drain from me like wax melting on a candle. Mac had the good sense to remain quiet and let me finish.

"I just could not bring myself to believe it, but it all makes sense now," I said, by way of excuse. "Oddly enough, I saw her again for the first time since school on the day I was appointed here."

"Had you been offered the appointment then?" Perking up, Mac turned to face me, curiosity in his voice.

I watched his gentle eyes in the moonlight; he seemed to be fitting the pieces together nicely.

"No, but it had been approved," I replied, seeing the path he was on.

"Do you believe it was just a coincidence?" Mac asked, his eyebrows up, then he smiled slightly before chuckling and shaking his head—the incredulity was dripping off of him.

"It's hard to, but why would anyone have wanted to know where I was being posted?" I wondered aloud.

"You saw they had a picture of you and Irina kissing," Mac spoke softly, almost to himself. "So, they kept an eye on you after the Surtees business. Is it too much of a stretch to suppose that they knew Elena and you had some background and asked her to find an excuse to get in touch?"

I thought for a moment. "Elena said as much, and mentioned she had told Dimitri about the photo, but she might have been lying about that too. Perhaps she was watching me all along after the Surtees mess?" I realised I had more questions than answers. The little garden held peace, but none of the answers to my questions, and we had kept Anna waiting long enough.

We walked quietly for a while, the sound of our shoes echoing off the brick walls around us.

"I don't know," I confessed, sighing loudly, tired of the whole affair. "We would have to ask Elena. For now, I just want to enjoy the night air."

As we talked, Mac got a call. It seemed that Elena had wanted to give a statement. She'd spoken to one of the officers before the doctors had intervened and pushed them out of the room.

"She's in hospital, heavily sedated, and will be out for days, or so the doctors say. She might have internal bleeding; they won't know until they can run some tests tomorrow. But she's under guard twenty-four-seven." Mac laughed, a hollow one that lacked any joy. "Funny, now that one of our own is involved, I have a blank cheque. If it had only been there before..."

He didn't have to finish; I didn't have to be psychic to know we were both thinking of Marta. I couldn't help but wonder how many others there might have been before her.

"Don't beat yourself up, Mac." I was already flagellating myself enough on that score; I didn't need a teammate. "Even if you had all the resources in the world, we just didn't know Marta was in danger."

"I suppose you are right, as usual." He sighed. "One good thing, the clock for holding Elena is paused while she's sedated and unfit for questioning. We'll restart it once she's capable of being cautioned and questioned. So, no rush on that score; your prayer was answered; she will sleep the night at least."

"The hospital takes care of Elena, but what of Dimitri and the others? Dimitri will call his lawyer. Don't you have to get back now?" I asked, interested of course, but I knew nothing of the way police worked.

"All sorted. At this moment Dimitri and his thugs are in interview rooms having a chat with a DC. You are not the only one with hunches, Reverand Topham. I arranged a couple of extra DCs for the night, and a DS will sit in, they are all good lads." He actually smiled at me, a smile that was a happy one, the first of the evening. "I still have a couple of things I must do, and some things I should do, and one or two I want to do, but all in all, I am free for the evening, let those who have a fresh perspective, and a good deal more sleep, to handle the whole mess."

We walked on in silence for a while, coming to a break in the solid wall of buildings where we could see out into the bay. We stopped for a moment, looking out at the dark blackness of the sky over the rolling waves, illuminated only by the odd star and moonlight when the clouds shifted. That inky abyss reflected my mood.

When we got to the restaurant, Anna launched herself at me, her arms around me, pressing her breasts into mine as she lifted me clear of the ground. Eventually, she put me down. By this time, her makeup was ruined, but she was beaming and still looked beautiful.

"You know, Robin, it seems an awful shame not to have taken advantage of that dress." Anna had a mischievous tone in her voice.

"I said the same thing not thirty minutes ago, Anna, back of the queue," Mac was laughing.

Thank goodness the lighting was too subdued to see how pink my cheeks were, but I could not repress a smile. She returned it, her face lit only by the faint gleam of the streetlight.

"Maybe, but however tempting, I think I should resist, and so should you," I said, brushing aside a wayward strand of her hair.

"Spoilsport," she replied, grinning. "And there was me feeling… what is your English word? Horny?"

We both glanced at Mac; he had stopped short a step behind, his jaw just millimetres from the pavement. Both Anna and I burst into uncontrolled laughter. It felt marvellous, and Mac suddenly appeared bashful, the street light just bright enough to show his cheeks were pink, which began another laughing fit for Anna and me.

We walked back to Mac's car, and Anna said something about a shotgun. It meant nothing to me, but apparently, Mac understood, and he laughed; he said she now got to sit in the passenger seat beside him. Something to do with American Westerns. I was no more informed than I was before, but it meant I was relegated to the back seat, but I didn't care. It was a beautiful night; the sea air was clean, and I didn't want to talk anyway.

Unfortunately, the drive to the station was short, nowhere near as satisfying as a walk for sorting out my thoughts, sore ankles or no. We soon pulled up in front, the harsh lights of the building ruining my view of the stars.

"I have to go into the station to change, deposit my firearm, and check on Dimitri of course. Then I'll stop by the hospital to look in on Elena, make sure she is safe and secure. No idea how long all that will take, but if you two would like a lift or a drink. Unfortunately, it might be past pub closing time," he added with a very naughty grin. "We could all three go back to mine for a nightcap?" Mac was smiling broadly, twirling his keys.

Anna laughed and moved closer to Mac; I, on the other hand, blushed and shook my head emphatically.

"I am fine, Mac," I answered. I was actually fine. "I need to go to bed, *but alone*."

"Would that offer extend to a refugee?" Anna grinned broadly, arching her back to press her breasts out.

Both Mac and I noticed; Mac whistled, and I blushed more. Anna laughed, enjoying the attention.

"It would," Mac confirmed with a grin and raised eyebrows. "Come into the station, I will get you some coffee while you wait. Robin can tell you how good it is."

"It will take rust off an old iron fence, but I would not recommend drinking it," I responded, smiling. "I think I shall take myself home and get to bed."

I almost choked on how that sounded, but both Anna and Mac laughed.

Anna put her arm around Mac, who took that as a sign to reciprocate. They both walked to the station door, before Mac stopped and turned.

"Don't worry, Robin, your babysitters will see you home," he nodded towards a marked car that I had not noticed before. It had been a few metres behind us, apparently, and the interior light revealed Henry and Tom smiling and waving. One opened the window and whistled at Mac and Anna, both of whom laughed and waved, then turned to enter the station.

A girl did not need too much imagination to know how their night was going to end.

I went on, alone, or as alone as one could be with a car creeping along behind you. Before, with Mac and wrapped up in my own thoughts, it had been completely invisible. Now that I knew it was there, it seemed as distracting as a zeppelin in your garden.

I went about ten meters when my feet voted for a ride. The boys smiled bright and let me in the back. Both were chatty, and we didn't have far to go back to the Rectory, so I engaged a little, but mostly I was quiet. Tom and Henry carried on like giddy school boys—even with Elena, it had all been a great success.

They both saw me in. Henry did his accustomed sweep while Tom stood by, and they said they would be on watch again tonight and for the foreseeable. I thanked them, then closed the door thankful that there were such good men.

Finally, I texted Maddie to say I had a story for her. She texted right back that she would ring. I made a cup of tea and waited. It wasn't long before my mobile chirped with her photo.

I told her the story of the night's events.

"Robin, let me contact the *Daily Mail.* I do some work for them as a stringer. I just have time for them to change their front page. Let me get back to you."

I had never been so happy to reach my door. Now in the Rectory, warm and cozy, it truly felt like home. Curled up in a comfy, overstuffed chair, watching the fire while sipping my tea, I wondered, given everything, just how long this could last. As if in answer to my unspoken question, my mobile started dancing across the companion side table next to me.

"They want it. They will run it tomorrow—hope you don't mind your wet tee shot being used again. They said they had a picture of this Dimitri. Thanks, Robin, this will be great. I can follow up next week with the more reflective piece on your work. This will give it much more of a profile."

I smiled to myself. More Randy Rev in the morning papers. Perhaps I was in the wrong job? I had to admit I did look pretty good in the photo; they definitely got my girl's good side.

I undressed and showered before putting my nightdress on and, to yet again, spend a night alone; but at least it was by choice. I would need to phone Jane in the morning. But that, as they said, was sufficient unto the day thereof. I prayed and slept the sleep of the just.

Chapter 14

JUDGEMENT DAY FOR ROBIN

I woke with a start as the sunlight filtered through a gap in the curtains. Yet again, the dawn was beautiful. I slid my robe over my shoulders, then toddling into the kitchen, I put on a pot of coffee. I caught a movement, thinking it was the neighbour woman's cat again, trying to get at the bird feeder; she was a sweetheart but was brutal on the songbirds. I planned to shoo her off when I looked out of the window and realised why I had woken - there was a press pack outside my door.

My phone! I had left it off, and when I turned it on, I had three missed calls and a voicemail to call the BBC. Maddie had done her stuff. Someone must have seen the curtains twitch, as there was a tap, well not so much tap, but a knock, or perhaps a knock with intent, my poor door. Brushing my hair and glancing in the hall mirror, I went to answer it.

"Robin, can we talk with you?" asked a middle-aged man with a determined expression below his thinning comb-over and above the press badge in danger of falling off his prominent beer belly. I was so morning-addled I could not think.

"Can you all give me a few moments to freshen up and dress, and I promise I will be with you. Coffee all round?" I asked; at least, I think that is what I said.

I shuffled back to the kitchen, realising the coffee *was* on, then wandered to the bath to shower. I used cold to wake up and did so in record time, dressed in something suitably clerical then made ten cups of coffee. Started another pot and decided to put on the kettle, knowing it would be needed also.

Finally, I could stall no longer and went to the door, with a tray full of cups, where the pack was still there, now joined by a BBC van.

For the next half an hour, I told the press what had happened, omitting any mention of Elena and her role.

"But, Reverend, wasn't a police officer also taken into custody?" A handsome young man with blond hair, asked.

I had been steeling myself for just this question. "Whether that is true or not, I cannot say. From what I understand, there were a number of arrests but that is not for me to say. I would refer you to the police." I hoped that would thread the needle and leave Mac some room to manoeuvre.

As we wound up so I could do the BBC interview, the same tall man with a striking head of blond hair spoke up, "Rupert Myers from *The Times*. I wonder, Robin, whether we could do an in-depth story on this? There's a lot more to this, I am sure." He deployed what I could only assume was his most engaging smile.

Just at that point, Maddie arrived in a rush, her face flushed.

"Rupert, this," I said, "is Maddie Stone from the *Church Times*, who broke the story and is doing an in-depth on the project with the women. Could she work with you?"

I had said it in a way which implied that I would only cooperate if he would let Maddie in, and Rupert was quick enough to catch that and immediately agreed.

"If that's agreeable to you, Maddie, if I may make so bold." I smiled at Maddie, who was a bit stunned.

"You're Rupert Myers, aren't you? Love your stuff, yes, sure, be honoured to share the deep background. I don't think my stuff for the CT will take the same line as yours." Maddie was being modest; I had read both. I preferred hers, and that, after all, was partly why she was here.

"Look," I said, "I have to do something for the Beeb, so if you two want to settle down in the kitchen and have a chat, I'll be with you soonest."

"You might want to see the story first, Robin." Maddie smiled, and I did, it read:

"Daily Mail Exclusive: 'Randy Rev and the Revolting Russians', by our special reporter, Maddie Stone: see pp. 4, 5 and 6."

It was complete with that picture of me, my nipples prominent in the wet tee-shirt. Ah well, I thought, it was not as though everyone interested had not seen them before.

The BBC reporter did an interview for the radio and asked whether I'd be interested in doing the Sunday programme live in London. As I was initially down to help at St Mark's for the Sunday services, and that was not going to happen given Richard's injunction to me, I said I would.

"We can put you up overnight if that will help, and send a car."

"If you would, I shall happily do it. Will you bring me back?" I asked, upping the ante.

"Of course!" he replied happily.

I told the few remaining reporters that I didn't know I was busy and would not be answering any more questions, but I gave them Miriam's number to call if they wanted further comment. I did not feel badly as I doubted that number was correct, and Miriam's role was no secret. Still, I thought to text her a warning.

So, I would be in London later—which set my mind to working on Jane. Sunday was, of course, our busy day, and unlike me, she was not barred from services, but I decided to text her and see what happened.

Back in the house I made some breakfast for the three of us, and chatted to Maddie and Rupert about what had happened. It was rather pleasant to discuss the work and not just my breasts. While they talked a bit about who would do what and take which angles, I snuck away to give Mac a ring; he took some time to answer.

"Robin?" He sounded a bit groggy. I wondered how much sleep Anna had allowed him.

I told him what was happening, and he agreed to see Maddie and Rupert at the station later.

As Maddie made ready to leave, she suddenly paused and turned to me.

Whispering, "Robin, thanks, I think you just made my career." She was all smiles and hugged me.

That made me feel good. I smiled back and returned the hug before my whispered reply, "Just do what I know you can and will—be honest about what we are trying to do here, and try not to let Rupert get carried away."

Rupert checked that he could call me for *colour*, those little personal details that make the story more relatable. Since we were all headed in the same direction I went down to the station with them.

Roly, the newsagent waved as we went past and came to the door.

"I see you are in the papers again, vicar?" He was smiling, something unusual for him.

"I am, Roly, hope that helps you sell more papers," I responded, grinning and wondering if maybe I was becoming too comfortable with my nipples being on show.

"That picture of you does!" He chuckled with a rakish grin, and I blushed.

The weather looked threatening as we walked, but it didn't do much but threaten. It was too much to ask for the weather to hold indefinitely; this was, after all, England.

Mac looked a bit sheepish when I saw him, but I smiled nicely and introduced Maddie and Rupert to him, and agreed to meet them later for lunch.

I went over to the Retreat. Miriam was in—*catching up*, she said, but clearly burning with curiosity about the news, so I filled her in.

"Gosh, Robin," she said at the end, "you're becoming a celebrity."

"That," I said, with feeling, "is the last thing I want. But I will be on the BBC Sunday programme tomorrow, so if you get the chance…"

"Are you not at St Mark's?"

"I have effectively been banned from there, so I will go into town and, hopefully, see Bishop Jane."

As though uttering her name had been an incantation, my phone buzzed, and it was Jane.

"Excuse me, Miriam, that's the bishop!"

"Robin, what on earth is going on? I had the press office on the line, and was going to phone you. They'd like a briefing." Her voice was different, but I could not put my finger on it.

"Look, Jane, I am on the BBC tomorrow and am coming into town. Are you free later in the afternoon or early evening?" I asked, a bit hopeful that there was still a chance for us.

"I can be, and if you can Zoom with the press office in a few minutes, that will help us all," Jane responded, papers shuffling in the background.

And that, was that. Short, pleasant, business like. I could now put my finger on the difference; Jane's voice was cool, bordering on indifferent. That train had clearly left the station.

I did the Zoom meeting as ordered and expected, but they were not happy. I was told in no uncertain terms that I was a naughty girl for getting involved in another crime and police investigation without informing the church. Their frustration was palpable about maintaining the church's reputation. To make matters worse, the press office was uninformed, and the church was caught off guard.

After licking my wounds a bit, I then phoned my BBC contact and asked if they could send the car after lunch as my bishop wanted to see me before the programme. They agreed.

So, all of a sudden, I had a few moments to myself.

I hated loose ends; there was one, and it was a very big one.

Elena had known I was being posted to this Mission before I had known. Someone had told her. I could understand those arrested with Surtees wanting to keep an eye on me, but how could they have known where I was being sent before I did? It would have had to have been signed off by the Archbishop, but there could not have been that many people in the loop. I needed to find out who they were.

I wandered out into the lobby to think, when down the stairs came Anna, who smiled at me.

"Hope you did not mind?" she said, coming up to sit by me. She looked both worn and delighted. Anna's hair was slightly tousled, and her cheeks were flushed. Despite dark circles hinting at a lack of sleep, her eyes sparkled with a contented glow. "Anna, darling, you had your needs, I hope Mac was the man to satisfy them?" I tried to keep a straight face; it certainly was not a question I could imagine Father Richard asking.

She grinned, and I chuckled while shaking my head.

"Was he *so*! He's dishy, and we're meeting again. I see you are in the papers again?" Anna was almost breathless.

"Yes, we have some journalists in town, and I am going up to London later, so I shall be away overnight."

"You really have no problem with my seeing Mac?"

"Really." I smiled, leaning in to hug her. "I'm delighted for you both."

I genuinely was. I was hopeful that *someone* I knew was having a good relationship. I hoped that they would be good to—and for—each other.

The phone buzzed. It was Irina.

"Robin, I have seen the news. Been trying to get through, but your phone seems permanently busy."

"It's been that sort of day," I replied with a sigh. "What can I do for you?"

"Really just wanted to congratulate you on getting Dimitri and company out of the way. It will really help us."

I told her about Elena, which was still surprisingly difficult.

"So that was how the bastards knew who to target back in Ukraine. How could anyone do that?"

"Baffles me too. Greed and fear are powerful things, I suppose. But I wonder if your services could help me with a problem?"

I told her that Elena had confessed about the Russians knowing about my new situation before I had, and asked if her people could dig around. She promised to help. I found myself still wondering who those *people* might be, but I decided to let her tell me in her own time—my own form of 'don't ask, don't tell' I supposed.

"I shall be going back to Ukraine for a while next week. Any chance of seeing you before then?" A note in her voice sounded hopeful, but with my recent experience, I was not exactly confident about even this relationship.

"Yes, every chance. I am off to London later, but will be back for the week ahead. Let me know what evening you'd like."

"I shall," she promised.

I met Maddie and Rupert as agreed at my beloved haunt on the seafront. Already, the autumnal coolness was militating against my favourite place, sitting outside, and watching the sea and sky. We got a table by the window. They both seemed happy with their morning.

"Robin, I have to thank you for access to Macduff, from what he was saying there is much more to this story, although he refused to share the information as the investigation is ongoing," Rupert said, getting down to business as Maddie and I scanned the menu.

Considering how much fishing Rupert was doing, it was convenient we were at the seaside.

"Oh, there is, and if your editor has the stamina for it, I think there is a really good story here," I responded, my eyes never leaving the menu.

"Actually," Maddie interjected, "there are two, and that's what Rupert and I have been discussing. I will have a word with my editor about doing a couple of church-orientated pieces on you and your work, and Rupert wants to do a short series on the wider context."

"That sounds marvellous," I said, thankful that the focus was shifting away from me to what I was doing. And it'd perhaps, give my breasts a break.

"There's a *but*, coming, Robin," Rupert said in a tone anticipating opposition from me.

I sighed. *There always is.* Putting down my menu, I leaned back in my chair, crossed my arms, and subconsciously protected myself.

"Alright, what is it?" I asked, trying to at least be open to the suggestion.

"Robin," Rupert began tentatively, presumably hoping his charm would soften me up. "Editors and readers like a personal angle, and we'd love to do a profile piece on you to preface the articles covering your work and the Russians."

I could not help but sigh again.

And, just when I supposed the focus was shifting from me, back it swivels.

But, of course, what Rupert said made sense, and if it would help get his editor on our side, then how could I say no?

"I think I can trust you both." Doing my best to look genuine, I smiled, hoping I was correct. "So yes, by all means."

We spent the rest of the lunch discussing my least favourite subject — *me*. They both had their phones recording and promised I could see the final version. Although, I did realise that might be the same as the executioner graciously showing you the sword if they chose to take that role.

"I'm not naïve enough to think I have a veto, but that's kind of you both." I wasn't a fool.

"We'll get it done in time for the deadline, and it will advertise a two-part feature on you and the Russians over the next fortnight. How does that suit you?" Rupert asked, flashing me his broad smile.

"I am off to London soon," I said, still trying to be positive. I would let them prove their mettle. "But I can pick it up on my phone, so just text me when you're sending it."

Seeing the time, I thanked them both, returned home, then packed an overnight bag, just in time for my lift to arrive.

Had I done the right thing, or was I being naïve? I'd told them about my life up to now, and been honest about my sex life, or to be truthful, lack thereof. Had I opened myself up too much? But I did, I really did, want to highlight the plight of the women I had been working with, and to get the focus to shift onto them. If my privacy was the price I had to pay, so be it.

The journey to London was pleasant enough. My driver did not try to chat me up and left me to my own devices for the most part. I pondered what to wear for my interview, but even more, what to say to Jane.

It only took a couple of hours to get me to the hotel, and once I had unpacked there, I caught a cab to Lambeth. I was nervous about what I would find. I guessed I still had some small hope of a relationship but knew it was foolishness, after all, hope and wisdom were not always compatible.

The door keeper let me in and directed me to Jane's quarters. To my surprise, the Archbishop was also there.

"Robin, you know the Archbishop? Julian, this is Robin." Jane wore a soft, welcoming smile.

I'd thought she might be glad to see me, but I could not see it in her eyes.

"Welcome, Robin. I wanted to meet and talk with you. Will you take some tea with us?" Julian was all politeness; he held his hand out to me, and I was taken aback, shocked, really.

Getting over my surprise at the top man wanting to talk to me, I said that of course I would.

After we sat down and tea was served, Jane began. "His Grace and I have been considering what to do about the situation, Robin. I will let him expand on that."

I was being set up, and I knew it.

My heart lurched before descending to my stomach and making somersaults there, leaving me slightly sick.

"You will understand, Robin, that we have a safeguarding duty to you and those with whom you have dealings. All this publicity must be stressful for you, and now there are the added weights of this business with the Russians and the whole gay issue. It is too much to ask you to bear. We think a period of rest and relaxation might help. We can then consider where your gifts might be best applied." He was smiling with his best fatherly look of faux concern; it was like the gleam of metal on a coffin lid.

This masterpiece of mealymouthed doublespeak effectively meant: '*You are a troublesome young woman, and we want to use the excuse that you must be stressed, to take you out of the public eye and calm down the furore*'. All the while, Jane maintained a beatific expression of benign concern she could not quite make convincing; the strain at the corners of her mouth told the tail.

For my part, I struggled to retain control of myself, fighting the rapidly increasing need to vomit.

Will I go to hell for projectile vomiting on an Archbishop? Maybe it depends on the archbishop. I glanced at the only one in the room.

So, to keep from discovering the answer to that question, I bit into the scone, and then took a sip of tea, letting the rchbishop rabbit on in the same vein.

It was clear enough. I had become a source of controversy, and there were various ways of dealing with me. The kind option was the one they were proposing, namely that 'out of pastoral concern', they wanted to move me from the eye of the storm. But I knew there were other, less kind options. 'Safeguarding' was, at best, a double-edged sword, and in reality, it usually meant safeguarding the church and would effectively be a headsman's axe for me.

"It must be hard for you, Robin, and we are aware that there may be some safeguarding issues concerning you and one of the Ukrainian women. We have had a report of inappropriate behaviour, which, unfortunately, we may have to explore if you were to stay." His smile shifted to show his fangs.

And there it was, the other option laid bare: *Go, or we shall make you go.*

My mind was in turmoil. There had been those few moments with Anna, but no one else had been in the room, and it had not gone anywhere, and we had done nothing, and Anna had taken the lead, and so on and so forth. But that was the point, of course—it would go on until I agreed. I could *agree* in a way that would not damage my career, or I could *agree* once my prospects had been damaged. What hurt most was that Jane had bought into this. She had not warned me. She did not want to see me; she had called me in for a chat with *the boss.* I was unsure which betrayal hurt worse, Elena's or Jane's. I could not recall that Elena had ever said she loved me, but Jane had.

We must have had *very different* opinions of what that word meant.

As someone said to me a few hours later:

"You should have told them where to stuff their job and left; that was disgraceful of them!"

Maybe. What happened? Well, it would take longer to write than the minutes it actually took.

Perhaps I was too much of an Anglican, but I actually understood. Under my mounting anger, I saw two good people trying to protect the church and me. They had put their minds together and come up with what they thought was the best way of doing it. *Keep quiet, be a good girl and all will yet be well.* I had no doubt they'd have found me something somewhere. *Make a noise and be a bad girl, and it will be the worse for you, and you will be harming the church.* Jane knew how I thought and was banking on my being a good girl, as I had been brought up to be. But they were both wrong. They were thinking small.

I looked at them both.

"We all know that all you have on that last is Miriam peeping in through keyholes. Nothing happened beyond a kiss, and the woman concerned, Anna, will not only not confirm whatever Miriam told you, she will tell you the truth!"

I could see the Archbishop beginning to reply and, rather rudely, I cut him off, "It's okay, I'll go!"

Sighs of relief all around, except for me, of course. They had not wanted to go down the *bad girl* route.

"Why would I want to stay where my assistant behaves like that, and my parish priest treats me like a pariah because I kissed a girl and liked it?" I replied with more heat than I should have, considering the situation.

Both of my companions' mouths were open.

I took a breath to calm myself before I continued, "But I have a suggestion to which I would like you to agree."

The Archbishop looked even more taken aback, his mouth opening and closing like a gasping fish. I thought I saw a smile flicker across Jane's lips, but strangely, I did not care.

"I am in town because tomorrow I am being interviewed on the BBC's *Sunday* programme. That morning, *The Sunday Times* is running a profile on me and a piece on what is being done in Suffolk; it is the first of two. The *Church Times* is running a piece contextualising our work, and saying something about the treatment of gay women in the Church." As they say, I was *on a roll* and unwilling to be interrupted or shuffled off.

I could see all of that had gripped the Archbishop's attention, just as his white knuckles gripped the chair's arms.

"I *want* to be able to say that the Church is helping and doing Christ's work in the world, but if what I *have* to say is that I am being moved away, well, I don't have to tell either of you how that will be received." I fixed each with a cold stone stare; I was not playing for scraps but the whole pie. "We can all see Monday's headlines now. Moreover, the Home Office is also taking an interest in what we are doing, and I daresay MPs might ask what is going on and how are we being so successful."

Both Jane and the Archbishop sat as stiff as if they were tied to their chairs. They exchanged quick, nervous glances—clear signs they knew what cards I held, and it was trumps. Better still, they knew I knew. So, I paused a moment for dramatic effect, then continued.

"But of course, there is a way in which moving me can be part of a good news story."

The Archbishop leaned forward, I knew I had his interest. I had not threatened anything, I had not lost my temper, much anyway, and I had agreed to do as asked—I was going to go, as they wanted—but at a price.

"If it were to be announced that as part of the Strategic Mission and Ministry Investment Scheme, a new Ministry of Service to abused refugee women and girls was being set up, and I was being appointed as its first director, don't you think that might play rather well with the media and MPs?" It was my turn to smile as sweetly as I knew how.

The Archbishop's thin lips broke into a genuine smile for the first time since I had entered the room.

"Jane told me you were clever. She was *not* wrong. What you are outlining would, of course, achieve some of the objectives we need, but *where* would this be based?"

"London is probably the most *gay-friendly* diocese, and as it so happens, there is a vacant large church building in Southwest London looking for a use. There are some church flats in the complex next to it; it sounds to me as though that would work. It would put me out in the leafy suburbs, look like a promotion, help the refugees, and burnish the church's reputation. Moreover, one more gay woman priest in liberal middle class Teddington would make no great stir, would it?"

He looked at me, then at Jane, then back at me. "If we agreed to that now, you could get that onto the programme tomorrow?" he asked, hopefully, but I would need to box him in and remove his weasel room.

"Not only could I, I would. And I just have time to get it to my journalist contact to go with tomorrow's story. What do you say, your Grace?" I responded, hoping the box would hold him.

"I say you are an extremely bold and resourceful young woman. I am setting up a commission to see what more we should be doing for refugees; I want you to be on it. If you agree, you can tell them that, too. I will brief the press office immediately after this," he answered, seeming to add more work as a reward; if I was busy, I might not cause as much trouble. He did not know me very well.

I wondered if he was using the adage of keeping your friends close and your enemy closer. No matter, I grinned all the same.

"Deal, your Grace!" I responded.

He stood up, and I did the same. He looked me in the eye and shook my hand.

"I meant it, your idea was much better than mine. God be with you!" He appeared to honestly mean both. And with that he left, rushing off to brief the press.

"Jane, can I have a moment to tell my press person?" I asked, unsure if I wanted to speak to her alone.

"Of course," she answered, the corners of her mouth lifting in a relieved smile.

I phoned Maddie who was delighted and who promised to tell Rupert.

"We'll send you the final piece in about an hour," she responded; I could almost hear her bouncing in her chair.

Ending the call, I sat and looked at Jane. I was left with the prospect of facing her now, with no other options.

"I am sorry, truly I am." Her voice trembled, hands clutched together, and I believed her. "But you understand why we could not leave you where you were."

"I do," I responded flatly. "I really do, but I think my idea is a better way of doing it."

"You're disappointed in me?" She actually sounded like she cared if I was, her voice still trembling slightly.

I took a deep breath; of course I was. I was done lying, especially to myself. What I had to decide was whether I gained anything by saying so. I had always wondered where I would stand with Jane, but I could see now that she loved her career more than she had or could love me. That meant that even if all of this had not happened, I would have always been her mistress with her career, her true love.

"I am human, Jane, so I would lie if I said I wasn't. I am not a saint." I shifted and paused to collect my thoughts. "I understand you must consider the broader implications for the church."

"It's like my hopes that we could have a relationship. Robin. I really wanted that, but the damage it would now do to my position is too great," she continued, and I wondered if she was trying to convince me or herself.

"Like the damage I did to mine, letting that picture be published?" Leaving the truth that I had no power to prevent it unsaid, I knew my permission was not required.

"That's different. You have only yourself to consider, I have the whole benefice over which I preside." Clearly, she was trying to convince me she was in the right.

"I know," I said, somewhat weakly, not wanting to end this with an argument. "I know."

"I will tell Bishop Sarah on Monday, Robin, and we shall try to get you in for Advent. How would that be?" She was offering an olive branch.

"Thank you." I meant it.

The Church bureaucracy moved at a glacial pace. I could still have been in Felixstowe for Easter, and the longer the move took, the greater the chance it would not happen. Jane's final gift to me *as my bishop* was to help me one last time. Still, I was sorrowful. It must have shown on my face.

"I am sorry, truly, Robin. If I can do anything to help in the future, just ask."

She seemed sincere; I hoped she was.

"I shall," I said, "let me show myself out; I know the way."

We leaned in for an awkward air hug and pecks on the cheek.

On leaving Jane's office, I closed the door behind me. I took a breath to calm my nerves. When I opened my eyes, I realised something that had bothered me when I'd entered.

The outer office was different. Major furniture was as it always was, but there were subtle differences, primarily small things, but one object stood out to me. It was a detail I had missed because when I'd entered the outer office, I'd been preoccupied with my concerns but also because a filing cabinet had screened the object from casual view. What had caught my attention?

A Russian icon was on display, causing me to take more careful note of the outer office and its present occupant, particularly the nameplate on the desk: *Anya Rostov*.

I would have put money on Ms Rostov being the origin of the *leak*. The question I had to wrestle with now was whether and how I would tell Jane.

As I left and walked to Lambeth bridge, a wave of feeling passed over me. It was that strange time, late on a Saturday afternoon, when the business of the everyday world began to run down. I had always felt a sort of melancholy, as though time itself was slipping away. I wanted company, and yet had none. The phone buzzed. Assuming it had to be Rupert or Maddie, I just took it.

"Robin?"

I heard a voice that was both familiar and strange, one that I had known my whole life, yet it was strange to me.

"Mama?" I exclaimed, shocked. Apart from Christmas and birthday cards, we had not spoken in two years. She had excommunicated me from the family when I'd come to her with my ambivalence at my sexual uncertainty. I had hoped for her understanding and guidance, from the one person I'd desperately wanted to accept and understand. She had not, and the pain of that memory was still a dagger in my heart.

"Oh, Robin, I read the papers. Are you okay?"

I could hear genuine concern; I didn't know why that surprised me.

"Yes, yes, Mama, I am. How good to hear your voice again." Choking up; I swallowed hard, trying to control myself.

"Robin, I am sorry."

I stood in the street, stunned, on the edge of tears.

Part of me wanted to say: '*Who are you and what have you done with my infallible Mama?*' but I simply said, my voice cracking, "About what?"

"Doing what I did to you. Your witness to Jesus is exemplary." She paused, clearing her throat. "I am proud to be your Mama. Next time you are in London, you must pop in."

For a moment, I looked around to see if I had fallen and hit my head. I pinched myself; as far as I could tell, I was neither dreaming nor dead. She had to have thought I was thinking of a way to refuse.

"Please, Robin, do come to see me." Her voice wavered, like she was holding back tears by a thread.

I knew my mother; this was as close to a plea as I would ever receive. It broke my heart.

"Mama, thank you. You are not going to believe this, but I am in London; I have just left Lambeth Palace and the Archbishop."

"You are? Oh, how Lovely! Well, let me get cook to get something on for the two of us. Will you pop straight over?" She honestly sounded hopeful.

I briefly wondered whether my real mother *was* locked in a closet somewhere.

"I can be in Arlington Street in about half an hour if I take a brisk walk. See you then!"

My heart was singing, I actually danced in the street, and my cheeks hurt from smiling.

The prodigal mother had reached out to me with love. I was, indeed, blessed.

The traffic and the people faded into the background as I said a prayer of thanks to God, who had sustained me through the worst trial I had ever had.

I started walking. I still had things to do, and a walk would do me good.

I read the piece by Maddie and Rupert as I trekked home. It was good. It would do, and I told them so. Maddie seemed relieved.

Suddenly, I was standing before the door of the home of my youth. I briefly considered running, but then the door opened.

Mother's maid, Helen, holding the door open and smiling, had not changed in the two years I had been banished.

"Miss Robin, please come in; your mother is waiting in the library," she said and took my things.

My palms were sweating. I took a moment at the library door to steady my nerves and take a breath.

I need not have bothered; Mama was Mama, and in a heartbeat, it was as if the time of my banishment had never been.

It felt so good to see Mama again, and she was so welcoming. That alone warmed my heart and salved many wounds.

"My darling girl, you have become quite a beauty. I knew you had it in you, you get it from my side of the family, of course, your Papa had a nose like a hawk! Now, sherry?"

Dear Mama, she would never change, I thought, but then of course, she had—that was why I was back in the bosom of the family.

Over supper, I told her of the events of the afternoon, and it was she who told me I should have told them to stuff it. I chuckled; she had iron in her spine, which I'd also inherited.

"I will be moving to town, Mama, and will be based out Teddington way, so I can see you more often, if you like." I tried not to push or sound least not as hopeful, certainly not too desperate.

"Like? My darling girl, you are too kind to your silly old Mama. Forgive me, I was brought up to think it was wrong for women to go to bed with other women." She was being as contrite as possible; we were all products of our experiences.

I smiled, shaking my head a little. I knew it was an excuse but a forgivable one.

"You were also brought up to think it was wrong for women to go to bed with a man before they were married!" I reminded, giving her what I hoped was a knowing smile.

Mama had the grace to blush. "Stuff and nonsense! Much like my view on your being gay. What matters is who you are, and I am proud to be your Mama. You say there will be stuff in the papers?"

I told her what I had told the Archbishop and Jane.

"Well, I shall make sure to get a couple of copies. I am sure the aunts would like to see it. Would you really like to see more of me?" There it was again, a note of apprehension that I might not.

"Yes, Mama, I'll only be an hour on the tube, and you can come out. I know you like Richmond, and I will only be a station or so down the line."

The look on her face made my heart melt. I went over and hugged her.

"I've been a foolish old woman," she said, appearing to hold back tears, and failing for one or two.

"Not so much of the old," I said. "You simply had firm views, firmly held. Where do you think I get it from?"

It was her turn to smile.

We chatted into the evening. We had so much to catch up on. So much needed to be said, so much I had longed to say.

"Next time you're in town for the night, give me a ring and you can stay here, my darling girl."

"I shall, Mama." I hugged her again at the door, and she did not pull away as I thought she might but held it for a very long time.

I took a cab to the hotel. My heart singing. However, this time, it was an entire symphony rather than the tentative tune during my walk to the family pile. As the streets passed, it suddenly occurred to me that maybe, just maybe, God still performed the occasional miracle.

Chapter 15

ENDGAME BUT A NEW PROSPECT

The hotel bed was comfortable, and after an evening with my Mama, I slept well. I realised how much her rejection of me had hurt. It was no wonder no one else wanted me if my own mother didn't. I felt a balm of healing descend. I said a heartfelt prayer of thanks.

I knew I had to be up early, so I showered, dressed in my best 'lady vicar' outfit—clerical blouse and collar, mid-thigh tartan skirt and heels; respectable but not dull.

At the hotel, I had the chance to read *The Sunday Times*. The headline caught my eye: '*Rev Robin's Story – Read More Inside.*' And there it was, the profile, complete with a rather nice drawing of me. *Must get the original,* I thought to myself. I texted Maddie and Rupert and thanked them. They had done a great job. Of course, there was stuff about me, personally, but they'd put it all in the context I had wanted. I breathed a heartfelt sigh of relief. I started to wonder if I was becoming cynical.

I checked out, had a coffee in the lounge, looked at the other papers, which also mentioned me, and waited for the car, which arrived at eight on the dot. The journey to Broadcasting House felt strange, the usually busy London streets hushed, the noise and bustle giving way to an unaccustomed calmness.

At the Studio, I was met by a nice young woman and shown to the make-up room, where some kind soul had the task of taming my hair and making me presentable. From there, it was into the Green Room, where coffee and Danish pastries were on tap.

Kim Lysander, the presenter, popped in. "Robin, I take it?" She smiled and held out her hand.

"Yes, nice to meet you," I replied, shaking hands.

"And you. You have certainly made a splash." Kim gave a small chuckle.

I could only blush.

"I wanted to ask whether you could stay and help with the paper review? We have copies here and if you want to leaf through them after your interview, that will do, and we can get your car ready after that. Would that suit?"

I was flattered and, of course, agreed.

I was joined by a politician whom I knew I *ought* to recognise, but didn't, and an actress who was famous for her portrayal of alpha women, who assumed I knew who she was, which was a huge help, as I could not recall her name either. As insular as it sounds, I enjoy my own pursuits rather than more popular ones. Give me a good book, a glass of wine, and a happily burning little fire on the grate; then I am content.

"Oh, darling," the actress said, "I saw that profile in *The Times*, so lovely. A delight to meet you, don't you think, Minister?"

The Minister was hardly likely to dissent. We were then joined by two journalists who were there to review the papers. I was the first one up, the main interviewee. I supposed I should have been nervous, but somehow, I wasn't.

I was fitted with a mic, and then sat facing Kim. After the opening credits came the news, and then it was over to Kim. My butterflies settled surprisingly quickly.

"Our main guest today is, for once, not a politician or entertainer or sports personality. The Reverend Robin Topham is front page news in most of the papers, and there is a profile of her in this morning's *Sunday Times*, along with an article about her work. For those of you who have been on a Desert Island these last few days, Reverand Topham has been involved in bringing to justice a group of Russian mafia thugs who have been trafficking Ukrainian women. Reverend Topham, thank you for being here." With that utterly 'neutral' introduction, Kim turned to me.

"Thank you for having me, Kim." I smiled but tried to keep my professional demeanour. "And most of all, for not using the title the Mail, seems to prefer."

She laughed, and it was a genuine laugh, and it made my smile broader, which nicely broke the ice.

"Please, Robin, if I might call you that, tell us what has transpired in the last few days," Lisa opened the door for me and invited me to walk through.

"Please do. Well, I suppose it all began…" I felt more in control, telling our little story. I restrained myself and gave as succinct an account as I could.

"Robin, as you know, there is some controversy about you because you are gay. Rumours are that the Church is rather embarrassed by some of the publicity and that you are to be shunted off somewhere you can be kept quiet. Would you like to comment on that?"

"Rumours," I said, "which are the opposite of the truth. Indeed, later today, the Archbishop of Canterbury, whom I saw yesterday, will be announcing the setting up of a new initiative, the Rahab Centre, which will deal with the issues we have been discussing. I am to be its first director, and it will be based here, in London. If that is someone's idea of the Church hiding me, it is an odd one!"

"Is that hot off the press, Robin?" Kim asked. Clearly, this was not the answer she had expected. Someone was feeding them with false information. I already had my suspicions about whose office was the source.

"It is, only *The Times*, and now yourselves have it. I think it shows that the Church has its priorities and heart in the right place, don't you? There is a lot of careless talk about the Church being remote from the concerns of the people, and its middle-class nature and its new initiatives being self-referential; I think this shows how wrong such criticisms are." I was being a very good girl for the Church; I hoped that I was also telling the truth about its motives and future actions.

I could almost hear the Archbishop and Jane cheering, either or both punching the air with tightly clenched fists.

That led us into a discussion of refugees and how we should deal with them, which allowed me to reference Maddie's forthcoming article and the subsequent Sunday Times article next week.

I got the full fifteen minutes, and it passed like a flash. As Kim turned away to the second camera, I was allowed to retreat to the Green Room while the Minister came in. Idiot that I was, I only realised when I saw the screen that it was the Home Secretary!

"Home Secretary," Kim said, "you will, I am sure, have been as impressed as we all were with the Reverend Robin. What do you think of her announcement of what the Church is doing?"

"I was, Kim, and it is an excellent example of what the Prime Minister calls the *Common Good Approach or CGA*, working with the communities locally. I shall, by the way, be speaking to Robin personally, and will welcome her help with our own highly successful initiatives." His patented smile showed he thought he had just drawn trumps. I'd set him up, and he'd just taken the glory.

I stood there shaking my head.

Oh my! Oh well, I thought, at least my not having the foggiest idea who he was had not stopped him from wanting to welcome what I was doing. Indeed, when he came back into the Room for a post interview coffee, he could not have been more welcoming, and he gave me his card, took my number, and said his office would be in touch. After that we chatted like old friends. I sat amazed at the ability of the politician to seem so at ease with someone who was a total stranger. Still, what mattered was that I had some access to the Government.

The paper review was fascinating. The three of us sat about a spartan but clean conference room, with stacks of recent editions all about us. As I was in nearly all of them, the two journalists were exceptionally polite, which meant that the project got more publicity. However, it was also clear that I would receive my own amount of publicity bordering on scrutiny; whether I added anything to the story was debatable at best.

Afterwards, Kim invited me to join her for a coffee.

"Thank you," I said, now more nervous without the camera. "You were a breath of fresh air."

"Thank you," she said, a slight blush creeping onto her cheeks. "I wanted you to stay for the papers to ensure that neither of the journos made any comments you would not like. It's so odd; we were being fed leaks yesterday that you were going to be moved, and there was nothing about the new project."

"That would be before I talked to the Archbishop," I responded with a slight smile, just before sipping my coffee. It was delicious coffee.

Kim returned my smile with a knowing, wry grin. "I see." Her grin held. "Would that be because all the publicity shifted things in your favour?"

"It would. However tiresome some of the stuff was, it helped," I responded, finally reaching the bottom of my coffee and putting it down.

"You mean you *made* it help." She moved forward, leaning into me. "Look, Robin, if you are moving to London, please keep in touch. I have a feeling we have not heard the last of you. Here's my card."

I thanked her and gave her my mobile number. We shook hands one final time, and I said my goodbyes and went out into the sun for some air and a think.

As I waited for the car, Mama phoned me, all excited.

"Darling girl, you were wonderful, and I love the piece in *The Times*. Give me a ring when you get back home, and we can see when we can meet up again."

Of all the compliments I was to get for that interview, Mama's was the one I treasured most. But as valuable as her compliment was, it was hearing her voice again that brought the greatest thrill to my heart.

The driver on the return leg was, alas, much chattier but not very skilled at it, so I was relieved when the phone buzzed again. It was Mac.

"Just wanted to say how well we thought that went." He genuinely sounded pleased for me, but I could also hear another familiar voice in the background.

"We?" I grinned.

"I gave that away, didn't I? Anna would like a word."

I had always wondered if you could hear someone blushing through a phone; now I knew you could.

"Robin, darling, you were so good. But what is all this about a new project in London? How long have you known?" Anna managed to sound thrilled for me, but a little sadness seemed to tinge her enthusiasm.

"Oh, since about four o'clock yesterday!" I responded. I had to say I was naturally warming to all the developments. It had been a last-ditch attempt to avoid proverbial Siberia; now it seemed I was drinking my homemade lemon twists.

"Wow! Let's meet soon. I'll put Mac back on."

Anna did not even wait for me to give her my love before I heard the phone passing hands. It made me chuckle—they were undoubtedly a matched set; I hoped it would last and wondered if I could do the honours.

"Can we meet up for supper tomorrow?" Mac asked, something different in his tone.

"Tell you what," I said, "why don't all three of us meet at the usual place?"

"Wouldn't that make you gooseberry?" Mac was always thoughtful.

"Don't be silly. You are both my friends, and it would be nice to see you two together, unless, that is, I am presuming too much?" I cast my net to see if I might land a fish.

"No, not at all, that would be nice," Mac answered a little too quickly.

"Okay, well let's fix seven at the usual then?" I made a mental note.

"See you then, but probably before," he responded, and the line was dead.

The driver seemed able to carry on both sides of the chat with only an occasional comment from me.

My thoughts drifted to many things only to settle on the sheer strangeness of it all, and how easily one's life could be derailed.

I had trained for the Ministry because I'd wanted to serve. My ideal had been where I had served my ticket, a rural Suffolk Parish where I could be part of the community and serve those to whom God had sent me. I realised, with a sigh and great sadness, that would now never happen.

The ways of the Church of England were quite as mysterious as those of the God it served. Those who decided these things had moved me after the Surtees business, and now, scarcely six months later, here I was, on the move again. One advantage of living in church accommodation was it was possible to manage the moving easily. But so soon? How did one make friends, find lovers, become part of a community if one was constantly on the move? Rolling stones and all, it seemed terribly lonely, and at that moment, I felt the weight of it acutely.

Still, I reflected that *they*, whoever *they* were, would find it difficult to move me on so soon again. I was genuinely grateful to Jane for promising to expedite the move. She was right—the longer it took, the more *they* might find an excuse to change *their* minds. After all, it was me who had made *their* mind up, and I doubted that would be forgiven.

What I had to do now was to exploit my notoriety for all it was worth. I would *talk* to the Home Secretary, I would *talk* with Maddie and Rupert, I would go on this Commission, and I would make sure that the Rahab Centre got the funding it deserved. I realised that the publicity blaze had given me access to a level of influence and even temporary power that nothing else could have done. God moved in mysterious ways, his wonders to perform. I would, I promised him, do all I could to deserve his grace.

St Mary Magdalen's had been the big parish church in the Teddington area, but had been replaced in the seventies with a smaller church. The original neo-Gothic building had been converted into an arts centre, and a complex of apartments built on its grounds. The Church had retained control of the complex and the building, but latterly, the arts centre had failed, and rumour had it that the Church was looking to sell the whole thing. Well, I was putting a stop to that. I doubted the money men would be pleased, I was depriving them of the income from selling assets off, and wanting more of those assets for a cause I doubted they approved of. My heart bled for them; I was pretty sure it did, I think it did, a little — somewhere. Still, I smiled; there were different funding departments, so who even knew if the right hand was aware of the existence of the left one? One hardly needed to divide and rule - the bureaucracy had done it to itself.

I was in no doubt that Mary Mags would be hard work—the hardest I had ever done. I would need to get a small team to help; otherwise it would be beyond me. I needed someone who could do the money, someone to do the administration, someone to keep things running smoothly, and most of all, I needed people I could trust and who shared my sense of purpose.

I thought back to Miriam; part of me knew she meant me no ill will. She was a product of her times. She'd told the Church what she'd seen or had *thought* she'd seen. And in her mind, she was doing exactly what Jane and the Archbishop were doing, protecting the Church they loved, and had possibly thought she was saving me from myself.

Laughing at myself, I caused the driver to ask what was funny?

"Life," I answered, knowing the honest answer would have bewildered him. That was: *'And just who do you think you are, Robin Topham?'* The answer to that was: 'God's handmaiden'.

As the Psalmist asked, 'What is man that thou art mindful of him?' We were as grass, and like the flowers of the field, we would fade, and yet God loved us. That was why I loved him; I could do no other. That being so, I had to do his work, and if that meant I would be denied the comforts and reassurances of everyday parish life, and be plunged into this world of woe, then so be it. Through all seasons, I would endeavour to be faithful to that mission. It would not be easy, but then what was in this life?

How ironic it was, I thought. I had no idea what the Archbishop and Jane had been proposing to do with me, but it probably would have tucked me away somewhere far away to get on with it. But the scheme I had put to them was not of my devising — it was His inspiration. *So, girl,* I told myself, *pull yourself together, pull up your big girl knickers and get on with it!* Mama would have approved.

My phone buzzed with a text. It was from the Archbishop:

'Thank you, Robin. That was great for the Church. Well done!'

I could not help chuckling, my head leaning on the car window, watching the old city flow by.

Golly, now I was the blue-eyed girl. Was it only yesterday that they had been proposing to hide me away? Life in all its ironies!

The driver dropped me off at the Rectory.

The town felt cold and empty after London's hustle and bustle. For a moment I had nothing to do, no one to see and nowhere I ought to have been, so I took a walk along the seafront. The North Sea wind was bracing now; I felt it cut into me. They called it the 'lazy wind' in East Anglia because it was too lazy to go round you, preferring to go straight through you. But I did not mind. It felt refreshing. As strange as it sounded I would miss it terribly. It occurred to me that the wind was like me; I went straight at things.

I prayed as I walked, asking for whatever the next best thing to wisdom might be. But I know that the die had been cast. Already, as I looked around, all this seemed to be fading. I would miss Mac, Anne, Irina, and the women who had helped me as much as I had supported them. I ought to have felt a tinge of autumnal melancholy, but I didn't.

I took myself to the chapel at the Retreat to celebrate evening prayer alone, but to my amazement, within minutes of my arrival, most of the women staying there had joined me. Their presence spoke volumes to me, and we went through Cranmer's sonorous English together. As I finished, I prepared to pack, but one of them came up to me.

"I'm Kateryna, and the girls and I wondered if you'd like to join us for supper. We want to thank you." She was so earnest, so severe, so gentle.

So, instead of the quiet evening I had envisaged, I had a wonderful one with the Ukrainian women, sharing their food and fellowship. They had seen me on TV and thought I had 'done well'. It made it all worthwhile. That evening reminded me why I was doing what I was doing. I reassured them that far from it being the case that, with me gone, they'd be forgotten—it would be the other way round. The corps that they had formed would be the model for the one I would use with the new centre. Their delight at that made my day, and after night prayers, I went to bed a good deal happier than I had been for a long time.

The morning would bring me back into contact with Miriam, and I had to decide what to do about her. The 'inappropriate behaviour' with which I would have been charged could only have come from that encounter with Anna, and there had been no witnesses—or so I had thought.

I got there early, doing morning prayer with those women who wanted it. That meant that Miriam was already in the office when I had finished.

"I saw you on TV, Mother Robin. Thought you did very well. Was that news about the move?" Miriam actually sounded like she meant it, though I wasn't sure which part she was happiest about.

"Glad you liked it," I said perhaps a little colder than I previously would have but I could not help myself. "And yes, good news at that. I was a little concerned at one point."

She looked at me. "Well, it is a big responsibility." Her voice was more tentative.

"It is, but what worried me was that there was some talk about an inappropriate relationship with one of the women." I fixed her with a stare, my arms folded. "Any idea where that might have originated?"

Her eyes darted to the floor, and a faint blush spread across her cheeks as she glanced up at me through her lashes. "But I was *told* to report anything that seemed unusual or wrong to me," Miriam softly replied, her eyes carefully studying the desktop.

Well, at least she did not lie to me. I unfolded my arms, shaking them out, trying to release the tension in my shoulders. I glanced away, was mildly cross but mostly disappointed in Miriam; I'd thought we were closer than this.

"By whom?" I kept my eyes fixed, willing her to look at me.

She did, but her gaze flickered uncertainly, betraying her doubt. As to those she served, I had my own guesses.

"That policewoman, Elena. She gave me the number for the bishop's secretary and said to report anything untoward. I did not mean to eavesdrop, but I was about to knock when I heard you and that Anna woman. I felt that was the sort of thing I should report." She sounded plaintive. Again, someone trying to protect the Church, but in this case, on orders from the state.

"Well, I ought to tell you now that the police officer who was arrested was Elena," I informed.

The colour drained from Miriam's face and she began to shake, her eyes filling with unshed tears. She fell back into her chair.

"She was using me?" Miriam whispered more to herself than I.

"She was using your prejudices, Miriam." I was going to lift a mirror for her to look.

"I am sorry, Mother Robin. I was only following orders." She sounded so pathetic.

"I know," I said, hearing, mentally, the echoes of that worst of all excuses; how many had said those exact words before mounting the gallows steps? "And for that, I forgive you. But please, with my successor, talk with them first. I did not think I was unapproachable."

"I am sorry," she said, shaking and on the verge of tears. "Mother Robin, I thought you'd dismiss me."

I sighed. There really was no dealing with prejudices.

"I wouldn't. Personal contact should come first, Miriam. I hope you will be happy to help me with the process of finishing here."

She glanced down, her cheeks reddening, unable to meet my eyes. "Am I the reason you are going?"

I let the question hang in the air, allowing Miriam a moment to contemplate her actions. I would allow her to flog herself for a bit, but not too long.

"No, I am," I said, not thinking that the intricacies of it were a matter for her.

She was as good as her word to me, and over the following weeks, she was a help. But interestingly, I was not replaced by another priest; they put a social worker in charge of the Retreat and the other houses. That, for me, was a sign of how seriously the Church took my work. *Well, I should do something about that in my next posting.*

What I had to keep in perspective was that Miriam was just the puppet; I had to focus on removing the puppeteer.

The immediate question for me was what to do about Jane's secretary? Was it simply a coincidence that she was Russian, and that Elena had contacted her? Or was it more sinister? I was not a great believer in coincidences.

How deep did this cancer go? I would have to ponder it.

Supper that evening with Anna and Mac was a delight but bittersweet. I could feel the separation already growing. As both of them had, at different times, expressed interest in me, I put their minds at rest at once by saying that I was delighted to be dining with two of my favourite people. The only sadness was in the fact that I would soon be leaving, but I told them both that it would be open house in London, and I hoped they would both visit me there. I told Anna that I wanted to use the corps as a model for my new enterprise and hoped that she would be able to come and talk about what we had been doing; she seemed as delighted to accept as I was that she had done so.

Anna and I went to the bathroom together, prompting Mac to ask why women always did that in groups. Anna smiled. "Much more fun that way, Mac. I presume men go alone for the same reason?" She giggled.

"You are awful!" I whispered as we walked to the bathroom.

"Oh, Robin, I like him. He is actually a nice man, so gentle and considerate." Her smile was so bright when she spoke of Mac; it made me feel good.

"I should clearly have snapped him up," I chuckled, holding her arm.

"I am glad you didn't. He seems to actually like me for me, not just for the sex—great as that is!" She smiled wistfully, clearly lost in memory. "He does not see me for… he does not see me for what I did."

I felt the slightest sliver of regret. But no, I reflected; perhaps Mac was the man to bring healing to Anna after all she had been through. I very much prayed that was true.

Walking back, she thanked me again.

"You were right, Robin. We would not have worked, but it might have been fun trying." She beamed when she saw Mac waiting.

"It would have been," I concurred, giving the easy answer. There seemed no point complicating things at this stage. Besides, I knew we would not have worked—neither Anna and me or Mac and me—and I would never know if it would have been 'fun trying' with either.

At the end of the evening, Mac said that he hoped I did not mind, but that before I went, they wanted to throw a farewell party for me. Far from minding, I was deeply touched.

The next few days were hectic as the appointment to London came through, along with a request to see the bishop. That, I thought, would give me a chance to enquire about the secretary; I hated untidy ends.

It seemed as though I had a free hand with the new initiative. I had enough funding to appoint a finance person, an administrative assistant, and a publicity officer. Just as I was wondering what to do first, Irina rang.

"Robin, there has been a development. Can I see you soon?" Irina sounded severe, the customary humour in her voice utterly absent.

"I'm free this afternoon. Why don't you come over? What is it?" My curiosity was getting the better of me.

"I'll tell you when I see you," she replied and rang off before I could respond.

I stood there looking at my phone as if it would give me a clue; it remained annoyingly secretive.

I hated mysteries, but contained my impatience. I spent the late morning and lunch with Miriam and Anna discussing arrangements for the handover. Whoever took over, it was essential for the women and the rest of the community that the corps continued.

I had texted Irina to meet at the seafront café. She was already there when I arrived.

"I got us something to drink. Do you mind if we sit in the corner. I don't want to be overheard." Irina walked toward the spot she'd picked.

We ordered from the menu, and then I asked her what she had found.

"Robin, were you and the bishop involved—romantically, I mean?"

My breath caught, and my eyes involuntarily darted away, a flush creeping across my face.

"Sort of." I was about to explain it had been very early days in the relationship when things had gone sideways, but she went on.

"I shan't ask what that means." She actually sounded upset, which took me aback.

"Why is it important? As it happens, she and I had talked about being an item, but had not gone far before my world exploded." I finished my earlier thought.

Irina's eyes dropped to the floor, a hint of redness creeping up her neck as her lips pressed into a thin line, then she gave a sigh, "Look at these; they came from one of our agents who is shadowing a woman called Rostov, Anya Rostov."

She handed me an envelope with some photographs. They were clearly from a club. That was the only clear thing, as the room was poorly lit. But what they showed was Jane, kissing another woman. The other woman was small and elfin-like. The sequence showed them getting very close. My stomach ached. So did my heart.

"These were taken a month or so ago in a lesbian bar in Soho. That is your bishop, isn't it?" Her voice was soft, her hand on mine; she was trying to be gentle. How did you gently rip someone's heart out?

With an effort, I pulled myself together and said it was. I knew deep down something had changed between Jane and me some time back, but this? I could never have imagined.

"Rostov is a Russian agent, a honey trap if you like. She and your bishop are having an affair." Irina paused. She glanced at me; our eyes met, and her expression softened in sympathy, her voice dropping in volume and tenor,

"We are unsure which agency she is affiliated with, probably GRU, but perhaps the FSB, but that makes less sense."

Shock brought numbness. Numbness was necessary at times like this, although, of course, one ached all the more afterwards. I felt unutterably desolate.

"Do you think the bishop knows?" I asked, hoping Jane might salvage something.

"We can't be sure. But Jane is in deep with Rostov. We have proof, photos you may not want to see." Irina looked away from me, her fingers absent-mindedly drawing patterns on the table.

Who to trust? Of late, my ability to trust had become seriously tested.

Was Irina playing me? I had to trust someone, and from Surtees onwards, Irina had come through.

"Show me." I hoped my voice sounded firm, but my stomach certainly was not.

She showed me four more. Each was worse than the last, and each alone would destroy Jane.

I had seen Jane in her dog collar, but not the collar of an *actual* dog. There she was, on all fours with a studded collar around her neck, a name tag with *Bitch* clearly visible, being led by the smaller woman. There was one of her being taken from behind; one of her being sat on; and one of her bringing the other woman to orgasm.

I shook, my stomach rolling and my eyes swimming.

I felt Irina's hand on mine.

"Robin, I am *so* sorry."

I could hear her sincerity; I needed it.

"How." My throat tightened. I cleared it and went on, "How did you get these?"

"We have an undercover woman who works there; she keeps an eye on anything to do with the Russians; she came across this a month or so back. The club has very high-quality CCTV, and she got these images from there. I am sorry, Robin." Irina put away all the photos. "I fear that the club may be used to gather material to blackmail more than your bishop, but I do not know for certain."

I wanted to say, '*it's okay*'. I wanted to say, '*it's fine*'. I wanted to, but I couldn't. I could not lie. I was not 'okay', nor was I 'fine'. I had looked to Jane as an example, as a mentor, and had wanted to be her lover; now this, seeing her that way, turned my stomach.

The irony was not lost on me; some part of me was judging Jane for her actions, but I had not just this morning admonished Miriam for judging me and Anna for a kiss. Clearly, my eye needed some lumber removal.

Irina just held my hand. It was all she could do. The sense of loss was overwhelming.

"One good bit of news, perhaps, Robin," she continued.

"I could do with one, what is it?" I half-laughed.

"As our agent in London is getting some good information and I am her handler, they have said I can stay once suitable cover is found for me," Irina added, taking a long-delayed sip of her drink.

An idea came into my head. I must have given a little smile. I was going to make lemonade again.

"Would being my assistant in London work as cover?" I asked; it should work, given everything.

Irina's face lit up. "Yes, yes it would. Can you arrange that?" She was so excited; it cheered me… a little.

"I can. It will be an actual job, though, working with the women." I added, I could feel the broad smile and knew my hope gleamed in my eyes.

"Even better," she said, returning my smile. "That would suit me, that would suit me very nicely, and my service, of course."

"Well then," I said, beaming, "consider yourself hired."

She squeezed my hand.

"You know." A very naughty look came to her face. "If you ever want to do what we did before, I am here for you." Her offer was genuine.

"I do," I said, "and thank you."

"Can I ask you a question?"

"Yes, of course," I replied.

"How did those pictures make you feel?"

"I was upset." Stupid questions, stupid answers.

"That was not what I meant, Robin." She almost sounded exhausted with my being thick.

"What did you mean?" I asked, stirring my drink, feeling my body responding to her implied meaning.

"Did you identify more with Anya or Jane?" There was a sort of half smile and a hungry look in Irina's eyes.

Blood rushed to my cheeks as usual but furiously this time.

"That," I said, parrying, "is for another occasion. Now, let's get on with lunch. We have a lot to do in the next fortnight. I am down in London to see my new bishop, and I need a CV from you."

Irina gave me that look, her eyes darkening and lips parting slightly, a gaze that seemed to reach into my soul, igniting a familiar, electric shiver down my spine. Then she slid an envelope to me. Within it I found a neatly folded two-page resume, with the name, Irina Ivanova in bold.

"I was going to suggest this arrangement, if you did not." She gave me her most dazzling smile, then gently reached over, closing my jaw, and came close to whisper, "I trust you with my life, Reverend Robin Topham, my real name is Irina Kovalenko."

Looking into those eyes, all I could muster was a whisper in reply, "It is *such* a pleasure to meet you, Ms. Irina Ivanova."

She kissed me gently. I tilted my head for another, before adding, "I am going to need an electronic copy."

She burst into laughter, then grinning broadly, Irina said, "Here's to working together!"

La fin

About the Authors

Kate Robins

Kate Robins is the nom de plume of a former academic busily writing while living quietly with her wife in blissful rural obscurity.

Artemis Taylor

Artemis Taylor is the nom de plume for a late bloomer who has always loved stories but never thought she could write. A proud mother of strong, brilliant daughters and wife of an extraordinary spouse.

Printed in Great Britain
by Amazon

ff1e8c64-e903-4817-9f7b-0c59be9a1127R01